KU-714-770

STORIES FOR GIRLS

First published in 2005 by Miles Kelly Publishing Ltd
Harding's Barn, Bardfield End Green, Thaxted, Essex, CM6 3PX, UK

This edition printed in 2011

4 6 8 10 9 7 5 3

Publishing Director Belinda Gallagher
Creative Director Jo Cowan
Assistant Editors Rosalind McGuire, Hannah Todd
Design and Graphic Artwork Louisa Leitao
Cover Designer Michelle Foster
Picture Research Manager Liberty Newton
Picture Researcher Laura Faulder
Production Manager Elizabeth Collins
Reprographics Anthony Cambray, Mike Coupe,
Stephan Davis, Ian Paulyn
Assets Lorraine King, Cathy Miles

ISBN 978-1-84810-143-2

Printed in China

British Library Cataloguing-in-Publication Data
A catalogue record for this book is available from the British Library

Made with paper from a sustainable forest

www.mileskelly.net
info@mileskelly.net

www.factsforprojects.com

STORIES FOR GIRLS

Miles Kelly

Contents

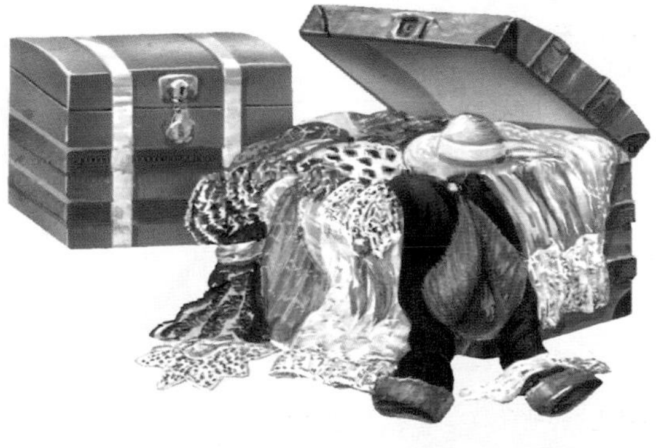

Introduction

Stories for Girls is a timeless collection of some of the most beloved classics of children's literature. Characters such as Dorothy, Heidi, Lorna Doone and Black Beauty have delighted generations of readers, and are here reinterpreted with charming new illustrations by established children's artists.

With authors ranging from Lewis Carroll and Kenneth Grahame to Charlotte Brontë and George Eliot, even the youngest child will love to hear the stories read aloud, while older girls will enjoy reading them for themselves.

Authors who successfully capture a child's imagination can lead the reader into extraordinary imaginary worlds, and many of the stories included started out as bedtime stories – often created for the sons and daughters of the authors themselves. *The Wind in the Willows* was originally written for

Kenneth Grahame's son, Alastair, and Grahame would probably have been astonished to think his simple stories now form one of the best-loved children's classics. Similarly, Lewis Carroll invented his series of strange and extraordinary stories to amuse 10-year-old Alice Liddell and her sisters, and they were eventually published as *Alice's Adventures in Wonderland* and *Through the Looking Glass.*

Most of the stories here are extracts, which will encourage readers to seek out the books for themselves. Chosen by renowned children's author and anthologist Fiona Waters, each story is accompanied by an introduction to the book and its characters, as well as a short biography of the author, making it a rich family resource to which children will return. *Stories for Girls* will be treasured by girls of all ages for many years to come.

A Little Princess

An extract
by Frances Hodgson Burnett

Written by Frances Hodgson Burnett (1849–1924) A Little Princess *is the story of Sara Crewe, who arrives at Miss Minchin's Select Seminary for Young Ladies as the adored daughter of the rich Captain Crewe, only to have her world turned upside down when her father dies and there is no money left to pay her school fees. How Sara survives and the turn her fortunes take, makes this a wonderful 'happy ever after' story.*

Sara

Once on a dark winter's day, when the yellow fog hung so thick and heavy in the streets of London that the lamps were lighted and the shop windows blazed with gas as they do at night, a little girl sat in a cab with her father and was driven rather slowly through the big thoroughfares.

She sat with her feet tucked under her, and leaned against her father, who held her in his arm as she stared out of the window at the passing people with a queer old-fashioned thoughtfulness in her big eyes.

She was such a little girl that one did not expect to see such a look on her small face. It would have been an old look for a child of twelve, and Sara Crewe was only seven. The fact was, however, that she was always dreaming and thinking odd things and could not herself remember any time when she had not been thinking things about grown-up people and the world they belonged to. She felt as if she had lived a long, long time.

"Papa," she said in a low, mysterious little voice which was almost a whisper, "papa".

"What is it, darling?" Captain Crewe answered, holding her closer and looking down into her face. "What is Sara thinking of?"

"Is this the place?" Sara whispered, cuddling still closer to him. "Is it, papa?"

"Yes, little Sara, it is. We have reached it at last." And though she was only seven years old, she knew that he felt sad when he said it.

It seemed to her many years since he had begun to prepare her mind for 'the place', as she always called it. Her mother had died when she was born, so she had never known or missed her. Her young, handsome, rich, doting father seemed to be the only relation she had in the world. They had always played together and been fond of each other. She only knew he was rich because she had heard people say so when they thought she was not listening, and she had also heard them say that when she grew up she would be rich, too. She did not know all that being rich meant. She had always lived in a beautiful bungalow, and had been used to seeing many servants who made salaams to her and called her 'Missee Sahib' and let her have her own way in everything. She had had toys and pets and an ayah who worshipped her, and she had gradually learned that people who were rich had these things. That, however, was all she knew about it.

During her short life only one thing had troubled her, and that thing was 'the place' she was to be taken to some day. The climate of India was very bad for children, and as soon as possible they were sent away from it – generally to England and to school. She had seen other children go away, and had heard their fathers and mothers talk about the letters they received from them. She had known that she would be obliged to go also, and she had been troubled by the thought that her father could not stay with her.

"Couldn't you go to that place with me, papa?" she had asked when she was five years old. "Couldn't you go to school, too? I would help you with your lessons."

"But you will not have to stay for a very long time, little Sara," he had always said. "You will go to a nice house where there will be a lot of little girls, and you will play together, and I will send you plenty of books, and you will grow so fast that it will seem scarcely a year before you are big enough and clever enough to come back and take care of papa."

"Well, papa" she said softly, "if we are here I suppose we must be resigned."

He laughed at her old-fashioned speech and kissed her. He was really not resigned himself, though he knew he must keep that a secret. His little Sara had been a great companion to him, and he felt he should be lonely when, on his return to India, he went into his house knowing he need not expect to see the small figure come to meet him. So he held her in his arms as the cab rolled into the square in which stood the house which was their destination.

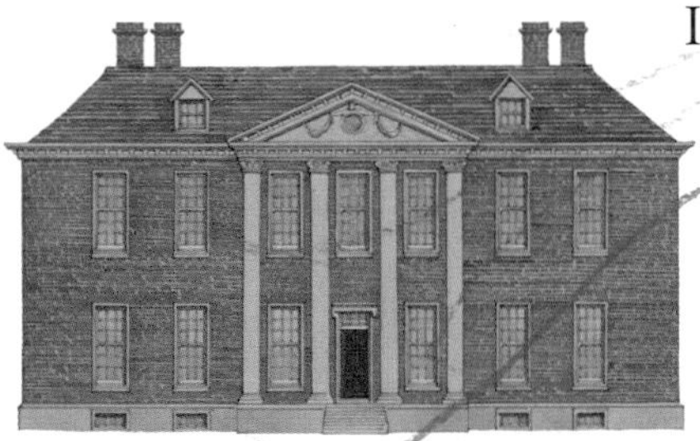

It was a big, dull, brick house exactly like all the others in its row, but when they got close to the door they could see there shone a brass plate on which was engraved in black letters:

Miss Minchin
Select Seminary for Young Ladies

"Here we are, Sara" said Captain Crewe, making his voice sound as cheerful as possible. Then he lifted her out of the cab and they mounted the steps and rang the bell. Sara often thought afterwards that the house was somehow exactly like Miss Minchin. It was respectable and well furnished, but everything in it was ugly, and the very armchairs seemed to have hard bones in them. In the hall everything was hard and polished – even the red cheeks of the moon face on the tall clock in the corner had a severe varnished look. The drawing room into which they were ushered was covered by a carpet with a square pattern upon it, the chairs were square, and a heavy marble timepiece stood upon the heavy marble mantel.

As she sat down in one of the stiff mahogany chairs, Sara cast one of her quick looks about her.

"I don't like it, papa," she said. "But then I dare say soldiers – even brave ones – don't really *like* going into battle."

Captain Crewe laughed outright at this. He was young and full of fun, and he never tired of hearing Sara's queer speeches.

"Oh, little Sara," he said. "What shall I do when I have no one to say solemn things to me? No one else is as solemn as you are."

"But why do solemn things make you laugh?" inquired Sara.

"Because you are such fun when you say them," he answered, laughing still more. And then suddenly he swept her into his arms and kissed her, stopping laughing all at once and looking almost as if tears had come into his eyes.

It was just then that Miss Minchin entered the room. She was very like her house, Sara felt – tall and dull, and respectable and ugly. She had large, cold, fishy eyes, and a large, cold, fishy smile. It spread itself into a very large smile when she saw Sara and Captain Crewe. She had heard a great many desirable things of the young soldier from the lady who had recommended her school to him. Among other things, she had heard that he was a rich father who was willing to spend a great deal of money on his little daughter.

"It will be a great privilege to have charge of such a beautiful and promising child, Captain Crewe," she said, taking Sara's hand and stroking it. "Lady Meredith has told me of her unusual cleverness. A clever child is a great treasure in an establishment like mine."

Sara stood quietly, with her eyes fixed upon Miss Minchin's face. She was thinking something odd, as usual.

'Why does she say I am a beautiful child?' she was thinking. 'I am not beautiful at all. Colonel Grange's little girl, Isobel, is beautiful. She has dimples and rose-coloured cheeks, and long hair the colour of gold. I have short black hair and green eyes; besides which, I am a thin child and not fair in the least. I am one of the ugliest children I ever saw. She is beginning by telling a story.'

She was mistaken, however, in thinking she was an ugly child. She was not in the least like Isobel Grange, who had been the beauty of the regiment, but she had an odd charm of her own. She was a slim, supple creature, rather tall for her age, and had an intense, attractive little face. Her hair was heavy and quite black and only curled at the tips; her eyes were greenish grey, it is true, but they were big, wonderful eyes with long, black lashes, and though she herself did not like the colour of them, many other people did. Still she was very firm in her belief that she was an ugly little girl, and she was not at all elated by Miss Minchin's flattery.

'I should be telling a story if I said she was beautiful,' she thought; 'and I should know I was telling a story. I believe I am as ugly as she is – in my way. What did she say that for?'

After she had known Miss Minchin longer she learned why she had said it. She discovered that she said the same thing to each papa and mamma who brought a child to her school.

Sara stood near her father and listened while he and Miss Minchin talked. She had been brought to the seminary because Lady Meredith's two little girls had been educated there, and Captain Crewe had a great respect for Lady Meredith's experience. Sara was to be what was known as a 'parlour boarder', and she was to enjoy even greater privileges than parlour boarders usually did. She was to have a pretty bedroom and sitting room of her own; she was to have a pony and a carriage, and a maid to take the place of the ayah who had been her nurse in India.

"I am not in the least anxious about her education," Captain Crewe said with a light laugh, as he held Sara's hand and patted it. "The difficulty will be to keep her from learning too fast and too much. She is always sitting with her little nose burrowing into books. She doesn't read them, Miss Minchin; she gobbles them up as if she were a little wolf instead of a little girl. She is always starving for new books to gobble, and she wants grown-up books – great, big, fat ones – French and German as well as English – history and biography and poets, and all sorts of things. Drag her away from her books when she reads too much. Make her ride her pony in the Row or go out and buy a new doll. She ought to play more with dolls."

"Papa," said Sara, "you see, if I went out and bought a new doll every few days I should have more than I could be fond of. Dolls ought to be intimate friends. Emily is going to be my intimate friend."

Captain Crewe looked at Miss Minchin and Miss Minchin looked at Captain Crewe.

"Who is Emily?" she inquired.

"Tell her, Sara," Captain Crewe said, smiling.

Sara's green-grey eyes looked very solemn and quite soft as she answered.

"She is a doll I haven't got yet," she said. "She is a doll papa is going to buy for me. We are going out together to find her. I have called her Emily. She is going to be my friend when papa is gone. I want her to talk to about him."

Miss Minchin's large, fishy smile became very flattering indeed.

"What an original child!" she said. "What a darling little creature!"

"Yes," said Captain Crewe, drawing Sara close. "She is a darling little creature. Take great care of her for me, Miss Minchin."

Sara stayed with her father at his hotel for several days; in fact, she remained with him until he sailed away again to India. They went out and visited many big shops together, and bought a great many things. They bought, indeed, a great many more things than Sara needed, but Captain Crewe was a rash, innocent young man and wanted his little girl to have everything she admired and everything he admired himself, so between them they collected a wardrobe much too grand for a child of seven. There were velvet dresses trimmed with costly furs, and lace dresses, and embroidered ones, and hats with great, soft ostrich feathers, and ermine coats and muffs, and boxes of tiny gloves and handkerchiefs and silk stockings in such abundant supplies that the polite young women behind the counters whispered to each other that the odd little girl with the big, solemn eyes must be at least some foreign princess – perhaps the little daughter of an Indian rajah.

And at last they found Emily, but they went to a number of toy shops and looked at a great many dolls before they discovered her.

"I want her to look as if she wasn't a doll really," Sara said. "I want her to look as if she *listens* when I talk to her. The trouble with dolls, papa" – and she put her head on one side and reflected as she said it – "the trouble with dolls is that they never seem to *hear*." So they looked at big ones and little ones – at dolls with black eyes and dolls with blue – at dolls with brown curls and dolls with golden braids, dolls dressed and dolls undressed.

"You see," Sara said when they were examining one who had no clothes. "If, when I find her, she has no frocks, we can take her to a dressmaker and have her things made to fit. They will fit better if they are tried on."

After a number of disappointments they decided to walk and look in at the shop windows and let the cab follow them. They had passed two or three places without even going in, when, as they were approaching a shop which was really not a very large one, Sara suddenly started and clutched her father's arm.

"Oh, papa!" she cried. "There is Emily!"

A flush had risen to her face and there was an expression in her green-grey eyes as if she had just recognized someone she was intimate with and fond of.

"She is actually waiting there for us!" she said. "Let us go in to her."

"Dear me," said Captain Crewe, "I feel as if we ought to have someone to introduce us."

"You must introduce me and I will introduce you," said Sara. "But I knew her the minute I saw her – so perhaps she knew me, too."

Perhaps she had known her. She had certainly a very intelligent expression in her eyes when Sara took her in her arms. She was a large doll, but not too large to carry about easily. She had naturally curling golden-brown hair, which hung like a mantle about her, and her eyes were a deep, clear, grey-blue, with soft, thick eyelashes that were real eyelashes and not mere painted lines.

"Of course," said Sara, looking into her face as she held her on her knee, "of course papa, this is Emily."

So Emily was bought and actually taken to a children's outfitter's shop and measured for a wardrobe as grand as Sara's own. She had lace frocks, too, and velvet and muslin ones, and hats and coats and beautiful lace-trimmed underclothes, and gloves and handkerchiefs and furs.

"I should like her always to look as if she was a child with a good mother," said Sara. "I'm her mother, though I am going to make a companion of her."

Captain Crewe would really have enjoyed the shopping tremendously, but that a sad thought kept tugging at his heart. This all meant that he was going to be separated from his beloved, quaint little comrade.

He got out of his bed in the middle of that night and went and stood looking down at Sara, who lay asleep with Emily in her arms. Her black hair was spread out on the pillow and Emily's golden-brown hair mingled with it, both of them had lace-ruffled nightgowns, and both had long eyelashes which lay and curled up on their cheeks. Emily looked so like a real child that Captain Crewe felt glad she was there. He drew a big sigh and pulled his mustache with a boyish expression.

"Heigh-ho, little Sara!" he said to himself. "I don't believe you know how much your daddy will miss you."

The next day he took her to Miss Minchin's and left her there. He was to sail away the next morning. He explained to Miss Minchin that his solicitors, Messrs. Barrow & Skipworth, had charge of his affairs in England and would give her any advice she wanted, and that they would pay the bills she sent in for Sara's expenses. He would write to Sara twice a week, and she was to be given every pleasure she asked for.

"She is a sensible little thing, and she never wants anything it isn't safe to give her," he said.

Then he went with Sara into her little sitting room and they bade each other goodbye. Sara sat on his knee and held the lapels of his coat in her small hands, and looked long and hard at his face.

"Are you learning me by heart, little Sara?" he said, stroking her hair.

"No," she answered. "I know you by heart. You are inside my heart." And they put their arms round each other and hugged as if they would never let each other go.

When the cab drove away from the door, Sara was sitting on

the floor of her sitting room, with her hands under her chin and her eyes following it until it had turned the corner of the square. Emily was sitting by her, and she looked after it, too. When Miss Minchin sent her sister, Miss Amelia, to see what the child was doing, she found she could not open the door.

"I have locked it," said a queer, polite little voice from inside. "I want to be quite by myself, if you please."

Miss Amelia was fat and dumpy, and stood very much in awe of her sister. She was really the better-natured person of the two, but she never disobeyed Miss Minchin. She went downstairs again, looking almost alarmed.

"I never saw such a funny, old-fashioned child, sister," she said. "She has locked herself in, and she is not making the least particle of noise."

"It is much better than if she kicked and screamed, as some of them do," Miss Minchin answered. "I expected that a child as much spoiled as she is would set the whole house in an uproar. If ever a child was given her own way in everything, she is."

"I've been opening her trunks and putting her things away," said Miss Amelia. "I never saw anything like them – sable and ermine on her coats, and beautiful lace on her underclothing.

You have seen some of her clothes. What *do* you think of them?"

"I think they are perfectly ridiculous," replied Miss Minchin, sharply; "but they will look very well at the head of the line when we take the schoolchildren to church on Sunday. She has been provided for as if she were a little princess."

And upstairs in the locked room Sara and Emily sat on the floor and stared at the corner round which the cab had disappeared, while Captain Crewe looked backward, waving and kissing his hand as if he could not bear to stop.

A French Lesson

When Sara entered the schoolroom the next morning everybody looked at her with interested eyes. By that time every pupil – from Lavinia Herbert, who was nearly thirteen and felt quite grown up, to Lottie Legh, who was only just four and the baby of the school – had heard a great deal about her. They knew very certainly that she was Miss Minchin's show pupil and was considered a credit to the establishment. One or two of them had even caught a glimpse of her French maid, Mariette, who had arrived the evening before. Lavinia had managed to pass Sara's room when the door was open, and had seen Mariette opening a box which had arrived late from some shop.

"It was full of petticoats with lace frills on them," she whispered to her friend Jessie as she bent over her geography. "I saw her shaking them out. I heard Miss Minchin say to Miss Amelia that her clothes were too grand for a child. My mamma says that children should be dressed simply. She has got one of those petticoats on now. I saw it when she sat down."

"She has silk stockings on!" whispered Jessie, bending over her geography also. "And what little feet! I never saw such little feet."

"Oh," sniffed Lavinia, spitefully, "that is the way her slippers are made. My mamma says that even big feet can be made to look small if you have a clever shoemaker. I don't think she is pretty at all. Her eyes are such a queer colour."

"She isn't pretty as other pretty people are," said Jessie,

stealing a glance across the room; "but she makes you want to look at her again. She has tremendously long eyelashes, but her eyes are almost green."

Sara was sitting quietly in her seat, waiting to be told what to do. She had been placed near Miss Minchin's desk. She was not abashed at all by the many pairs of eyes watching her. She was interested and looked back quietly at the children who looked at her. She wondered what they were thinking of, and if they liked Miss Minchin, and if they cared for their lessons, and if any of them had a papa at all like her own. She had had a long talk with Emily about her papa that morning.

"He is on the sea now, Emily," she had said. "We must be very great friends to each other and tell each other things. Emily, you have the nicest eyes I ever saw. But I wish you could speak."

She was a child full of imaginings and whimsical thoughts, and one of her fancies was that there would be a great deal of comfort in even pretending that Emily was alive and really heard and understood. After Mariette had dressed her in her dark-blue schoolroom frock and tied her hair with a dark-blue ribbon, she went to Emily, who sat in a chair of her own, and gave her a book.

"You can read that while I am downstairs," she said; and,

seeing Mariette looking at her curiously, she spoke to her with a serious little face.

"What I believe about dolls," she said, "is that they can do things they will not let us know about. Perhaps, really, Emily can read and talk and walk, but she will only do it when people are out of the room. That is her secret. You see, if people knew that dolls could do things, they would make them work. So, perhaps, they have promised each other to keep it a secret. If you stay in the room, Emily will just sit there and stare; but if you go out, she will begin to read, perhaps, or go and look out of the window. Then if she heard either of us coming, she would just run back and jump into her chair and pretend she had been there all the time."

"What an odd child!" Mariette said to herself. But she had already begun to like this odd little girl who had such an intelligent small face and such perfect manners. She had taken care of children before who were not so polite. Sara was a very fine little person, and had a gentle, appreciative way of saying, 'If you please, Mariette,' and 'Thank you, Mariette,' which was very charming. Mariette told the head housemaid that she thanked her as if she was thanking a lady.

"She has the air of a princess, this little one," she said. Indeed, she was very much pleased with her new little mistress and liked her place greatly.

After Sara had sat in her seat in the schoolroom for a few minutes, being looked at by the pupils, Miss Minchin rapped in a dignified manner upon her desk.

"Young ladies," she said, "I wish to introduce you to your new companion." All the little girls rose in their places, and Sara rose also. "I shall expect you all to be very agreeable to Miss Crewe. As soon as lessons are over you must make each other's acquaintance."

The pupils bowed ceremoniously, and Sara made a little curtsy, and then they sat down and looked at each other again.

"Sara," said Miss Minchin in her schoolroom manner, "come here to me." She had taken a book from the desk and was turning over its leaves. Sara went to her politely.

"As your papa has engaged a French maid for you," she began, "I conclude that he wishes you to make a special study of the French language."

Sara felt a little awkward.

"I think he engaged her," she said, "because he – he thought I would like her, Miss Minchin."

"I am afraid," said Miss Minchin, with a slightly sour smile, "that you have been a very spoiled little girl and always imagine that things are done because you like them. My impression is that your papa wished you to learn French."

If Sara had been older or less punctilious about being quite polite to people, she could have explained herself in a very few words. But, as it was, she felt a flush rising on her cheeks. Miss Minchin was a very severe and imposing person, and she seemed so absolutely sure that Sara knew nothing whatever of French that she felt as if it would be almost rude to correct her. The truth was that Sara could not remember the time when she had not seemed to know French. Her father had often spoken it to her when she had been a baby. Her mother had been a French woman, and Captain Crewe had loved her language, so it happened that Sara had always heard and been familiar with it.

"I – I have never really learned French, but – but—" she began, trying shyly to make herself clear.

One of Miss Minchin's chief secret annoyances was that she did not speak French herself, and she wished to conceal the irritating fact. She, therefore had no intention of discussing the matter and laying herself open to questioning by a new pupil.

"That is enough," she said with polite tartness. "If you have not learned, you must begin at once. The French master, Monsieur Dufarge, will be here in a few minutes. Take this book and look at it until he arrives."

Sara's cheeks felt warm. She went back to her seat and opened the book. She looked at the first page with a grave face. She knew it would be rude to smile, and she was very determined not to be rude. But it was very odd to find herself expected to study a page which told her that 'le pere' meant 'the father,' and 'la mere' meant 'the mother.'

'When Monsieur Dufarge comes,' she thought, 'I can make him understand.'

Monsieur Dufarge arrived very shortly afterward. He was a very nice, intelligent, middle-aged Frenchman, and he looked interested when his eyes fell upon Sara.

"Is this a new pupil for me, madame?" he said to Miss Minchin. "I hope that is my good fortune."

"Her papa – Captain Crewe – is very anxious that she should begin the language. But I am afraid she has a childish prejudice against it. She does not seem to wish to learn," said Miss Minchin.

"I am sorry of that, mademoiselle," he said kindly to Sara. "Perhaps, when we begin to study together, I may show you that it is a charming tongue."

Little Sara rose in her seat. She was beginning to feel rather desperate, as if she were in disgrace. She looked up into Monsieur Dufarge's face with her green-grey eyes, and they were quite appealing. She knew that he would understand as soon as she spoke. She began to explain in pretty and fluent French. Madame had not understood. She had not learned French exactly – not out of books – but her papa had always spoken it to her, and she had read it and written it as she had read and written English. Her papa loved it, because her dear mamma, who had died when she was born, had been French. She would be glad to learn anything monsieur would teach her, but what she had tried to explain to madame was that she already knew the words in this book – and she held out the little book of phrases.

When she began to speak Miss Minchin started quite violently and sat staring at her over her eyeglasses, until she had finished. Monsieur Dufarge began to smile, and his smile was one of great pleasure. To hear this pretty voice speaking his own language so charmingly made him feel almost as if he were in his native land – which in foggy days in London sometimes seemed worlds away. When she had finished, he took the phrase book from her, with a look almost affectionate. But he spoke to Miss Minchin.

"Ah, madame," he said, "there is not much I can teach her. She has not learned French; she is French. Her accent is exquisite."

"You ought to have told me," exclaimed Miss Minchin, much mortified, turning to Sara.

"I – I tried," said Sara. "I – I suppose I did not begin right."

Miss Minchin knew she had tried, and that it had not been her fault that she was not allowed to explain. And when she saw that the pupils had been listening and that Lavinia and Jessie were giggling behind their French grammars, she felt infuriated.

"Silence, young ladies!" she said severely, rapping upon the desk. "Silence at once!"

And she began from that minute to feel rather a grudge against her show pupil.

The Caravan Siege

by Alice Massie

Introduction

Sadly we don't know very much about Alice Massie. She was writing around 1920 and her work appeared mainly in collections of stories. When Alice Massie wrote The Caravan Siege, *children's books often had a strong moral behind the story. In this story the reader is encouraged to see that it is not wise to make judgements based on appearances and gossip.*

The Caravan Siege

The door of the country school was open, and the grey-green hills could peep right in, and see the children came from fairly prosperous farms – for the valley was a rich one – and some of them were sent on afterwards to boarding schools. By some unwritten law the children of the farm labourers went chiefly to the school at the other end of the valley, where the schoolmistress had not such the reputation for learning. Both schools were free. No one could say why the children were divided up like this; no one perhaps realized they were; but the fact remained that the only badly dressed and hungry-looking child in the south school was Tom Darrington, and he was lame, so that he could not be expected to tramp up to the north end of the valley as his sisters and brothers had done before him.

Tom was rather a pet in the school, and the girls from Croft Farm always shared their lunch with him. They were twins, and they rode in on ponies, which they put up themselves in stables at the back of the school.

Miss Bolt, the school mistress, with her eyes upon the lovely view the school-door framed, said: “I think you could sing your fairy chorus with great expression on a day like this. Now then, seconds, be very careful on the second line of ‘pitter-pats’. Trebles, take one long look at the beautiful hills before you start, and then fix your eyes on me.” The voices lifted very prettily:

“Fairy folk, fairy folk, down from the mountains,
Pitter pat – fairy feet ringing along.
Pitter pat – pitter pat – like fairy fountains –
Why do you hurry, still singing your song?”

“Now, Ida.”

Ida blushed and coughed, and began the solo part awkwardly, but her voice was full, and rich, and rather mournful:

“People of earth, we have lost a fair daughter,
Say have you seen her – oh say if you can—”

Ida stopped short half-way through her solo; there was a sudden movement through the class; everybody stared. Miss Bolt turned

her head towards the door at the side. Leaning against the doorframe was a slender, graceful girl. She wore shoes but no stockings, and a shabby cotton frock. Her hair stood out like an aureole, and the sun shone through it.

Tommy Darrington said out loud, not knowing that he had spoke: "It's the fairy daughter!" Someone tittered. Miss Bolt said: "What is it, dear?" The girl stepped into the room and came to Miss Bolt's desk. The whole school watched her.

"Oh if you please," said the girl, "I want to come to school. We've just moved into the valley, and Father thought I'd better come."

The whole school gasped. No one had moved into the valley.

Didn't they live here? Didn't they know? Was Tommy right – was this a fairy? The Croft Farm girls believed she might be; she was very pretty.

Miss Bolt said: "Ida, take my book and make the class repeat the words of the other verses – they don't know them properly. I will speak to you outside," and she led the newcomer out into the sunshine.

When Miss Bolt came in again every eye was fixed upon her. She smiled. She said: "Tomorrow we shall have a new schoolfellow. Her name is Olga Grey. Now we will go on with the singing."

The next morning, Olga Grey came to school early. She was just as pretty, very eager to make friends, very bright at her lessons. At the luncheon hour all the girls hung round her; she was something new – something fresh.

Ella Croft said: "Where do you live, Olga?"

Olga replied: "In London really, but we're staying here while Daddy's ill."

"She lives—" said Ida, and then stopped.

"Then you're in lodgings?" said Ella. That, of course, explained it. One of the farmers had taken them.

"Sort of," said Olga, smiling.

"Sort of!" repeated Ida. Ida, with her lovely voice, had been the unofficial head of the school; she could see at once that this new girl, who spoke differently from all of them, who could sing nearly as well as she could herself, would be their queen at once. Suppose – oh, suppose they gave her a chief part in the fairy opera!

"She doesn't live anywhere," said Betty Croft. "She's the fairy down from the hills."

Ida sniffed.

When school was over, the Croft girls wanted to ride up the valley with Olga, but she would not let them. She said: "Daddy will come down to meet me, and he can't bear strangers – not till he's stronger if you don't mind."

So the Croft girls watched her running up the little track beside the silver birches, looking more than ever like a fairy, and when she had passed out of sight, Ida Burman spoke.

She said: "I tell you why that girl won't let you go with her; she is a common gypsy; she lives in a caravan!"

Ella and Betty Croft looked at each other, and they laughed.

"A gypsy!" said Betty.

"With fair hair like that and speaking as she does! You're only jealous, Ida, because she's prettier than you."

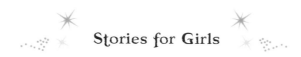

"If you had said she was a fairy now—" said Ella.

"I can tell you," said Ida, "they came down that hill track two days ago. My Uncle Tom, he wouldn't let them camp on his land – he said he didn't want his chickens and things stolen. Old Mr Graham let them have his little spinney place."

Ella started her pony. "They're certainly not gypsies," she said.

"They are!" said Ida. "You'll have Olga selling clothes pegs at your door, you see! A girl like that ought not to come to our school."

"Rubbish!" said Betty. But all the same she stopped in the middle of a game of tennis that evening to stare at a pedlar woman who was going to the back door with a basket. Was she possibly a relative of Olga Grey's?

Olga, too, at school was very reticent. Her mother was dead, she and her father lived together and a 'man' of father's cooked for them and looked after them. That startled the school. What sort of man? Rumours floated about of a strange, bent, dark man seen in Mr Graham's spinney, where the van was. Someone had seen the van, or said they had, but was hardly believed, because to get to Mr Graham's spinney you had to go practically across his lawn, and Mr Graham was touchy about his land and trespassers.

On the 23rd of June the school was reading part of Shakespeare's *A Midsummer Night's Dream*, and Tommy Darrington put up his hand.

"Please, teacher," he said, "I seen a fairy dance."

"Have you, Tommy? That is very interesting. Where?"

"Back of Mr Graham's house, miss, please. And there was lovely fairy music."

"How delightful! Well, as this is really midsummer-eve now, you'd better look out again tonight."

Betty Croft was watching Olga. She often did, because Olga's profile was so dainty. She saw Olga half turn to Tommy with a startled look in her eye, and a soft flush mounted to her face.

"I believe she is a fairy – really I believe she is," thought Betty.

Ida Burman put her hand on Betty's rein at close of school.

"Look here," she said, "Doris, and Hetty, and Bill Smith, and myself, and one or two more, we're going up to that caravan tonight – to find out things. They've cut the grass in Graham's long meadow now; we can sneak up between the haycocks and no one will see us. Like to come?"

"No – yes – I don't know," said Betty.

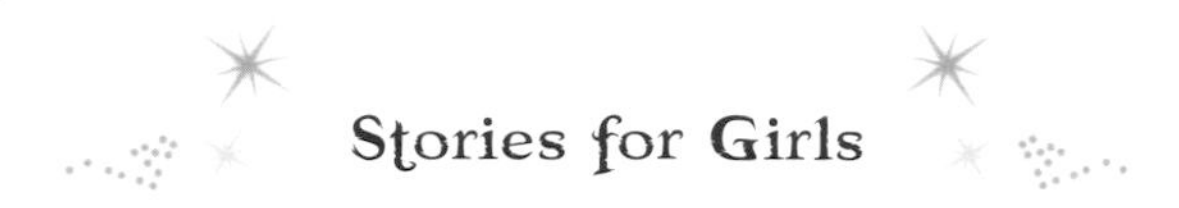

"If they're witches or gypsies we shall smash the windows. They've no right – people like that – to send children to this school."

"Ella and I will come," said Betty, and she put her lips firmly together. She wouldn't let anyone smash Olga's windows. Her brother Jim, the midshipman, was home on leave; she'd make him

come to Graham's spinney. Smash the windows! Who cared if Olga's people sold clothes pegs or not! Olga was a dear.

Up through the hayfield came the conspirators, in threes, and twos and ones. Betty and Ella and Jim were together.

There was the caravan at last, looking ghostly in the evening summer light, and there upon the steps sat Tommy Darrington. Just behind him, on a little stool, there was the bent, dark man, and he was playing on a violin. From the tent there came a fairy dressed in something that floated and shimmered. She glided to the steps of the caravan and then began to sway. The violin laughed and sobbed and wilted, and the fairy danced and danced.

"It's Olga, and she is a fairy then!" breathed Betty.

The violinist rose; his back was very crooked. Someone in the hayfield cried: "They're witches. Look – he's humped!" And threw a stone. The dancer hesitated, and then ran into the caravan.

Betty, Jim and Ella rose. "Stop that!" cried Jim, in what should have been a splendid naval voice, only it would end in a squeak, because Jim's voice was breaking.

"Mind your own business," cried the stone-thrower. "We're not going to have mad people here and coming to our school. Hi, witches!"

Jim and the boy who had thrown grappled with each other; little Tommy Darrington, on the caravan steps, stood up and shut the caravan steps and the caravan door, standing against it, outside, waving his crutch.

"Come on!" he cried. "Come on there, if you dare!"

No one came; they could hear Jim and the other boy scuffling, pummelling, breathing hard; they could see Tommy waving his crutch; they could hear unearthly music; and had seen fairy dancing; they were scared; they were angry because they were scared. Under the hedgerow were stones, cleared from the field; some of the children picked them up and threw them at the caravan; many missed, some pattered on the caravan; one hit Tommy.

The evening had clouded over badly and it was getting dark. A light suddenly appeared in the caravan – a bright light. The door was opened and a woman stood on the steps. A little cry of amazement went up from the children. It was Miss Bolt, their schoolmistress.

No more stones were thrown. Jim Croft hit his opponent on the nose once more and let him go. Miss Bolt just stood there, looking towards them. Nearly all the children ran away. Betty and

Ella thought of going to see Miss Bolt and saying they had come to save the caravan, not to attack it, but that seemed too much like boasting. They, too, turned round and went away.

In school next morning most of the children looked worried. Olga Grey did not appear; Tommy Darrington did not appear; Miss Bolt seemed late. If you spent the evening before throwing stones at the wooden roof that sheltered your schoolmistress, what happened to you?

Miss Bolt came. When prayers were over she said: "Children, your fairy opera performance won't take place. Up to last night I had some hope that Sir Gilbert Grey, who is a world-famous musician, and Olga's father, would have helped us. By your own actions you have now made that impossible."

A gasp went round the school. Ida Burman murmured: "She should have told us."

Miss Bolt said: "I think that Olga feared to seem superior. She wanted to make friends of you."

Betty Croft said: "Oh, Miss Bolt, isn't she coming any more?"

Miss Bolt shook her head. "No," she said, "they're moving on. The violinist, who is an old friend of Sir Gilbert's, thinks it better to find—" she hesitated, "a more hospitable valley. They are taking Tommy with them – Sir Gilbert thinks he knows a surgeon who can cure Tommy's leg."

"Teacher, we didn't know."

Miss Bolt rapped the desk. "Know!" she said, "Know! Couldn't you have trusted?" Her eyes rested on Tommy's empty place and softened. "It's better to believe in fairies and take things on trust," she said. "We'll miss the singing lesson. Get out your arithmetic books. Ida Burman, there were three sums wrong in your homework book; you will stay behind and get them right. Billy, close the door – I do not think we wish to see the hills today."

"No, miss," said Billy mournfully, and, as he closed the door, he thought he heard the creaking of a caravan upon the distant track.

Through the Looking Glass

An extract

by Lewis Carroll

Introduction

Through the Looking Glass *was written by Lewis Carroll, the pseudonym of Charles Lutwidge Dodgson (1832–1898). It is the sequel to* Alice's Adventures in Wonderland *and is full of brilliantly funny characters such as Tweedledum and Tweedledee. Alice climbs through the mirror on the sitting room mantlepiece and finds herself in a strange world where everything is in reverse. Her entire adventure is based on a game of chess.*

Alice looked at the Queen as her voice rose to a squeak. "Much be-etter! Be-etter! Be-e-e-etter! Be-e-ehh!" The last word ended in a long bleat, so like a sheep that Alice quite started.

She looked at the Queen, who seemed to have suddenly wrapped herself up in wool. Alice rubbed her eyes, and looked again. She couldn't make out what had happened at all. Was she in a shop? And was that really – was it really a *sheep* that was sitting on the other side of the counter? Rub as she could, she could make nothing more of it. She was in a little dark shop, leaning with her elbows on the counter, and opposite to her was an old sheep, sitting in an arm-chair knitting, and every now and then leaving off to look at her through a great pair of spectacles.

"What is it you want to buy?" the sheep said at last, looking up for a moment from her knitting.

"I don't *quite* know yet," Alice said, very gently. "I should like to look all round me first, if I might."

"You may look in front of you, and on both sides, if you like," said the sheep: "but you can't look *all* round you – unless you've got eyes at the back of your head."

But these, as it happened, Alice had *not* got, so she contented herself with turning round, looking at the shelves as she came to them.

The shop seemed to be full of all manner of curious things – but the oddest part of it all was, that whenever she looked hard at any shelf, to make out exactly what it had on it, that particular shelf was always quite empty, though the others round it were crowded as full as they could hold.

"Things flow about so here!" she said at last in a plaintive tone, after she had spent a minute or so vainly pursuing a large bright thing, that looked sometimes like a doll and sometimes like a work-box, and was always in the shelf next above the one she was looking at. "And this one is the most provoking of all – but I'll tell you what—" she added, as a sudden thought struck her, "I'll follow it up to the very top shelf of all. It'll puzzle it to go through the ceiling, I expect!"

But even this plan failed: the 'thing' went through the ceiling as quietly as possible, as if it were quite used to it.

"Are you a child or a teetotum?" the sheep said, as she took up another pair of needles. "You'll make me giddy soon, if you go on turning round like that." She was now working with fourteen pairs at once, and Alice couldn't help looking at her in great astonishment.

"How *can* she knit with so many?" the puzzled child thought to herself. "She gets more and more like a porcupine every minute!"

"Can you row?" the sheep asked, handing her a pair of knitting-needles as she spoke.

"Yes, a little. But not on land – and not with needles—" Alice was beginning to say, when suddenly the needles turned into oars in her hands, and she found they were in a little boat, gliding along between banks, so there was nothing for it but to do her best.

"Feather!" cried the sheep, as she took up another pair of needles.

This didn't sound like a remark that needed any answer, so Alice said nothing, but pulled away. There was something very queer about the water, she thought, as every now and then the oars got fast in it, and would hardly come out again.

"Feather! Feather!" the sheep cried again, taking more needles. "You'll be catching a crab directly."

'A dear little crab!' thought Alice. 'I should like that.'

"Didn't you hear me say 'Feather'?" the sheep cried angrily, taking up quite a bunch of needles.

"Indeed I did," said Alice: "you've said it very often – and very loud. Please, where *are* the crabs?"

"In the water, of course!" said the sheep, sticking some of the needles into her hair, as her hands were full. "Feather, I say!"

"*Why* do you say 'feather' so often?" Alice asked at last, rather vexed. "I'm not a bird!"

"You are," said the sheep: "you're a little goose."

This offended Alice a little, so there was no more conversation for a minute or two, while the boat glided gently on, sometimes among beds of weeds (which made the oars stick fast in the water, worse then ever), and sometimes under trees, but always with the same tall river-banks frowning over their heads.

"Oh, please! There are some scented rushes!" Alice cried in a sudden transport of delight. "There really are – and *such* beauties!"

"You needn't say 'please' to *me* about 'em" the sheep said, without looking up from her knitting: "I didn't put 'em there, and I'm not going to take 'em away."

"No, but I meant – please, may we wait and pick some?" Alice pleaded. "If you don't mind stopping the boat for a minute."

"How am I to stop it?" said the sheep. "If you leave off rowing, it'll stop of itself."

So the boat was left to drift down the stream as it would, till it glided gently in among the waving rushes. And then the little sleeves were carefully rolled up, and the little arms were plunged in elbow-deep to get the rushes a good long way down before breaking them off – and for a while Alice forgot all about the sheep and the knitting, as she bent over the side of the boat, with just the ends of her tangled hair dipping into the water, while with bright eager eyes she caught at one bunch after another of the darling scented rushes.

'I only hope the boat won't tipple over!' she thought to herself.

'Oh, *what* a lovely one! Only I couldn't quite reach it.' And it certainly *did* seem a little provoking – 'almost as if it happened on purpose,' she thought – that, though she managed to pick plenty of beautiful rushes as the boat glided by, there was always a more lovely one that she couldn't reach.

"The prettiest are always further!" she said at last, with a sigh at the obstinacy of the rushes in growing so far off, as, with flushed cheeks and dripping hair and hands, she scrambled back into her place, and began to arrange her new-found treasures.

What did it matter to her that the rushes had begun to fade, and to lose all their scent and beauty, from the very moment that she picked them? Even real scented rushes, you know, last only a very little while – and these, being dream-rushes, melted away almost like snow, as they lay in heaps at her feet – but Alice hardly noticed this, there were so many other curious things to think about.

They hadn't gone much farther before the blade of one of the oars got fast in the water and *wouldn't* come out again, and the consequence was that the handle of it caught her under the chin, and, in spite of a series of little shrieks of "Oh, oh, oh!" from poor Alice, it swept her off the seat, and down among the rushes.

However, she wasn't hurt, and was soon up again. The sheep went on with her knitting all the while, just as if nothing had happened. "That was a nice crab you caught!" she remarked, as Alice got back into her place, very much relieved to find herself still in the boat.

"Was it? I didn't see it," said Alice, peeping cautiously over the side of the boat into the dark water. "I wish it hadn't let go – I should so like to see a little crab to take home with me!" But the sheep only laughed scornfully, and went on with her knitting.

"Are there many crabs here?" said Alice.

"Crabs, and all sorts of things," said the sheep: "plenty of choice, only make up your mind. Now, what *do* you want to buy?"

"To buy!" Alice echoed in a tone that was half astonished and half frightened – for the boat, and the river, had vanished all in a moment, and she was back again in the little dark shop.

"I should like to buy an egg, please," she said timidly. "How do you sell them?"

"Fivepence farthing for one – twopence for two," the sheep replied.

"Then two are cheaper than one?" Alice asked, taking out her purse.

"Only you *must* eat them both, if you buy two," said the sheep.

"Then I'll have *one*, please," said Alice, as she put the money down on the counter. For she thought to herself, 'They mightn't be at all nice, you know.'

The sheep took the money, and put it away in a box. Then she said "I never put things into people's hands – that would never do – you must get it for yourself." And so saying, she went off to the other end of the shop, and set the egg upright on a shelf.

'I wonder *why* it wouldn't do?' thought Alice, as she groped her way among the tables and chairs, for the shop was very dark towards the end. 'The egg seems to get further away the more I walk towards it. Let me see, is this a chair? Why, it's got branches, I declare! How very odd to find trees growing here! And actually here's a little brook! Well, this is the very queerest shop I ever saw!'

So she went on, wondering more and more at every step, as everything turned into a tree the moment she came up to it, and she quite expected the egg to do the same.

Black Beauty

An extract
by Anna Sewell

Introduction

Black Beauty *was the only book written by Anna Sewell (1820–1878). Anna was a Quaker who suffered all her life from a chronic disease and was unable to walk unaided for any distance.* Black Beauty *is written as the autobiography of a young horse. At the beginning of this extract Black Beauty had just met Ginger, a chestnut filly who was to become a lifelong companion, and all was well in his life as he had a good and kind owner.*

Ginger

One day when Ginger and I were standing alone in the shade, we had a great deal of talk; she wanted to know all about my bringing up and breaking in, and I told her.

"Well," said she, "if I had had your bringing up I might have had as good a temper as you, but now I don't believe I ever shall."

"Why not?" I said.

"Because it has been all so different with me," she replied. "I never had any one, horse or man, that was kind to me, or that I cared to please, for in the first place I was taken from my mother as soon as I was weaned, and put with lots of other young colts; none of them cared for me, and I cared for none of them. There was no kind master like yours to look after me, and talk to me, and bring me nice things to eat. The man that had the care of us never gave me a kind word in my life. I do not mean that he ill-used me, but he did not care for us one bit further than to see that we had plenty to eat, and shelter. A footpath ran through our field, and very often the great boys passing through would fling stones to make us gallop. I was never hit, but one fine young colt was badly cut in the face. We did not care for them, but of course it made us more wild, and we settled it in our minds that boys were our enemies. We had very good fun in the meadows, galloping up and down and chasing each other round and round the field; then standing still under the shade of the trees. But when it came to breaking in, that was a bad time for me; several men came to catch me, and when at last they closed me in at one corner of the field, one caught me by the forelock, another caught me by the nose and held it so tight I could hardly draw my breath; then another took my under jaw in his hard hand and wrenched my mouth open, and so by force they got on the halter and the bar into my mouth; then one dragged me along by the halter, another flogging behind, and this was the first experience I had of men's kindness; it was all force. They did not give me a chance to know what they wanted. I was high bred and had a great deal of spirit, and was very wild, no doubt, and gave them, I dare say, plenty of trouble, but then it was dreadful to be shut up in a stall day after day instead of having my liberty, and I fretted and pined and wanted to get loose. You know yourself it's bad enough when you have a kind master and plenty of coaxing, but there was nothing of that sort for me.

"There was one – the old master, Mr Ryder – who, I think, could soon have brought me round, and could have done anything with me; but he had given up all the hard part of the trade to his son and to another experienced man, and he only came at times to oversee. His son was a strong, tall, bold man; they called him Samson, and he used to boast that he had never found a horse that could throw him. There was no gentleness in him, as there was in his father, but only hardness, a hard voice, a hard eye, a hard hand; and I felt from the first that what he wanted was to wear all the spirit out of me, and just make me into a quiet, humble, obedient piece of horseflesh. 'Horseflesh!' Yes, that is all that he thought about," and Ginger stamped her foot as if the thought of him made her angry. Then she went on:

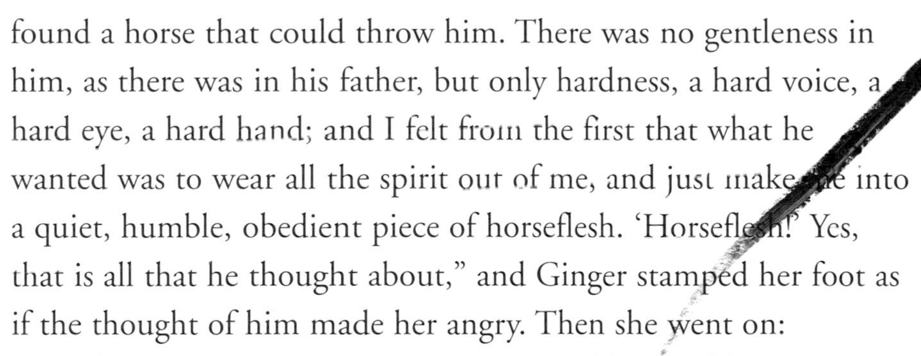

"If I did not do exactly what he wanted he would get put out,

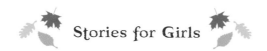

and make me run round with that long rein in the training field till he had tired me out. I think he drank a good deal, and I am quite sure that the oftener he drank the worse it was for me. One day he had worked me hard in every way he could, and when I lay down I was tired, and miserable, and angry; it all seemed so hard. The next morning he came for me early, and ran me round again for a long time. I had scarcely had an hour's rest, when he came again for me with a saddle and bridle and a new kind of bit. I could never quite tell how it came about; he had only just mounted me on the training ground, when something I did put him out of temper, and he chucked me hard with the rein. The new bit was very painful, and I reared up suddenly, which angered him still more, and he began to flog me. I felt my whole spirit set against him, and I began to kick, and plunge, and rear as I had never done before, and we had a regular fight; for a long time he stuck to the saddle and punished me cruelly with his whip and spurs, but my blood was thoroughly up, and I cared for nothing he could do if only I could get him off. At last after a terrible struggle I threw him off backward. I heard him fall heavily on the turf, and without looking behind me, I galloped off to the other end of the field; there I turned round and saw my persecutor

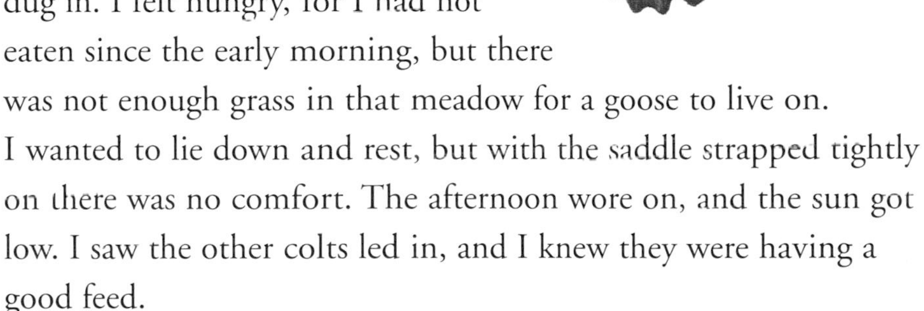

slowly rising from the ground and going into the stable. I stood under an oak tree and watched, but no one came to catch me. The time went on, and the sun was very hot; the flies swarmed round me and settled on my bleeding flanks where the spurs had dug in. I felt hungry, for I had not eaten since the early morning, but there was not enough grass in that meadow for a goose to live on. I wanted to lie down and rest, but with the saddle strapped tightly on there was no comfort. The afternoon wore on, and the sun got low. I saw the other colts led in, and I knew they were having a good feed.

"At last, just as the sun went down, I saw the old master come out with a sieve in his hand. He was a very fine old gentleman with quite white hair, but his voice was what I should know him by among a thousand. It was not high, nor yet low, but full, and clear, and kind, and when he gave orders it was so steady and decided that every one knew, both horses and men, that he expected to be obeyed. He came quietly along, now and then shaking the oats about that he had in the sieve, and speaking cheerfully and gently to me: 'Come along, lassie, come along, lassie; come along, come along.' I stood still and let him come up; he held the oats to me, and I began to eat without fear. He stood by, patting and stroking me while I was eating, and seeing the clots of blood on my side he seemed very vexed. 'Poor lassie! it was a bad business;' then he quietly took the rein and led me to the stable; just at the door stood Samson. I laid my ears back and snapped at him. 'Stand back,' said the master, 'and keep out of her way; you've done a bad day's work for this filly.' He growled out something about a vicious brute. 'Hark ye,' said the father, 'a bad-tempered man will never make a good-tempered horse. You've not learned your trade yet, Samson.' Then he led me into my box, took off the saddle and bridle with his own hands, and tied me up; then he called for a pail of warm water and a sponge, took off his coat, and while the stable-man held the pail, he sponged my sides so tenderly that I was sure he knew how sore and bruised they were. 'Whoa! my pretty one,' he said, 'stand still, stand still.' His very voice did me good, and the bathing was very comfortable. The skin was so broken at the corners of my mouth that I could not eat the hay. He looked closely at it, shook his head, and told the man to fetch a good bran mash and put some meal into it. How good that mash was! So soft and healing to my mouth. He stood by all the time I was eating, stroking me and talking to the man. 'If a high-mettled creature like this,' said he, 'can't be broken by fair means, she will never be good for anything.'

"After that he often came to see me, and when my mouth was healed the other breaker, Job, went on training me; he was steady and thoughtful, and I soon learned what he wanted." And so Ginger finished telling me about her bad start in life.

A Stormy Day

One day late in the autumn my master had a long journey to go on business. I was put into the dog-cart, and John went with his master. I always liked to go in the dog-cart, it was so light and the high wheels ran along so pleasantly. There had been a great deal of rain, and now the wind was very high and blew the dry leaves across the road in a shower. We went along merrily till we came to the toll-bar and the low wooden bridge. The river banks were rather high, and the bridge, instead of rising, went across just level, so that in the middle, if the river was full, the water would be nearly up to the woodwork, but as there were good substantial rails on each side, people did not mind it.

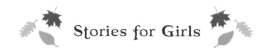

The man at the gate said the river was rising fast, and he feared it would be a bad night. In one low part of the road the water was halfway up to my knees. The bottom was good, and master drove gently, so it was no matter.

When we got to the town of course I had a good bait, but as the master's business engaged him a long time we did not start for home till late in the afternoon. The wind was then much higher, and I heard the master say to John that he had never been out in such a storm. And so I thought, as we went along the skirts of a wood, where the great branches were swaying about like twigs, and the rushing sound was terrible.

"I wish we were well out of this wood," said my master.

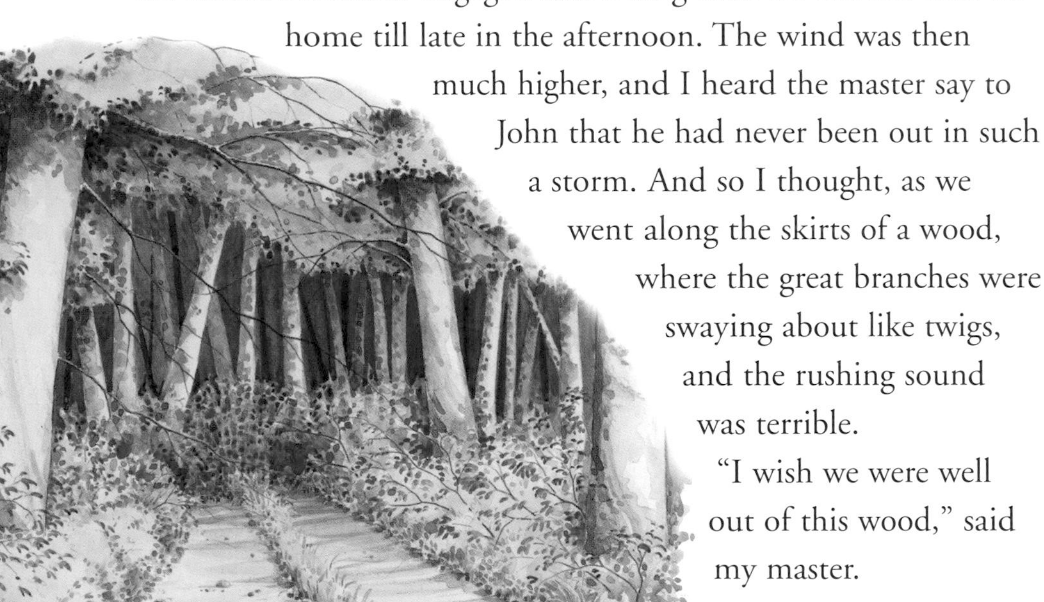

"Yes, sir," said John, "it would be rather awkward if one of these branches came down upon us."

The words were scarcely out of his mouth when there was a groan, and a crack, and a splitting sound, and tearing, crashing down among the other trees came an oak, torn up by the roots, and it fell right across the road just before us. I will never say I was not frightened, for I was. I stopped still, and I believe I trembled; of course I did not turn round or run away – I was not brought up to that. John jumped out and was in a moment at my head.

"That was a very near touch," said my master. "What's to be done now?"

"Well, sir, we can't drive over that tree, nor yet get round it. There will be nothing for it, but to go back and that will be a good six miles before we get round to the wooden bridge again."

So back we went and round by the crossroads, but by the time we got to the bridge it was very nearly dark; we could just see that the water was over the middle of it; but as that happened sometimes when the floods were out, master did not stop. We were going along at a good pace, but the moment my feet touched the first part of the bridge I felt sure there was something wrong. I dare not go forward, and I made a dead stop. "Go on, Beauty,"

said my master, and he gave me a touch with the whip, but I dare not stir. He gave me a sharp cut; I jumped, but I dare not go forward.

"There's something wrong, sir," said John, and he sprang out of the dog-cart and came to my head and looked all about. He tried to lead me forward. "Come on, Beauty, what's the matter?" Of course I could not tell him, but I knew very well that the bridge was not safe.

Just then the man at the toll-gate on the other side ran out of the house, tossing a torch about like one mad.

"Hoy, hoy, hoy! Halloo! Stop!" he cried.

"What's the matter?" shouted my master.

"The bridge is broken in the middle, and part of it is carried away; if you come on you'll be into the river."

"Thank God!" said my master.

"You Beauty!" said John, and took the bridle and gently turned me round. The wind seemed to have lulled off after that furious blast which tore up the tree. It grew darker and darker, stiller and stiller. I trotted quietly along, the wheels hardly making a sound on the soft road. For a good while neither master nor John spoke, and then master began in a serious voice. I could not understand much of what they said, but I found they thought, if I had gone on as the master wanted me, most likely the bridge would have given way under us, and horse, chaise, master, and man would have fallen into the river; and as the current was flowing very strongly, it was more than likely we should all have been drowned. Master said, 'God had given men reason by which they could find out things for themselves; but he had given animals knowledge that did not depend on reason, and which was much more prompt and perfect in its way, and by which they had often saved the lives of men.' John thought people did not value their animals half enough nor make friends of them as they ought to do.

At last we came to the park gates and found the gardener looking out for us. He said that mistress had been in a dreadful way ever since dark, fearing some accident had happened, and that she had sent James off on Justice, the roan cob, toward the bridge to enquire after us. As we approached, mistress ran out, saying,

"Have you had an accident?"

"No, my dear; but if your Black Beauty had not been wiser than we were we should all have been carried down the river at the wooden bridge."

Oh, what a good supper he gave me that night – a good bran mash and some crushed beans with my oats, and such a thick bed of straw! And I was glad of it, for I was tired.

The Witch in the Stone Boat

Retold by Fiona Waters

Introduction

This story comes from Iceland and was collected by Andrew Lang (1844–1912) in his Yellow Fairy Book *which was the fourth of his 'Colour Fairy Books'. It was during his study of myths and legends that he began collecting the fairy tales that made his name famous. He said, "nobody can write a new fairy tale; you can only mix up and dress the old stories and put characters into new dresses".*

Long, long ago when the winter winds blew icy cold from the north, there lived a king and queen who had a son called Sigurd. He was a mighty warrior but he had a kind heart. The king was growing old and frail and it was his great desire that Sigurd should have a wife by his side when he came to rule after him. The king had a fine girl in mind, Princess Gullveig, but she lived in another kingdom, far across the seas. Sigurd was happy to embark on this quest for his bride and so he set off to sail for several weeks until he reached the shores of Gullveig's home.

Sigurd's father had made a fine choice in Gullveig. She was not only beautiful, but she was courteous and gentle, and she possessed a quiet determination which, as you will see, was to stand her in good stead.

Sigurd and Gullveig were married and in time they had a child – a son whom they called Agnar. He was a happy child and he never cried or fretted.

News came that Sigurd's father was near death so Sigurd and Gullveig took Agnar and set sail with great haste. Sigurd piled on the sails so the boat would make good time, taking no rest for himself and staying on deck to encourage the sailors to keep up speed. But eventually he could not stay awake a moment longer so he went below and lay down, leaving Gullveig and Agnar on deck. He was not long gone before Gullveig saw a black boat sailing over the horizon. As it came nearer, she could see the boat was made of stone, with only one person on board. The stone boat drew alongside and the most dreadfully ugly witch clambered up beside the princess. In her terror, Gullveig became as stone herself, quite unable to move or cry out. The witch took hold of her and pulled off all her fine clothes that she then put on herself. Covering Gullveig with a dirty old cloak, the witch pushed her into the stone boat and with a shove set the boat sailing back from whence it came. Before long the boat was quite out of sight.

As soon as the stone boat was no longer visible, Agnar began to cry. The witch tried to hush the baby but he just kept on wailing and in the end Sigurd awoke and came up on deck to see what was the matter. The witch had taken on a human form so

Sigurd did not notice anything amiss although he was astonished when the supposed princess spoke to him in great anger, complaining that Sigurd should not have left her alone. She had never raised her voice to him before, but he was so busy trying to calm Agnar that he thought no more of it.

When they finally sailed into port it was to be greeted with the sad news that the old king had died. Sigurd was crowned king in his place and he set about restoring his kingdom to happiness. All went well except that Agnar hardly ever stopped crying from morn to night, though he had been such a good child before. Sigurd decided the child needed a nurse and as soon as she took over looking after him, Agnar stopped crying.

After a while it seemed to Sigurd that his princess, who was now the queen, had changed towards him since the voyage. He began to think that perhaps he had not made such a good choice of wife after all. She was always grumpy and spiteful, and spent a great deal of time locked away in her own room.

The nurse looked after Agnar as though he were her own and she could not help but notice that the boy always cried whenever the queen was near. But she kept quiet about this. Then one evening as she was putting Agnar to bed, there was a flash of pure

white light and a great hole opened up in the floor. A beautiful woman, dressed all in white with a great iron chain round her waist, rose up through the hole, took Agnar in her arms and covered him with kisses, tears falling down her face all the while. Then she sank back through the floor that closed up behind her.

The nurse was very frightened but did not dare say anything about this strange occurrence in case people thought she was not fit to look after Agnar.

The very next evening, the same thing happened. But this time the beautiful woman spoke as she held Agnar in her arms.

"Two are gone, and only one is left," she sighed sadly, then the floor closed over her again.

This time the nurse felt she could not keep these events secret so she went to the king and told him all that had happened. He trusted her completely and believed her strange tale. The next evening he joined the nurse and Agnar in the nursery, his sword drawn in his hand. Soon the white light filled the room again and as the beautiful woman came up through the floor, Sigurd could see that it was his own dear wife. He leapt to her side, severed the iron chain round her waist and caught her in his arms. There was a great rattling sound as the iron chain fell through the floor and seemed to tumble over and over again through the darkness. Agnar laughed with delight.

Gullveig told Sigurd the whole terrible story of how the witch had sailed up in the stone boat and taken her place. The stone boat had sailed through the darkness until it reached the gates of a huge stone castle where a three-headed giant had taken her prisoner, demanding that she marry him forthwith. She refused over and over again, plotting all the while how she might escape. Eventually she promised the three-headed giant that she would indeed marry him if he would only let her return for three nights to see Agnar, her son, first. The giant agreed but had tied the great iron chain round her waist so she could not escape.

The king now understood why his supposed queen had been so bad-tempered, and he ordered that she be brought into the nursery immediately. No longer in the guise of his beautiful wife, the witch stood spitting and scratching with rage in front of everyone, and then with a great cry she flung herself through the floor after the iron chain. She was never seen again in all the land. The king and queen ruled their kingdom for many years and lived in great happiness. Agnar grew up to become a fine young man – who always took special care of his mother.

Lorna Doone

An extract

by R D Blackmore

Introduction

Richard Doddridge Blackmore (1825–1900) wrote fourteen novels but his fame today rests solely on Lorna Doone. *Set in Exmoor, it is the story of an outlawed family – the Doones. They have murdered the father of John Ridd, who is twelve at the time of this extract, which chronicles his first meeting with Lorna. He takes Lorna to be a Doone, but she was kidnapped by them as a child, and is in fact a wealthy heiress. She and John eventually fall in love.*

Lorna Doone

When I came to myself again, my hands were full of young grass and mould, and a little girl kneeling at my side was rubbing my forehead tenderly with a dock-leaf and a handkerchief.

"Oh, I am so glad," she whispered softly, as I opened my eyes and looked at her; "now you will try to be better, won't you?"

I had never heard so sweet a sound as came from between her bright red lips, while there she knelt and gazed at me; neither had I ever seen anything so beautiful as the large dark eyes intent upon me, full of pity and wonder. And then, my nature being slow, and perhaps, for that matter, heavy, I wandered with my hazy eyes down the black shower of her hair, as to my jaded gaze it seemed; and where it fell on the turf, among it (like an early star) was the first buttercup of the season. And since that day I think of her, through all the rough storms of my life, when I see an early buttercup.

Perhaps she liked my countenance, and indeed I know she did, because she said so afterwards, although at the time she was too young to know what made her take to me. Not that I had any beauty, or ever pretended to have any, only a solid healthy face, which many girls have laughed at.

Thereupon I sat upright, with my little trident still in one hand, and was much afraid to speak to her, being conscious of my country-brogue, lest she should cease to like me. But she clapped her hands, and made a trifling dance around my back, and came to me on the other side, as if I were a great plaything.

"What is your name?" she said – as if she had every right to ask me – "and how did you come here, and what are these wet things in this great bag?"

"You had better let them alone," I said. "They are loaches for my mother. But I will give you some, if you like."

"Dear me, how much you think of

them! Why, they are only fish. But how your feet are bleeding! Oh, I must tie them up for you. And no shoes nor stockings! Is your mother very poor, poor boy?"

"No," I said, being vexed at this. "We are rich enough to buy all this great meadow, if we chose; and here my shoes and stockings be."

"Why, they are quite as wet as your feet, and I cannot bear to see your feet. Oh, please to let me manage them – I will do it very softly."

"Oh, I don't think much of that," I replied; "I shall put some goose-grease to them. But how you are looking at me! I never saw anyone like you before. My name is John Ridd. What is your name?"

"Lorna Doone," she answered, in a low voice, as if afraid of it, and hanging her head so that I could see only her forehead and eyelashes; "if you please, my name is Lorna Doone, and I thought you must have known it."

Then I stood up and touched her hand, and tried to make her look at me, but she only turned away the more. Young and harmless as she was, her name alone made guilt of her. Nevertheless I could not help looking at her tenderly, and the more when her blushes turned into tears, and her tears to long, low sobs.

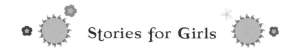

"Don't cry," I said, "whatever you do. I am sure you have never done any harm. I will give you all my fish Lorna, and catch some more for mother – only don't be angry with me."

She flung her little soft arms up in the passion of her tears, and looked at me so piteously, that what did I do but kiss her. It seemed to be a very odd thing, when I came to think of it, because I hated kissing so, as all honest boys must do. But she touched my heart with a sudden delight, like a cowslip-blossom (although there were none to be seen yet), and the sweetest flowers of spring. She gave me no encouragement, as my mother in her place would have done; nay, she even wiped her lips (which I thought was rather rude of her), and drew away, and smoothed her dress, as if I had used a freedom. Then I felt my cheeks grow burning red, and I gazed at my legs and was sorry. For although she was not at all a proud child (at any rate in her countenance), I knew that she was by birth a thousand years in front of me. They might have taken and framed me, or (which would be more to the purpose) my sisters, until it was time for us to die, and then have trained our children after us, for many generations; yet never could we have gotten that look upon our faces which Lorna Doone had naturally, as if she had been born to it.

Here was I, a yeoman's boy, a yeoman every inch of me, from head to foot; and there was she, a lady born, and thoroughly aware of it, and dressed by people of rank and taste, who took pride in her beauty and set it to advantage. For though her hair was fallen down by reason of her wildness, and some of her frock was touched with wet where she had tended me so, behold her dress was pretty enough for the queen of all the angels. The colours were bright and rich indeed, and the substance very sumptuous, yet simple and free from gaudy stuff, and matching most harmoniously. All from her waist to her neck was white, plaited in close like a curtain, and the dark soft weeping of her hair, and the shadowy light of her eyes (like a wood rayed through with sunset), made it seem yet whiter, as if it were done on purpose. As for the rest, she knew what it was a great deal better than I did, for I never could look far away from her eyes when they were opened upon me.

Now, seeing how I heeded her, and feeling that I had kissed her, although she was such a little girl, eight years old or thereabouts, she turned to the stream in a bashful manner, and began to watch the water, and rubbed one leg against the other.

I, for my part, being vexed at her behaviour to me, took up all my things to go, and made a fuss about it; to let her know I was going. But she did not call me back at all, as I had made sure she would do; moreover, I knew that to try the descent was almost certain death to me, and it looked as dark as pitch; and so at the mouth I turned round again, and came back to her, and said,

"Lorna."

"Oh, I thought you were gone," she answered. "Why did you ever come here? Do you know what they would do to us, if they found you here with me?"

"Beat us, I dare say, very hard – or me, at least. They could never beat you,"

"No. They would kill us both outright, and bury us here by the water; and the water often tells me that I must come to that."

"But what should they kill me for?"

"Because you have found the way up here, and they never could believe it. Now, please to go – oh, please to go. They will kill us both in a moment. Yes, I like you very much" – for I was teasing her to say it – "very much indeed, and I will call you John Ridd, if you like. Only please to go, John. And when your feet are

well, you know, you can come and tell me how they are."

"But I tell you, Lorna, I like you very much indeed – nearly as much as Annie, and a great deal more than Lizzie. And I never saw anyone like you, and I must come back again tomorrow, and so must you, to see me, and I will bring you such lots of things – there are apples still, and a thrush I caught, and our dog has just had puppies—"

"Oh, dear, they won't let me have a dog. There is not a dog in the valley. They say they are such noisy things—"

"Only put your hand in mine – what little things they are, Lorna! And I will bring you the loveliest dog – I will show you just how long he is."

"Hush!" A shout came down the valley, and all my heart was trembling, like water after sunset, and Lorna's face was altered from pleasant play to terror. She shrank to me, and looked up at me with such a power of weakness, that I at once made up my mind to save her or to die with her. A tingle went through all my bones, and I only longed for my carbine. The little girl took courage from me, and put her cheek quite close to mine.

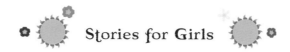

"Come with me down the waterfall. I can carry you easily and mother will take care of you."

"No, no," she cried, as I took her up: "I will tell you what to do. They are only looking for me. You see that hole, that hole there?"

She pointed to a little niche in the rock that verged the meadow, about fifty yards away from us. In the fading of the twilight I could just descry it.

"Yes, I see it, but they will see me crossing the grass to get there."

"Look! look!" She could hardly speak. "There is a way out from the top of it – they would kill me if I told it. Oh, here they come, I can see them."

The little maid turned as white as the snow which hung on the rocks above her, and she looked at the water and then at me, and she cried, "Oh dear! oh dear!" And then she began to sob aloud, being so young and unready. But I drew her behind the withy-bushes, and close down to the water, where it was quiet and shelving deep, where it came to the lip of the chasm. Here they could not see either of us from the upper valley, and might have sought a long time for us, even when they came quite near, if the trees had been clad with their summer clothes. Luckily I had picked up my fish and taken my three-pronged fork away.

Crouching in that hollow nest, as children get together in ever so little compass, I saw a dozen fierce men come down, on the other side of the water, not bearing any fire-arms, but looking lax and jovial, as if they were come from riding and a dinner taken hungrily. "Queen, queen!" they were shouting, here and there, and now and then: "where the pest is our little queen gone?"

"They always call me 'queen,' and I am to be queen by-and-by," Lorna whispered to me, with her soft cheek on my rough one, and her little heart beating against me: "oh, they are crossing by the timber there, and then they are sure to see us."

"Stop," said I. "Now I see what to do. I must get into the water, and you must go to sleep."

"To be sure, yes, away in the meadow there. But how bitter cold it will be for you!"

She saw in a moment the way to do it, sooner than I could tell her, and there was no time to lose.

"Now mind you never come again," she whispered over her shoulder, as she crept away with a childish twist hiding her white front from me; "only I shall come sometimes – oh, here they are, Madonna!"

Daring scarce to peep, I crept into the water, and lay down bodily in it, with my head between two blocks of stone, and some flood-drift combing over me. The dusk was deepening between the hills and a white mist lay on the river, but I, being in the channel of it, could see every ripple, and twig, and rush, and glazing of twilight above it, as bright as in a picture; so that to my ignorance there seemed no chance at all but what the men must find me. For all this time they were shouting and swearing, and keeping such a hullabaloo, that the rocks all round the valley rang, and my heart quaked, so (what with this and the cold) that the water began to gurgle round me, and to lap upon the pebbles.

Neither in truth did I try to stop it, being now so desperate, between the fear and the wretchedness; till I caught a glimpse of the little maid, whose beauty and whose kindliness had made me yearn to be with her. And then I knew that for her sake I was

bound to be brave and hide myself. She was lying beneath a rock, thirty or forty yards from me, feigning to be fast asleep, with her dress spread beautifully, and her hair drawn over her.

Presently one of the great, rough men came round a corner upon her, and there he stopped and gazed awhile at her fairness and her innocence. Then he caught her up in his arms, and kissed her so that I heard him – and if I had only brought my gun, I would have tried to shoot him.

"Here our queen is! Here's the queen, here's the captain's daughter!" he shouted to his comrades. "Fast asleep, by God, and hearty! Now I have first claim to her, and no one else shall touch the child. Back to the bottle, all of you!"

He set her dainty little form upon his great square shoulder, and her narrow feet in one broad hand, and so in triumph marched away, with the purple velvet of her skirt ruffling in his long black beard, and the silken length of her hair fetched out, like a cloud by the wind behind her. This way of her going vexed me so, that I leaped upright in the water, and must have been spied by some of them, but for their haste to the wine bottle. Of their little queen they took small notice, being in this urgency; although they had thought to find her drowned; but trooped away after one

another with kindly challenge to gambling, so far as I could make them out; and I kept sharp watch, I assure you.

Going up that darkened glen, little Lorna, riding still the largest and most fierce of them, turned and put up a hand to me, and I put up a hand to her, in the thick of the mist and the willows.

She was gone, my little dear, and when I got over my terrible fright, I longed to have more to say to her. Her voice to me was so different from all I had ever heard before, as might be a sweet silver bell intoned to the small chords of a harp. But I had no time to think about this, if I hoped to have any supper.

I crept into a bush for warmth, and rubbed my shivering legs on bark, for I was freezing cold. Then as daylight sank below the forget-me-not of stars, with a sorrow to be quit, I knew that now must be my time to get away, if there were any.

Therefore, wringing my sodden breeches, I managed to crawl from the bank to the niche in the cliff that Lorna had shown me.

Through the dusk I had trouble to see the mouth, at even the five land-yards of distance. Nevertheless, I entered well, and held on by some dead fern-stems, and did hope that no one would shoot me.

But while I was hugging myself like this, with a boyish manner of reasoning, my joy was like to have ended in sad grief both to myself and my mother, and haply to all honest folk who shall love to read this history. For hearing a noise in front of me, and like a coward not knowing where, but afraid to turn round or think of it, I felt myself going down some deep passage into a pit of darkness. It was no good to catch the sides, the whole thing seemed to go with me. Then, without knowing how, I was leaning over a night of water.

This water was of black radiance, as are certain diamonds, spanned across with vaults of rock, and carrying no image, neither showing marge nor end, but centred (at it might be) with a bottomless indrawal.

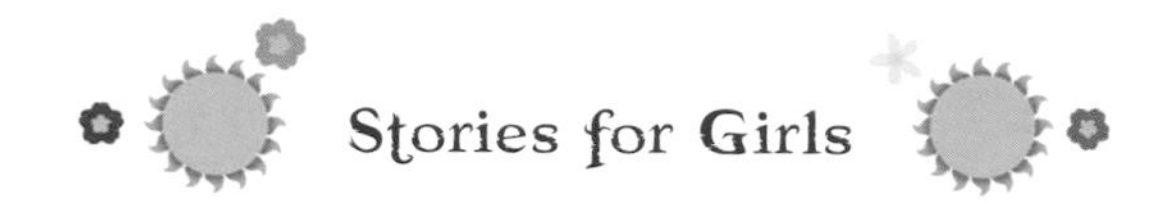

With that chill and dread upon me, and the sheer rock all around, and the faint light heaving wavily on the silence of this gulf, I must have lost my wits and gone to the bottom, if there were any.

But suddenly a robin sang (as they will do after dark, towards spring) in the brown fern and ivy behind me. I took it for our little Annie's voice (for she could call any robin), and gathering quick warm comfort, sprang up the steep way towards the starlight. Climbing back, as the stones glid down, I heard the cold greedy wave go japping, like a blind black dog, into the distance of arches and hollow depths of darkness.

The Railway Children

An extract
by Edith Nesbit

Introduction

Edith Nesbit (1858–1924) wrote many stories for children, mostly after she was forty. She used the initial E rather than Edith in order to disguise the fact that she was a woman.

In The Railway Children *Roberta (Bobbie), Peter and Phyllis have to move to the country with their mother when their father is suddenly taken away. The children spend much of their time watching the trains that pass by their cottage.*

Saviours of the Train

Their mother was so delighted with the cherries that they had picked that the three children racked their brains to find some other surprise for her. But all the racking did not bring out any idea more novel than wild strawberries. And this idea occurred to them next morning. They had seen the flowers on the plants in the spring, and they knew where to find wild strawberries. The plants grew all up and along the rocky face of the cliff out of which the mouth of the tunnel opened. There were all sorts of trees there – birches and beeches and baby oaks and hazels – and among them the red strawberries glistened on the ground like rubies in the sun.

The mouth of the tunnel was some way from Three Chimneys, so Mother let them take their lunch with them in a basket. And the basket would do to bring the strawberries back in if they found any. She also lent them her silver watch so that they should not be late for tea – Peter's Waterbury had taken it into its head not to go since the day when Peter dropped it into the water-

butt. And they started. When they got to the top of the cutting, they leaned over the fence and looked down to where the railway lines lay at the bottom of what, as Phyllis said, was exactly like a mountain gorge.

"If it wasn't for the railway at the bottom, it would be as though the foot of man had never been there, wouldn't it?" she said.

The sides of the cutting were of grey stone, very roughly hewn. Indeed the top part of the cutting had been a little natural glen that had been cut deeper to bring it down to the level of the tunnel's mouth. Among the rocks, grass and flowers grew, and seeds dropped by birds in the crannies of the stone had taken root and grown into bushes and trees that overhung the cutting. Near the tunnel was a flight of steps leading down to the line – just wooden bars roughly fixed into the earth – a very steep and narrow way, more like a ladder than a stair.

"We'd better get down," said Peter; "I'm sure the strawberries would be quite easy to get at from the side of the steps. You remember it was there we picked the cherry blossoms that we put on the rabbit's funeral grave."

So they went along the fence towards the little swing gate that is at the top of these steps. And they were almost at the gate when Bobbie said: "Hush. Stop! What's that?"

'That' was a very odd noise indeed – a soft noise, but quite plainly to be heard through the sound of the wind in the tree branches, and the hum and whirr of the telegraph wires. It was a sort of rustling, whispering sound. As they listened it stopped, and then it began again.

And this time it did not stop, but it grew louder and more rustling and rumbling. "Look," cried Peter, suddenly; "the tree over there!"

The tree he pointed at was one of those that have rough grey leaves and white flowers. The berries, when they come, are bright scarlet, but if you pick them, they disappoint you by turning black before you get them home. And, as Peter pointed, the tree was moving – not just the way trees ought to move when the wind blows through them, but all in one piece, as though it were a live creature and were walking down the side of the cutting.

"It's moving!" cried Bobbie. "Oh, look! And so are the others. It's like the woods in Macbeth."

"It's magic," said Phyllis, breathlessly. "I always knew this railway was enchanted."

It really did seem a little like magic. For all the trees for about twenty yards of the opposite bank seemed to be slowly walking down towards the railway line, the tree with the grey leaves bringing up the rear like some old shepherd driving a flock of green sheep.

"What is it? Oh, what is it?" said Phyllis; "it's much too magic for me. I don't like it. Let's go home."

But Bobby and Peter clung fast to the rail and watched breathlessly. And Phyllis made no movement towards going home by herself.

The trees moved on and on. Some stones and loose earth fell down and rattled on the railway metals far below.

"It's all coming down," Peter tried to say, but he found there was hardly any voice to say it with. And, indeed, just as he spoke, the great rock, on the top of which the walking trees were, leaned slowly forward. The trees, ceasing to walk, stood still and shivered. Leaning with the rock, they seemed to hesitate a moment, and then rock and trees and grass and bushes, with a rushing sound, slipped right away from the face of the cutting and fell on the line with a blundering crash that could have been heard half a mile off. A cloud of dust rose up.

"Oh," said Peter, in awestruck tones, "isn't it exactly like when coals come in? If there wasn't any roof to the cellar and you could see down."

"Look what a great mound it's made!" said Bobbie.

"Yes, it's right across the down line," said Phyllis.

"That'll take some sweeping up," said Bobbie.

"Yes," said Peter, slowly. He was still leaning on the fence.

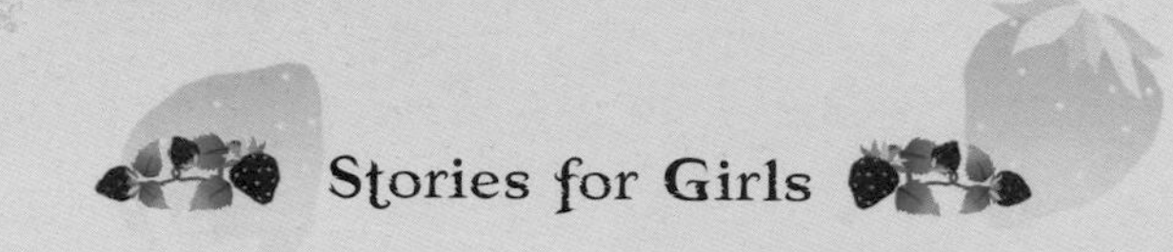

"Yes," he said again, still more slowly.

Then he stood upright. "The 11.29 hasn't gone by yet. We must let them know at the station, or there'll be a most frightful accident."

"Let's run," said Bobbie, and began.

But Peter cried, "Come back!" and looked at Mother's watch. He was very prompt and businesslike, and his face looked whiter than they had ever seen it.

"No time," he said; "it's two miles away, and it's past eleven."

"Couldn't we," suggested Phyllis, breathlessly, "couldn't we climb up a telegraph post and do something to the wires?"

"We don't know how," said Peter.

"They do it in war," said Phyllis; "I know I've heard of it."

"They only cut them, silly," said Peter, "and that doesn't do any good. And we couldn't cut them even if we got up, and we couldn't get up. If we had anything red, we could get down on the line and wave it."

"But the train wouldn't see us till it got round the corner, and then it could see the mound just as well as us," said Phyllis. "Better, because it's much bigger than us."

"If we only had something red," Peter repeated, "we could

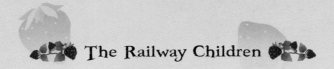

go round the corner and wave to the train."

"We might wave, anyway."

"They'd only think it was just us, as usual. We've waved so often before. Anyway, let's get down."

They got down the steep stairs. Bobbie was pale and shivering. Peter's face looked thinner than usual. Phyllis was red-faced and damp with anxiety.

"Oh, how hot I am!" she said; "and I thought it was going to be cold. I wish we hadn't put on our—" she stopped short, and then ended in quite a different tone "our flannel petticoats."

Bobbie turned at the bottom of the stairs. "Oh, yes," she cried. "They're red! Let's take them off."

They did, and with the petticoats rolled up under their arms, ran along the railway, skirting the newly fallen mound of stones and rock and earth, and bent, crushed, twisted trees. They ran at their best pace. Peter led, but the girls were not far behind. They reached the corner that hid the mound from the straight line of railway that ran half a mile without curve or corner.

"Now," said Peter, taking hold of the largest flannel petticoat.

"You're not—" Phyllis faltered, "you're not going to tear them?"

"Shut up," said Peter, with brief sternness.

"Oh, yes," said Bobbie, "tear them into little bits if you like. Don't you see, Phil, if we can't stop the train, there'll be a real live accident, with people killed. Oh, horrible! Here, Peter, you'll never tear it through the band!"

She took the red flannel petticoat from him and tore it off an inch from the band. Then she tore the other in the same way.

"There!" said Peter, tearing in his turn. He divided each petticoat into three pieces. "Now, we've got six flags." He looked at the watch again. "And we've got seven minutes. We must have flag-staffs."

The knives given to boys are, for some odd reason, seldom of the kind of steel that keeps sharp. The young saplings had to be broken off. Two came up by the roots. The leaves were stripped from them.

"We must cut holes in the flags, and run the sticks through the holes," said Peter. And the holes were cut. The knife was sharp enough to cut flannel with. Two of the flags were set up in heaps of loose stones between the sleepers of the down line. Then Phyllis and Roberta took each a flag, and stood ready to wave it as soon as the train came in sight.

"I shall have the other two myself," said Peter, "because it was my idea to wave something red."

"They're our petticoats, though," Phyllis was beginning, but Bobbie interrupted:

"Oh, what does it matter who waves what, if we can only save the train?"

Perhaps Peter had not rightly calculated the number of minutes it would take the 11.29 to get from the station to the place where they were, or perhaps the train was late. Anyway, it seemed a very long time that they waited.

Phyllis grew impatient. "I expect the watch is wrong, and the train's gone by," said she.

Peter relaxed the heroic attitude he had chosen to show off his two flags with. And Bobbie began to feel sick with suspense.

It seemed to her that they had been standing there for hours and hours, holding those silly little red flannel flags that no one would ever notice. The train wouldn't care. It would go rushing by them and tear round the corner and go crashing into that awful mound. And everyone would be killed. Her hands grew very cold and trembled so that she could hardly hold the flag. And then came the distant rumble and hum of the metals, and a puff of

white steam showed far away along the stretch of line.

"Stand firm," said Peter, "and wave like mad! When it gets to that big furze bush step back, but go on waving! Don't stand on the line, Bobbie!"

The train came rattling along very, very fast.

"They don't see us! They won't see us! It's all no good!" cried Bobbie.

The two little flags on the line swayed as the nearing train shook and loosened the heaps of loose stones that held them up. One of them slowly leaned over and fell on the line. Bobbie jumped forward and caught it up, and waved it; her hands did not tremble now.

"Keep off the line, you silly cuckoo!" said Peter, fiercely.

It seemed that the train came on as fast as ever. It was very near now.

"It's no good," Bobbie said again.

"Stand back!" cried Peter, suddenly, and he dragged Phyllis back by the arm.

But Bobbie cried, "Not yet, not yet!" and waved her two flags right over the line. The front of the engine looked black and enormous. It's voice was loud and harsh.

"Oh, stop, stop, stop!" cried Bobbie. No one heard her. At least Peter and Phyllis didn't, for the oncoming rush of the train covered the sound of her voice with a mountain of sound. But afterwards she used to wonder whether the engine itself had not heard her. It seemed almost as though it had, for it slackened swiftly, slackened and stopped, not twenty yards from the place where Bobbie's two flags waved over the line. She saw the great black engine stop dead, but somehow she could not stop waving the flags. And when the driver and the fireman had got off the engine and Peter and Phyllis had gone to meet them and pour out their excited tale of the awful mound just round the corner, Bobbie still waved the flags but more and more feebly and jerkily.

When the others turned towards her she was lying across the line with her hands flung forward and still gripping the sticks of the little red flannel flags.

The engine-driver picked her up, carried her to the train, and laid her on the cushions of a first-class carriage.

"Gone right off in a faint," he said, " Poor little woman. And no wonder. I'll just 'ave a look at this 'ere mound of yours, and then we'll run you back to the station and get her seen to."
It was horrible to see Bobbie lying so white and quiet, with her lips blue, and parted.

"I believe that's what people look like when they're dead," whispered Phyllis.

"Don't!" said Peter, sharply.

They sat by Bobbie on the blue cushions, and the train ran back. Before it reached their station Bobbie had sighed and opened her eyes, and rolled herself over and begun to cry. This cheered the others wonderfully. They had seen her cry before, but they had never seen her faint, nor anyone else, for the matter of that. They had not known what to do when she was fainting, but now she was only crying they could thump her on the back and tell her not to, just as they always did. And presently, when she stopped crying, they were able to laugh at her for being such a coward as to faint.

When the station was reached, the three were the heroes of an

agitated meeting on the platform.

The praises they got for their 'prompt action,' their 'common sense,' their 'ingenuity,' were enough to have turned anybody's head. Phyllis enjoyed herself thoroughly. She had never been a real heroine before, and the feeling was delicious. Peter's ears got very red. Yet he, too, enjoyed himself. Only Bobbie wished they all wouldn't. She wanted to get away.

"You'll hear from the Company about this, I expect," said the Station Master.

Bobbie wished she might never hear of it again. She pulled at Peter's jacket.

"Oh, come away, come away! I want to go home," she said. So they went. And as they went Station Master and Porter and guards and driver and fireman and passengers sent up a cheer.

"Oh, listen," cried Phyllis; "that's for us!"

"Yes," said Peter, "I say, I am glad I thought about something red, and waving it."

"How lucky we did put on our red flannel petticoats!" said Phyllis.

Bobbie said nothing. She was thinking of the horrible mound, and the trustful train rushing towards it.

"And it was us that saved them," said Peter.

"How dreadful if they'd all been killed!" said Phyllis, with enjoyment; "Wouldn't it, Bobbie?"

"We never got any strawberries, after all," said Bobbie.

The others thought her rather heartless.

The Terrible Secret

When they first went to live at Three Chimneys, the children had talked a great deal about their Father, and had asked a great many questions about him, and what he was doing and where he was and when he would come home. Mother always answered their questions as well as she could. But as the time went on they grew to speak less of him. Bobbie had felt almost from the first that for some strange miserable reason these questions hurt Mother and made her sad. And little by little the others came to have this feeling, too, though they could not have put it into words.

One day, when Mother was working so hard that she could not leave off even for ten minutes, Bobbie carried up her tea to the big bare room that they called Mother's workshop. It had hardly

any furniture. Just a table and a chair and a rug. But always big pots of flowers on the window-sills and on the mantelpiece. The children saw to that. And from the three long uncurtained windows the beautiful stretch of meadow and moorland, the far violet of the hills, and the unchanging changefulness of cloud and sky.

"Here's your tea, Mother-love," said Bobbie. "Do drink it while it's hot."

Mother laid down her pen among the pages that were scattered all over the table, pages covered with her writing, which was almost as plain as print, and much prettier. She ran her hands into her hair, as if she were going to pull it out by handfuls.

"Poor dear head," said Bobbie, "does it ache?"

"No – yes – not much," said Mother. "Bobbie, do you think Peter and Phil are *forgetting* Father?"

"No," said Bobbie, indignantly. "Why?"

"You none of you ever speak of him now."

Bobbie stood first on one leg and then on the other.

"We often talk about him when we're by ourselves," she said.

"But not to me," said Mother. "Why?"

Bobbie did not find it easy to say why.

"I – you—" she said and stopped. She went over to the

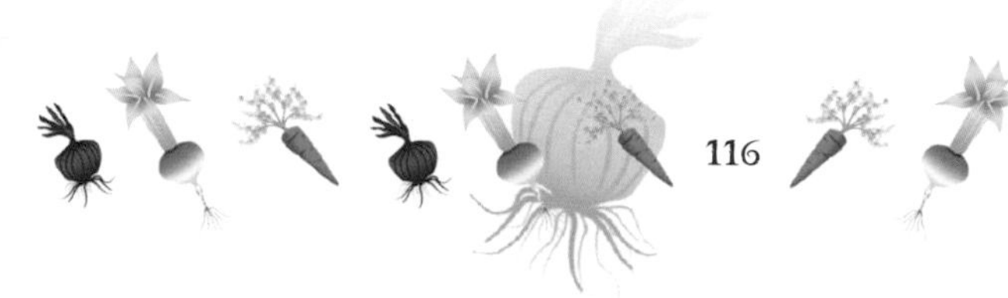

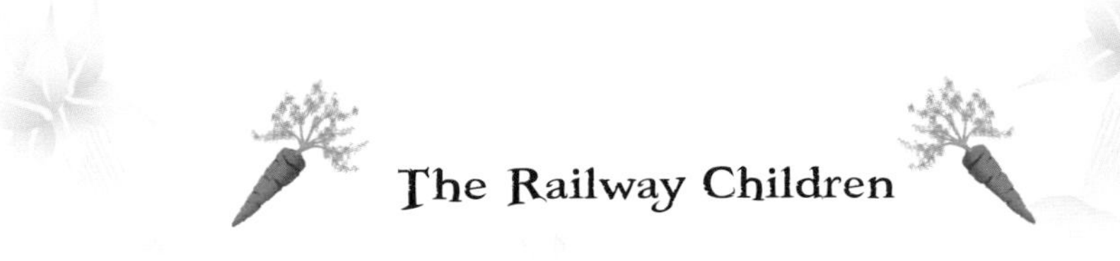

window and looked out.

"Bobbie, come here," said her Mother, and Bobbie came.

"Now," said Mother, putting her arm round Bobbie and laying her ruffled head against Bobbie's shoulder, "try to tell me, dear."

Bobbie fidgeted.

"Tell Mother."

"Well, then," said Bobbie, "I thought you were so unhappy about Daddy not being here, it made you worse when I talked about him. So I stopped doing it."

"And the others?"

"I don't know about the others," said Bobbie. "I never said anything about *that* to them. But I expect they felt the same about it as me."

"Bobbie dear," said Mother, still leaning her head against her, "I'll tell you. Besides parting from Father, he and I have had a great sorrow – oh, terrible – worse than anything you can think of, and at first it did hurt to hear you all talking of him as if everything were just the same. But it would be much more terrible if you were to forget him. That would be worse than anything."

"The trouble," said Bobbie, in a very little voice, "I promised I would never ask you any questions, and I never have, have I? But

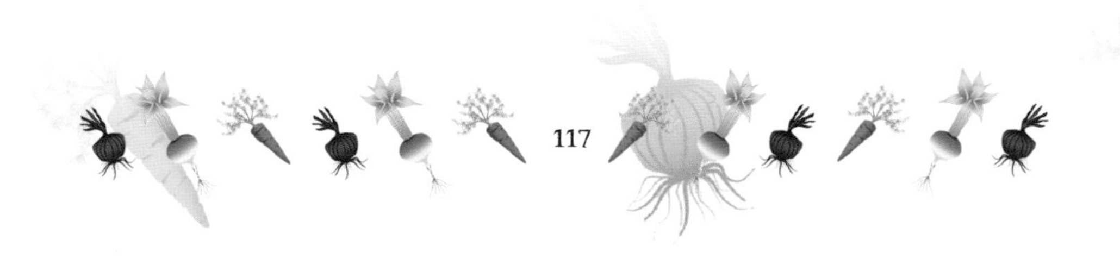

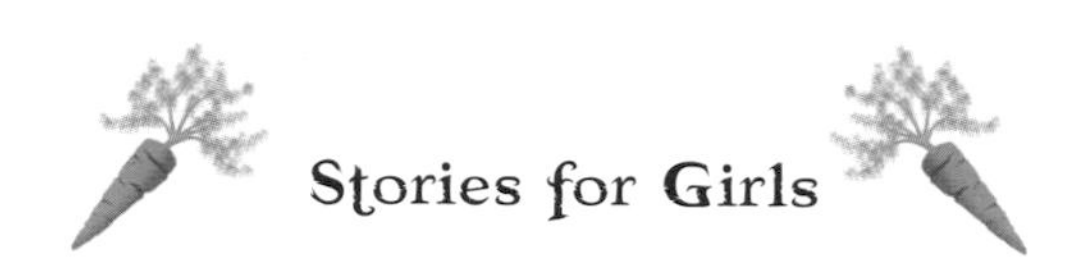

– the trouble – it won't last always?"

"No," said Mother, "the worst will be over when Father comes home to us."

"I wish I could comfort you," said Bobbie.

"Oh, my dear, do you suppose you don't? Do you think I haven't noticed how good you've all been, not quarrelling nearly as much as you used to – and all the little kind things you do for me – the flowers, and cleaning my shoes, and tearing up to make my bed before I get time to do it myself?"

Bobbie *had* sometimes wondered whether Mother noticed these things.

"That's nothing," she said, "to what—"

"I *must* get on with my work," said Mother, giving Bobbie one last squeeze. "Don't say anything to the others."

That evening in the hour before bedtime instead of reading to the children Mother told them stories of the games she and Father used to have when they were children and lived near each other in the country – tales of the adventures of Father with Mother's brothers when they were all boys together. Very funny stories they were, and the children laughed as they listened.

"Uncle Edward died before he was grown up, didn't he?" said

Phyllis, as Mother lighted the bedroom candles.

"Yes, dear," said Mother, "you would have loved him. He was such a brave boy, and so adventurous. Always in mischief, and yet friends with everybody in spite of it. And your Uncle Reggie's in Ceylon, and Father's away, too. But I think they'd all like to think we'd enjoyed talking about the things they used to do. Don't you think so?"

"Not Uncle Edward," said Phyllis, in a shocked tone, "he's in heaven."

"You don't suppose he's forgotten us and all the old times, because God has taken him, any more than I forget him. Oh, no, he remembers. He's only away for a little time. We shall see him some day."

"And Uncle Reggie – and Father, too?" said Peter.

"Yes," said Mother. "Uncle Reggie and Father, too. Goodnight, my darlings."

"Good night," said everyone. Bobbie hugged her mother more closely even than usual, and whispered in her ear, "Oh, I do love you so, Mummy – I do – I do—"

When Bobbie came to think it all over, she tried not to wonder what the great trouble was. But she could not always help it. Father was not dead – like poor Uncle Edward – Mother had said so. And he was not ill, or Mother would have been with him. Being poor wasn't the trouble. Bobbie knew it was something nearer the heart than money could be.

"I mustn't try to think what it is," she told herself, "no, I mustn't. I *am* glad Mother noticed about us not quarrelling so much. We'll keep that up."

But alas, that very afternoon she and Peter had what Peter called a first-class shindy.

They had not been a week at Three Chimneys before they had asked Mother to let them have a piece of garden each for their very own, and she had agreed, and the south border under the peach trees had been divided into three pieces and they were allowed to plant whatever they liked there.

Phyllis had planted mignonette and nasturtium and Virginia Stock in hers. The seeds came up, and though they looked just like weeds, Phyllis believed that they would bear flowers some day. The Virginia Stock justified her faith quite soon, and her garden was bright with a band of vivid little flowers, pink and white and red and mauve.

"I can't weed for fear I pull up the wrong things," she used to say comfortably, "it saves such a lot of work."

Peter sowed vegetable seeds in his – carrots and onions and turnips. The seed was given to him by the farmer who lived in the nice black-and-white, wood-and-plaster house just beyond the bridge. He kept turkeys and guinea fowls, and was a most amiable man. But Peter's vegetables never had much of a chance, because he liked to use the earth of his garden for digging canals, and making forts and earthworks for his toy soldiers. And the seeds of vegetables rarely come to much in a soil that is constantly disturbed for the purposes of war and irrigation.

Bobbie planted rose-bushes in her garden, but all the little new leaves of the rose-bushes shrivelled and withered, perhaps because she moved them from the other part of the garden in May, which is not at all the right time of year for moving roses. But she would not own that they were dead, until the day when Perks came up to see the garden, and told her quite plainly that all her roses were as dead as doornails.

"Only good for bonfires, Miss," he said. "You just dig 'em up and burn 'em, and I'll give you some nice fresh roots outer my garden – pansies, and stocks, and sweet willies, and forget-me-nots. I'll bring 'em along tomorrow if you get the ground ready."

So next day she set to work, and that happened to be the day when Mother had praised her and the others about not quarrelling. She moved the rose-bushes and carried them to the other end of the garden, where the rubbish heap was that they meant to make a bonfire of when Guy Fawkes' Day came.

Meanwhile Peter had decided to flatten out all his forts and earthworks, with a view to making a model of the railway-tunnel, cutting, embankment, canal, aqueduct, bridges and all.

So when Bobbie came back from her last thorny journey with the dead rose-bushes, he had got the rake and was using it busily.

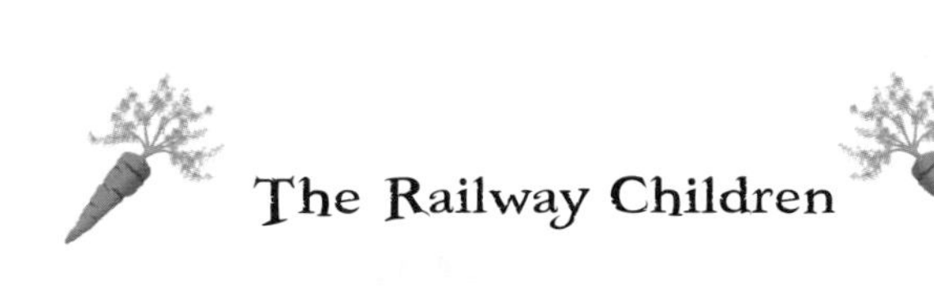

"I was using the rake," said Bobbie.

"Well, I'm using it now," said Peter.

"But I had it first," said Bobbie.

"Then it's my turn now," said Peter. And that was how the quarrel began. "You're always being disagreeable about nothing," said Peter, after some heated argument.

"I had the rake first," said Bobbie, flushed and defiant, holding onto its handle.

"Don't – I tell you I said this morning I meant to have it. Didn't I, Phil?"

Phyllis said she didn't want to be mixed up in their rows. And instantly, of course, she was.

"If you remember, you ought to say."

"Of course she doesn't remember – but she might say so."

"I wish I'd had a brother instead of two whiny little kiddy sisters," said Peter. This was always recognised as indicating the high-water mark of Peter's rage.

Bobbie made the reply she always made to it.

"I can't think why little boys were ever invented," and just as she said it she looked up, and saw the three long windows of Mother's workshop flashing in the red rays of the sun. The sight

brought back those words of praise: 'You don't quarrel like you used to do.'"

"*Oh!*" cried Bobbie, just as if she had been hit, or had caught her finger in a door, or had felt the hideous sharp beginnings of toothache.

"What's the matter?" said Phyllis.

Bobbie wanted to say: 'Don't let's quarrel. Mother hates it so,' but she couldn't. Peter was looking too disagreeable and insulting.

"Take the horrid rake, then," was the best she could manage. And she suddenly let go her hold on the handle. Peter had been holding on to it too firmly, and now that the pull the other way was suddenly stopped, he staggered and fell over backward, the teeth of the rake between his feet.

"Serve you right," said Bobbie, before she could stop herself.

Peter lay still for half a moment – long enough to frighten Bobbie a little. Then he frightened her a little more, for he sat up, screamed once, turned rather pale, and then lay back and began to shriek, faintly but steadily. It sounded exactly like a pig being killed a quarter of a mile off.

Mother put her head out of the window, and it wasn't half a minute after that she was in the garden kneeling by the side of

Peter, who never for an instant ceased to squeal.

"What happened, Bobbie?" Mother asked.

"It was the rake," said Phyllis. "Peter was pulling at it, so was Bobbie, and she let go and he went over."

"Stop that noise, Peter," said Mother. "Come. Stop at once."

Peter used up what breath he had left in a last squeal and stopped.

"Now," said Mother, "are you hurt?"

"He must be really hurt, or he wouldn't make such a fuss," said Bobbie, still trembling with fury, "he's not a coward!"

"I think my foot's broken off, that's all," said Peter, huffily, and sat up. Then he turned quite white. Mother put her arm round him.

"He *is* hurt," she said, "he's fainted. Here, Bobbie, sit down and take his head on your lap."

Then Mother undid Peter's boots. As she took the right one off, something dripped from his foot on to the ground. It was red blood. And when the stocking came off there were three red wounds in Peter's foot and ankle, where the teeth of the rake had bitten him, and his foot was covered with red smears.

"Run for water – a basinful," said Mother, and Phyllis ran. She

upset most of the water out of the basin in her haste, and had to fetch more in a jug.

Peter did not open his eyes again till Mother had tied her handkerchief round his foot, and she and Bobbie had carried him in and laid him on the brown wooden settle in the dining room. By this time Phyllis was halfway to the Doctor's.

Mother sat by Peter and bathed his foot and talked to him, and Bobbie went out and got tea ready, and put on the kettle.

'It's all I can do,' she thought to herself. 'Oh, suppose Peter should die, or be a helpless cripple for life, or have to walk with crutches, or wear a boot with a sole like a log of wood!'

She stood by the back door reflecting on these gloomy

possibilities, her eyes fixed on the water-butt.

"I wish I'd never been born," she said, and she said it out loud.

The Doctor came and looked at the foot and bandaged it beautifully, and said that Peter must not put it to the ground for at least a week.

"He won't be lame, or have to wear crutches or a have a lump on his foot, will he?" whispered Bobbie, breathlessly, at the door.

"My aunt! No!" said Dr. Forrest, "he'll be as nimble as ever on his pins in a fortnight. Don't you worry, little Mother Goose."

It was when Mother had gone to the gate with the Doctor to take his last instructions and Phyllis was filling the kettle for tea, that Peter and Bobbie found themselves alone.

"He says you won't be lame or anything," said Bobbie.

"Oh, course I shan't, silly," said Peter, very much relieved all the same.

"Oh, Peter, I *am* so sorry," said Bobbie, after a pause.

"That's all right," said Peter, gruffly.

"It was *all* my fault," said Bobbie.

"Rot," said Peter.

"If we hadn't quarrelled, it wouldn't have happened. I knew it was wrong to quarrel. I wanted to say so, but somehow I couldn't."

"Don't drivel," said Peter. "I shouldn't have stopped if you *had* said it. Not likely."

"But I knew it was wrong to quarrel," said Bobbie, in tears, "and now you're hurt and—"

"Now look here," said Peter, firmly, "you just dry up. If you're not careful, you'll turn into a beastly little Sunday-school prig, so I tell you."

"I don't mean to be a prig. But it's so hard not to be when you're really trying to be good."

"Not it," said Peter, "it's a jolly good thing it wasn't you was hurt. I'm glad it was *me*. There! If it had been you, you'd have been lying on the sofa looking like a suffering angel and being the light of the anxious household and all that. And I couldn't have stood it."

"No, I shouldn't," said Bobbie.

"Yes, you would," said Peter.

"I tell you I shouldn't."

"I tell you you would."

"Oh, children," said Mother's voice at the door. "Quarrelling again? Already?"

"We aren't quarrelling – not really," said Peter. "I wish you

wouldn't think it's rows every time we don't agree!" When Mother had gone out again, Bobbie broke out,

"Peter, I *am* sorry you're hurt. But you *are* a beast to say I'm a prig."

"Well," said Peter unexpectedly, "perhaps I am. You did say I wasn't a coward, even when you were in such a wax. The only thing is – don't you be a prig, that's all. You keep your eyes open and if you feel priggishness coming on just stop in time. See?"

"Yes," said Bobbie, "I see."

"Then let's call it Pax," said Peter, magnanimously. "Bury the hatchet. I say, Bobbie, old chap, I am tired."

At first Bobbie found it quite hard to be as nice to him as she wanted to be, for fear he should think her priggish. But that soon wore off, and both she and Phyllis were, as he observed, jolly good sorts. Mother sat with him when his sisters were out. And the words, 'he's not a coward,' made Peter determined not to fuss about the pain in his foot, though it was rather bad. Praise helps people very much, sometimes.

There were visitors, too. Mrs Perks came up to ask how he was, and so did the Station Master, and several of the village people. But the time went slowly, slowly.

"I do wish there was something to read," said Peter. "I've read all our books fifty times over."

"I'll go to the Doctor's," said Phyllis, "he's sure to have some."

"Only about how to be ill, and about people's nasty insides, I expect," said Peter.

"Perks has a whole heap of magazines that came out of trains when people are tired of them," said Bobbie. "I'll run down and ask him."

So the girls went their two ways.

Bobbie found Perks busy cleaning lamps.

"And how's the young gent?" he asked.

"Better, thanks," said Bobbie, "but he's most frightfully bored. I came to ask if you'd got any magazines you could lend him."

"There, now," said Perks, regretfully, rubbing his ear with a black and oily lump of cotton waste, "why didn't I think of that, now? I was trying to think of something as 'ud amuse him only this morning, and I couldn't think of anything better than a guinea-pig. And a young chap I know's going to fetch that over for him this teatime."

"How lovely! A real live guinea! He will be pleased. But he'd like the magazines as well."

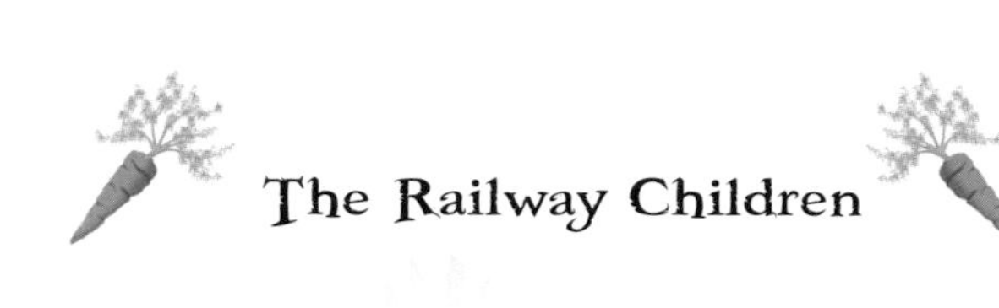

"That's just it," said Perks. "I've just sent the pick of 'em to Snigson's boy – him what's just getting over the pewmonia. But I've lots of illustrated papers left."

He turned to the pile of papers in the corner and took up a heap six inches thick.

"There!" he said. "I'll just slip a bit of string and a bit of paper round 'em."

He pulled an old newspaper from the pile and spread it on the table, and made a neat parcel of it.

"There," said he, "there's lots of pictures, and if he likes to mess 'em about with his paint-box, or coloured chalks or what not, why, let him. I don't want 'em."

"You're a dear," said Bobbie, took the parcel, and started off for home. The papers were heavy, and when she had to wait at the level-crossing while a train went by, she rested the parcel on the top of the gate. And idly she looked at the printing on the paper that the parcel was wrapped in.

Suddenly she clutched the parcel tighter and bent her head over it. It seemed like some horrible dream. She read on – the bottom of the column was torn off – she could read no farther.

She never remembered how she got home. But she went on

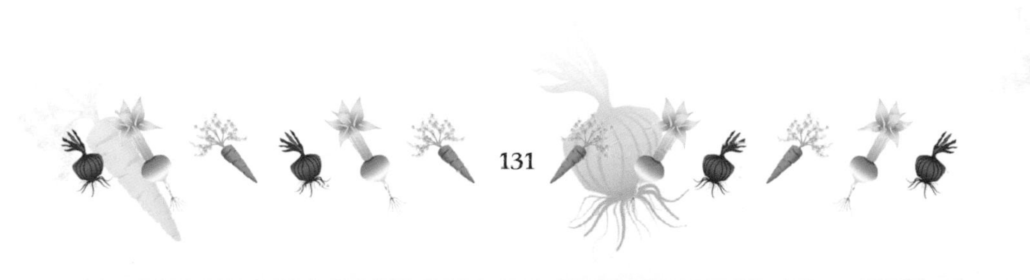

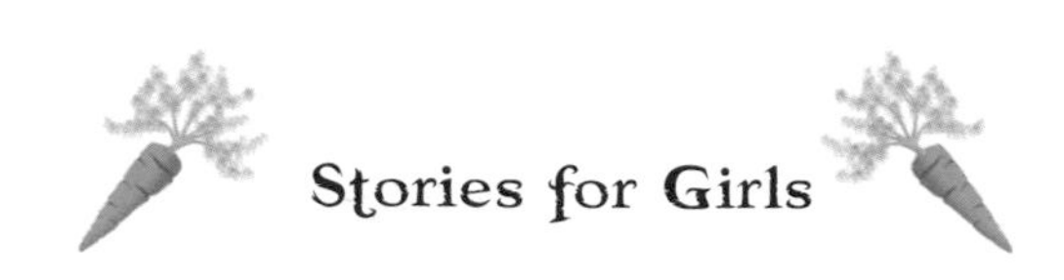

tiptoe to her room and locked the door. Then she undid the parcel and read that printed column again, sitting on the edge of her bed. When she had read all there was, she drew a long breath.

"So now I know," she said.

What she had read was headed, 'End of the Trial. Verdict. Sentence.'

The name of the man who had been tried was the name of her Father. The verdict was 'Guilty.' And the sentence was 'Five years' Penal Servitude.'

"Oh, Daddy," she whispered, crushing the paper hard, "it's not true – I don't believe it. You never did it! Never, never, never!"

There was a hammering on the door.

"What is it?" said Bobbie.

"It's me," said the voice of Phyllis; "tea's ready, and a boy's brought Peter a guinea-pig. Come along down."

And Bobbie had to.

Vanity Fair

An extract
by William Makepeace Thackeray

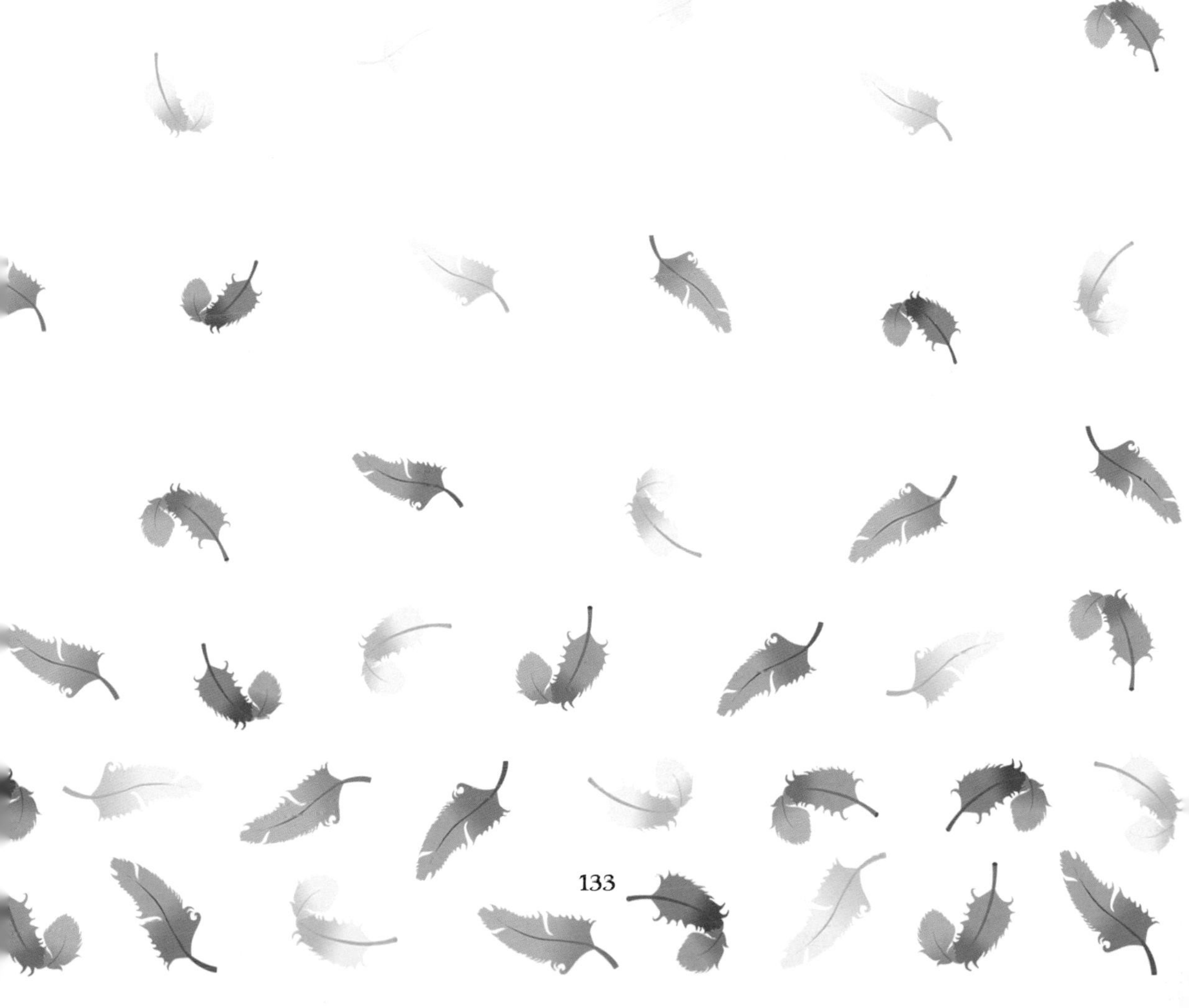

Introduction

William Makepeace Thackeray (1811–1863) began his career after a spell at Trinity College, Cambridge, as a journalist. Vanity Fair *was his first major novel and was published in 1847. It tells the tale of the fortunes of two young women at the time of the Napoleonic Wars. Becky Sharp is a penniless orphan, while Amelia Sedley is the sheltered daughter of a city merchant. This extract sees them leaving their academy for ladies.*

On one sunshiny morning in June, there drove up to the great iron gate of Miss Pinkerton's academy for young ladies, on Chiswick Mall, a large family coach, with two fat horses in blazing harness, driven by a fat coachman in a three-cornered hat and wig, at the rate of four miles an hour. A servant, who reposed on the box beside the fat coachman, uncurled his bandy legs as soon as the equipage drew up opposite Miss Pinkerton's shining brass plate, and as he pulled the bell at least a score of young heads were seen peering out of the narrow windows of the stately old brick house. Nay, the acute observer might have recognized the little red nose of good-natured Miss Jemima Pinkerton herself, rising over some geranium pots in the window of that lady's own drawing-room.

"It is Mrs Sedley's coach, sister," said Miss Jemima. "James, the servant, has just rung the bell; and the coachman has a new red waistcoat."

"Have you completed all the preparations necessary for Miss Sedley's departure, Miss Jemima?" asked Miss Pinkerton herself, that majestic lady, the friend of Doctor Johnson, the correspondent of Mrs Chapone herself.

"The girls were up at four this morning, packing her trunks, sister," replied Miss Jemima; "we have made her a bow-pot."

"Say a bouquet, sister Jemima, 'tis more genteel."

"Well, a booky as big almost as a haystack; I have put up two bottles of the gillyflower water for Mrs Sedley, and the receipt for making it, in Amelia's box."

"And I trust, Miss Jemima, you have made a copy of Miss Sedley's account. This is it, is it? Very good – ninety-three pounds, four shillings. Be kind enough to address it to John Sedley, Esquire, and to seal this letter which I have written to his lady."

In Miss Jemima's eyes an autograph letter of her sister, Miss Pinkerton, was an object of as deep veneration as would have been a letter from a sovereign. Only when her pupils quitted the establishment, or when they were about to be married, and once, when poor Miss Birch died of the scarlet fever, was Miss Pinkerton known to write personally to the parents of her pupils; and it was Jemima's opinion that if anything could console Mrs Birch for her daughter's loss, it would be that pious and eloquent composition in which Miss Pinkerton announced the event.

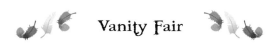

In the present instance Miss Pinkerton's "letter" was to the following effect:

The Mall, Chiswick, 15th June

Madam,

After her six years' residence at the Mall, I have the honour and happiness of presenting Miss Amelia Sedley to her parents, as a young lady not unworthy to occupy a fitting position in their polished and refined circle. Those virtues which characterize the young English gentlewoman, those accomplishments which become her birth and station, will not be found wanting in the amiable Miss Sedley, whose industry and obedience have endeared her to her instructors, and whose delightful sweetness of temper has charmed her aged and her youthful companions.

In music, in dancing, in orthography, in every variety of embroidery and needlework, she will be found to have realized her friends' fondest wishes. In geography there is still much to be desired, and a careful and undeviating use of the backboard, for four hours daily during the next three years, is recommended as necessary to the acquirement of that dignified deportment and carriage, so requisite for every young lady of fashion.

In the principles of religion and morality, Miss Sedley will be found worthy of an establishment which has been honoured by the presence of The Great Lexicographer, and the patronage of the admirable Mrs Chapone. In leaving the Mall, Miss Amelia carries with her the hearts of her companions, and the affectionate regards of her mistress, who has the honour to subscribe herself,

Madam, Your most obliged humble servant,
Barbara Pinkerton

P.S. Miss Sharp accompanies Miss Sedley. It is particularly requested that Miss Sharp's stay in Russell Square may not exceed ten days. The family of distinction with whom she is engaged, desire to avail themselves of her services as soon as possible.

This letter completed, Miss Pinkerton proceeded to write her own name, and Miss Sedley's, in the fly-leaf of a Johnson's Dictionary – the interesting work which she invariably presented to her scholars, on their departure from the Mall. On the cover was inserted a copy of 'Lines addressed to a young lady on quitting Miss Pinkerton's school, at the Mall; by the late revered Doctor

Samuel Johnson.' In fact, the Lexicographer's name was always on the lips of this majestic woman, and a visit he had paid to her was the cause of her reputation and her fortune.

Being commanded by her elder sister to get the Dictionary from the cupboard, Miss Jemima had extracted two copies of the book from the receptacle in question. When Miss Pinkerton had finished the inscription in the first, Jemima, with rather a dubious and timid air, handed her the second.

"For whom is this, Miss Jemima?" said Miss Pinkerton, with awful coldness.

"For Becky Sharp," answered Jemima, trembling very much, and blushing over her withered face and neck, as she turned her back on her sister. "For Becky Sharp. She's going too."

"MISS JEMIMA!" exclaimed Miss Pinkerton, in the largest capitals. "Are you in your senses? Replace the dictionary in the closet, and never venture to take such a liberty in future."

"Well, sister, it's only two-and-ninepence, and poor Becky will be miserable if she don't get one."

"Send Miss Sedley instantly to me," said Miss Pinkerton. And so venturing not to say another word, poor Jemima trotted off, exceedingly flurried and nervous.

Miss Sedley's papa was a merchant in London, and a man of some wealth; whereas Miss Sharp was an articled pupil, for whom Miss Pinkerton had done, as she thought, quite enough, without conferring upon her at parting the high honour of the dictionary.

Although schoolmistresses' letters are to be trusted no more nor less than churchyard epitaphs, it sometimes happens that a person departs this life who is really deserving of all the praises the stone cutter carves over his bones. Miss Amelia Sedley was a young lady of this singular species, and deserved not only all that Miss Pinkerton said in her praise, but had many charming qualities which that pompous old Minerva of a woman could not see, from the differences of rank and age between her pupil and herself.

For she could not only sing like a lark, dance gracefully, embroider beautifully and spell as well as a dictionary itself; she also had such a kindly, smiling, tender, gentle, generous heart of her own, as won the love of everybody who came near her, from Minerva herself down to the poor girl in the scullery, and the one-eyed tart-woman's daughter. She had twelve intimate and bosom friends out of the twenty four young ladies. Even envious Miss Briggs never spoke ill of her, high and mighty Miss Saltire (Lord Dexter's granddaughter) allowed that her figure was genteel, and as for Miss Swartz, on the day Amelia went away, she was in such a passion of tears that they were obliged to send for Dr Floss, and try to revive her with smelling salts. Miss Pinkerton's attachment was, as may be supposed from the high position and eminent virtues of that lady, calm and dignified, but Miss Jemima had already whimpered several times at the idea of Amelia's departure and, but for fear of her sister, would have gone off in downright hysterics. Such luxury of grief, however, is only allowed to parlour-boarders. Honest Jemima had all the bills, and the washing, and the mending, and the puddings, and the plate and crockery, and the servants to superintend. But why speak about her? It is probable that we shall not hear of her again from this moment to the end of time, and that when the great filigree iron gates are once closed on her, she and her awful sister will never issue therefrom into this little world of history.

But as we are to see a great deal of Amelia, there is no harm in saying, at the outset of our acquaintance, that she was a dear little creature, and a great mercy it is, both in life and in novels, which (and the latter especially) abound in villains of the most sombre sort, that we are to have for a constant companion so guileless and good-natured a person. As she is not a heroine, there is no need to describe her person. Indeed I am afraid that her nose was rather short and her cheeks a great deal too round and red for a heroine. However, her face blushed with rosy health, and her lips with the freshest of smiles. She had a pair of eyes that sparkled with the brightest good-humour, except indeed when they filled with tears – and that was a great deal too often – for the silly thing would cry over a dead canary-bird or the end of a novel, were it ever so stupid. As for saying an unkind word to her, were any persons hard-hearted enough to do so – why, so much the worse for them. Even Miss Pinkerton, that austere and godlike woman, ceased scolding her after the first time, and though she no more comprehended sensibility than she did Algebra, gave all masters and teachers particular orders to treat Miss Sedley with the utmost gentleness, as harsh treatment was injurious to her.

So that when the day of departure came, between her two customs of laughing and crying, Miss Sedley was greatly puzzled how to act. She was glad to go home, and yet most woefully sad at leaving school. For three days before, little Laura Martin, the orphan, followed her about like a little dog. She had to make and receive at least fourteen presents – to make fourteen solemn promises of writing every week: "Send my letters under cover to my grandpapa, the Earl of Dexter," said Miss Saltire (who, by the way, was rather shabby). "Never mind the postage, but write every day, you dear darling," said the impetuous and scatty, but generous and affectionate Miss Swartz and the orphan little Laura Martin took her friend's hand and said, looking up in her face wistfully, "Amelia, when I write to you I shall call you Mamma."

Well, then. The flowers, and the presents, and the trunks, and bonnet-boxes of Miss Sedley having been arranged by Mr James in the carriage, together with a very small and weather-beaten old cow's-skin case with Miss Sharp's card neatly nailed upon it, which was delivered by James with a grin, and packed by the coachman with a corresponding sneer – the hour for parting came and the grief of that moment was considerably lessened by the admirable discourse that Miss Pinkerton addressed to her pupil. Not that the parting speech caused Amelia to philosophise – it was intolerably dull, pompous, and tedious and having the fear of her schoolmistress greatly before her eyes.

"You'll go in and say goodbye to Miss Pinkerton, Becky!" said Miss Jemima to a young lady of whom nobody took any notice, and who was coming downstairs with her own bandbox.

"I suppose I must," said Miss Sharp calmly, and much to the wonder of Miss Jemima; and the latter having knocked at the door, and receiving permission to come in, Miss Sharp advanced in a very unconcerned manner, and said in French, and with a perfect accent, "Mademoiselle, je viens vous faire mes adieux."

Miss Pinkerton did not understand French, but biting her lips and throwing up her venerable and Roman-nosed head she said, "Miss Sharp, I wish you a good morning." As Miss Pinkerton spoke, she waved one hand to give Miss Sharp an opportunity of shaking the hand that was left out for that purpose.

Miss Sharp only folded her own hands with a very frigid bow, and quite declined to accept the proffered honour; on which Miss Pinkerton tossed up her head more indignantly than ever. "Heaven bless you, my child," said she, embracing Amelia, and scowling the while over the girl's shoulder at Miss Sharp. "Come away, Becky," said Miss Jemima, pulling the young woman away and the drawing room door closed upon them for ever.

Then came the struggle and parting below. There was such a scuffling, and hugging, and kissing, and crying, as no pen can depict, and as the tender heart would fain pass over. The embracing was over, they parted – that is, Miss Sedley parted from her friends. Miss Sharp had demurely entered the carriage some minutes before. Nobody cried for leaving her.

James slammed the carriage door on his young weeping mistress. He sprang up behind the carriage. "Stop!" cried Miss Jemima, rushing to the gate with a parcel.

"It's some sandwiches, my dear," said she to Amelia. "You may be hungry, you know. And Becky, Becky Sharp, here's a book for you that my sister – that is, I – Johnson's Dictionary, you know you mustn't leave us without that. Goodbye. Drive on, coachman. God bless you!"

And the kind creature retreated into the garden, overcome with emotion.

But, lo! and just as the coach drove off, Miss Sharp put her pale face out of the window and actually flung the book back into the garden.

This almost caused Jemima to faint with terror. "Well, I never..." said she "what an audacious..." Emotion prevented her from completing either sentence. The carriage rolled away, the great gates were closed and the bell rang for the dancing lesson. The world is before the two young ladies, and so, farewell to Chiswick Mall.

The Giant Sisters and the Silver Swan

Retold by Fiona Waters

Introduction

This fairy tale puts a new spin on many familiar fairy tale ingredients. Here we find a prince under a spell, a penniless heroine who embarks on a quest to rescue him and devious female giants hiding in their lair. The story probably originates from eastern Europe.

Prince Locket lived with his parents, King Roland and Queen Rosalind the Fair, in a castle deep in an ancient forest. The castle had stout wooden gates, but they were never closed as King Roland did not believe in pomp and ceremony. He always wanted his people to feel they could walk in whenever they wanted to see him and discuss the weather, or how best to cure a cow who had hiccups.

The village well was a stone's throw from the gates and simple wooden cottages were huddled around the marketplace. In one of these lived Lynnet, whose father was a cheesemaker. She often used to see Prince Locket as he went out with his sleek hunting dogs and a band of cheerful companions. Lynnet was a quiet girl but when she smiled her eyes crinkled in a most attractive way and she was possessed of a kind heart and great good sense.

One day, a very curious thing happened. As Prince Locket was riding home with his friends, a sudden and mysterious mist enveloped him, and him only. His friends were at first puzzled and then alarmed. When the mist lifted, as inexplicably as it had fallen, Prince Locket was nowhere to be seen. His friends shouted his name until they were hoarse, and the sleek hunting dogs ran around in ever-increasing circles, noses to the ground, but Prince Locket appeared to have vanished. With heavy hearts, his friends sped back to the castle to break the dreadful news to King Roland and Queen Rosalind the Fair.

The King and Queen were distraught. Prince Locket was their only son and they loved him dearly. Queen Rosalind the Fair took to her bed, the dark green velvet curtains drawn against the light, while the King wandered disconsolately round the market square, wringing his hands, with tears running down his face. Lynnet saw his grief and immediately decided, in her usual way, to do something practical. She put on her heavy clogs, wrapped a shawl round her shoulders, and packed a bag with one of her father's best cheeses and some freshly baked bread. She kissed her parents goodbye, telling them that she would find Prince Locket however long it took her, and walked resolutely into the forest.

She walked for days along paths dappled with light as the sun

filtered through the thick canopy of leaves. She drank water from the clear streams and when her bread and cheese were finished, she ate the berries and nuts that she found along her way. Eventually she came to the forest edge and before her lay a rocky valley. Curiously misshapen and stunted bushes clustered round a group of caves nearby, and the grass was all flattened as if a herd of raggedy sheep had trampled it down.

Dusk was falling, and so Lynnet decided to shelter in one of the caves for the night. The first one she looked in didn't smell very nice, and the second was full of damp moss, but the third looked dry and went back quite a way so Lynnet stepped in cautiously and looked around. The cave was large, and fireflies provided a soft light that reached even into the far corners. Something glittered in the gloom and when she tiptoed towards it. To her astonishment, Lynnet found two huge great beds, one with a silver quilt and one a golden quilt. Lying fast asleep on the bed with the silver quilt, was Prince Locket. She called his name and, when there was no response, tried to climb up onto the bed to shake him awake. But the bed was so tall that she couldn't reach him. As she stood pondering how she might climb up, she noticed strange lettering carved round the bedhead. Lynnet could not read

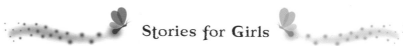

the words which appeared to be in some ancient runic script.

As she gazed at the curious letters, she felt the ground begin to tremble beneath her feet, and loud voices sounded outside the cave. She looked over her shoulder, and there in the entrance stood two very big and very ugly giant women. Quick as a mouse, Lynnet slipped under one of the huge beds.

The giant women lumbered into the cave.

"I can smell a human being," said one.

"Well, of course you can, stupid," said the younger of the two. "It's the prince, isn't it?" They stumped over to the bed where Prince Locket lay.

And then the giant women began to sing, in terrible cracked voices,

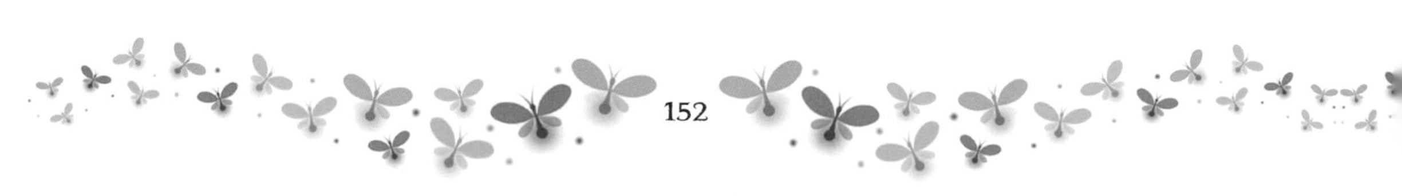

"Silver swan, silver swan, come swift as you may,
For Locket must open his eyes straight away."

And into the cave flew a magnificent silver swan, swooping down to the end of the bed. Prince Locket opened his eyes and sat up. He looked pale. The younger woman offered him food from a silver plate, but he would have none of it. Then with a dreadful smile, she asked him if he would marry her.

"Certainly not," he said with great determination.

The giant women muttered angrily.

"That is the only way you will ever be free, young Prince," and they cackled horribly, before singing again.

"Silver swan, silver swan, go swift as light.
For Locket must close his eyes here tonight."

And Locket fell once more into his enchanted sleep as the silver swan flew off out of the cave. The giant women squashed up together in the other bed and the cave was soon filled with appalling snoring. Lynnet stayed where she was, but was quite unable to sleep with such a noise reverberating round the cave.

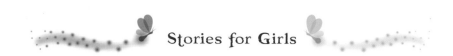

In the morning, the women rose with a great deal of grumbling and creaking of huge bones.

"Have you got the speckled egg safely?" the younger one asked.

"Of course I have," replied the other crossly, and they stomped out of the cave.

After what seemed like an eternity, Lynnet decided it was safe enough to come out from her hiding place.

"Nothing ventured, nothing gained," she said to herself and, looking all the while at the sleeping Prince Locket, she repeated the verse she had memorised from the night before.

> "Silver swan, silver swan, come swift as you may
> For Locket must open his eyes straightway."

The silver swan flew into the cave and landed on the bed. Instantly, Prince Locket sat up in bed.

Great was his astonishment and delight when he saw Lynnet standing there. Questions tumbled out one after another as Lynnet tried to find out how Prince Locket came to be in the cave in the first place, and Prince Locket asked for news from home.

It transpired that the mist which had enveloped Prince Locket had been conjured up by the younger woman who wanted a husband to look after the cave while she and her sister were out during the day.

Lynnet thought for a while and then said to Prince Locket,

"This is what we must do. Tonight when the giant woman asks you to marry her, you must agree—" At this point Prince Locket spluttered in protest but Lynnet carried on. "You must agree on condition that she tells you what she and her sister do all day." And with that she summoned the silver swan again to put Prince Locket to sleep once more, crawled under the bed, and fell fast asleep for she was very tired, having been awake all night.

In the evening when the giant women came back, they called the silver swan once more.

"Silver swan, silver swan,
come swift as you may,
For Locket must open his eyes
straightway."

In flapped the magnificent swan, and landed on the end of the bed. Prince Locket opened his eyes and sat up. The younger woman offered him food from a silver plate, but as before he would have none of it. Then with a dreadful smile, she asked him if he would marry her.

Trying very hard not to look at her tangled hair and her broken teeth and, worst of all the huge wart at the end of her nose, Prince Locket said,

"Certainly I will," with great determination.

At first the younger woman could not believe her ears. A ghastly smile crossed her face, revealing all her broken teeth, and Prince Locket crossed his fingers behind his back, hoping fervently that Lynnet knew what she was doing.

"I will marry you," he repeated, "but you must tell me what you do all day."

"We hunt for food and then when we have enough, we guard our speckled egg. It is our most precious possession for if it ever breaks we will die immediately."

Ah-hah, thought Lynnet hiding under the bed.

The giant women ate a very hearty meal and then, having summoned the silver swan to put Prince Locket back to sleep once more, they tumbled once more into the other bed, and were soon fast asleep and snoring deafeningly.

The next morning, the women summoned the silver swan as usual and when Prince Locket was awake, told him that they would leave him awake to explore if he chose.

As soon as they were gone, Lynnet crept out from under the bed to join Prince Locket and the silver swan.

"Silver swan, please help us," said Lynnet. "We need to escape from these terrible giant women. Can you help us?"

"Of course I can," murmured the swan and her voice was as soft as the wind in the reeds. "You know that you must destroy the speckled egg. In the chest by the cave mouth you will find my silver bow and arrow. Take that, Prince Locket, and follow the giant women, and when they rest you will see that they lay the speckled egg down on a flat rock. You must take very careful aim indeed, for you will only have the one chance to hit it. As soon as you have done that you must come back here where Lynnet and I will be waiting for you."

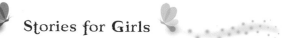

Prince Locket needed no second bidding. He rushed to the great chest by the cave mouth and there indeed was the gleaming silver bow and arrow. He took it up carefully and, with a cheery wave, ran out of the cave after the women. He soon came across them, stretched out on the grass, the speckled egg balanced on a flat rock nearby. Prince Locket drew back the silver bow very, very slowly and carefully, then let the arrow fly. Straight and true it went, and the speckled egg shattered with a crack. Before Prince Locket's eyes, the giant women turned to stone and then crumbled to dust.

Meanwhile, back at the cave, the silver swan was explaining to Lynnet that she had once been the familiar of a wonderful magician from the eastern lands, but she had been stolen by an ogre – the father of the giant women. The great bed with the silver quilt had also belonged to the magician and the strange lettering carved round the bedhead was a spell to make it fly.

Under the sheepskin rug in the great chest where the silver bow and arrow had lain, Lynnet found a magnificent hoard of treasure. Chests of silver and gold coins, golden claret glasses, silver spoons and sparkling crowns of precious jewels lay all jumbled together. Together the silver swan and Lynnet piled it all up on the bed with the silver quilt, and in her voice soft as the wind in the reeds, the swan read out the spell written on the bed.

"Turn around, turn around, great bed I implore
Fly through the air and straight out the door."

The bed rose straight in the air and out of the cave. They soon found Prince Locket and he scrambled up onto the quilt and sat laughing with Lynnet among all the treasure. Lynnet then asked the bed very politely to fly them back home.

The silver swan flew alongside the bed, her great wings thrumming in the air. Soon the bed began to fly lower and dropped gently into the market place by the castle. Great was the rejoicing when the people saw Prince Locket and Lynnet both safely returned, and it was not long before King Roland himself heard all the commotion and came rushing up to hug his beloved son. Everyone was cheering and laughing and as the sound reached the queen's chamber, the dark green velvet curtains were drawn back. There stood Queen Rosalind the Fair, smiling joyfully at the window.

Prince Locket asked Lynnet to marry him, but she said she would rather travel the world on the magical bed. This she did often, a little bag with one of her father's best cheeses and some freshly baked bread by her side. The silver swan took up residence on the river by the flower strewn meadows and was to be seen every evening, walking through the stout wooden gates into the castle to visit Prince Locket, King Roland and Queen Rosalind the Fair. So everyone lived happily ever after!

Heidi

An extract

by Johanna Spyri

Introduction

Johanna Spyri (1827–1901) was born in Switzerland. She began writing as a means of earning money to help the refugees from the Franco-Prussian war. Aged five, the orphan Heidi is taken by her cousin to live with her grandfather, a herdsman who lives up the side of a mountain in the Swiss Alps. Grandfather and Heidi live contentedly until the outside world intrudes and threatens to separate them.

Quickly the winter passed, and still more quickly the bright glad summer, and now another winter was drawing to its close. Heidi was still as light-hearted as the birds, and looked forward with more delight each day to the coming spring, when the warm south wind would blow away the snow, and the sun would entice the blue and yellow flowers, and the long days out on the mountain would come again, which seemed to Heidi the greatest joy that the earth could give. Heidi was now in her eighth year; she had learnt all kinds of useful things from her grandfather; she knew how to look after the goats as well as any one, and Little Swan and Bear would follow her like two faithful dogs, giving bleats of pleasure when they heard her voice. Twice during the course of this last winter Peter had brought up a message from the schoolmaster at Dorfli, who sent word to Alm-Uncle that he ought to send Heidi to school, as she was over the usual age, and ought to have gone the winter before. Uncle had sent word back each time that the schoolmaster would find him at home if he had anything he wished to say to him, but that he did not intend to send Heidi to school, and Peter had delivered his message.

When the March sun had melted the snow on the mountain side and the snowdrops were peeping out all over the valley, and the fir trees had shaken off their burden of snow and were again waving their branches in the air, Heidi ran backwards and forwards with delight first to the goat-shed then to the fir-trees, and then to the hut-door, in order to let her grandfather know how much larger a piece of green there was under the trees, and then would run off to look again, for she could hardly wait till everything was green and the full summer had clothed the mountain with grass and flowers. As Heidi was running about one sunny March morning, and had just jumped over the water-trough for the tenth time, she nearly fell backwards into it with fright, for there in front of her, looking gravely at her, stood an old gentleman dressed in black. When he saw how startled she was, he said in a kind voice, "Don't be afraid of me. You must be Heidi; where is your grandfather?"

"He is sitting by the table, making round wooden spoons," Heidi informed him, as she opened the door.

He was the old village pastor from Dorfli who had been a

neighbour of Uncle's when he lived down there, and had known him well. He stepped inside the hut, and going up to the old man, who was bending over his work, said, "Good morning, neighbour."

The grandfather looked up in surprise, and then rising said, "Good morning" in return. He pushed his chair towards the visitor as he continued, "If you do not mind a wooden seat there is one for you."

The pastor sat down. "It is a long time since I have seen you, neighbour," he said.

"Or I you," was the answer.

"I have come today to talk over something with you," continued the pastor. "I think you know already what it is that has brought me here," and as he spoke he looked towards the child who was standing at the door, gazing with interest and surprise at the stranger.

"Heidi, go off to the goats," said her grandfather. You take them a little salt and stay with them till I come."

Heidi vanished on the spot.

"The child ought to have been at school a year ago, and most certainly this last winter," said the pastor. "The schoolmaster sent you word about it, but you gave him no answer. What are you thinking of doing with the child, neighbour?"

"I am thinking of not sending her to school," was the answer.

The visitor, surprised, looked across at the old man, who was sitting on his bench with his arms crossed and a determined expression about his whole person.

"How are you going to let her grow up then?" he asked.

"I am going to let her grow up and be happy among the goats and birds; with them she is safe, and will learn nothing evil."

"But the child is not a goat or a bird, she is a human being. She ought not to grow up in ignorance, and it is time she began her lessons. I have come now that you may have leisure to think over it, and to arrange about it during the summer. This is the last winter that she must be allowed to run wild; next winter she must come regularly to school every day."

"She will do no such thing," said the old man.

"Do you mean that by no persuasion can you be brought to see reason, and that you intend to stick obstinately to your decision?" said the pastor, growing somewhat angry. "You have been about the world, and must have seen and learnt much, and I should have given you credit for more sense, neighbour."

"Indeed," replied the old man, and there was a tone in his voice that betrayed a growing irritation on his part too, "and does the worthy pastor really mean that he would wish me next winter to send a young child like that some miles down the mountain on ice-cold mornings through storm and snow, and let her return at night, when even one like ourselves would run a risk of being buried in the snow? And perhaps he may not have forgotten the child's mother, Adelaide? She was a sleep-walker, and had fits. Might not the child be attacked in the same way if obliged to over-exert herself? And someone thinks they can come and force me to send her? I will go before all the courts of justice in the country, and then we shall see who will force me to do it!"

"You are quite right, neighbour," said the pastor in a friendly tone of voice. "I see it would have been impossible to send the child to school from here. But I perceive that the child is dear to you; for her sake do what you ought to have done long ago: come down into Dorfli and live again among your fellowmen. What sort of a life is this you lead, alone, and with bitter thoughts towards God and man! If anything were to happen to you up here who would there be to help you? I cannot think but what you must be half frozen to death in this hut in the winter, and I do not know how the child lives through it!"

"The child has young blood in her veins and a good roof over her head, and let me further tell the pastor, that I know where wood is to be found, and when is the proper time to fetch it; the pastor can go and look inside my woodshed; the fire is never out in my hut the whole winter through. As to going to live below that is far from my thoughts; the people despise me and I them; it is therefore best for all of us that we live apart."

"No, no, it is not best for you; I know what it is you lack," said the pastor in an earnest voice. "As to the people down there looking on you with dislike, it is not as bad as you think. Believe me, neighbour; seek to make your peace with God, pray for forgiveness where you need it, and then come and see how differently people will look upon you, and how happy you may yet be."

The pastor had risen and stood holding out his hand to the

old man as he added with renewed earnestness, "I will wager, neighbour, that next winter you will be down among us again, and we shall be good neighbours as of old. I should be very grieved if any pressure had to be put upon you; give me your hand and promise me that you will come and live with us again and become reconciled to God and man."

Alm-Uncle gave the pastor his hand and answered him calmly and firmly, "You mean well by me I know, but as to that which you wish me to do, I say now what I shall continue to say, that I will not send the child to school nor come and live among you."

"Then God help you!" said the pastor, and he turned sadly away and left the hut and went down the mountain.

Alm-Uncle was out of humour. When Heidi said as usual that afternoon, "Can we go down to grandmother now?" he answered, "Not today." He did not speak again the whole of that day, and the following morning when Heidi again asked the same question, he replied, "We will see." But before the dinner bowls had been cleared away another visitor arrived, and this time it was Cousin Dete. She had a fine feathered hat on her head, and a long trailing skirt to her dress which swept the floor, and on the floor of a goatherd's hut there are all sorts of things that do not belong to a dress.

The grandfather looked her up and down without uttering a word. But Dete was prepared with an exceedingly amiable speech and began at once to praise the looks of the child. She was looking so well she should hardly have known her again, and it was evident that she had been happy and well-cared for with her grandfather; but she had never lost sight of the idea of taking the child back again, for she well understood that the little one must be much in his way, but she had not been able to do it at first. Day and night, however, she had thought over the means of placing the child somewhere, and that was why she had come today, for she had just heard of something that would be a lucky chance for Heidi beyond her most ambitious hopes. Some immensely wealthy relatives of the people she was serving, who had the most splendid house, had an only daughter, young and an invalid, who was always obliged to go about in a wheeled chair. She was therefore very much alone and had no one to share her lessons. Her father had spoken to Dete's mistress about finding a companion for her, and her mistress was anxious to help in the matter, as she felt so sympathetic about it. The lady housekeeper

had described the sort of child they wanted, simple-minded and unspoilt. Dete had thought at once of Heidi and had gone off without delay to see the lady housekeeper, and after Dete had given her a description of Heidi, she had immediately agreed to take her. And no one could tell what good fortune there might not be in store for Heidi, for if she was once with these people and they took a fancy to her, and anything happened to their own daughter – one could never tell, the child was so weakly – and they did not feel they could live without a child, why then the most unheard of luck –

"Have you nearly finished what you had to say?" broke in Alm-Uncle, who had allowed her to talk on uninterruptedly so far.

"Ugh!" exclaimed Dete, throwing up her head in disgust, "one would think I had been talking to you about the most ordinary matter; why there is not one person in all Prattigau who would not thank God if I were to bring them such a piece of news as I am bringing you."

"You may take your news to anybody you like, I will have nothing to do with it."

But now Dete leaped up from her seat like a rocket and cried, "If that is all you have to say about it, why then I will give you a bit of my mind. The child is now eight years old and knows nothing, and you will not let her learn. You will not send her to church or school, and she is my own sister's child. I am responsible for what happens to her, and when there is such a good opening for a child, as this which offers for Heidi, only a person who cares for nobody and never wishes good to anyone would think of not jumping at it. But I am not going to give in, and that I tell you. I have everybody in Dorfli on my side. There is not one person there who will not take my part against you; and I advise you to think well before bringing it into court, if that is your intention; there are certain things which might be brought up against you which you would not care to hear, for when one has to do with law courts there is a great deal raked up that had been forgotten."

"Be silent!" thundered the Uncle, and his eyes flashed with

anger. "Go and be done with you! Never let me see you again with your hat and feather, and such words on your tongue as you come with today!" And with that he strode out of the hut.

"You have made grandfather angry," said Heidi, and her dark eyes had anything but a friendly expression in them as she looked at Dete.

"He will soon be all right again; come now," said Dete hurriedly, "and show me where your clothes are."

"I am not coming," said Heidi.

"Nonsense," continued Dete; then altering her tone to one half-coaxing, half-cross, "Come, come, you do not understand any better than your grandfather; you will have all sorts of good things that you never dreamed of." Then she went to the cupboard and taking out Heidi's things rolled them up in a bundle. "Come along now, there's your hat – it is very shabby but will do for the present. Put it on and let us make haste off."

"I am not coming," repeated Heidi.

"Don't be so stupid and obstinate, like a goat; I suppose it's from the goats you have learnt to be so. Listen to me: you saw your grandfather was angry and heard what he said, that he did not wish to see us ever again. He wants you now to go away with me and you must not make him angrier still. You can't think what a lot of things you will see, and if you do not like it you can come back again.

"Can I return at once and be back home again here this evening?" asked Heidi.

"What are you talking about, come along now! I tell you that you can come back here when you like. Today we shall go as far as Mayenfeld, and early tomorrow we shall start in the train, and that will bring you home again in no time when you wish it, for it goes as fast as the wind."

Dete had now got the bundle under her arm and the child by the hand, and so they went down the mountain together.

As it was still too early in the year to take his goats out, Peter continued to go to school at Dorfli, but now and again he stole a holiday, for he could see no use in learning to read, while to wander about a bit and look for stout sticks which might be wanted some day he thought a far better employment. As Dete and Heidi neared the grandmother's hut they met Peter coming round the corner; he had evidently been well rewarded that day for his labours, for he was carrying an immense bundle of long thick hazel sticks on his shoulders. He stood still and stared at the two approaching figures; as they came up to him, he exclaimed, "Where are you going, Heidi?"

"I am only just going over to Frankfurt for a little visit with Dete," she replied; "but I must first run in to grandmother, she will be expecting me."

"No, no, you must not stop to talk; it is already too late," said Dete, holding Heidi, who was struggling to get away, fast by the hand. "You can go in when you come back, you must come along now," and she pulled the child on with her, fearing that if she let her go in Heidi might take it into her head again that she did not wish to come, and that the grandmother might stand by her. Peter ran into the hut and banged against the table with his bundle of sticks with such violence that everything in the room shook, and his grandmother leaped up with a cry of alarm from her spinning wheel. Peter had felt that he must give vent to his feelings somehow.

"What is the matter? What is the matter?" cried the frightened old woman, while his mother, who had also started up from her seat at the shock, said in her usual patient manner, "What is it, Peter? Why do you behave so roughly?"

"Because she is taking Heidi away," explained Peter.

"Who? Who? Where to, Peter, where to?" asked the grandmother, growing still more agitated; but even as she spoke she guessed what had happened, for Brigitta had told her shortly before that she had seen Dete going up to Alm-Uncle. The old woman rose hastily and with trembling hands opened the window and called out beseechingly, "Dete, Dete, do not take the child away from us! Do not take her away!"

The two who were hastening down the mountain heard her voice, and Dete evidently caught the words, for she grasped Heidi's hand more firmly. Heidi struggled to get free, crying, "Grandmother is calling, I must go to her."

But Dete had no intention of letting the child go, and quieted her as best she could; they must make haste now, she said, or they would be too late and not able to go on the next day to Frankfurt, and there the child would see how delightful it was, and Dete was sure would not wish to go back when she was once there. But if Heidi wanted to return home she could do so at once, and then she could take something she liked back to grandmother. This was a new idea to Heidi, and it pleased her so much that Dete had no longer any difficulty in getting her along.

After a few minutes' silence, Heidi asked, "What could I take back to her?"

"We must think of something nice," answered Dete; "a soft roll of white bread; she would enjoy that, for now she is old she can hardly eat the hard, black bread."

"No, she always gives it back to Peter, telling him it is too hard, for I have seen her do it myself," affirmed Heidi. "Do let us make haste, for then perhaps we can get back soon from Frankfurt, and I shall be able to give her the white bread today." And Heidi started off running so fast that Dete with the bundle under her arm could scarcely keep up with her. But she was glad, nevertheless, to get along so quickly, for they were nearing Dorfli, where her friends would probably talk and question in a way that might put other ideas into Heidi's head. So she went on straight ahead through the village, holding Heidi tightly by the hand, so that they might all see that it was on the child's account she was hurrying along at such a rate. To all their questions and remarks she made answer as she passed "I can't stop now, as you see, I must make haste with the child as we have yet some way to go."

"Are you taking her away?" "Is she running away from Alm-Uncle?" "It's a wonder she is still alive!" "But what rosy cheeks she has!" Such were the words which rang out on all sides, and Dete was thankful that she had not to stop and give any distinct answers to them, while Heidi hurried eagerly forward without saying a word.

From that day forward Alm-Uncle looked fiercer and more forbidding than ever when he came down and passed through Dorfli. He spoke to no one, and looked such an ogre as he came along with his pack of cheeses on his back, his immense stick in his hand, and his thick, frowning eyebrows, that the women would call to their little ones, "Take care! Get out of Alm-Uncle's way or he may hurt you!"

The old man took no notice of anybody as he strode through

the village on his way to the valley below, where he sold his cheeses and bought what bread and meat he wanted for himself. After he had passed the villagers all crowded together looking after him, and each had something to say about him; how much wilder he looked than usual, how now he would not even respond to anybody's greeting, while they all agreed that it was a great mercy the child had got away from him, and had they not all noticed how the child had hurried along as if afraid that her grandfather might be following to take her back? Only the blind grandmother would have nothing to say against him, and told those who came to her to bring her work, or take away what she had spun, how kind and thoughtful he had been with the child, how good to her and her daughter, and how many afternoons he had spent mending the house which, but for his help, would certainly by this time have fallen down over their heads. And all this was repeated down in Dorfli; but most of the people who heard it said that grandmother was too old to understand, and very likely had not heard rightly what was said; as she was blind she was probably also deaf.

Alm-Uncle went no more now to the grandmother's house, and it was well that he had made it so safe, for it was not touched again for a long time. The days were sad again now for the old blind woman, and not one passed but what she would murmur complainingly, "Alas! all our happiness and pleasure have gone with the child, and now the days are so long and dreary! Pray God, I see Heidi again once more before I die!"

At the Back of the North Wind

An extract
by George MacDonald

Introduction

George MacDonald (1824–1905) was the great-grandson of a piper who fought for Prince Charles at Culloden in 1746. At the Back of the North Wind *was published in 1871. Diamond is the son of a coachman who sleeps in the hayloft over the stable. One night he is woken by the voice of the North Wind, who is then revealed as a beautiful young woman with long dark hair.*

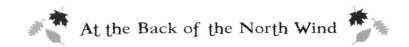

As she stood looking towards London, Diamond saw that she was trembling.

"Are you cold, North Wind?" he asked.

"No, Diamond," she answered, looking down upon him with a smile; "I am only getting ready to sweep one of my rooms. Those careless, greedy, untidy children make it in such a mess."

As she spoke he could have told by her voice, if he had not seen with his eyes, that she was growing larger. Her head went up and up towards the stars; and as she grew, still trembling through all her body, her hair also grew – longer and longer, lifting itself from her head, and went out in black waves. The next moment it fell back around her, and she grew less and less till she was only a tall woman. Then she put her hands behind her head, and gathered some of her hair, and began weaving and knotting it together. When she had done, she bent down her beautiful face close to his, and said,

"Diamond, I am afraid you would not keep hold of me, and if I were to drop you, I don't know what might happen; so I have been making a place for you in my hair. Come."

Diamond held out his arms and the wind took him in her hands, threw him over her shoulder, and said, "Get in, Diamond."

And Diamond parted her hair with his hands, crept between, and feeling about soon found the woven nest. It was just like a pocket. North Wind put her hands to her back, felt all about the nest, and finding it safe, said,

"Are you comfortable Diamond?"

"Yes, indeed," answered Diamond.

The next moment he was rising in the air. North Wind grew towering up to the place of the clouds. Her hair went streaming out from her, till it spread like a mist over the stars. She flung herself abroad in space.

Diamond held on by two of the twisted ropes which formed his shelter, for he could not help being a little afraid. As soon as he had come to himself, he peeped through the woven meshes – he did not dare to look over the top of the nest. The earth was rushing past like a river below him. Trees and water and green grass hurried away beneath. A great roar of wild animals rose as they rushed over the Zoological Gardens, mixed with a chattering of monkeys and a screaming of birds; but it died away in a moment behind them. And now there was nothing but the roofs of houses, sweeping along like a great torrent of stones and rocks. Chimney-pots fell, and tiles flew from the roofs; but it looked to him as if they were left behind by the roofs and the chimneys as they scudded away. There was a great roaring, for the wind was dashing against London like a sea; but at North Wind's back Diamond, of course, felt nothing of it all. He was in a perfect calm. He could hear the sound of it, that was all.

By and by he raised himself and looked over the edge of his nest. There were the houses rushing up and shooting away below him, like a fierce torrent of rocks instead of water. Then he looked up to the sky, but could see no stars; they were hidden by the blinding masses of the lady's hair which swept between. He began to wonder whether she would hear him if he spoke. He would try.

"Please, North Wind," he said, "what is that noise?"

From high over his head came the voice of North Wind, answering him, gently,

"The noise of my broom. I am the old woman that sweeps the cobwebs from the sky; only I'm busy with the floor now."

"What makes the houses look as if they were running away?"

"I am sweeping so fast over them."

"But, please, North Wind, I knew London was very big, but I didn't know it was so big as this. It seems as if we should never get away from it."

"We are going round and round, else we should have left it long ago."

"Is this the way you sweep, North Wind?"

"Yes; I go round and round with my great besom."

"Please would you mind going a little slower, for I want to see the streets?"

"You won't see much now."

"Why?"

"Because I have nearly swept all the people home."

"Oh! I forgot," said Diamond, and was quiet after that, for he did not want to be troublesome.

But she dropped a little towards the roofs of the houses, and Diamond could see down into the streets. There were very few people about, though. The lamps flickered and flared again, but nobody seemed to want them.

Suddenly Diamond espied a little girl coming along a street. She was dreadfully blown by the wind, and a broom she was trailing behind her was very troublesome. It seemed as if the wind had a spite at her – it kept worrying her like a wild beast, and tearing at her rags. She was so lonely there!

"Please, North Wind," he cried, "won't you help that girl?"

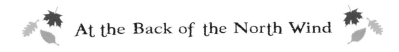

"No, Diamond; I mustn't leave my work."

"But why shouldn't you be kind to her?"

"I am kind to her. I am sweeping the wicked smells away."

"But you're kinder to me, dear North Wind. Why shouldn't you be as kind to her as you are to me?"

"There are reasons, Diamond. Everybody can't be done to all the same. Everybody is not ready for the same thing."

"But I don't see why I should be kinder used than she."

"Do you think nothing's to be done but what you can see, Diamond, you silly! It's all right. Of course you can help her if you like. You've got nothing particular to do at this moment; I have."

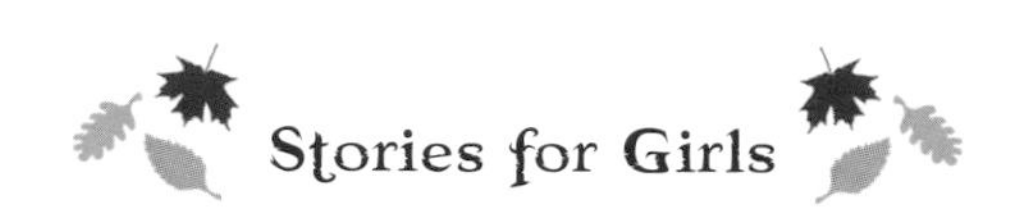

"Oh! Do let me help her, then. But you won't be able to wait, perhaps?"

"No, I can't wait; you must do it yourself. And, mind, the wind will get a hold of you, too."

"Don't you want me to help her, North Wind?"

"Not without having some idea what will happen. If you break down and cry, that won't be much of a help to her, and it will make a goose of little Diamond."

"I want to go," said Diamond. "Only there's just one thing – how am I to get home?"

"If you're anxious about that, perhaps you had better go with me. I am bound to take you home again, if you do."

"There!" cried Diamond, who was still looking after the little girl; "I'm sure the wind will blow her over, and perhaps kill her. Do let me go."

They had been sweeping more slowly along the line of the street. There was a lull in the roaring.

"Well, though I cannot promise to take you home," said North Wind, as she sank nearer and nearer to the tops of the houses, "I can promise you it will be all right in the end. You will get home somehow. Have you made up your mind what to do?"

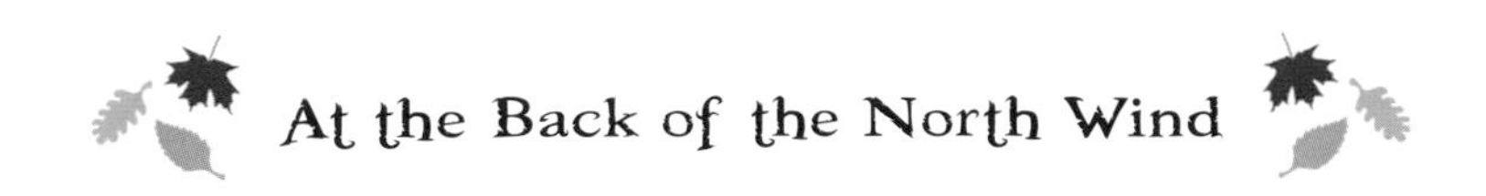

"Yes; to help the little girl," said Diamond firmly.

The same moment North Wind dropped into the street and stood, only a tall lady, but with her hair flying up over the housetops. She put her hands to her back, took Diamond, and set him down in the street. The same moment he was caught in the fierce coils of the blast, and all but blown away. North Wind stepped back a step, and at once towered in stature to the height of the houses. A chimney pot clashed at Diamond's feet. He turned in terror, but it was to look for the little girl, and when he turned again the lady had vanished, and the wind was roaring along the street. The little girl was scudding before the blast, and behind her she dragged her broom. Her little legs were going as fast as ever they could to keep her from falling. Diamond crept into the shelter of a doorway, thinking to stop her; but she passed him like a bird, crying gently and pitifully.

"Stop! Stop! Little girl," shouted Diamond, starting in pursuit.

"I can't," wailed the girl, "the wind won't leave go of me."

Diamond could run faster than she. In a few moments he had caught her by the frock, but it tore in his hand, and away went the little girl. So he had to run again, and this time he ran so fast that he got before her, and turning round caught her in his arms, when down they went both together, which made the little girl laugh in the midst of her crying.

"Where are you going?" asked Diamond, rubbing the elbow that had stuck farthest out. The arm it belonged to was twined round a lamp-post as he stood between the little girl and the wind.

"Home," she said, gasping for breath.

"Then I will go with you," said Diamond.

And then they were silent for a while, for the wind blew worse than ever, and they had both to hold on to the lamp-post.

"Where is your crossing?" asked the girl at length.

"I don't sweep," answered Diamond.

"What do you do, then?" asked she. "You ain't big enough for most things."

"I don't know what I do do," answered he, feeling rather ashamed. "Nothing, I suppose. My father's Mr Coleman's coachman."

"Have you a father?" she said, staring at him as if a boy with a father was a natural curiosity.

"Yes. Haven't you?" returned Diamond.

"No; nor mother neither. Old Sal's all I've got." And she began to cry again.

"I wouldn't go to her if she wasn't good to me," said Diamond.

"But you must go somewheres."

"Move on," said the voice of a policeman behind them.

"I told you so," said the girl. "You must go somewheres. They're always at it."

"But old Sal doesn't beat you, does she?"

"I wish she would."

"What do you mean?" asked Diamond, quite bewildered.

"She would if she was my mother. But she wouldn't lie abed a-cuddlin' of her ugly old bones, and laugh to hear me crying at the door."

"You don't mean she won't let you in tonight?"

"It'll be a good chance if she does."

"Why are you out so late, then?" asked Diamond.

"My crossing's a long way off at the West End, and I had been indulgin' in door-steps and mewses."

"We'd better have a try anyhow," said Diamond. "Come along."

As he spoke Diamond thought he caught a glimpse of North Wind turning a corner in front of them; and when they turned the corner too, they found it quiet there, but he saw nothing of the lady.

"Now you lead me," he said, taking her hand, "and I'll take care of you."

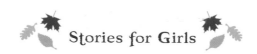

The girl withdrew her hand, but only to dry her eyes with her frock. She put it in his again, and led him, turning after turning, until they stopped at a cellar-door in a very dirty lane. There she knocked.

"I shouldn't like to live here," said Diamond.

"Oh, yes, you would, if you had nowhere else to go to," answered the girl. "I only wish we may get in."

"I don't want to go in," said Diamond. "I want to go home to my home."

"Where's that?"

"I don't exactly know."

"Then you're worse off than I am."

"Oh no, for North Wind—" began Diamond, and then stopped, although he hardly knew why he did.

"What?" said the girl, as she held her ear to the door listening.

But Diamond did not reply. Neither did old Sal.

"What will you do, then?" asked Diamond.

"Move on," she answered.

"Where?"

"Oh, anywheres. Bless you, I'm used to it."

"Hadn't you better come home with me, then?"

"That's a good joke, when you don't know where it is. Come on."

"But where?"

"Oh, nowheres in particular. Come on."

They wandered on and on, until they had got out of the thick of the houses into a waste kind of place. By this time Diamond felt a good deal inclined to cry, and thought he had been very silly to get down from the back of North Wind; not that he would have minded it if he had done the girl any good; but he thought he had been of no use to her. He was mistaken there, for she was far happier for having Diamond with her than if she had been wandering about alone.

"Do let us rest a bit," said Diamond.

"Let's see," she answered. "There's something like a railway there. Perhaps there's an open arch."

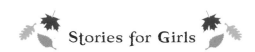

They went towards it and found one, and, better still, there was an empty barrel lying under the arch.

"Hello! Here we are!" said the girl. "A barrel's the jolliest bed going. We'll have forty winks, and then go on again."

She crept in, and Diamond crept in beside her. When he began to grow warm, Diamond's courage began to come back.

"This is jolly!" he said. "I'm so glad!"

"I don't think so much of it," said the girl. "I'm used to it, I suppose. But I can't think how a kid like you comes to be out all alone this time o' night."

"But I shouldn't have been out so late if I hadn't got down to help you," said Diamond. "North Wind is gone home long ago."

"You said something about the north wind afore that I couldn't get the rights of. I think you must ha' got out o' one o' them Hidget Asylms," said the girl.

So now, for the sake of his character, Diamond had to tell her the whole story.

She did not believe a word of it. She said he wasn't such a flat as to believe all that bosh.

"I thought we should have had a sleep," said Diamond; "but I can't say I'm very sleepy after all. Come, let's go on again."

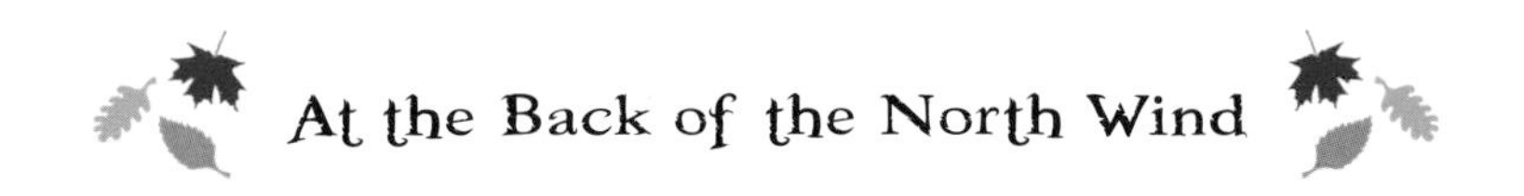

They wandered on and on, sometimes sitting on a doorstep, but always turning into lanes or fields when they had a chance.

They found themselves at last on a rising ground that sloped rather steeply on the other side. It was a waste kind of spot below, bounded by an irregular wall, with a few doors in it. When they reached the brow of the rising ground, a gust of wind seized them and blew them down hill as fast as they could run. Nor could Diamond stop before he went bang against one of the doors in the wall, which burst open. They peeped in – it was the back door of a garden.

"Ah, ah!" cried Diamond, after staring for a few moments, "I thought so! Here I am in master's garden! I tell you what, little girl, you just bore a hole in old Sal's wall, and put your mouth to it, and say, 'Please, North Wind, mayn't I go out with you?' and then you'll see what'll come."

"I dare say I shall. But I'm out in the wind too often already to want more of it."

"I said with the North Wind, not in it."

"It's all one."

"It's not all one."

"It is all one."

"But I know best."

"And I know better. I'll box your ears," said the girl.

Diamond got very angry. But he remembered that if she did box his ears, he musn't box hers for she was a girl. So he went in at the door.

"Goodbye, mister" said the girl.

"I'm sorry I was cross," he said. "Come in for breakfast."

"No, thank you. I must be off to my crossing."

"I'm very sorry for you," said Diamond.

"Well, it is a life to be tired of – what with old Sal, and so many holes in my shoes."

"I wonder you're so good. I should give up."

"Oh, no, you wouldn't! I always want to see what's coming next, and so I always wait till next is over. Goodbye!"

She ran up the hill and disappeared behind it. Then Diamond shut the door as he best could, and ran through the kitchen-garden to the stable. And wasn't he glad to get into his own blessed bed again!

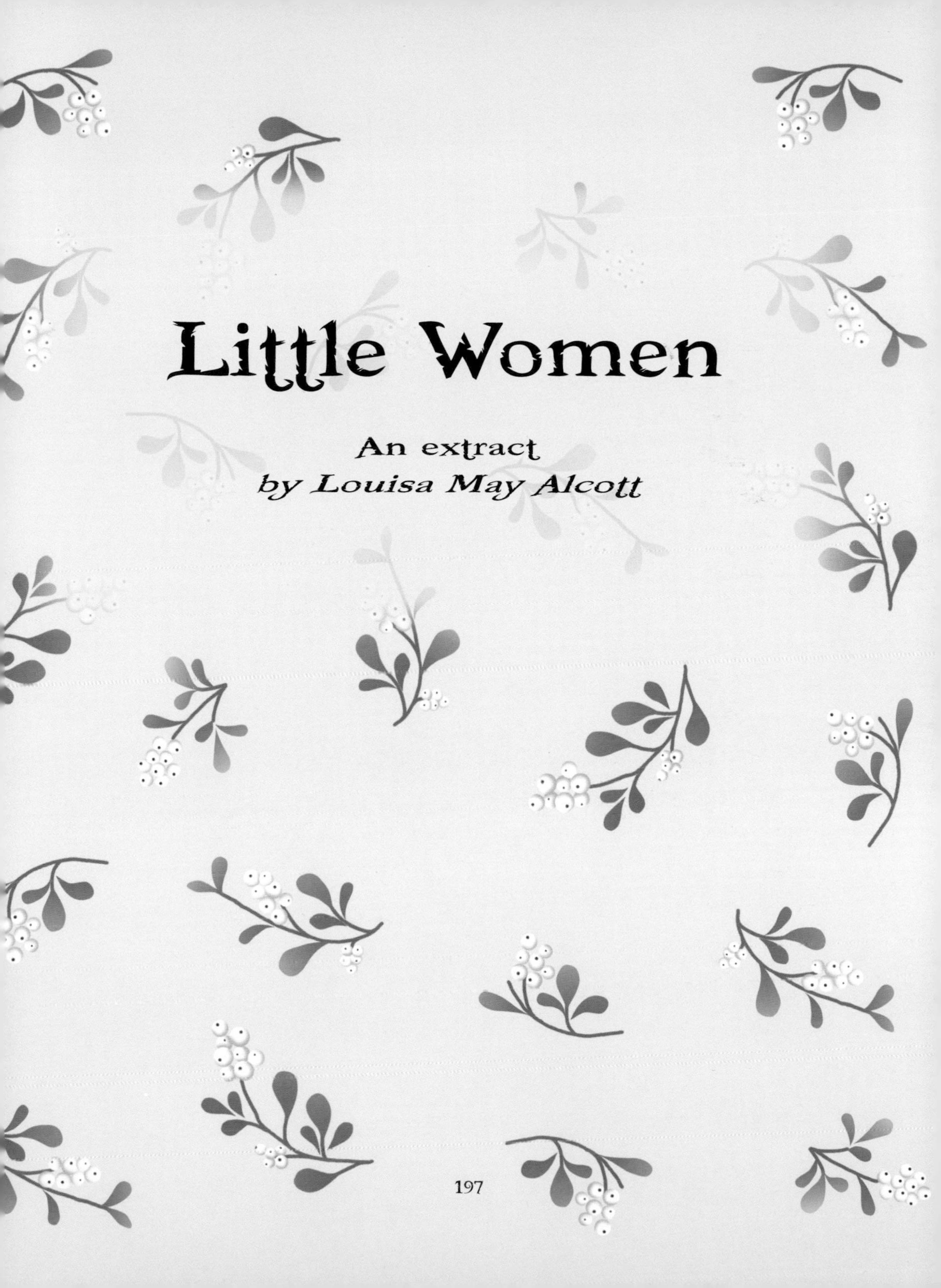

Little Women

An extract
by Louisa May Alcott

Introduction

Louisa May Alcott (1832–1888) was the second of four daughters of Amos Bronson Alcott. Louisa helped support the family through her writing for the popular market. Little Women, *published in 1868, was very largely based on her own experiences. The book describes a few months in the lives of the March sisters, living with their mother while their impoverished father is away from home as Army Chaplain in the Civil War.*

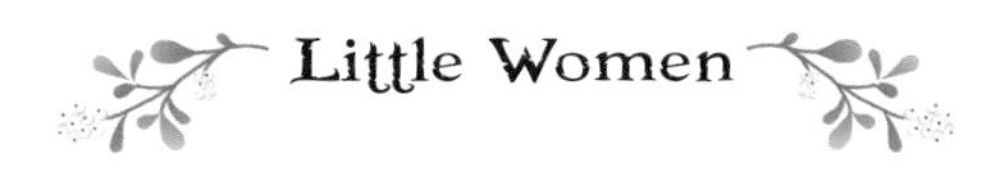

Jo lay on the rug and grumbled, "Christmas won't be Christmas without any presents."

"It's so dreadful to be poor!" sighed Meg, looking down at her old dress.

"I don't think it's fair for some girls to have plenty of pretty things, and other girls nothing at all," added little Amy, with an injured sniff.

"We've got Father and Mother, and each other," said Beth contentedly from her corner.

The four young faces on which the firelight shone brightened at the cheerful words, but darkened again as Jo said sadly, "We haven't got Father, and shall not have him for a long time." She didn't say perhaps never, but each silently added it, thinking of Father far away, where the fighting was.

Nobody spoke for a minute; then Meg said in an altered tone, "You know the reason Mother proposed not having any presents this Christmas was because it is going to be a hard winter for everyone; and she thinks we ought not to spend money for pleasure, when our men are suffering so in the army. We can't do much, but we can make our little sacrifices, and ought to do it gladly. But I am afraid I don't." And Meg shook her head, as she thought regretfully of all the pretty things she wanted.

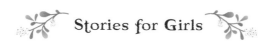

"But I don't think the little we should spend would do any good. We've each got a dollar, and the army wouldn't be much helped by our giving that. I agree not to expect anything from Mother or you, but I do want to buy *Undine and Sintram* for myself. I've wanted it so long", said Jo, who was a bookworm.

"I planned to spend mine in new music," said Beth, with a little sigh, which no one heard but the hearth brush and kettle holder.

"I shall get a nice box of Faber's drawing pencils. I really need them," said Amy decidedly.

"Mother didn't say anything about our money, and she won't wish us to give up everything. Let's each buy what we want, and have a little fun. I'm sure we work hard enough to earn it," cried Jo, examining the heels of her shoes in a gentlemanly manner.

"I know I do – teaching those tiresome children nearly all day, when I'm longing to enjoy myself at home," began Meg, in the complaining tone again.

"You don't have half such a hard time as I do", said Jo. "How would you like to be shut up for hours with great-aunt March – such a nervous, fussy old lady, who keeps you trotting, is never satisfied, and worries you till you're just about ready to fly out of the window or cry?"

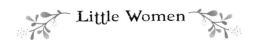

"It's naughty to fret, but I do think washing dishes and keeping things tidy is the worst work in the world. It makes me cross, and my hands get so stiff, I can't practice well at all." And Beth looked at her rough hands with a sigh that anyone could hear that time.

"I don't believe any of you suffer as I do," cried Amy. "For you don't have to go to school with impertinent girls, who plague you if you don't know your lessons, and laugh at your dresses, and label your father if he isn't rich, and insult you when your nose isn't nice."

"If you mean libel, I'd say so, and not talk about labels, as if Papa was a pickle bottle," advised Jo, laughing.

"I know what I mean, and you needn't be satirical about it. It's proper to use good words, and improve your vocabulary," returned Amy, with dignity.

"Don't peck at one another, children. Don't you wish we had the money Papa lost when we were little, Jo? Dear me! How happy and good we'd be, if we had no worries!" said Meg, who could remember better times.

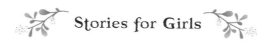

"You said the other day you thought we were a deal happier than the King children, for they were fighting and fretting all the time, in spite of their money."

"So I did, Beth. Well, I think we are. For though we do have to work, we make fun of ourselves, and are a pretty jolly set, as Jo would say."

"Jo does use such slang words!" observed Amy, with a reproving look at the long figure stretched on the rug.

Jo immediately sat up, put her hands in her pockets, and began to whistle.

"Don't, Jo. It's so boyish!"

"That's why I do it."

"I detest rude, unladylike girls!"

"I hate affected, niminy-piminy chits!"

"Birds in their little nests agree," sang Beth, the peacemaker, with such a funny face that both sharp voices softened to a laugh, and the pecking ended for that time.

"Really, girls, you are both to be blamed," said Meg, beginning to lecture in her elder-sisterly fashion. "You are old enough to leave off boyish tricks, and to behave better, Josephine. It didn't matter so much when you were a little girl, but now you are so tall, and turn up your hair, you should remember that you are a young lady."

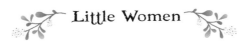

"I'm not! And if turning up my hair makes me one, I'll wear it in two tails till I'm twenty," cried Jo, pulling off her net, and shaking down a chestnut mane. "I hate to think I've got to grow up, and be Miss March, and wear long gowns, and look as prim as a China Aster! It's bad enough to be a girl, anyway, when I like boy's games and work and manners! I can't get over my disappointment in not being a boy. And it's worse than ever now, for I'm dying to go and fight with Papa. And I can only stay home and knit, like a poky old woman!"

And Jo shook the blue army sock till the needles rattled like castanets, and her ball bounded across the room.

"Poor Jo! It's too bad, but it can't be helped. So you must try to be contented with making your name boyish, and playing brother to us girls," said Beth, stroking the rough head with a hand that all the dish washing and dusting in the world could not make ungentle in its touch.

"As for you, Amy," continued Meg, "you are altogether too particular and prim. Your airs are funny now, but you'll grow up an affected little goose, if you don't take care. I like your nice

manners and refined ways of speaking, when you don't try to be elegant. But your absurd words are as bad as Jo's slang."

"If Jo is a tomboy and Amy a goose, what am I, please?" asked Beth, ready to share the lecture.

"You're a dear, and nothing else", answered Meg warmly, and no one contradicted her, for the 'Mouse' was the pet of the family.

As young readers like to know 'how people look', we will take this moment to give them a little sketch of the four sisters, who sat knitting away in the twilight, while the December snow fell

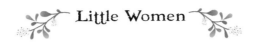

quietly without, and the fire crackled cheerfully within. It was a comfortable room, though the carpet was faded and the furniture very plain, for a good picture or two hung on the walls, books filled the recesses, chrysanthemums and Christmas roses bloomed in the windows, and a pleasant atmosphere of home peace pervaded it.

Margaret, the eldest of the four, was sixteen, and very pretty, being plump and fair, with large eyes, plenty of soft brown hair, a sweet mouth, and white hands, of which she was rather vain. Fifteen-year-old Jo was very tall, thin, and brown, and reminded one of a colt, for she never seemed to know what to do with her long limbs, which were very much in her way. She had a decided mouth, a comical nose, and sharp, grey eyes, which appeared to see everything, and were by turns fierce, funny, or thoughtful. Her long, thick hair was her one beauty, but it was usually bundled into a net, to be out of her way. Round shoulders had Jo, big hands and feet, a fly-away look to her clothes, and the uncomfortable appearance of a girl who was rapidly shooting up into a woman and didn't like it. Elizabeth, or Beth, as everyone called her, was a rosy, smooth-haired, bright-eyed girl of thirteen, with a shy manner, a timid voice, and a peaceful expression which

was seldom disturbed. Her father called her 'Miss Tranquillity', and the name suited her excellently, for she seemed to live in a happy world of her own, only venturing out to meet the few whom she trusted and loved. Amy, though the youngest, was a most important person, in her own opinion at least. A regular snow maiden, with blue eyes, and yellow hair curling on her shoulders, pale and slender, and always carrying herself like a young lady mindful of her manners. What the characters of the four sisters were we will leave to be found out.

The clock struck six and, having swept up the hearth, Beth put a pair of slippers down to warm. Somehow the sight of the old shoes had a good effect upon the girls, for Mother was coming, and everyone brightened to welcome her. Meg stopped lecturing, and lighted the lamp, Amy got out of the easy chair without being asked, and Jo forgot how tired she was as she sat up to hold the slippers nearer to the blaze.

"They are quite worn out. Marmee must have a new pair."

"I thought I'd get her some with my dollar," said Beth.

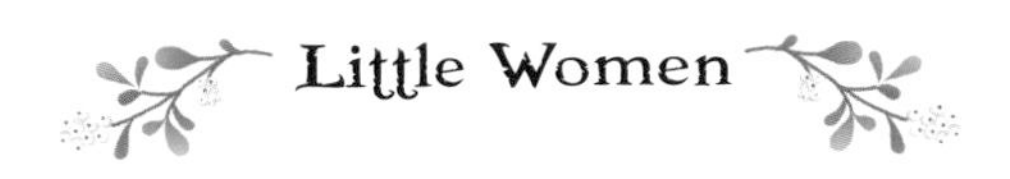

"No, I shall!" cried Amy.

"I'm the oldest," began Meg, but Jo cut in with a decided, "I'm the man of the family now Papa is away, and I shall provide the slippers, for he told me to take special care of Mother while he was gone."

"I'll tell you what we'll do," said Beth, "let's each get her something for Christmas, and not get anything for ourselves."

"That's like you, dear! What will we get?" exclaimed Jo.

Everyone thought soberly for a minute, then Meg announced, as if the idea was suggested by the sight of her own pretty hands, "I shall give her a nice pair of gloves."

"Army shoes, best to be had," cried Jo.

"Some handkerchiefs, all hemmed," said Beth.

"I'll get a little bottle of cologne. She likes it, and it won't cost much, so I'll have some left to buy my pencils," added Amy.

"How will we give the things?" asked Meg.

"Put them on the table, and bring her in and see her open the bundles. Don't you remember how we used to do on our birthdays?" answered Jo.

"I used to be so frightened when it was my turn to sit in the chair with the crown on, and see you all come marching round to

give the presents, with a kiss. I liked the things and the kisses, but it was dreadful to have you sit looking at me while I opened the bundles," said Beth, who was toasting her face and the bread for tea at the same time.

"Let Marmee think we are getting things for ourselves, and then surprise her. We must go shopping tomorrow afternoon, Meg. There is so much to do about the play for Christmas night," said Jo, marching up and down, with her hands behind her back, and her nose in the air.

"I don't mean to act any more after this time. I'm getting too old for such things," observed Meg, who was as much a child as ever about 'dressing-up' frolics.

"You won't stop, I know, as long as you can trail round in a white gown with your hair down, and wear gold-paper jewellery. You are the best actress we've got, and there'll be an end of everything if you quit the boards," said Jo. "We ought to rehearse tonight. Come here, Amy, and do the fainting scene, for you are as stiff as a poker in that."

"I can't help it. I never saw anyone faint, and I don't choose to make myself all black and blue, tumbling flat as you do. If I can go down easily, I'll drop. If I can't, I shall fall into a chair and be

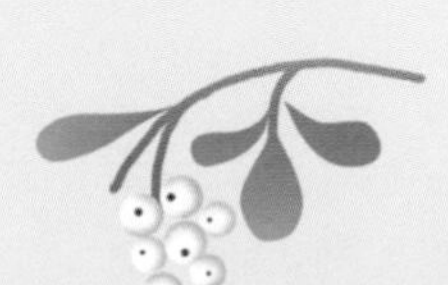

graceful. I don't care if Hugo does come at me with a pistol," returned Amy, who was not gifted with dramatic power, but was chosen because she was small enough to be borne out shrieking by the villain of the piece.

"Do it this way. Clasp your hands so, and stagger across the room, crying frantically, 'Roderigo Save me! Save me!'" and away went Jo, with a melodramatic scream that was truly thrilling.

Amy followed, but she poked her hands out stiffly before her, and jerked herself along as if she went by machinery, and her "Ow!" was more suggestive of pins being run into her than of fear and anguish. Jo gave a despairing groan, and Meg laughed outright, while Beth let her bread burn as she watched the fun with interest.

"It's no use! Do the best you can when the time comes, and if the audience laughs, don't blame me. Come on, Meg."
Then things went smoothly, for Don Pedro defied the world in a speech of two pages without a single break. Hagar, the witch, chanted an awful incantation over her kettleful of simmering toads, with weird effect. Roderigo rent his chains asunder manfully, and Hugo died in agonies of remorse and arsenic, with a wild, "Ha! Ha!"

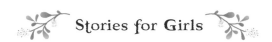

"It's the best we've had yet", said Meg, as the dead villain sat up and rubbed his elbows.

"I don't see how you can write and act such splendid things, Jo. You're a regular Shakespeare!" exclaimed Beth, who firmly believed that her sisters were gifted with wonderful genius in all things.

"Not quite," replied Jo modestly. "I do think *The Witches Curse*, an Operatic Tragedy is rather a nice thing, but I'd like to try *MacBeth*, if we only had a trapdoor for Banquo. I always wanted to do the killing part. 'Is that a dagger that I see before me?'" muttered Jo, rolling her eyes and clutching at the air, as she had seen a famous tragedian do.

"No, it's the toasting fork, with Mother's shoe on it instead of the bread. Beth's stage-struck!" cried Meg, and the rehearsal ended in a general burst of laughter.

"Glad to find you so merry, my girls," said a cheery voice at the door, and actors and audience turned to welcome a tall, motherly lady with a 'can I help you' look about her which was truly delightful. She was not elegantly dressed, but a noble-looking woman, and the girls thought the grey cloak and unfashionable bonnet covered the most splendid mother in the world.

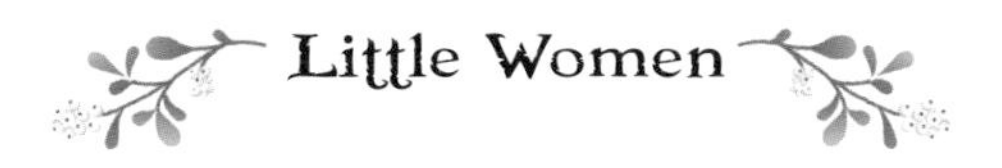

"Well, dearies, how have you got on today? There was so much to do, getting the boxes ready to go tomorrow, that I didn't come home to dinner. Has anyone called, Beth? How is your cold, Meg? Jo, you look tired to death. Come and kiss me, baby."

While making these maternal inquiries Mrs March got her wet things off, her warm slippers on, and sitting down in the easy chair, drew Amy to her lap, preparing to enjoy the happiest hour of her busy day. The girls flew about, trying to make things comfortable, each in her own way. Meg arranged the tea table, Jo brought wood and set chairs, dropping, over-turning, and clattering everything she touched. Beth trotted to and fro between parlour kitchen, quiet and busy, while Amy gave directions to everyone, as she sat with her hands folded.

As they gathered about the table, Mrs March said, with a particularly happy face, "I've got a treat for you after supper."

A quick, bright smile went round like a streak of sunshine. Beth clapped her hands, regardless of the biscuit she held, and Jo tossed up her napkin, crying, "A letter! A letter! Three cheers for Father!"

"Yes, a nice long letter. He is well, and thinks he shall get through the cold season better than we feared. He sends all sorts

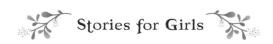

of loving wishes for Christmas, and an especial message to you girls", said Mrs March, patting her pocket as if she had got a treasure there.

"Hurry and get done! Don't stop to quirk your little finger and simper over your plate, Amy", cried Jo, choking on her tea and dropping her bread, butter side down, on the carpet in her haste to get at the treat.

Beth ate no more, but crept away to sit in her shadowy corner and brood over the delight to come, till the others were ready.

"I think it was so splendid in Father to go as chaplain when he was too old to be drafted, and not strong enough for a soldier," said Meg warmly.

"Don't I wish I could go as a drummer, a vivan – what's its name? Or a nurse, so I could be near him and help him," exclaimed Jo, with a groan.

"It must be very disagreeable to sleep in a tent, and eat all sorts of bad-tasting things, and drink out of a tin mug," sighed Amy.

"When will he come home, Marmee?" asked Beth, with a little quiver in her voice.

"Not for many months, dear, unless he is sick. He will stay and do his work faithfully as long as he can, and we won't ask for him back a minute sooner than he can be spared. Now come and hear the letter."

They all drew to the fire, Mother in the big chair with Beth at her feet, Meg and Amy perched on either arm of the chair, and Jo leaning on the back, where no one would see any sign of emotion if the letter should happen to be touching. Very few letters were written in those hard times that were not touching, especially those that fathers sent home. In this one little was said of the hardships endured, the dangers faced, or the homesickness conquered. It was a cheerful, hopeful letter, full of lively descriptions of camp life, marches, and military news, and only at the end did

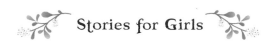

the writer's heart overflow with fatherly love and longing for the little girls at home:

Give them all of my dear love and a kiss. Tell them I think of them by day, pray for them by night, and find my best comfort in their affection always. A year seems a very long time to wait before I can see them again, but remind them that while we wait we may all work, so that these hard days need not be wasted. I know they will remember all that I said to them, that they will be loving children to you, will do their duty faithfully, fight their bosom enemies bravely, and conquer themselves so beautifully that when I come back to them I may be fonder and prouder than ever of my little women.

Everybody sniffed when they came to that part. Jo wasn't ashamed of the great tear that dropped off the end of her nose, and Amy never minded the rumpling of her curls as she hid her face on her mother's shoulder and sobbed, "I am a selfish girl! But I'll truly try to be better, so he mayn't be disappointed in me by-and-by."

"We all will," cried Meg. "I think too much of my looks and hate to work, but won't any more, if I can help it."

"I'll try hard to be what he loves to call me, 'a little woman' and not be rough and wild, and I shall try to do my duty here instead of wanting to be somewhere else," said Jo, thinking that keeping her temper at home was a much harder task than facing a rebel or two down South.

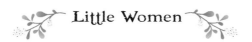

Beth said nothing, but wiped away her tears with the blue army sock and began to knit with all her might, losing no time in doing the duty that lay nearest her, while she resolved in her quiet little soul to be all that Father hoped to find her when the year brought round the happy coming home.

Mrs March broke the silence that followed Jo's words, by saying in her cheery voice, "Do you remember how you used to play Pilgrims Progress when you were little? Nothing delighted you more than to tie my piece bags on your backs for burdens, give you sticks and rolls of paper, and let you travel through the house from the cellar, which was the City of Destruction, to the housetop, where you had lovely things you could collect to make a Celestial City."

"I liked the place where the bundles fell off and tumbled downstairs," said Meg.

"I don't remember much about it, except that I was afraid of the cellar and the dark entry, and always liked the cake and milk we had up at the top. If I wasn't too old for such things, I'd rather

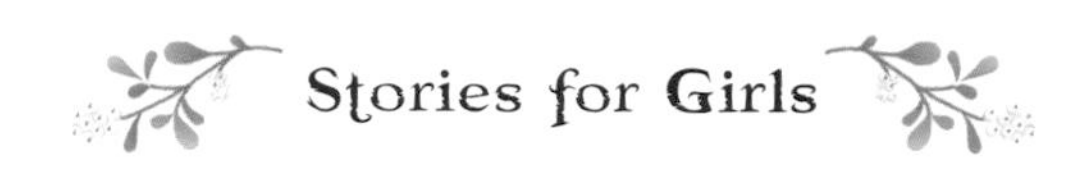

like to play it over again," said Amy, who began to talk of renouncing childish things at the mature age of twelve.

"We never are too old for this, my dear, because it is a play we are playing all the time in one way or another. Our burdens are here, our road is before us, and the longing for goodness and happiness is the guide that leads us through many troubles and mistakes to the peace which is a true Celestial City. Now, my little pilgrims, suppose you begin again, not in play, but in earnest, and see how far on you can get before Father comes home."

"Really, Mother? Where are our bundles?" asked Amy, who was a very literal young lady.

"Each of you told what your burden was just now, except Beth. I rather think she hasn't got any," said her mother.

"Yes, I have. Mine is dishes and dusters, and envying girls with nice pianos, and being afraid of people."

Beth's bundle was so funny that everybody wanted to laugh, but nobody did, for it would have hurt her feelings very much.

"Let us do it," said Meg thoughtfully. It is only another name for trying to be good, and the story may help us, for though we do want to be good, it is hard work and we sometimes forget, and don't do our best."

They talked over the new plan, then out came the four little work baskets, and the needles flew as the girls made sheets for Aunt March. It was uninteresting sewing, but tonight no one grumbled. They adopted Jo's plan of dividing the long seams into four parts, and calling the quarters Europe, Asia, Africa, and America, and in that way got on capitally, especially when they talked about the different countries as they stitched their way through them.

At nine they stopped work, and sang, before they went to bed. No one but Beth could get much music out of the old piano, but she had a way of softly touching the yellow keys and making a pleasant accompaniment to the simple songs they sang. Meg had a voice like a flute, and she and her mother led the little choir. Amy chirped like a cricket, and Jo wandered through the airs at her own sweet will, always coming out at the wrong place with a croak or a quaver that spoiled the most pensive tune. They had done this from the time they could lisp "Crinkle, crinkle, 'ittle 'tar", and it

had become a household custom, for mother was a born singer. The first sound in the morning was her voice as she went about the house singing like a lark, and the last sound at night was the same cheery sound, for the girls never grew too old for that familiar lullaby.

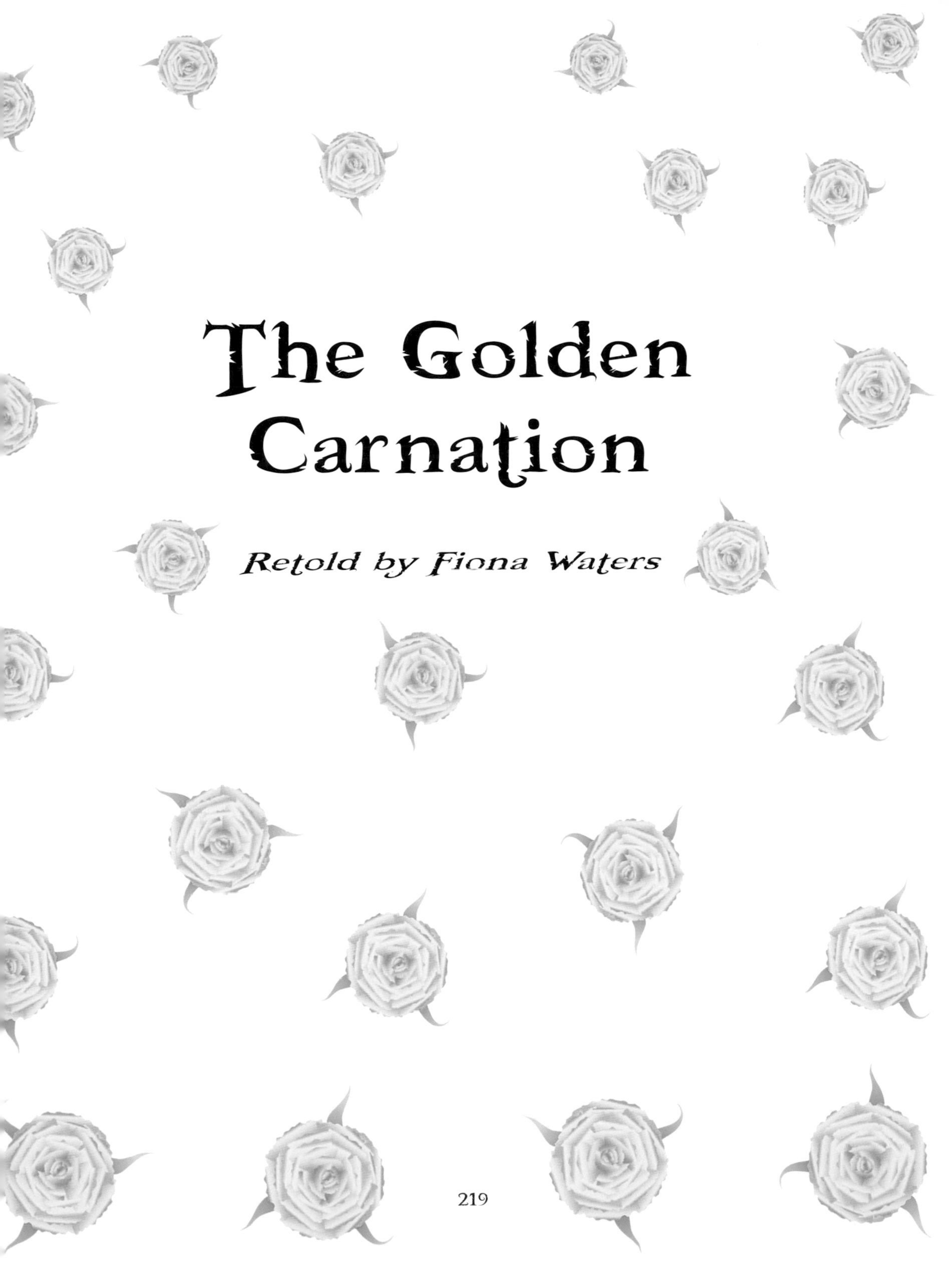

The Golden Carnation

Retold by Fiona Waters

Introduction

The Golden Carnation *is an Italian version of the old story of* Beauty and the Beast. *French aristocrat Madame Le Prince de Beaumont (1711–1780) wrote the first version of* Beauty and the Beast *to be published in 1756 as part of a collection of stories. Since its initial publishing the story has been revised many times. The nineteenth century saw a proliferation of retellings in France, England and America.*

The Golden Carnation

Many moons ago a wealthy merchant lived in Italy with his three daughters. The elder two daughters were sour and bitter like lemons, but the youngest was as sweet and pretty as a peach. As he set out on a long voyage to the Spice Islands the merchant asked each of his daughters what gifts they would like him to bring back.

"A dress covered in tiny golden bells," said the eldest, Maria.

"Silver slippers with glass heels," said the middle daughter, Lucia. (No 'please' and 'thank you' as I'm sure you have noticed.)

"And what would you like, my dear Florita?" said the merchant, turning to the youngest.

"I would only like you to come home safely, Father," she replied with a smile.

"But your sisters have made special requests; I would not leave you out," said the merchant.

"Very well, Father. I would like a golden carnation, please, and I would like you to come home safely!" she said laughing.

The merchant set sail the very next day and many weeks later reached port. He met many traders and soon the hold of the ship was groaning with the weight of all the rare and precious spices he had bought. Determined to return home on the next tide, he set off to find the presents for his daughters. In the bazaar he found great lengths of silk, all covered with tiny golden bells, and a dark-eyed tailor who promised to have the dress ready by dawn. In the leather market he found a cobbler whose stitches were so minute as to be invisible, and he too promised to have the silver slippers with glass heels ready by dawn. But nowhere was there a golden carnation to be found. The merchant searched the flower market and he searched the goldsmiths' vaults and he asked every trader he met but no one could help, so the merchant set sail on the early morning tide. The dress with the tiny golden bells lay in tissue paper in a sandalwood box. The silver slippers with glass heels were in a velvet drawstring bag, all lined with silk. But he had no golden carnation for Florita.

The ship had a safe passage, but it was with a heavy heart that the merchant stepped ashore once again. Where was he to find a golden carnation? He walked aimlessly away from the bustling harbour and after a while found himself in a completely unfamiliar wood. He looked around, greatly puzzled. He did not recognise a single landmark. Then ahead he saw a great gateway and filled with curiosity he stepped inside. The air seemed to crackle with magic and he knew he had somehow wandered into a garden of deep enchantment. And then, there in front of him, grew a great bush covered with golden carnations!

Without thinking the merchant stepped forward and broke off one of the gorgeous blooms. Instantly there was a huge flash of purple light and a roll of thunder, and there stood a mighty wizard. And he looked very cross indeed.

"Who are you, impudent man, and how dare you pick one of my precious carnations?" he asked, and his eyes flashed with anger.

Haltingly, the merchant explained about his promise to Florita. The wizard scowled. "As you have picked the carnation you may have it for your daughter, but the payment for this will be that you must bring your daughter here in three days. If you do not, it will be the worse for you and all your family," said the wizard before disappearing in a whirl of smoke.

When the merchant arrived home he gave his daughters their presents. The elder two rushed off to try on their gifts, but Florita could see that her father was worried about something.

Eventually the merchant poured out the whole story. Florita was quite undismayed. “Well, Father, you must take me to meet this wizard tomorrow before he becomes any crosser,” she said. “I shall go and pack a few things to take with us.”

The next day they set off, the merchant not even quite sure how to find the wizard again but somehow, just by wishing it, they found themselves in the enchanted garden. Just as suddenly as before, the wizard appeared.

“Well, Florita, to pay for your golden carnation you must stay here and look after my garden. I shall visit you every evening and we will dine together,” and so saying, the wizard vanished again. The merchant was heartbroken, but Florita told him she was quite happy to look after such a lovely garden. He went sadly back to Maria and Lucia, who were still so sour they were not at all sorry to see the back of their lovely younger sister.

Many days passed. Florita greatly enjoyed looking after the garden and began to look forward to her evenings with the wizard, who was not so terrifying once she got to know him. But after a

while she began to worry about her father. She was sure her selfish sisters would not be looking after him properly, and she missed him. She asked the wizard if she might go home for a few days, and at first he refused to let her go. But as she grew quieter and unhappier, he relented.

"I can see you are unhappy so I will let you return, but you must promise to come back in three days or it will be the worse for us both," and he looked sad as he sent her on her way in a golden carriage.

When Florita arrived home, her worse fears were realized. Her father looked ill, the house was a shambles and her sisters only said by way of greeting, "Oh, good! You can tidy the house and get us some supper. We can't find a thing!"

She made her father a bowl of good hot soup and set to the task of cleaning the house. She scrubbed and polished from top to bottom, looking after her father all the while. The three days slipped by without her noticing, and it was only when her father asked whether the golden carnations were still blooming in the wizard's garden that she remembered her promise. In great distress Florita dashed out of the house. The golden carriage had disappeared and she had to walk through the night, alone and

greatly afraid of what the wizard might say. Just as dawn was breaking, she reached the great gates.

But what had happened to the beautiful garden? Huge weeds and brambles were crushing the rare plants and flowers. There was no water in the fountains and the leafy trees drooped sadly. At the foot of the terrace steps, the wizard lay in a crumpled heap. His gorgeous robes were dusty and torn, and his eyes were closed.

Florita knelt by his side and whispered, “What have I done? I only stayed to help my father. I did mean to return to you,” and she bent forward and kissed his cheek. Immediately there was a shower of golden light, full of glittering stars, and there, instead of a great wizard, stood a rather ordinary but very pleasant-looking young man.

“Well, that was a close thing!” he said. “My name is Pietro and I have been under a spell which could only be broken by an act of kindness. Will you stay with me, Florita, and help me look after the garden?” Florita was delighted but first she collected her father so they could all live together. As for her two sisters, they couldn’t abide all the pollen from the flowers in the garden so they had to remain at home looking after each other which, of course, made them more sour than ever!

The Secret Garden

An extract
by Frances Hodgson Burnett

Frances Hodgson Burnett (1849–1924) published The Secret Garden *in 1911. Mary Lennox is the spoiled orphan daughter of a British official in India who is brought back to Misselthwaite Manor in Yorkshire, England, to live with her uncle, a disabled and reclusive man. In this episode Mary discovers the secret garden that has lain hidden and locked away since the tragic death of her uncle's wife ten years previously.*

The Key to the Garden

When Mary opened her eyes she sat upright in bed immediately, and called to Martha.

"Look at the moor! Look at the moor!"

The rainstorm had ended and the grey mist and clouds had been swept away in the night by the wind. The wind had ceased and a brilliant, deep blue sky arched high over the moorland. Never had Mary dreamed of a sky so blue. In India skies were hot and blazing; this was a deep cool blue which almost seemed to sparkle like the waters of some lovely bottomless lake. Here and there, high in the arched blueness floated small clouds of snow-white fleece. The far-reaching world of the moor itself looked softly blue instead of gloomy purple-black or dreary grey.

"Aye," said Martha with a cheerful grin. "Th' storm's over for a bit. It does like this at this time o' th' year. It goes off in a night like it was pretendin' it had never been here an' never meant to come again. That's because th' springtime's on its way. It's a long way off yet, but it's comin'."

"I thought perhaps it always rained or looked dark in England," Mary said.

"Eh! no!" said Martha, sitting up on her heels among her

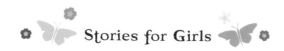

black lead brushes. "Nowt o' th' soart!"

"What does that mean?" asked Mary seriously. In India the natives spoke different dialects which only a few people understood, so she was not surprised when Martha used words she did not know.

"There now," Martha said. "I've talked broad Yorkshire again like Mrs. Medlock said I mustn't. 'Nowt o' th' soart' means 'nothin'-of-the-sort'," slowly and carefully, "but it takes so long to say it. Yorkshire's th' sunniest place on earth when it is sunny. I told thee tha'd like th' moor after a bit. Just you wait till you see th' gold-coloured gorse blossoms an' th' blossoms o' th' broom, an' th' heather flowerin', all purple bells, an' hundreds o' butterflies flutterin' an' bees hummin' an' skylarks soarin' up an' singin'. You'll want to get out on it as sunrise an' live out on it all day like Dickon does."

"Could I ever get there?" asked Mary wistfully, looking through her window at the far-off blue.

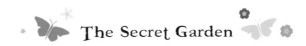

It was so new and big and wonderful and such a heavenly colour.

"I don't know," answered Martha. "Tha's never used tha' legs since tha' was born, it seems to me. Tha' couldn't walk five mile. It's five mile to our cottage."

"I should like to see your cottage."

Martha stared at her a moment curiously before she took up her polishing brush and began to rub the grate again. She was thinking that the small plain face did not look quite as sour at this moment as it had done the first morning she saw it.

"I'll ask my mother about it," she said. "She's one o' them that nearly always sees a way to do things. It's my day out today an' I'm goin' home. Eh! I am glad. Mrs Medlock thinks a lot o' mother. Perhaps she could talk to her."

"I like your mother," said Mary.

"I should think tha' did," agreed Martha, polishing away.

"I've never seen her," said Mary.

"No, tha' hasn't," replied Martha.

She sat up on her heels again and rubbed the end of her nose with the back of her hand as if puzzled for a moment, but she ended quite positively.

"Well, she's that sensible an' hard workin' an' goodnatured an' clean that no one could help likin' her whether they'd seen her or not. When I'm goin' home to her on my day out I just jump for joy when I'm crossin' the moor."

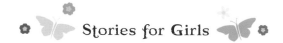

"I like Dickon," added Mary, "And I've never seen him."

"Well," said Martha stoutly, "I've told thee that th' very birds likes him an' th' rabbits an' wild sheep an' ponies, an' th' foxes themselves. I wonder," staring at her reflectively, "what Dickon would think of thee?"

"He wouldn't like me," said Mary in her stiff, cold little way. "No one does."

Martha looked reflective again.

"How does tha' like thysel'?" she inquired, really quite as if she were curious to know.

Mary hesitated a moment and thought it over.

"Not at all, really," she answered. "But I never thought of that before."

Martha grinned a little as if at some homely recollection.

"Mother said that to me once," she said. "She was at her wash-tub an' I was in a bad temper an' talkin' ill of folk, an' she turns round on me an' says: 'Tha' young vixen, tha'! There tha' stands sayin' tha' doesn't like this one an' tha' doesn't like that one. How does tha' like thysel'?' It made me laugh an' it brought me to my senses in a minute."

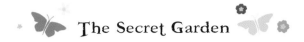

She went away in high spirits as soon as she had given Mary her breakfast. She was going to walk five miles across the moor to the cottage, and she was going to help her mother with the washing and do the week's baking and enjoy herself thoroughly. Mary felt lonelier than ever when she knew she was no longer in the house. She went out into the garden as quickly as possible, and the first thing she did was to run round and round the fountain flower garden ten times. When she had finished she felt in better spirits. The sunshine made the whole place look different. The high, deep, blue sky arched over Misselthwaite as well as over the moor, and she kept lifting her face and looking up into it. She went into the first kitchen-garden and found Ben Weatherstaff working there with two other gardeners. The change in the weather seemed to have done him good. He spoke to her of his own accord. "Springtime's comin'," he said. "Cannot tha' smell it?"

Mary sniffed and thought she could. "I smell something nice and fresh and damp," she said.

"That's th' good rich earth," he answered, digging away. "It's in a good humour makin' ready to grow things. It's glad when plantin' time comes. It's dull in th' winter when it's got nowt to do. In th' flower gardens out there things will be stirrin' down below in th' dark. Th' sun's warmin' 'em. You'll see bits o' green spikes stickin' out o' th' black earth after a bit."

"What will they be?" asked Mary.

"Crocuses an' snowdrops an' daffydowndillys. Has tha' never seen them?"

"No. Everything is hot, and wet, and green after the rains in India," said Mary. "And I think things grow up in a night."

"These won't grow up in a night," said Weatherstaff. "Tha'll have to wait for 'em. They'll poke up a bit higher here, an' push out a spike more there, an' uncurl a leaf this day an' another that. You watch 'em."

"I am going to," answered Mary.

Very soon she heard the soft rustling flight of wings again and she knew at once that the robin had come again. He was very pert and lively, and hopped about so close to her feet, and put his head on one side and looked at her so slyly that she asked Ben Weatherstaff a question.

"Do you think he remembers me?" she said.

"Remembers thee!" said Ben Weatherstaff indignantly. "He knows every cabbage stump in th' gardens, let alone th' people. He's never seen a little girl here before, an' he's bent on findin' out all about thee. Tha's no need to try to hide anything from him."

"Are things stirring down below in the dark in that garden where he lives?" Mary inquired.

"What garden?" grunted Ben Weatherstaff, becoming surly again.

"The one where the old rose-trees are." She could not help asking, because she wanted so much to know. "Are all the flowers dead, or do some of them come again in the summer? Are there ever any roses?"

"Ask him," said Ben Weatherstaff, hunching his shoulders toward the robin. "He's the only one as knows. No one else has seen inside it for ten year'."

Ten years was a long time, Mary thought. She had been born ten years ago.

She walked away, slowly thinking. She had begun to like the garden just as she had begun to like the robin and Dickon and Martha's mother. She was beginning to like Martha, too. That seemed a good many people to like – when you were not used to liking. She thought of the robin as one of the people. She went to her walk outside the long, ivy-covered wall over which she could see the tree-tops; and the second time she walked up and down the most interesting and exciting thing happened to her.

She heard a chirp and a twitter, and when she looked at the bare flower-bed at her left side there he was hopping about and pretending to peck things out of the earth to persuade her that he had not followed her. But she knew he had followed her and the surprise so filled her with delight that she almost trembled a little.

"You do remember me!" she cried out. "You do! You are prettier than anything else in the world!"

She talked, and coaxed and he hopped, and flirted his tail and twittered. It was as if he were talking. His red waistcoat was like satin and he puffed his tiny breast out and was so fine and so grand that it was really as if he were showing her how important and like a human person a robin could be. He allowed her to draw closer and closer to him, and bend down and talk and try to make something like robin sounds.

To think that he should actually let her come as near to him as that! He knew nothing in the world would make her put out her hand toward him or startle him in the least tiniest way. He knew it because he was a real person – only nicer than any other person in the world. The flower-bed was not quite bare. It was bare of flowers, but there were tall shrubs and low ones which grew together at the back of the bed, and as the robin hopped about under them she saw him hop over a small pile of freshly turned up earth. He stopped on it to look for a worm. The earth had been turned up because a dog had been trying to dig up a mole and he had scratched quite a deep hole.

Mary looked at it, not really knowing why the hole was there, and as she looked she saw something almost buried in the newly-turned soil. It was something like a ring of rusty iron or brass and when the robin flew up into a tree nearby she put out her hand and picked the ring up. It was more than a ring, however; it was an old key that looked as if it had been buried a long time.

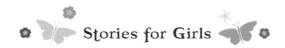

Mistress Mary stood up and looked at it with an almost frightened face as it hung from her finger.

"Perhaps it has been buried for ten years," she said in a whisper. "Perhaps it is the key to the garden!"

The Robin Who Showed the Way

She looked at the key quite a long time. As I have said before, she was not a child who had been trained to ask permission or consult her elders about things. All she thought about the key was that if it was the key to the closed garden, and she could find out where the door was, she could perhaps open it and see what was inside the walls, and what had happened to the old rose-trees. It was because it had been shut up so long that she wanted to see it. Besides that, if she liked it she could go into it every day and shut the door behind her, and could make up some play of her own and play it alone, because nobody would ever know where she was, but would think the door was still locked and the key buried in the earth. The thought of that pleased her very much.

Living as it were, all by herself in a house with a hundred mysteriously closed rooms and having nothing whatever to do to amuse herself, had set her inactive brain to working and was actually awakening her imagination. There is no doubt that the fresh, strong, pure air from the moor had a great deal to do with it. Just as it had given her an appetite, and fighting with the wind had stirred her blood, so the same things had stirred her mind. In India she had always been too hot and languid and weak to care much about anything, but in this place she was beginning to care and to want to do new things. Already she felt less 'contrary', though she did not know why.

She put the key in her pocket and walked up and down her walk. No one but herself ever seemed to come there, so she could walk slowly and look at the wall, or rather, at the ivy growing on it. The ivy was the baffling thing. However carefully she looked she could see nothing but thickly growing, glossy, dark green leaves. She was very disappointed. Something of her contrariness came back to her as she paced the walk and looked over it at the tree-tops inside. It seemed so silly, she said to herself, to be near it and not be able to get in. She took the key in her pocket when she went back to the house, and she made up her mind that she would always carry it with her when she went out, so that if she ever should find the hidden door she would be ready.

Mrs. Medlock had allowed Martha to sleep all night at the cottage, but she was back at her work in the morning with cheeks redder than ever and in the best of spirits.

"I got up at four o'clock," she said. "Eh! it was pretty on th' moor with th' birds gettin' up an' th' rabbits scamperin' about an' th' sun risin'. I didn't walk all th' way. A man gave me a ride in his cart an' I did enjoy myself."

She was full of stories of the delights of her day out. Her mother had been glad to see her and they had got all the baking and washing done. She had even made each of the children a doughcake with a bit of brown sugar in it.

"I had 'em all pipin' hot when they came in from playin' on

th' moor. An' th' cottage all smelt o' nice, clean hot bakin' an' there was a good fire, an' they just shouted for joy. Our Dickon he said our cottage was good enough for a king."

In the evening they had all sat round the fire, and Martha and her mother had sewed patches on torn clothes and mended stockings and Martha had told them about the little girl who had come from India and who had been waited on all her life until she didn't know how to put on her own stockings.

"Eh! they did like to hear about you," said Martha. "They wanted to know all about th' people you knew an' about th' ship you came in. I couldn't tell 'em enough."

Mary reflected a little.

"I'll tell you a great deal more before your next day out," she said, "so that you will have more to talk about. I dare say they would like to hear about riding on elephants and camels, and about the officers going to hunt tigers."

"My word!" cried delighted Martha. "It would set 'em clean off their heads. It would be same as a wild beast show like we heard they had in York once."

"India is quite different from Yorkshire," Mary said slowly, as she thought the matter over. "I never thought of that. Did Dickon and your mother like to hear you talk about me?"

"Why, our Dickon's eyes nearly started out o' his head, they got that round," answered Martha. "But mother, she was put out about your seemin' to be all by yourself like. She said, 'Hasn't Mr. Craven got no governess for her, nor no nurse?' and I said, 'No, he hasn't, though Mrs. Medlock says he will when he thinks of it, but she says he mayn't think of it for two or three years.'"

"I don't want a governess," said Mary sharply.

"But mother says you ought to be learnin' your book by this time an' you ought to have a woman to look after you, an' she says: 'Now, Martha, you just think how you'd feel yourself, in a big place like that, wanderin' about all alone, an' no mother. You do your best to cheer her up,' she says, an' I said I would."

Mary gave her a long, steady look.

"You do cheer me up," she said. "I like to hear you talk."

Presently Martha went out of the room and came back with something held in her hands under her apron.

"What does tha' think," she said, with a cheerful grin. "I've brought thee a present."

"A present!" exclaimed Mistress Mary. How could a cottage full of fourteen hungry people give anyone a present?

"A man was drivin' across the moor peddlin'," Martha explained. "An' he stopped his cart at our door. He had pots an' pans an' odds an' ends, but mother had no money to buy anythin'. Just as he was goin' away our 'Lizabeth Ellen called out, 'Mother, he's got skippin'-ropes with red an' blue handles.' An' mother she calls out quite sudden, 'Here, stop, mister! How much are they?' An' he says 'Tuppence', an' mother she began fumblin' in her pocket an' she says to me, 'Martha, tha's brought me thy wages like a good lass, an' I've got four places to put every penny, but I'm just goin' to take tuppence out of it to buy that child a skippin'-rope,' an' she bought one an' here it is."

She brought it out from under her apron and exhibited it quite proudly. It was a strong, slender rope with a striped red and blue handle at each end, but Mary Lennox had never seen a skipping-rope before. She gazed at it with a mystified expression.

"What is it for?" she asked curiously.

"For!" cried out Martha. "Does tha' mean that they've not got skippin'-ropes in India, for all they've got elephants and tigers and camels! This is what it's for; just watch me."

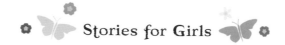

And she ran into the middle of the room and, taking a handle in each hand, began to skip, while Mary turned in her chair to stare at her, and the queer faces in the old portraits seemed to stare at her too, and wonder what on earth this common little cottager had the impudence to be doing under their very noses. But Martha did not even see them. The interest and curiosity in Mistress Mary's face delighted her, and she went on skipping and counted as she skipped until she had reached a hundred.

"I could skip longer than that," she said when she stopped. "I've skipped as much as five hundred when I was twelve, but I wasn't as fat then as I am now, an' I was in practice."

Mary got up from her chair beginning to feel excited herself.

"It looks nice," she said. "Your mother is a kind woman. Do you think I could ever skip like that?"

"You just try it," urged Martha, handing her the skipping-rope. "You can't skip a hundred at first, but if you practice you'll mount up. That's what mother said. She says, 'Nothin' will do her more good than skippin' rope. It's th' sensiblest toy a child can have. Let her play out in th' fresh air skippin' an' it'll stretch her legs an' arms an' give her some strength in 'em.'"

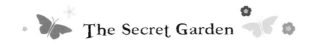

It was plain that there was not a great deal of strength in Mistress Mary's arms and legs when she first began to skip. She was not very clever at it, but she liked it so much that she did not want to stop.

"Put on tha' things and run an' skip out o' doors," said Martha. "Mother said I must tell you to keep out o' doors as much as you could, even when it rains a bit, so as tha' wrap up warm."

Mary put on her coat and hat and took her skipping-rope over her arm. She opened the door to go out, and then suddenly thought of something and turned back rather slowly.

"Martha," she said, "they were your wages. It was your two-pence really. Thank you." She said it stiffly because she was not used to thanking people or noticing that they did things for her. "Thank you," she said, and held out her hand because she did not know what else to do.

Martha gave her hand a clumsy little shake, as if she was not accustomed to this sort of thing either. Then she laughed.

"Run off outside an' play with thy rope."

Mistress Mary felt a little awkward as she went out of the

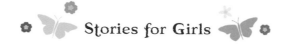

room. Yorkshire people seemed strange, and Martha was always rather a puzzle to her. At first she had disliked her very much, but now she did not. The skipping-rope was a wonderful thing. She counted and skipped, and skipped and counted, until her cheeks were quite red, and she was more interested than she had ever been since she was born. The sun was shining and a little wind was blowing – not a rough wind, but one which came in delightful little gusts and brought a fresh scent of newly turned earth with it. She skipped round the fountain garden, and up one walk and down another. She skipped at last into the kitchen-garden and saw Ben Weatherstaff digging and talking to his robin, which was hopping about him. She skipped down the walk toward him and he lifted his head and looked at her with a curious expression. She had wondered if he would notice her. She wanted him to see her skip.

"Well!" he exclaimed. "Upon my word. P'raps tha' art a young 'un, after all, an' p'raps tha's got child's blood in thy veins instead of sour buttermilk. Tha's skipped red into thy cheeks as sure as I'm Ben Weatherstaff. I wouldn't have believed tha' could do it."

"I never skipped before," Mary said. "I'm just beginning. I can only go up to twenty."

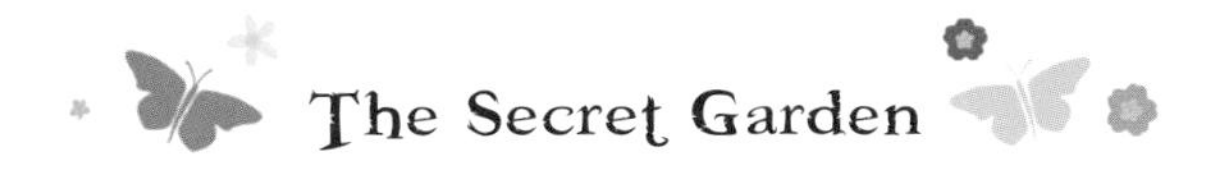

"Tha' keep on," said Ben. "Tha' shapes well enough at it for a young 'un that's lived in India. Just see how he's watchin' thee," jerking his head toward the robin. "He followed after thee yesterday. He'll be at it again today. He'll be bound to find out what th' skippin'-rope is. He's never seen one. Eh!" shaking his head at the bird, "tha' curiosity will be th' death of thee sometime if tha' doesn't look sharp."

Mary skipped round all the gardens and round the orchard, resting every few minutes. At length she went to her own special walk and made up her mind to see if she could skip the whole length of it. It was a good long skip and she began slowly, but before she had gone half-way down the path she was so hot and breathless that she was obliged to stop. She did not mind much, because she had already counted up to thirty. She stopped with a little laugh of pleasure, and there, lo and behold, was the robin swaying on a long branch of ivy. He had followed her and he greeted her with a chirp. As Mary had skipped toward him she felt something heavy in her pocket strike against her at each jump, and when she saw the robin she laughed again.

"You showed me where the key was yesterday," she said. "You ought to show me the door today, but I don't believe you know!"

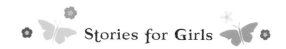

The robin flew from his swinging spray of ivy on to the top of the wall and he opened his beak and sang a loud, lovely trill, merely to show off. Nothing in the world is quite as adorably lovely as a robin when he shows off – and they are nearly always doing it.

Mary Lennox had heard a great deal about magic in her Ayah's stories, and she always said that what happened almost at that moment was magic. One of the nice little gusts of wind rushed down the walk, and it was a stronger one than the rest. It was strong enough to wave the branches of the trees, and it was more than strong enough to sway the trailing sprays of untrimmed ivy hanging from the wall. Mary had stepped close to the robin, and suddenly the gust of wind swung aside some loose ivy trails, and more suddenly still she jumped toward it and caught it in her hand. This she did because she had seen something under it – a round knob that had been covered by the leaves hanging over it. It was the knob of a door.

She put her hands under the leaves and began to pull and push them aside. Thick as the ivy hung, it nearly all was a loose and swinging curtain, though some had crept over wood and iron. Mary's heart began to thump and her hands to shake a little in her delight and excitement. The robin kept singing and twittering away and tilting his head on one side, as if he were as excited as she was. What was this under her hands which was square and made of iron and which her fingers found a hole in?

It was the lock of the door that had been closed ten years and she put her hand in her pocket, drew out the key and found it fitted the keyhole. She put the key in and turned it. It took two hands to do it, but it did turn. And then she took a long breath and looked behind her up the long walk to see if anyone was coming. No one ever did come, it seemed, and she took another long breath, because she could not help it, and she held back the swinging curtain of ivy and pushed back the door that opened slowly.

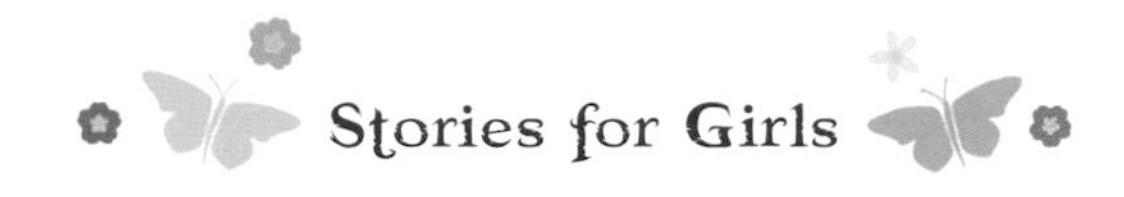

Then she slipped through it, and shut it behind her, and stood with her back against it, looking about her and breathing quite fast with excitement, and wonder, and delight.

She was standing inside the secret garden.

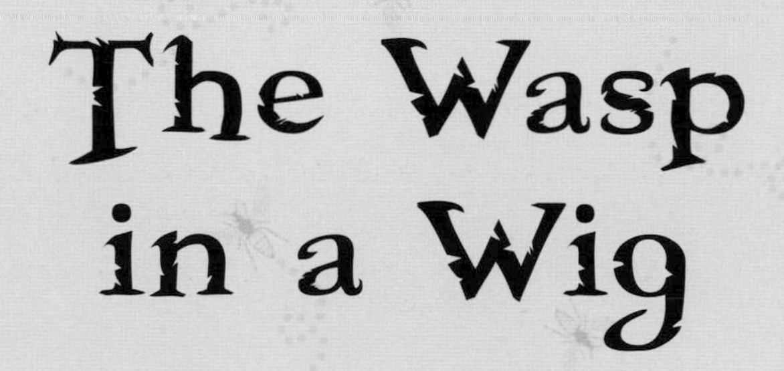

by Lewis Carroll

Introduction

The Wasp in a Wig *only came to light in 1974 and was first published in 1977. Lewis Carroll originally intended it to appear at the end of chapter eight of* Through the Looking Glass. *It was actually already set up in type but Carroll heeded the advice of John Tenniel, the original illustrator of Alice, who thought it should not be included in the final version of the story.*

The Wasp in a Wig

Alice heard a deep sigh, which seemed to come from the wood behind her.

"There's somebody very unhappy there," she thought, looking anxious. Something like a very old man (only that his face was more like a wasp) was sitting on the ground, leaning against a tree, all huddled up, and shivering as if he were very cold.

Alice went back to the Wasp.

"Oh, my old bones, my old bones!" he was grumbling as Alice came up to him.

"It's rheumatism, I should think," Alice said to herself, and she stooped over him, and said very kindly, "I hope you're not in much pain?"

The Wasp only shook his shoulders, and turned his head away. "Ah deary me!" he said to himself.

"Can I do anything for you?" Alice went on. "Aren't you rather cold here?"

"How you go on!" the Wasp said in a peevish tone. "Worrity, Worrity! There never was such a child!"

Alice felt rather offended at this answer, and was very nearly walking on and leaving him, but she thought to herself 'Perhaps it's only pain that makes him so cross.' So she tried once more.

"Won't you let me help you round to the other side? You'll be out of the cold wind there."

The Wasp took her arm, and let her help him round the tree, but when he got settled down again he only said, as before, "Worrity, worrity! Can't you leave a body alone?"

"Would you like me to read you a bit of this?" Alice went on, as she picked up a newspaper which had been lying at his feet.

"You may read it if you've a mind to," the Wasp said, rather sulkily. "Nobody's hindering you, that I know of."

So Alice sat down by him, and spread out the paper on her knees, and began. "Latest News. The Exploring Party have made another tour in the Pantry, and have found five new lumps of white sugar, large and in fine condition. In coming back they found a lake of treacle. The banks of the lake were blue and white, and looked like china. While tasting the treacle, they had a sad accident: two of their party were engulped—"

"Let's stop it here!" said the Wasp, fretfully turning away his head."It's all along of the wig," the Wasp said in a much gentler voice.

"Along of the wig?" Alice repeated, quite pleased to find that he was recovering his temper.

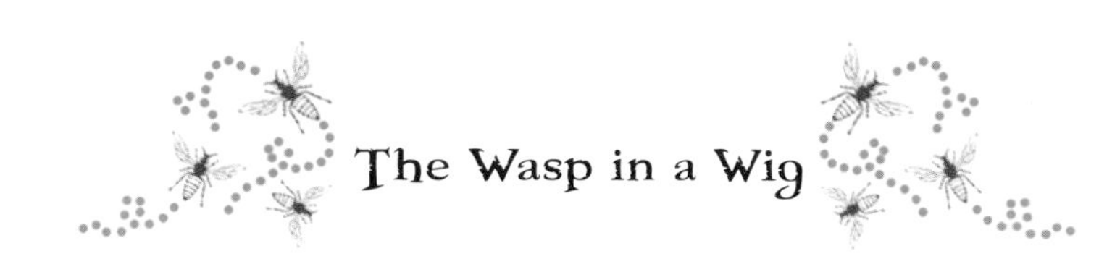

"You'd be cross too, if you'd a wig like mine," the Wasp went on. "They jokes, at one. And they worrits one. And then I gets cross. And I gets cold. And I gets under a tree. And I gets a yellow handkerchief. And I ties up my face – as at the present."

Alice looked pityingly at him. "Tying up the face is very good for the toothache," she said.

"And it's very good for the conceit," added the Wasp.

Alice didn't catch the word exactly. "Is that a kind of toothache?" she asked.

The Wasp considered a little. "Well, no," he said: "it's when you hold up your head – so – without bending your neck."

"Oh, you mean stiff-neck," said Alice.

The Wasp said "That's a new-fangled name. They called it conceit in my time."

"Conceit isn't a disease at all," Alice remarked.

"It is, though," said the Wasp, "wait till you have it. And when you catches it, just try tying a yellow handkerchief round your face. It'll cure you in no time!"

He untied the handkerchief as he spoke, and Alice looked at

his wig in great surprise. It was bright yellow like the handkerchief, and all tangled and tumbled about like a heap of seaweed. "You could make your wig much neater," she said, "if only you had a comb."

"What, you're a Bee, are you?" the Wasp said, looking at her with more interest. "And you've got a comb. Much honey?"

"It isn't that kind," Alice hastily explained. "It's to comb hair with – your wig's so very rough, you know."

"I'll tell you how I came to wear it," the Wasp said. "When I was young, you know, my ringlets used to wave—"

"Would you mind saying it in rhyme?" Alice asked politely.

"It aint what I'm used to," said the Wasp, "however I'll try; wait a bit." He was silent for a few moments, and then began again:

"When I was young, my ringlets waved
And curled and crinkled on my head:
And then they said 'You should be shaved,
And wear a yellow wig instead.'

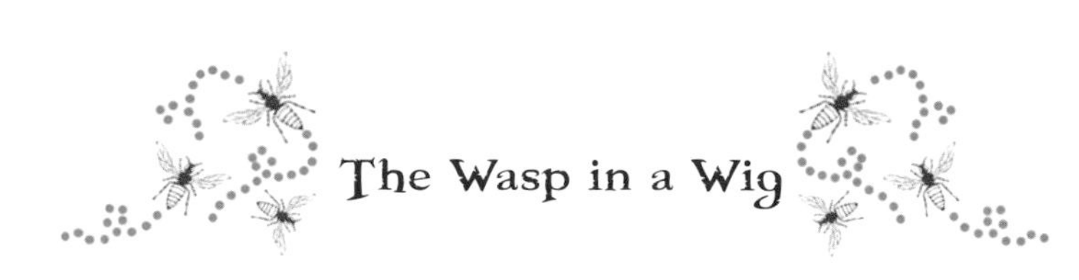

But when I followed their advice,
And they had noticed the effect,
They said I did not look so nice
As they had ventured to expect.

They said it did not fit, and so
It made me look extremely plain:
But what was I to do, you know?
My ringlets would not grow again.

So now that I am old and grey,
And all my hair is nearly gone,
They take my wig from me and say
'How can you put such rubbish on?'

And still, whenever I appear,
They hoot at me and call me 'Pig!'
And that is why they do it, dear,
Because I wear a yellow wig."

"I'm very sorry for you," Alice said heartily: "and I think if your wig fitted a little better, they wouldn't tease you so much."

"Your wig fits very well," the Wasp murmured, looking at her with an expression of admiration: "it's the shape of your head as does it. Your jaws aint well shaped, though – I should think you couldn't bite well?"

Alice managed to say gravely, "I can bite anything I want,"

"Not with a mouth as small as that," the Wasp persisted. "If you was a-fighting, now – could you get hold of the other one by the back of the neck?"

"I'm afraid not," said Alice.

"Well, that's because your jaws are too short," the Wasp went on: "but the top of your head is nice and round. Then, your eyes – they're too much in front, no doubt. One would have done as well as two, if you must have them so close."

Alice did not like having so many personal remarks made on her, as the Wasp had quite recovered his spirits, and was getting very talkative, she thought she might safely leave him. "I think I must be going on now," she said. "Goodbye."

"Goodbye, and thank-ye," said the Wasp, and Alice was quite pleased that she had made the poor old creature comfortable.

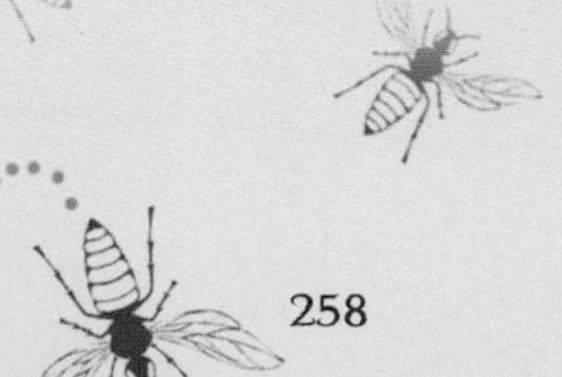

An extract
by Charlotte Brontë

Introduction

Jane Eyre, *written by Charlotte Brontë (1816–1855), was first published in 1847. In* Jane Eyre, *the heroine has been left a penniless orphan and is taken in by her aunt, Mrs Reed, who is harsh and unsympathetic to her plight. After a life of misery only occasionally interspersed with brief moments of happiness, Jane eventually finds peace and contentment in the last chapter of this wonderful book.*

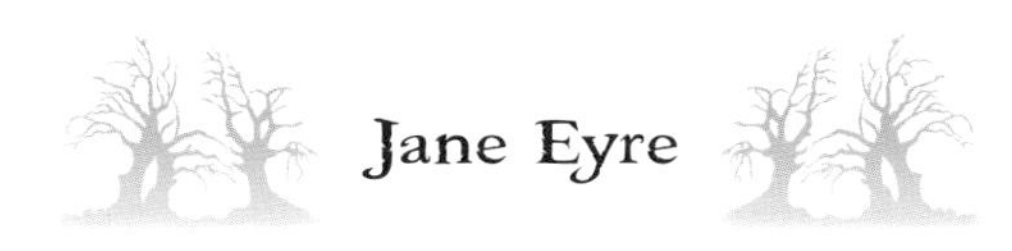

Eliza, John, and Georgiana were now clustered round their mama in the drawing room. She lay reclined on a sofa by the fireside, and with her darlings about her (for the time neither quarrelling nor crying) looked perfectly happy. Me, she had dispensed from joining the group, saying "She regretted to be under the necessity of keeping me at a distance, but that until she heard from Bessie, and could discover by her own observation, that I was endeavouring in good earnest to acquire a more sociable and childlike disposition, a more attractive and sprightly manner – something lighter, franker, more natural, as it were – she really must exclude me from privileges intended only for contented, happy, little children."

"What does Bessie say I have done?" I asked.

"Jane, I don't like cavillers or questioners; besides, there is something truly forbidding in a child taking up her elders in that manner. Be seated somewhere; and until you can speak pleasantly, remain silent."

A breakfast-room adjoined the drawing-room, I slipped in there. It contained a bookcase. I soon possessed myself of a volume, taking care that it should be one stored with pictures. I mounted into the window seat. Gathering up my feet, I sat cross-legged, and, having drawn the red curtain nearly close, I was shrined in double retirement. Folds of scarlet drapery shut in my view to the right hand; to the left were the clear panes of glass, protecting, but not separating me from the drear November day. At intervals, while turning over the leaves of my book, I studied the aspect of that winter afternoon. Afar, it offered a pale blank of mist and cloud; near a scene of wet lawn and storm-beat shrub, with ceaseless rain sweeping away wildly before a long and lamentable blast.

I returned to my book. With Bewick on my knee, I was then happy – happy at least in my way. I feared nothing but interruption, and that came too soon. The breakfast room door opened.

"Boh! Madam Mope!" cried the voice of John Reed. Then he paused – he found the room apparently empty.

"Where the dickens is she!" he continued. "Lizzy! Georgy! (calling to his sisters) Jane is not here. Tell mama she is run out into the rain – bad animal!"

'It is well I drew the curtain,' thought I, and I wished fervently he might not discover my hiding-place: nor would John Reed have found it out himself; he was not quick either of vision or conception; but Eliza just put her head in at the door, and said at once:

"She is in the window seat, to be sure, Jack."

And I came out immediately, for I trembled at the idea of being dragged forth by the said Jack.

"What do you want?" I asked, with awkward diffidence.

"Say, 'What do you want, Master Reed?'" was the answer. "I want you to come here," and seating himself in an armchair, he gestured that I was to approach and stand before him.

John Reed was a schoolboy of fourteen years old – four years older than I, for I was but ten – large and stout for his age, with a dingy and unwholesome skin, thick lineaments in a spacious visage, heavy limbs and large extremities. He gorged himself habitually at table, which made him bilious, and gave him a dim and bleared eye and flabby cheeks. He ought now to have been at school, but his mama had taken him home for a month or two, 'on account of his delicate health.' Mr Miles, the master, affirmed that he would do very well if he had fewer cakes and sweetmeats sent him from home; but the mother's heart turned from an opinion so harsh, and inclined rather to the more refined idea that John's sallowness was owing to over-application and, perhaps, to pining after home.

John had not much affection for his mother and sisters, and an antipathy to me. He bullied and punished me continually. Every nerve I had feared him, and every morsel of flesh in my bones shrank when he came near. There were moments when I was bewildered by the terror he inspired, because I had no appeal whatever against either his menaces or his inflictions – the servants did not like to offend their young master by taking my part against him, and Mrs Reed was blind and deaf on the subject: she never saw him strike or heard him abuse me, though he did both now and then in her very presence, more frequently, however, behind her back.

Habitually obedient to John, I came up to his chair. He spent some three minutes in thrusting out his tongue at me as far as he could without damaging the roots: I knew he would soon strike, and while dreading the blow, I mused on the disgusting and ugly appearance of him who would presently deal it. I wonder if he read that notion in my face, for all at once, without speaking, he struck suddenly and strongly. I tottered, and on regaining my equilibrium retired back a step or two from his chair.

"That is for your impudence in answering mama awhile since," said he, "and for your sneaking way of getting behind curtains, and for the look you had in your eyes two minutes since, you rat!"

Accustomed to John Reed's abuse, I never had an idea of replying to it. My care was how to endure the blow which would certainly follow the insult.

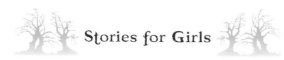

"What were you doing behind the curtain?" he asked.

"I was reading."

"Show the book."

I returned to the window and fetched it thence.

"You have no business to take our books. You are a dependent, mama says. You have no money. Your father left you none. You ought to beg, and not to live here with gentlemen's children like us, and eat the same meals we do, and wear clothes at our mama's expense. Now, I'll teach you to rummage my bookshelves – for they are mine – all the house belongs to me, or will do in a few years. Go and stand by the door, out of the way of the mirror and the windows."

I did so, not at first aware what was his intention, but when I saw him lift and poise the book and stand in act to hurl it, I instinctively started aside with a cry of alarm. Not soon enough, however; the volume was flung, it hit me, and I fell, striking my head against the door and cutting it. The cut bled, the pain was sharp: my terror had passed its climax, and other feelings succeeded.

"Wicked and cruel boy!" I said. "You are like a murderer."

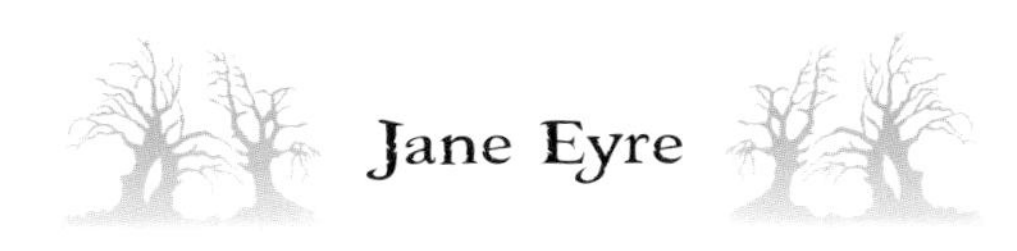

"What? What!" he cried. "Did she say that to me? Did you hear her, Eliza and Georgiana? I'll tell mama. But first—"

He ran headlong at me. I felt him grasp my hair and my shoulder: he had closed with a desperate thing. I really saw in him a tyrant, a murderer. I felt a drop or two of blood from my head trickle down my neck, and was sensible of somewhat pungent suffering. These sensations for the time predominated over fear, and I received him in frantic sort. I don't very well know what I did with my hands, but he called me "Rat! Rat!" and bellowed out aloud. Aid was near him – Eliza and Georgiana had run for Mrs Reed, who was gone upstairs. She now came upon the scene, followed by Bessie and her maid Abbot. We were parted. I heard the words:

"Dear! dear! What a fury to fly at Master John!"

"Did ever anybody see such a picture of passion!"

Then Mrs Reed subjoined:

"Take her away to the red-room, and lock her in there." Four hands were immediately laid upon me, and I was borne upstairs.

I resisted all the way: a new thing for me, and a circumstance that greatly strengthened the bad opinion Bessie and Miss Abbot were disposed to entertain of me. The fact is, I was a trifle beside myself, or rather out of myself, as the French would say. I was conscious that a moment's mutiny had already rendered me liable to strange penalties, and, like any other rebel slave, I felt resolved, in my desperation, to go all lengths.

"Hold her arms, Miss Abbot – she's like a mad cat."

"For shame! For shame!" cried the lady's-maid. "What shocking conduct, Miss Eyre, to strike a young gentleman, your benefactress's son! Your young master."

"Master! How is he my master? Am I a servant?"

"No, you are less than a servant, for you do nothing for your keep. There, sit down, and think over your wickedness."

They had got me by this time into the apartment indicated by Mrs Reed, and had thrust me upon a stool. My impulse was to rise from it like a spring, but their two pair of hands arrested me.

"If you don't sit still, you must be tied down," said Bessie. "Miss Abbot, lend me your garters; she would break mine."

Miss Abbot turned to divest a stout leg of the necessary ligature. This preparation for bonds, and the additional ignominy it inferred, took a little of the excitement out of me.

"Don't take them off," I cried, "I will not stir."

In guarantee whereof, I attached myself to my seat.

"Mind you don't," said Bessie; and when she had ascertained that I was really subsiding, she loosened her hold of me; then she and Miss Abbot stood with folded arms, looking darkly and doubtfully on my face, as incredulous of my sanity.

"She never did so before," at last said Bessie, turning to Abigail.

"But it was always in her," was the reply. "I've told Missis often my opinion about the child, and Missis agreed with me. She's an underhand little thing. I never saw a girl of her age with so much cover."

Bessie answered not; but ere long, addressing me, she said: "You ought to be aware, Miss, that you are under obligations to Mrs Reed. She keeps you. If she were to turn you off, you would have to go to the poorhouse."

I had nothing to say to these words. They were not new to me – my very first recollections of existence included hints of the same kind. This reproach of my dependence had become a vague sing-song in my ear: very painful and crushing, but only half

intelligible. Miss Abbot joined in, "And you ought not to think yourself on an equality with the Misses Reed and Master Reed, because Missis kindly allows you to be brought up with them. They will have a great deal of money, and you will have none: it is your place to be humble, and to try to make yourself agreeable to them."

"What we tell you is for your good," added Bessie, in no harsh voice, "you should try to be useful and pleasant, then, perhaps, you would have a home here. But if you become passionate and rude, Missis will send you away, I am sure."

"Besides," said Miss Abbot, "God will punish her. He might strike her dead in the midst of her tantrums, and then where would she go? Come, Bessie, we will leave her: I wouldn't have her heart for anything. Say your prayers, Miss Eyre, when you are by yourself, for if you don't repent, something bad might be permitted to come down the chimney and fetch you away."

They went, shutting the door, and locking it behind them.

The red-room was a square chamber, very seldom slept in. I might say never, indeed, unless when a chance influx of visitors at Gateshead Hall rendered it necessary to turn to account all the accommodation it contained, yet it was one of the largest and

stateliest chambers in the mansion. A bed supported on massive pillars of mahogany, hung with curtains of deep red damask, stood out like a tabernacle in the centre; the two large windows, with their blinds always drawn down, were half shrouded in festoons and falls of similar drapery. The carpet was red; the table at the foot of the bed was covered with a crimson cloth; the walls were a soft fawn colour with a blush of pink in it; the wardrobe, the toilet-table, the chairs were of darkly polished old mahogany. Out of these deep surrounding shades rose high, and glared white, the piled-up mattresses and pillows of the bed, spread with a snowy white counterpane. Scarcely less prominent was an ample cushioned easy-chair near the head of the bed, also white, with a footstool before it, and looking like a pale throne.

This room was chill, because it seldom had a fire; it was silent, because it was remote from the nursery and kitchen; solemn, because it was known to be so seldom entered. The house-maid alone came here on Saturdays, to wipe from the mirrors and the furniture a week's quiet dust; and Mrs Reed herself, at far intervals, visited it to review the contents of a certain secret drawer in the wardrobe, where were stored divers parchments, her jewel-casket, and a miniature of her deceased husband. And in those last words

lies the secret of the red-room – the spell which kept it so lonely in spite of its grandeur.

Mr Reed had been dead nine years. It was in this chamber he breathed his last; here he lay in state; hence his coffin was borne by the undertaker's men; and, since that day, a sense of dreary consecration had guarded it from frequent intrusion.

My seat, to which Bessie and the bitter Miss Abbot had left me riveted, was near the marble chimney-piece. The bed rose before me. To my right hand there was the high, dark wardrobe, with subdued, broken reflections varying the gloss of its panels. To my left were the muffled windows; a great looking glass between them repeated the vacant majesty of the bed and room. I was not quite sure whether they had locked the door, and when I dared move I got up and went to see. Alas! yes – no jail was ever more secure. Returning, I had to cross before the looking glass. All looked colder and darker in that visionary hollow than in reality. The strange little figure there gazing at me, with a white face and arms specking the gloom, and glittering eyes of fear moving where all else was still, had the effect of a real spirit – I thought it like one of the tiny phantoms, half fairy, half imp, Bessie's evening stories represented as coming out of lone, ferny dells in moors,

and appearing before the eyes of belated travellers. I returned to my stool.

Superstition was with me at that moment, my blood was still warm, the mood of the revolted slave was still bracing me with its bitter vigour. I had to stem a rapid rush of retrospective thought before I quailed to the dismal present.

All John Reed's violent tyrannies, all his sisters' proud indifference, all his mother's aversion, all the servants' partiality,

turned up in my disturbed mind like a dark deposit in a turbid well. Why was I always suffering, always browbeaten, always accused, forever condemned? Why could I never please? Why was it useless to try to win anyone's favour? Eliza, who was headstrong and selfish, was respected. Georgiana, who had a spoiled temper, a very acrid spite, a captious and insolent carriage, was universally indulged. Her beauty, her pink cheeks and golden curls, seemed to give delight to all who looked at her, and to purchase indemnity for every fault. John no one thwarted, much less punished; though he twisted the necks of the pigeons, killed the little pea-chicks, set the dogs at the sheep, stripped the hothouse vines of their fruit, and broke the buds off the choicest plants in the conservatory. He bluntly disregarded her wishes, not unfrequently tore and spoiled her silk attire, and he was still 'her own darling.'
I dared commit no fault: I strove to fulfil every duty, and I was termed naughty and tiresome, sullen and sneaking, from morning to night.

My head still ached and bled with the blow and fall I had received: no one had reproved John for wantonly striking me, and because I had turned against him to avert farther irrational violence, I was loaded with general opprobrium.

"Unjust! Unjust!" said my reason, forced by the agonising stimulus into precocious though transitory power, and resolve instigated some strange expedient to achieve escape from insupportable oppression by running away.

What a consternation of soul was mine that dreary afternoon! How all my brain was in tumult, and all my heart in insurrection! Yet in what darkness, what dense ignorance, was the mental battle fought! I could not answer the ceaseless inward question – why I thus suffered. Now, at the distance of – I will not say how many years – I see it clearly.

I was a discord in Gateshead Hall. I was like nobody there. I had nothing in harmony with Mrs Reed or her children, or her servants. If they did not love me, in fact, as little did I love them. They were not bound to regard with affection a thing that could not sympathise with one amongst them; a heterogeneous thing, opposed to them in temperament, in capacity, in propensities. A useless thing, incapable of serving their interest, or adding to their pleasure. I know that had I been a sanguine, brilliant, careless, exacting, handsome, romping child – though equally dependent and friendless – Mrs Reed would have endured my presence more complacently, her children would have entertained

for me more of the cordiality of fellow-feeling, the servants would have been less prone to make me the scapegoat of the nursery.

Daylight began to forsake the red-room. It was past four o'clock, and the beclouded afternoon was tending to drear twilight. I heard the rain still beating continuously on the staircase window, and the wind howling in the grove behind the hall. I grew by degrees cold as a stone, and my courage sank. All said I was wicked, and perhaps I might be so – what thought had I been but just conceiving of starving myself to death? That certainly was a crime, and was I fit to die? Or was the vault under the chancel of Gateshead Church an inviting resting place? In such vault I had been told did Mr Reed lie buried, and led by this thought to recall his idea I dwelt on it with gathering dread. I could not remember him, but I knew that he was my own uncle – my mother's brother – that he had taken me when a parentless infant to his house, and that in his last moments he had required a promise of Mrs Reed that she would rear and maintain me as one of her own children. Mrs Reed probably considered she had kept this promise, and so she had, I dare say, as well as her nature would permit her. But how could she really like an interloper not of her race, and unconnected with her, after her husband's death, by any tie? It must have been most irksome to find herself bound by a hard-wrung pledge to stand in the stead of a parent to a strange child she could not love, and to see an uncongenial alien permanently intruded on her own family group.

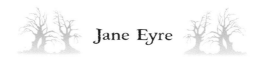

A singular notion dawned upon me. I never doubted that if Mr Reed had been alive he would have treated me kindly; and now, as I sat looking at the white bed and overshadowed walls – occasionally also turning a fascinated eye towards the dimly gleaning mirror – I began to recall what I had heard of dead men, troubled in their graves by the violation of their last wishes, revisiting the earth to punish the perjured and avenge the oppressed. I thought Mr Reed's spirit, harassed by the wrongs of his sister's child, might quit its abode – whether in the church vault or in the unknown world of the departed – and rise before me in this chamber. I wiped my tears and hushed my sobs, fearful lest any sign of violent grief might waken a preternatural voice to comfort me, or elicit from the gloom some haloed face, bending over me with strange pity. This idea, consolatory in theory, I felt would be terrible if realised: with all my might I endeavoured to stifle it – I endeavoured to be firm. Shaking my hair from my eyes, I lifted my head and tried to look boldly round the dark room. At this moment a light gleamed on the wall. Was it, I asked myself, a ray from the moon penetrating some aperture in the blind? No – moonlight was still, and this stirred. While I gazed, it glided up to the ceiling and quivered over my head. I can now conjecture readily that this streak of light was, in all likelihood, a gleam from a lantern carried by someone across the lawn, but then, prepared as my mind was for horror, shaken as my nerves were by agitation, I thought the swift darting beam was a herald of some coming vision from another world. My heart beat thick, my head grew hot, a sound filled my ears, which I deemed the rushing of wings, something seemed near me. I was oppressed, suffocated: endurance broke down. I rushed to the door and shook the lock in desperate effort. Steps came running along the outer passage – the key turned, and Bessie and Abbot entered.

"Miss Eyre, are you ill?" said Bessie.

"What a dreadful noise! It went quite through me!" exclaimed Abbot.

"Take me out! Let me go into the nursery!" was my cry.

"What for? Are you hurt? Have you seen something?" again demanded Bessie.

"Oh! I saw a light, and I thought a ghost would come." I had now got hold of Bessie's hand, and she did not snatch it from me.

"She has screamed out on purpose," declared Abbot, in some disgust. "And what a scream! If she had been in great pain one would have excused it, but she only wanted to bring us all here – I know her naughty tricks."

"What is all this?" demanded another voice peremptorily, and Mrs Reed came along the corridor, her cap flying wide, her gown rustling stormily. "Abbot and Bessie, I believe I gave orders that Jane Eyre should be left in the red-room till I came to her myself."

"Miss Jane screamed so loud, ma'am," pleaded Bessie.

"Let her go," was the only answer. "Loose Bessie's hand, child. You cannot succeed in getting out by these means, be assured. I abhor artifice, particularly in children. It is my duty to show you that tricks will not answer. You will now stay here an hour longer, and it is only on condition of perfect submission and stillness that I shall liberate you then."

"Oh aunt! Have pity! Forgive me! I cannot endure it. Let me

be punished some other way! I shall be killed if—"

"Silence! This violence is all most repulsive," and so, no doubt, she felt it. I was a precocious actress in her eyes. She sincerely looked on me as a compound of virulent passions, mean spirit, and dangerous duplicity.

Bessie and Abbot having retreated, Mrs Reed, impatient of my now frantic anguish and wild sobs, abruptly thrust me back and locked me in, without farther parley. I heard her sweeping away and soon after she was gone, I suppose I had a species of fit – unconsciousness closed the scene.

The Children of the New Forest

An extract
by Captain Marryat

Introduction

The Children of the New Forest, *published in 1847, was the last book to be written by Captain Frederick Marryat (1792–1848). Edward, Humphrey, Alice and Edith are left orphaned at their family home in the New Forest. They are given shelter by an old forester, Jacob Armitage, who passes them off as his own grandchildren. In this extract Edward rescues a young boy after robbers have broken into his house.*

Edward took the counterpane off the bed, and went with it into the next room. He gently drew the body to the corner of the room, and covered it up with the counterpane, and then proceeded to examine the cupboards. In one he found a good store of books, in another there was linen of all sorts, two suits of bright armour such as worn in those times, pistols and guns, and ammunition. On the floor of one of the cupboards was a locked iron chest about two feet by eighteen inches. Edward immediately concluded that this chest held the money of the unfortunate man – but where was the key? Most likely about his person. He did not like to afflict the poor boy by putting the question to him, but he went to the body and examined the pockets of the clothes. He found a bunch of several keys, which he took. He tried one of the keys, which appeared to be of the right size, to the lock of the iron chest, and found that it fitted it. Satisfied with this, he did not raise the lid of the chest, but dragged it out into the centre of the room. There were many things of value about the room – the candlesticks were silver, and there were goblets of the same metal. Edward collected all these articles, and a timepiece, and put them into a basket, of which there were two large ones at the end of the room, apparently used for holding firewood. Everything that he thought could be useful, or of value, he gathered together for the benefit of the poor orphan boy. He afterwards went into another small room, where he found small trunks and cases locked-up. These he brought out without examining, as he presumed that what they contained was of value, or they would not be locked. When he had collected everything, he found that he had already more than the cart could carry in one trip; and he wanted to take some bedding with him, as he had not a spare bed in the cottage to give to the boy. Edward decided in his own mind that he would take the most valuable articles away that night, and return with the cart for the remainder early on the following morning. It was now past noon, and Edward took out of the cupboard what victuals were left, and then went into the chamber where the boy was, and begged that he would eat something, and at last prevailed upon him to eat some bread and drink a glass of wine. The poor fellow shuddered as he saw the body covered up in the corner of the room, but said nothing. Edward was trying to make him eat a little more when Pablo made his appearance at the door.

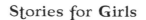

"Have you put up all that you want in the bed-chamber?" said Edward.

"Yes, I have put up everything."

"Then we will bring them out. Come, Pablo, you must help us."

Pablo made signs, and pointed to the door. Edward went out.

"First pull body away from this."

"Yes," replied Edward, "we must do so."

Edward and Pablo pulled the body of the robber on one side of the doorway, and threw over it some dried fern which lay by. They then backed the cart down to the door. The iron chest was first got in, then all the heavy articles, such as armour, guns and books, and by that time the cart was more than half-loaded. Edward then went into the chamber, and brought out the packages the boy had made up, and put them all in the cart until it was loaded high up. They brought out some blankets, and laid over all, to keep things steady, and then Edward told the boy that all was ready, and that they had better go.

"Yes, I am willing," replied he, with streaming eyes, "but let me see him once more."

"Come, then," said Edward, leading him to the corpse, and uncovering the face.

The boy knelt down, kissed the forehead and cold lips, covered up the face again, and then rose and wept bitterly on Edward's shoulder. Edward did not attempt to check his sorrow –

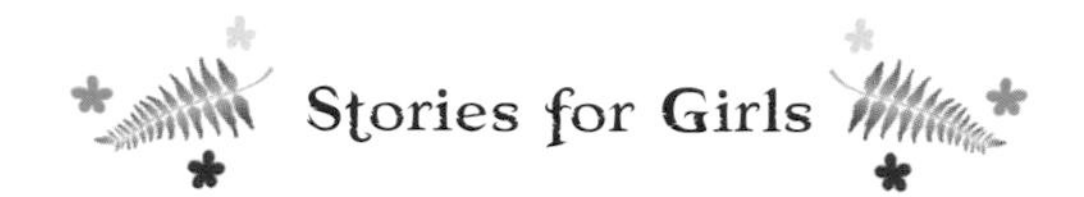

he thought it better it should have vent – but, after a time, he led the boy by degrees till they were out of the cottage.

"Now, then," said Edward, "we must go, or we shall be late. My poor little sisters have been dreadfully alarmed at my not having come home last night, and I long to see them."

"Indeed you must," replied the boy, wiping away his tears, "and I am very selfish. Let us go on."

"No room for cart to get through wood," said Pablo. "Hard work, cart empty – more hard work, cart full."

And so it proved to be. It required all the united efforts of Billy, Edward and Pablo, to force a passage for the cart through the narrow pathway, but at last it was effected, and then they went on at a quick pace, and in less than two hours the cottage was in sight. When within two hundred yards of it, Edith, who had been on the watch, came bounding out, flew into Edward's arms, and covered him with kisses.

"You naughty Edward, to frighten us so!"

"Look, Edith, I have brought you a nice little play-fellow. Welcome him, dearest."

Edith extended her hand as she looked into the boy's face.

"He is a pretty boy, Edward, much prettier than Pablo."

"No, Missy Edith," said Pablo; "Pablo more man than he."

"Yes, you may be more man, Pablo, but you are not pretty."

"And where is Alice?"

"She was getting supper ready, and I did not tell her that I saw you coming, because I wanted first kiss."

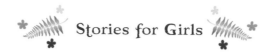

"You little jealous thing! But here comes Alice. Dear Alice, you have been very uneasy, but it was not my fault," said Edward, kissing her. "If I had not been where I was this poor boy would have been killed as well as his father. Make him welcome, Alice, for he is an orphan now, and must live with us. I have brought many things in the cart, and tomorrow we will bring more, for we have no bed for him."

"We will make him as happy as we can, Edward, and we will be sisters to him," said Alice, looking at the boy, who was blushing deeply. "How old are you? And what is your name?"

"I am thirteen years old next January," replied the boy.

"And your Christian name?"

"I will tell you by and by," replied he.

They arrived at the cottage, and Edward and Pablo were busy unpacking the cart, and putting all the contents into the inner chamber, where Pablo now slept, when Alice, who, with Edith, had been talking to the boy, came to Edward and said:

"Edward, she's a girl!"

"A girl!" replied Edward, astonished.

"Yes, she has told me so, and wished me to tell you."

"But why does she wear boys' clothes?"

"It was her father's wish, as he was very often obliged to send her to Lymington to a friend's house, and he was afraid of her getting into trouble. But she has not told me her story as yet – she says that she will tonight."

"Well, then," replied Edward, "you must make up a bed for her in your room tonight. Take Pablo's bed, and he shall sleep with me. Tomorrow morning I will bring some more bedding from her cottage."

"How Humphrey will be surprised when he comes back!" said Alice, laughing.

"Yes – she will make a nice little wife for him some years hence – and she may prove an heiress perhaps, for there is an iron chest with money in it."

Alice returned to her new companion, and Edward and Pablo continued to unload the cart.

"Well, Pablo, I suppose you will allow that, now that you know she is a girl, she is handsomer than you?"

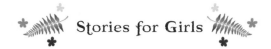

"Oh yes," replied Pablo, "very handsome girl, but too much girl for handsome boy."

At last everything was out of the cart, the iron chest dragged into Pablo's room, and Billy put into his stable and given his supper, which he had well earned, for the cart had been very heavily loaded. They then all sat down to supper, Edward saying to their new acquaintance, "So I find that I am to have another sister instead of another brother. Now you will tell me your name?"

"Yes; Clara is my name."

"And why did you not tell me that you are a girl?"

"I did not like, because I was in boys' clothes, and felt ashamed. Indeed I was too unhappy to think about what I was. My poor dear father!" and she burst into tears.

Alice and Edith kissed her and consoled her, and she became calm again. After supper was over they busied themselves making arrangements for her sleeping in their room, and then they went to prayers.

They were up on the following morning at dawn, and, putting Billy in the cart, set off for the cottage of Clara. They found everything as they had left it, and, having loaded the cart with what had been left behind the day before, the bedding for two beds, with several articles of furniture which Edward thought might be useful, there being still a little room left, Edward packed up in a wooden case with dried fern all the wine that was in the cupboard and left Pablo to return home with the cart, while he remained to wait the arrival of Humphrey, and whoever might come with him from the Intendant's. About ten o'clock, as he was watching outside of the wood, he perceived several people approaching him, and soon made out that Humphrey, the Intendant, and Oswald were among the number. When they came up to him Edward saluted the Intendant in a respectful manner, shook hands with Oswald, and then led the way by the narrow path through the wood to the cottage. The Intendant was on horseback, but all the rest were on foot.

The Intendant left his horse to the care of one of the verderers, and went through the wood on foot, preceded by Edward. He appeared to be very grave and thoughtful, and Edward thought that

there was a coolness in his manner towards himself, for it must be recollected that Mr Heatherstone had not seen Edward since he had rendered him such service in saving the life of his daughter. The consequence was, that Edward felt somewhat indignant, but he did not express his feelings, by his looks even, but conveyed the party in silence to the cottage. On their arrival, Edward pointed to the body of the robber, which had been covered with fern, and the verderers exposed it.

"By whose hand did that man fall?" said the Intendant.

"By the hand of the party who lived in the cottage."

Edward then led the way round to the back of the cottage where the other robber lay. "And this man was slain by my hand," he said. "We have one more body to see." Edward led the way into the cottage and uncovered the corpse of Clara's father.

Mr Heatherstone looked at the face and appeared much moved. "Cover it up," said he, turning away, and then sitting down on a chair close to the table.

"And how was this found?" he said.

"I neither saw this person killed nor the robber you first saw, but I heard the report of the firearms at almost the same moment, and I presume that they fell by each other's hands."

The Intendant called his clerk, who had accompanied him, and desired him to get ready his writing materials, and then said:

"Edward Armitage, we will now take down your deposition as to what has occurred."

Edward then commenced by stating that he was out in the forest and had lost his way, and was seeking his way home—

"You were out in the forest during the night?"

"Yes, sir, I was."

"With your gun?"

"I always carry my gun," replied Edward.

"In pursuit of game?"

"No, sir, I was not. I have never been out in pursuit of game during night-time in my life."

Edward met with no more interruption in his narrative. He stated briefly all that had taken place, from the time he fell in with the robbers till the winding up of the catastrophe.

The clerk took down all that Edward had stated, and then read it over to him, to ascertain if he had written it down correctly, and then inquired of Edward if he could read and write.

"I should hope so," replied Edward, taking the pen and signing his name.

The clerk stared, and then said, "People in your condition do not often know how to read and write, Mr Forester, and therefore you need not be offended at the question."

"Very true," replied Edward. "May I ask if my presence is considered any longer to be necessary?"

"You stated that there was a boy in the house, young man," said the Intendant, "what has become of him?"

"He is removed to my cottage."

"Why did you do so?"

"Because when his father died I promised to him that I would take care of his child, and I intend to keep my word."

"May I ask, did you remove any valuables?"

"I cannot tell. The lad packed up his own things; there were some boxes removed, which were locked-up, and the contents are to me wholly unknown. I did as I considered right for the benefit of the boy, and in accordance with the solemn promise which I made to his father."

"Still the property should not have been removed. The party who now lies dead there is a well-known Malignant."

"How do you know that, sir?" interrupted Edward. "Did you recognise him when you saw the body?"

"I did not say that I did," replied the Intendant.

"You either must have so done, sir," replied Edward, "or you must have been aware that he was residing in this cottage. You have to choose between."

"You are bold, young man," replied the Intendant, "I did recognise the party when I saw his face, and I knew him to be one who was condemned to death, and who escaped from prison a few days before the one appointed for his execution. I heard search had been made for him, but in vain, and it was supposed that he had escaped beyond the seas.

"You have surprised me by stating that Major Ratcliffe had a son here. There must be some mistake, or the boy must be an impostor. He had a daughter, an only daughter, as I have, but he never had a son."

"It is a mistake that I fell into, sir, by finding a boy here, as I stated to you before, and I considered it to be a boy until I brought her home, and she then discovered to my sisters that she was a girl dressed in boys' clothes. I did not give that as explanation, as it was not necessary."

"I am right, then. I must relieve you of that charge, Edward Armitage. She shall be to me as a daughter, I was a great friend of

her father's and it is what he would have wanted. I trust that you will agree with me, without any disparagement to your feelings, that my house will be a more fit residence for her than your cottage."

"I will not prevent her going, if she wishes it Mr Heatherstone."

"Let us move on then young man," said the Intendant aside.

They then proceeded through the wood. The Intendant mounted his horse, and they set off for the cottage, where they arrived at about two o'clock in the afternoon.

The Tale of the Tsarevna and the Seven Giants

Retold by Fiona Waters

Introduction

The earliest version of Snow White *was written by Jacob and Wilhelm Grimm. This version of* Snow White, *with giants instead of the usual dwarves, appears in a collection of fairy tales written in verse by the great Russian poet Alexander Sergevitch Pushkin (1799–1837).*

The Tsar had gone on a long journey, leaving the Tsarina behind in the great cold and glittering palace. She was expecting their first child so she was particularly sad to see the Tsar's cavalcade of horses disappear over the snowy steppe. From that moment on, she sat every day at her window, gazing over the white landscape but of the returning Tsar there was no sign. Every day she watched and waited, but all she saw was swirling snow as the drifts grew ever deeper.

Nine long months passed. Then, on Christmas Eve, the Tsarina gave birth to a tiny daughter. Just as midnight was striking, and with the wind howling round his head, the Tsar strode in through the palace, stamping his great boots and shaking the snow off his wolfskin clothes as he rushed upstairs to the room where his Tsarina and their new baby daughter lay together wrapped warmly in rugs by a blazing log fire. The Tsarina gave the Tsar one sad smile, and then closed her eyes, never to open them again. The birth of her daughter and the strain of waiting for the Tsar to return had used all her strength and she died that morning.

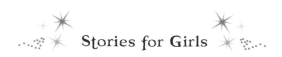

The Tsar was heartbroken. For months he wandered through the palace aimlessly, seemingly oblivious to all that went on around him. Meanwhile his tiny daughter the Tsarevna enchanted all who met her. Ever smiling, she had the fairest hair and deep blue eyes, and her skin was as white as the snow that her mother had gazed out on for all those months.

A year passed and the Tsar was persuaded to take a new wife. She was tall and very beautiful, with long black hair that she wore in two great plaits that fell past her waist. Her eyes were deep green and she always wore black velvet robes with silver braiding and silver fox fur round the neck and cuffs. A silver crown glittered on her head, and on her feet she wore silver boots. She looked every inch a Tsarina, but her heart was as cold as the icy steppe. She was proud and vain, and she hated the tiny Tsarevna.

In amongst her many trunks of clothes and perfumes and the like, the new Tsarina had brought with her a very special mirror.

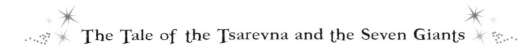

Now this mirror could speak, and whenever the Tsarina would look into it, which she did several times a day, she would ask it how beautiful she was, and the mirror would purr softly and say,

"Your beauty is astounding, my lady. There is no one on earth who can compare with you," and other such ridiculously flattering things, all of which the Tsarina would listen to with a greedy look in her green eyes and laughter in her throat. Then she was happy for a while.

Years passed and the Tsarevna grew into a lovely young woman. Her father adored her and bought her beautiful rich brocaded dresses, and the softest woollen wraps made of the finest cashmere. Finally he arranged for her to be betrothed to Nikolai, the son of a fabulously wealthy merchant. Nikolai adored the Tsarevna and she him, so plans were made for their wedding. On the morning of the wedding, the Tsarina asked the mirror her usual question, and the answer was not at all what she wanted to hear.

"Your beauty is astounding, my lady, but the Tsarevna is lovelier by far," and the mirror sniggered softly. The Tsarina flung her hairbrush at the mirror in a huge temper, but still it said, "The Tsarevna is lovelier by far."

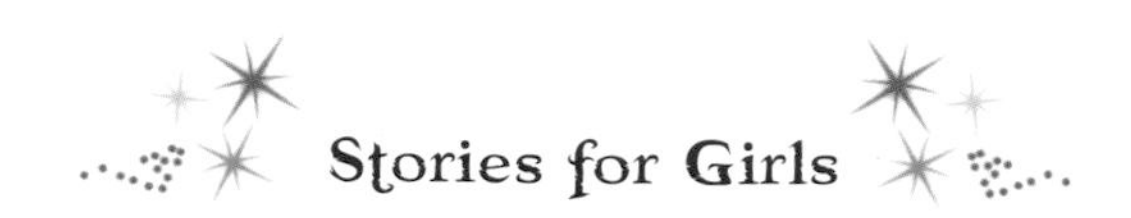

The Tsarina was beside herself. Never had the mirror denied her, and now it was her hated step-daughter who had usurped her. She called angrily for her servant-girl, Chernavka. When she appeared, looking fearfully down at the floor so great was her mistress' rage, the Tsarina hissed her instructions in a low whisper.

"Get hold of the Tsarevna and take her to the deepest, darkest part of the forest where you must leave her tied to a tree so she will be taken by the wolves."

Chernavka was horrified and this must have shown on her face.

"Do it, and do it now or will be the worse for you," snarled the Tsarina, and she certainly did not look beautiful as she spoke, her face all contorted with rage. "If you fail me in this, I shall have you nailed up in a barrel and rolled off into the deepest snowdrift," the Tsarina added.

With a heavy heart, Chernavka went in search of the Tsarevna. She wrapped her in the warmest furs and scarves, and pushed her feet into her thick boots, then she took the surprised Tsarevna by the hand

and led her far away from the palace and deep into the forest.

The Tsarevna was at first puzzled, but then she became frightened and as she began to cry she asked Chernavka where they were going. Before long Chernavka was crying too and then she spilled out the whole terrible story to the Tsarevna. The Tsarevna could see nothing was to be gained by her tears so she dried her eyes, sent Chernavka back to the palace and determinedly set about walking as fast as she could in the opposite direction as she now understood that the wicked Tsarina would stop at nothing to ensure her beauty remained unchallenged.

Chernavka stumbled back to the palace and told the Tsarina that she had taken the Tsarevna into the forest and, crossing her fingers behind her back suggested that even now she was probably being set upon by wolves. The Tsarina confronted the mirror. It simpered, "Your beauty is astounding my lady."

So delighted was the Tsarina that she did not notice the mirror appeared to hesitate after it spoke, as if there was something else it wanted to say. The Tsarina primped and preened for a while, and then joined the Tsar in the pale blue and silver ballroom to celebrate the wedding of Nikolai and the Tsarevna. But, of course, the Tsarevna did not appear, and after an increasingly frantic search of the palace it was decided that she must have been kidnapped. Nikolai wasted no time in saddling up his big black horse and galloping off to seek out the old wise woman who lived in the nearest village. He felt sure she would give him guidance as he sought to track down the Tsarevna, wherever she might have been taken.

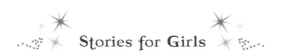

She, meanwhile, was tramping through the forest, increasingly anxious to find somewhere to shelter for the night. She thought she could hear wolves howling in the distance, and she was growing very tired. But then she heard a dog barking, and it seemed quite near.

"Where there is a dog, there must also be people," she said to herself, and she walked faster toward the sound. Suddenly she came across a clearing and there in front of her stood a house, quite ordinary in every aspect except its size. The windows were huge, the front door was huge, and the bench outside the door was huge. The dog, however, was very pleased to see her. It bounded up and licked her hand, then trotted in through the huge front door which lay slightly ajar. The dog looked over its shoulder and seemed to be encouraging her to come in so the Tsarevna followed cautiously behind.

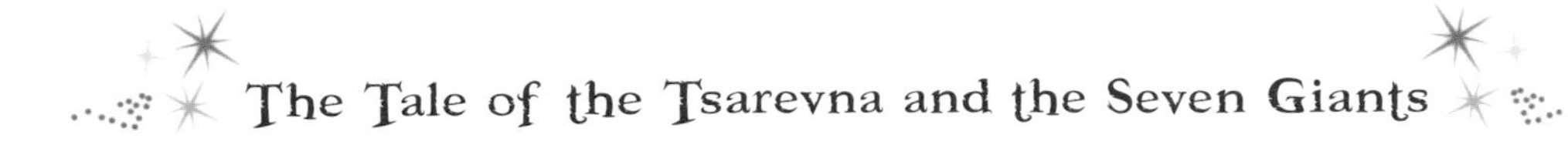

Inside everything was once again quite ordinary in aspect except its size. The table covered in dirty dishes was huge. Seven huge stools were scattered around and seven huge armchairs were ranged round the unlit stove. The dog danced at her feet and then seemed to invite the Tsarevna to climb up the huge staircase where she found seven huge and unmade beds.

The Tsarevna felt no fear, somehow it was a friendly house.

She went back downstairs and set about tidying up. She straightened the huge stools round the table. She cleared the table and washed up the seven huge bowls and the seven huge goblets and the seven huge knives and forks, and then she piled the stove high with logs and soon had a warming fire going. She made the seven huge beds. She lit the candle in front of the icon just inside the huge door and then she and the little dog curled up together on the huge rug in front of the stove and both fell fast asleep. From outside after a while came the sound of cheerful singing and the tramp of huge boots and as the door burst open, seven huge young giants tumbled inside. They made so much noise that both

the dog and the Tsarevna awoke with a start. The dog rushed up to the huge young men, wagging his tail in delight.

For a moment they all looked at each other in utter silence and then everyone started talking at once. The giants were delighted with their tidy house, and the Tsarevna was delighted to find seven champions for, of course, they were very angry when they heard why the Tsarevna had ended up in their home.

Everyone rushed around and soon supper was on the table. The Tsarevna could not be persuaded to drink any vodka but she did have a very, very small slice of the huge game pie that the giants set upon the table. After the meal, one of the giants, who were all brothers, made a simple bed out of logs and furs and it was placed carefully behind the stove so that the Tsarevna might have a cosy corner all of her own. The Tsarevna smiled to herself for the first time in what had been a very dark day.

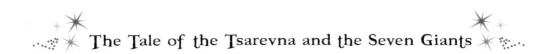

The next day, and the next, and the next after that, the seven giants and the Tsarevna all settled down into a happy routine. The giants would go out in the morning to patrol the forest. Sometimes they might meet a band of fierce Tartars and that night the Tsarevna would have cuts and bruises to attend to, but mostly the brothers came home with vegetables and fruits, and rabbits and sometimes a wild boar for the Tsarevna to turn into delicious meals for them all. She often thought of her beloved Nikolai, for she was sure he would try to find her, but then she remembered her terrible step-mother and so resigned herself to her new life.

And what of the Tsarina? Everyone was still preoccupied with the loss of the Tsarevna – no word had come from Nikolai, and the Tsar was plunged into gloom at the loss of his beloved daughter. The Tsarina hadn't looked in the mirror for a very long while, so sure was she that her beauty was the most outstanding. But one afternoon she was bored and so she smirked at the mirror and asked it,

"How beautiful am I?"

The mirror replied, "Your beauty is astounding my lady." The Tsarina smirked some more, but the mirror continued, "but lovelier by far is the Tsarevna."

The Tsarina flew into the most awful rage. She screamed for Chernavka and boxed her ears until the poor girl was seeing stars.

"You deceitful girl! How could you betray me so? Tell me where the Tsarevna is hiding at once!" and bit by bit she wormed out of Chernavka that the Tsarevna had been alive and well when she left her in the forest and in all probability had not been eaten by wolves. The Tsarina realised that she would need to seek out the Tsarevna herself and so she flung Chernavka out of her room and began to make some very terrible plans.

Some days later the Tsarevna looked out of the huge window, and there coming through the clearing was an old beggar woman dressed all in black. The Tsarevna fetched a hunk of bread to give to the old woman and opened the huge door. The little dog hurtled out and snarled and growled at the old woman.

"I am so sorry, I don't know what has possessed him," apologised the Tsarevna. "I have some bread for you, can you catch it if I throw it over his head?"

"Bless you," muttered the old woman. "You are very kind,

perhaps you would accept this apple as a thank you for your generosity?" And she threw the apple into the Tsarevna's outstretched hands, then scuttled away back into the forest.

The little dog whined and tried to push the apple out of the Tsarevna's hands, but she just laughed at him and took a great bite out of it. In an instant she fell to the ground, and lay quite still, no longer breathing. When the seven giants came back home later they found their friend stretched out on the floor lifeless, the little dog howling by her side. They tried everything they could think of to revive the Tsarevna but all to no avail.

"This is the evil Tsarina's doing," said one.

The others nodded, for who else would want to harm the gentle Tsarevna? The giants kept watch over the Tsarevna through the night, and then the next day discussed how to bury her. She looked as if she were only asleep and as beautiful as when she was alive and they were very reluctant to place her in a dark coffin. So they made her a special casket of crystal and laid her in that, placing it close by the house near a swiftly flowing river with flower strewn banks that the Tsarevna had often walked along. They took turns in watching over the coffin so that the Tsarevna was never alone, and a great sadness descended over the huge

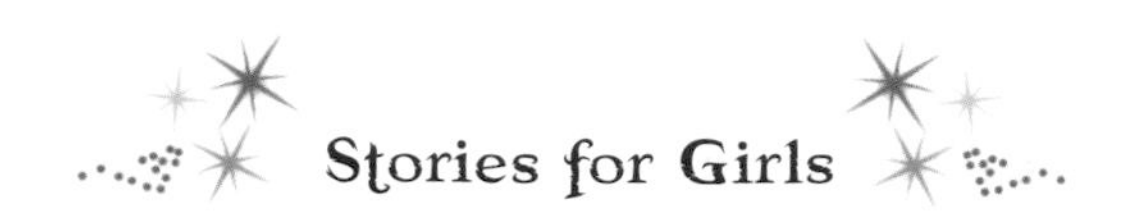

house in the forest clearing.

Meanwhile, back at the palace the Tsarina glared at her mirror.

"Your beauty is astounding, my lady. There is no one on earth who can compare with you," said the mirror.

Now, I hope you haven't forgotten poor Nikolai? He had searched the land for his Tsarevna, over mountains and through valleys, under rivers and across forests, but not a trace did he find. He asked every wise old babushka that he met, every rusalka swimming in the rivers, every wolf and even every fierce brown bear he stood before, but no one knew where she was. He asked the sun to shine in every dark corner, but she did not know where the Tsarevna was. He asked the secret moon to look behind the clouds but the moon had not seen her either. The day came when he thought he could look no longer for he was heart-sore and utterly weary. As he sat on the grass, his head cradled in his hands, a little bird chirruped in his ear.

"One more step, brave Nikolai. I know where your Tsarevna lies. She is in a special casket of crystal, close by a huge house near a swiftly flowing river with flower strewn banks and she is guarded by a loving giant."

When Nikolai looked up, the little bird cocked his head as if to say, 'Follow me,' and so he did. He scrambled to his feet and where the bird flew, Nikolai went. Finally the brave little bird led Nikolai right up to the giant who was guarding the crystal coffin. When he saw the Tsarevna lying there, Nikolai caught his breath in wonder.

"She looks as if she is merely sleeping!" he cried to the giant, and he laid his hand tenderly on the crystal coffin. There was a great crack, and the coffin splintered into a million pieces. The Tsarevna opened her eyes, and looked about her in wonderment. There in front of her stood her beloved Nikolai, and then all the giants came running up for they had heard the coffin shattering. The news spread like wildfire.

"The Tsarevna is alive!"

A very happy party made its way back to the palace. The giants were singing at the top of their voices, but Nikolai and the Tsarevna just looked at each other in total silence, blissfully happy but unable to believe that they were really reunited once again.

Inside the palace, the Tsarina was plaiting her hair before the mirror. It suddenly spoke of its own volition.

"Oh wicked lady, here comes the Tsarevna. Her beauty is astounding. There is no one on earth who can compare with her."

The Tsarina grew white as the driven snow and then smashed her hand against the mirror in her towering rage. The mirror flew into tiny pieces, showering the Tsarina in a glassy dust that snuffed out her breath. So that was the end of her!

Nikolai and the Tsarevna were married the very next day, with the giant brothers forming a guard of honour and the little dog and the little bird perched on their broad shoulders. The Tsar was overjoyed to have not only his dear daughter back again, but to have the strong young Nikolai by his side as well. And they really did all live happily ever after.

The Wind in the Willows

An extract
by Kenneth Grahame

Introduction

Kenneth Grahame (1859–1932) was born in Edinburgh. He had an unsettled childhood – his mother died when he was five and his father abandoned the family with their grandmother. Unable to afford a university education, Kenneth took a clerkship in the Bank of England. The Wind in the Willows *was written for his son. These simple stories now form one of the best-loved children's classics.*

The Wind in the Willows

The Riverbank

The Mole had been working very hard all the morning, spring-cleaning his little home. First with brooms, then with dusters; then on ladders and steps and chairs, with a brush and a pail of whitewash; till he had dust in his throat and eyes, and splashes of whitewash all over his black fur, and an aching back and weary arms. Spring was moving in the air above and in the earth below and around him, penetrating even his dark and lowly little house with its spirit of divine discontent and longing. It was small wonder, then, that he suddenly flung down his brush on the floor, said "Bother!" and "Oh blow!" and also "Hang spring-cleaning!" and bolted out of the house without even waiting to put on his coat. Something up above was calling him imperiously, and he made for the steep little tunnel, which answered in his case to the gravelled carriage-drive owned by animals whose residences are nearer to the sun and air. So he worked busily with his little paws and muttering to himself, "Up we go! Up we go!" till at last, pop! His snout came out into the sunlight, and he found himself rolling in the warm grass of a great meadow.

"This is fine!" he said to himself. "This is better than

whitewashing!" The sunshine struck hot on his fur, soft breezes caressed his heated brow, and after the seclusion of the cellarage he had lived in so long the carol of happy birds fell on his dulled hearing almost like a shout. Jumping off all his four legs at once, in the joy of living and the delight of spring without its cleaning, he pursued his way across the meadow till he reached the hedge on the further side.

It all seemed too good to be true. Hither and thither through the meadows he rambled busily, along the hedgerows, across the copses, finding everywhere birds building, flowers budding, leaves thrusting – everything happy, and progressive, and occupied. And instead of having an uneasy conscience pricking him and whispering 'whitewash!' he somehow could only feel how jolly it was to be the only idle dog among all these busy citizens. After all, the best part of a holiday is perhaps not so much to be resting yourself, as to see all the other fellows busy working.

He thought his happiness was complete when, as he meandered aimlessly along, suddenly he stood by the edge of a full-fed river. Never in his life had he seen a river before – this sleek, sinuous, full-bodied animal, chasing and chuckling, gripping things with a gurgle and leaving them with a laugh, to fling itself on fresh playmates that shook themselves free, and were caught and held again. All was a-shake and a-shiver – glints and gleams and sparkles, rustle and swirl, chatter and bubble. The Mole was bewitched, entranced, fascinated. By the side of the river he trotted as one trots, when very small, by the side of a man who holds one spell-bound by exciting stories; and when tired at last, he sat on the bank, while the river still chattered on to him, a babbling procession of the best stories in the world, sent from the heart of the earth to be told at last to the insatiable sea.

As he sat on the grass and looked across the river, a dark hole in the bank opposite, just above the water's edge, caught his eye, and dreamily he fell to considering what a nice snug dwelling-place it would make for an animal with few wants and fond of a bijo riverside residence, above flood level and remote from noise and dust. As he gazed, something bright and small seemed to twinkle down in the heart of it, vanished, then twinkled once more like a tiny star. But it could hardly be a star in such an unlikely situation, and it was too glittering and small for a glow-worm. Then, as he looked, it winked at him, and so declared itself to be an eye, and a small face began gradually to grow up round it, like a frame round a picture.

A brown little face, with whiskers.

A grave round face, with the same twinkle in its eye that had first attracted his notice.

Small neat ears and thick silky hair.

It was the Water Rat!

Then the two animals stood and regarded each other cautiously.

"Hullo, Mole!" said the Water Rat.

"Hullo, Rat!" said the Mole.

"Would you like to come over?" enquired the Rat presently.

"Oh, its all very well to *talk*," said the Mole, rather pettishly, he being new to a river and riverside life and its ways.

The Rat said nothing, but stooped and unfastened a rope and hauled on it; then lightly stepped into a little boat, which the Mole had not observed. It was just the size for two animals; and the Mole's whole heart went out to it at once, even though he did not yet fully understand its uses.

The Rat sculled smartly across and made fast. Then he held up his forepaw as the Mole stepped gingerly down. "Lean on that!" he said. "Now then, step lively!" and the Mole to his surprise and rapture found himself actually seated in the stern of a real boat.

"This has been a wonderful day!" said he, as the Rat shoved off and took to the sculls again. "Do you know, I've never been in a boat before in all my life."

"What?" cried the Rat, open-mouthed: "Never been in a – you never – well I – what have you been doing, then?"

"Is it so nice as all that?" asked the Mole shyly, though he was quite prepared to believe it as he leant back in his seat and surveyed the cushions, the oars, the rowlocks, and all the fascinating fittings, and felt the boat sway lightly under him.

"Nice? It's the *only* thing," said the Water Rat solemnly, as he leant forward for his stroke. "Believe me, my young friend, there is *nothing* – absolute nothing – half so much worth doing as simply messing about in boats. Simply messing..." he went on dreamily, "messing...about...in...boats...messing..."

"Look ahead, Rat!" cried the Mole suddenly.

It was too late. The boat struck the bank full tilt. The dreamer, the joyous oarsman, lay on his back at the bottom of the boat, his heels in the air.

"—about in boats or *with* boats," the Rat went on composedly, picking himself up with a pleasant laugh. "In or out of 'em, it doesn't matter. Nothing seems really to matter, that's the charm of it. Whether you get away, or whether you don't; whether you arrive at your destination or whether you reach somewhere else, or whether you never get anywhere at all, you're always busy, and you never do anything in particular; and when you've done it there's always something else to do, and you can do it if you like, but you'd much better not. Look here! If you've really nothing else on hand this morning, supposing we drop down the river together, and have a long day of it?"

The Mole waggled his toes from sheer happiness, spread his chest with a sigh of full contentment, and leaned back blissfully into the soft cushions.

"*What* a day I'm having!" he said. "Let us start at once!"

"Hold hard a minute, then!" said the Rat. He looped the painter through a ring in his landing-stage, climbed up into his hole above, and after a short interval reappeared staggering under a fat, wicker luncheon-basket.

"Shove that under your feet," he observed to the Mole, as he passed it down into the boat. Then he untied the painter and took the sculls again.

"What's inside it?" asked the Mole, wriggling with curiosity.

"There's cold chicken inside it," replied the Rat briefly; "coldtonguecoldhamcoldbeefpickledgherkinssaladfrenchrollscresssandwichespottedmeatgingerbeerlemonadesodawater—"

"Oh stop, stop," cried the Mole in ecstacies: "This is too much!"

"Do you really think so?" enquired the Rat seriously. "It's only what I always take on these little excursions; and the other animals are always telling me that I'm a mean beast and cut it *very* fine!"

The Mole never heard a word he was saying. Absorbed in the new life he was entering upon, intoxicated with the sparkle, the ripple, the scents and the sounds and the sunlight, he trailed a paw in the water and dreamed long waking dreams. The Water Rat, like the good little fellow he was, sculled steadily on and forebore to disturb him.

"I like your clothes awfully, old chap," he remarked after some half an hour or so had passed. "I'm going to get a black velvet smoking-suit myself some day, as soon as I can afford it."

"I beg your pardon," said the Mole, pulling himself together with an effort. "You must think me very rude, but all this is so new to me. So...this...is...a...river!"

"*The* River," corrected the Rat.

"And you really live by the river? What a jolly life!"

"By it and with it and on it and in it,' said the Rat. "It's brother and sister to me, and aunts, and company, and food and drink, and (naturally) washing. It's my world, and I don't want any other. What it hasn't got is not worth having, and what it doesn't know is not worth knowing. Lord! The times we've had together! Whether in winter or summer, spring or autumn, it's always got its fun and its excitements. When the floods are on in February, and my cellars and basement are brimming with drink that's no good to me, and the brown water runs by my best bedroom window; or again when it all drops away and, shows patches of mud that smells like plum-cake, and the rushes and weed clog the channels, and I can potter about dry shod over most of the bed of it and find fresh food to eat, and things careless people have dropped out of boats!"

"But isn't it a bit dull at times?" the Mole ventured to ask. "Just you and the river, and no one else to pass a word with?"

"No one else to – well, I mustn't be hard on you," said the Rat with forbearance. "You're new to it, and of course you don't know. The bank is so crowded nowadays that many people are moving

away altogether. Oh no, it isn't what it used to be, at all. Otters, kingfishers, dabchicks, moorhens, all of them about all day long and always wanting you to *do* something, as if a fellow had no business of his own to attend to!"

"What lies over *there*?" asked the Mole, waving a paw towards a background of woodland that darkly framed the water-meadows on one side of the river.

"That? Oh, that's just the Wild Wood," said the Rat shortly. "We don't go there very much, we river-bankers."

"Aren't they – aren't they very *nice* people in there?" said the Mole, a trifle nervously.

"W-e-ll," replied the Rat, "let me see. The squirrels are all right. *And* the rabbits, but rabbits are a mixed lot. And then there's Badger, of course. He lives right in the heart of it – wouldn't live anywhere else, either, if you paid him to do it. Dear old Badger! Nobody interferes with *him*. They'd better not," he added.

"Why, who *should* interfere with him?" asked the Mole.

"Well, of course, there are others," explained the Rat in a hesitating sort of way.

"Weasels and stoats and foxes and so on. They're all right in a way – I'm very good friends with them – pass the time of day when we meet, and all that – but they break out sometimes, there's no denying it, and then – well, you can't really trust them, and that's the fact."

The Mole knew well that it is quite against animal-etiquette to dwell on possible trouble ahead, or even to allude to it, so he dropped the subject.

"And beyond the Wild Wood again?" he asked. "Where it's all blue and dim, and one sees what may be hills or perhaps they mayn't, and something like the smoke of towns, or is it only cloud drift?"

"Beyond the Wild Wood comes the Wide World," said the Rat. "And that's something that doesn't matter, either to you or me. I've never been there, and I'm never going, nor you either, if you've got any sense at all. Don't ever refer to it again, please, especially not on sunny days. Now then! Here's our backwater at last, where we're going to lunch."

Leaving the main stream, they now passed into what seemed at first sight like a little land-locked lake. Green turf sloped down to either edge, brown snaky tree-roots gleamed below the surface of the quiet water, while ahead of them the silvery shoulder and foamy tumble of a weir, arm-in-arm with a restless dripping mill-wheel, that held up in its turn a grey-gabled mill-house, filled the air with a soothing murmur of sound, dull and smothery, yet with little clear voices speaking up cheerfully out of it at intervals. It was so very beautiful that the Mole could only hold up both forepaws and gasp, "Oh my! Oh my! Oh my!"

The Rat brought the boat alongside the bank, made her fast, helped the still awkward Mole safely ashore, and swung out the luncheon-basket. The Mole begged as a favour to be allowed to unpack it all by himself, and the Rat was very pleased to indulge him, and to sprawl at full length on the grass and rest, while his excited friend shook out the table cloth and spread it, took out all the mysterious packets one by one and arranged their contents in due order, still gasping, "Oh my! Oh my!" at each fresh revelation.

When all was ready, the Rat said, "Now, pitch in, old fellow!" and the Mole was indeed very glad to obey, for he had started his spring-cleaning at a very early hour that morning, as people *will*

do, and had not paused for bite or sup; and he had been through a very great deal since that distant time, which now seemed so many days ago.

"What are you looking at?" said the Rat presently, when the edge of their hunger was somewhat dulled, and the Mole's eyes were able to wander off the table cloth a little.

"I am looking," said the Mole, "at a streak of bubbles that I see travelling along the surface of the water. That is a thing that strikes me as funny."

"Bubbles? Oho!" said the Rat, and chirruped cheerily in an inviting sort of way.

A broad glistening muzzle showed itself above the edge of the bank, and the Otter hauled himself out and shook the water from his coat.

"Greedy beggars!" he observed, making for the provender. "Why didn't you invite me, Ratty?"

"This was an impromptu affair," explained the Rat. "By the way – my friend Mr Mole."

"Proud, I'm sure," said the Otter, and the two animals were friends forthwith.

"Such a rumpus everywhere!" continued the Otter. "All the world seems out on the river today. I came up this backwater to try and get a moment's peace, and then stumble upon you fellows! At least – I beg pardon – I don't exactly mean that, you know."

There was a rustle behind them, proceeding from a hedge wherein last year's leaves still clung thick, and a stripy head, with high shoulders behind it, peered forth on them.

"Come on, old Badger!" shouted the Rat.

The Badger trotted forward a pace or two; then grunted, "H'm! Company," and turned his back and disappeared from view.

"That's *just* the sort of fellow he is!" observed the disappointed Rat. "Simply hates Society! Now we shan't see any more of him today. Well, tell us, *who's* out on the river?"

"Toad's out, for one," replied the Otter. "In his brand-new wager-boat – new togs, new everything!" The two animals looked at each other and laughed.

"Once, it was nothing but sailing," said the Rat, "Then he tired of that and took to punting. Nothing would please him but to punt all day and every day, and a nice mess he made of it. Last year it was house-boating, and we all had to go and stay with him in his house-boat, and pretend we liked it. He was going to spend the rest of his life in a house-boat. It's all the same, whatever he takes up; he gets tired of it, and starts on something fresh."

"Such a good fellow, too," remarked the Otter reflectively. "But no stability – especially in a boat!"

From where they sat they could get a glimpse of the main stream across the island that separated them; and just then a wager-boat flashed into view, the rower – a short, stout figure – splashing badly and rolling a good deal, but working his hardest. The Rat stood up and hailed him, but Toad – for it was he – shook his head and settled sternly to his work.

"He'll be out of the boat in a minute if he rolls like that," said the Rat, sitting down again.

"Of course he will," chuckled the Otter. "Did I ever tell you that good story about Toad and the lock-keeper? It happened this way. Toad..."

An errant May-fly swerved unsteadily athwart the current in the intoxicated fashion affected by young bloods of May-flies seeing life. A swirl of water and a 'cloop!' and the May-fly was visible no more.

Neither was the Otter.

The Mole looked down. The voice was still in his ears, but the turf whereon he had sprawled was clearly vacant. Not an Otter to be seen, as far as the distant horizon.

But again there was a streak of bubbles on the surface of the river.

The Rat hummed a tune, and the Mole recollected that animal-etiquette forbade any sort of comment on the sudden disappearance of one's friends at any moment, for any reason or no reason whatever.

"Well, well," said the Rat, "I suppose we ought to be moving. I wonder which of us had better pack the luncheon-basket?" He did not speak as if he was frightfully eager for the treat.

"Oh, please let me," said the Mole. So, of course, the Rat let him.

Packing the basket was not quite such pleasant work as unpacking the basket. It never is. But the Mole was bent on enjoying everything, and although just when he had got the basket packed and strapped up tightly he saw a plate staring up at him from the grass, and when the job had been done again the Rat pointed out a fork which anybody ought to have seen, and last of all, behold! the mustard pot, which he had been sitting on without

knowing it – still, somehow, the thing got finished at last, without much loss of temper.

The afternoon sun was getting low as the Rat sculled gently homewards in a dreamy mood, murmuring poetry-things over to himself, and not paying much attention to Mole. But the Mole was very full of lunch, and self-satisfaction, and pride, and already quite at home in a boat (so he thought) and was getting a bit restless besides, and presently he said, "Ratty! Please, I want to row, now!"

The Rat shook his head with a smile. "Not yet, my young friend," he said. "Wait till you've had a few lessons. It's not so easy as it looks."

The Mole was quiet for a minute or two. But he began to feel more and more jealous of Rat, sculling so strongly and so easily along, and his pride began to whisper that he could do it every bit as well. He jumped up and seized the sculls, so suddenly, that the Rat, who was gazing out over the water and saying more poetry-things to himself, was taken by surprise and fell backwards off his seat with his legs in the air for the second time, while the triumphant Mole took his place and grabbed the sculls with entire confidence.

"Stop it, you *silly* ass!" cried the Rat, from the bottom of the boat. "You can't do it! You'll have us over!"

The Mole flung his sculls back with a flourish, and made a great dig at the water. He missed the surface altogether, his legs flew up above his head, and he found himself lying on the top of the prostrate Rat. Greatly alarmed, he made a grab at the side of the boat, and the next moment – Sploosh!

Over went the boat, and he found himself struggling in the river.

Oh my, how cold the water was, and oh, how *very* wet it felt. How it sang in his ears as he went down, down, down! How bright and welcome the sun looked as he rose to the surface coughing and spluttering! How black was his despair when he felt himself sinking again! Then a firm paw gripped him by the back of his neck. It was the Rat, and he was evidently laughing – the Mole could *feel* him laughing, right down his arm and through his paw, and so into his – the Mole's – neck.

The Rat got hold of a scull and shoved it under the Mole's arm; then he did the same by the other side of him and, swimming behind, propelled the helpless animal to shore, hauled him out, and set him down on the bank, a squashy, pulpy lump of misery.

When the Rat had rubbed him down a bit, and wrung some of the wet out of him, he said, "Now, then, old fellow! Trot up and down the towing-path as hard as you can, till you're warm and dry again, while I dive for the luncheon-basket."

So the dismal Mole, wet without and ashamed within, trotted about till he was fairly dry, while the Rat plunged into the water again, recovered the boat, righted her and made her fast, fetched his floating property to shore by degrees, and finally dived successfully for the luncheon-basket and struggled to land with it.

When all was ready for a start once more, the Mole, limp and dejected, took his seat in the stern of the boat; and as they set off, he said in a low voice, broken with emotion, "Ratty, my generous friend! I am very sorry indeed for my foolish and ungrateful conduct. My heart quite fails me when I think how I might have lost that beautiful luncheon-basket. Indeed, I have been a complete ass, and I know it. Will you overlook it this once and forgive me, and let things go on as before?"

"That's all right, bless you!" responded the Rat cheerily. "What's a little wet to a water rat? I'm more in the water than out of it most days. Don't you think any more about it. Look here! I really think you had better come and stop with me for a little time. It's very plain and rough, you know – not like Toad's house at all – but you haven't seen that yet. Still, I can make you comfortable. And I'll teach you to row, and to swim, and you'll soon be as handy on the water as any of us."

The Mole was so touched by his kind manner of speaking that he could find no voice to answer him, and he had to brush away a tear or two with the back of his paw. But the Rat kindly looked in another direction, and presently the Mole's spirits revived again.

When they got home, the Rat made a bright fire in the parlour, and planted the Mole in an arm-chair in front of it, having fetched down a dressing-gown and slippers for him, and told him river

stories till supper-time. Very thrilling stories they were, too, to an earth-dwelling animal like Mole. Stories about weirs, and sudden floods, and leaping pike, and steamers that flung hard bottles – at least bottles were certainly flung, and *from* steamers, so presumably *by* them; and about herons, and how particular they were whom they spoke to; and about adventures down drains, and night-fishings with Otter, or excursions far afield with Badger. Supper was a most cheerful meal; but very shortly afterwards a terribly sleepy Mole had to be escorted upstairs by his considerate host, to the best bedroom, where he soon laid his head on his pillow in great peace and contentment, knowing that his new-found friend the River was lapping the sill of his window.

This day was only the first of many similar ones for the emancipated Mole, each of them longer and full of interest as the ripening summer moved onward. He learnt to swim and to row, and entered into the joy of running water; and with his ear to the reed-stems he caught, at intervals, something of what the wind went whispering so constantly among them.

The Wild Wood

The Mole wanted to make the acquaintance of the Badger. He seemed, by all accounts, to be such an important personage and, though rarely visible, to make his unseen influence felt by everybody about the place. But whenever the Mole mentioned his wish to the Water Rat he always found himself put off. "It's all right," the Rat would say. "Badger'll turn up some day or other – he's always turning up – and then I'll introduce you. The best of fellows! But you must not only take him *as* you find him, but *when* you find him."

"Couldn't you ask him here dinner or something?" said the Mole.

"He wouldn't come," replied the Rat simply. "Badger hates Society, and invitations, and dinner, and all that sort of thing."

"Well, then, supposing we go and call on *him*?" suggested the Mole.

"Oh, I'm sure he wouldn't like that at *all*," said the Rat, quite alarmed. "He's so very shy, he'd be sure to be offended. I've never even ventured to call on him at his own home myself, though I know him so well. Besides, we can't. It's quite out of the question, because he lives in the very middle of the Wild Wood."

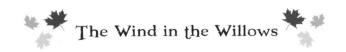

"Well, supposing he does," said the Mole. "You told me the Wild Wood was all right, you know."

"Oh, I know, I know, so it is," replied the Rat evasively. "But I think we won't go there just now. Not *just* yet. It's a long way, and he wouldn't be at home at this time of year anyhow, and he'll be coming along some day, if you'll wait quietly."

The Mole had to be content with this. But the Badger never came along, and every day brought its amusements, and it was not till summer was long over, and cold and frost and miry ways kept them much indoors, and the swollen river raced past outside their windows with a speed that mocked at boating of any sort or kind, that he found his thoughts dwelling again with much persistence on the solitary grey Badger, who lived his own life by himself, in his hole in the middle of the Wild Wood.

In the winter time the Rat slept a great deal, retiring early and rising late. During his short day he sometimes scribbled poetry or did other small domestic jobs about the house; and, of course, there were always animals dropping in for a chat, and consequently there was a good deal of story-telling and comparing notes on the past summer and all its doings.

Such a rich chapter it had been, when one came to look back

on it all! With illustrations so numerous and so very highly coloured! The pageant of the river bank had marched steadily along, unfolding itself in scene-pictures that succeeded each other in stately procession. Purple loosestrife arrived early, shaking luxuriant tangled locks along the edge of the mirror whence its own face laughed back at it. Willow-herb, tender and wistful, like a pink sunset cloud, was not slow to follow. Comfrey, the purple hand-in-hand with the white, crept forth to take its place in the line; and at last one morning the diffident and delaying dog-rose stepped delicately on the stage, and one knew, as if string-music had announced it in stately chords that strayed into a gavotte, that June at last was here. One member of the company was still awaited; the shepherd-boy for the nymphs to woo, the knight for whom the ladies waited at the window, the prince that was to kiss the sleeping summer back to life and love. But when meadow-sweet, debonair and odorous in amber jerkin, moved graciously to his place in the group, then the play was ready to begin.

And what a play it had been! Drowsy animals, snug in their holes while wind and rain were battering at their doors, recalled still keen mornings, an hour before sunrise, when the white mist, as yet undispersed, clung closely along the surface of the water; then the shock of the early plunge, the scamper along the bank, and the radiant transformation of earth, air, and water, when suddenly the sun was with them again, and grey was gold and colour was born and sprang out of the earth once more. They recalled the languorous siesta of hot midday, deep in green undergrowth, the sun striking through in tiny golden shafts and spots; the boating and bathing of the afternoon, the rambles along dusty lanes and through yellow cornfields; and the long, cool evening at last, when so many threads were gathered up, so many friendships rounded, and so many adventures planned for the morrow. There was plenty to talk about on those short winter days when the animals found themselves round the fire; still, the Mole had a good deal of spare time on his hands, and so one afternoon, when the Rat in his arm-chair before the blaze was alternately dozing and trying over rhymes that wouldn't fit, he formed the resolution to go out by himself and explore the Wild Wood, and perhaps strike up an acquaintance with Mr Badger.

It was a cold, still afternoon with a hard steely sky overhead, when he slipped out of the warm parlour into the open air. The country lay bare and entirely leafless around him, and he thought that he had never seen so far and so intimately into the insides of things as on that winter day when Nature was deep in her annual slumber and seemed to have kicked the clothes off. Copses, dells, quarries and all hidden places, which had been mysterious mines for exploration in leafy summer, now exposed themselves and their secrets pathetically, and seemed to ask him to overlook their shabby poverty for a while, till they could riot in rich masquerade as before, and trick and entice him with the old deceptions. It was pitiful in a way, and yet cheering – even exhilarating. He was glad that he liked the country undecorated, hard, and stripped of its finery. He had got down to the bare bones of it, and they were fine and strong and simple. He did not want the warm clover and the play of seeding grasses; the screens of quickset, the billowy drapery of beech and elm seemed best away; and with great cheerfulness of spirit he pushed on towards the Wild Wood, which lay before him low and threatening, like a black reef in some still southern sea.

There was nothing to alarm him at first entry. Twigs crackled under his feet, logs tripped him, funguses on stumps resembled caricatures, and startled him for the moment by their likeness to something familiar and far away; but that was all fun, and exciting. It led him on, and he penetrated to where the light was less, and trees crouched nearer and nearer, and holes made ugly mouths at him on either side.

Everything was very still now. The dusk advanced on him

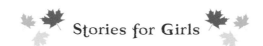

steadily, rapidly, gathering in behind and before; and the light seemed to be draining away like flood-water.

Then the faces began.

It was over his shoulder, and indistinctly, that he first thought he saw a face; a little evil wedge-shaped face, looking out at him from a hole. When he turned and confronted it, the thing had vanished.

He quickened his pace, telling himself cheerfully not to begin imagining things, or there would be simply no end to it. He passed another hole, and another, and another; and then – yes! – no! – yes! certainly a little narrow face, with hard eyes, had flashed up for an instant from a hole, and was gone. He hesitated – braced himself up for an effort and strode on. Then suddenly, and as if it had been so all the time, every hole, far and near, and there were hundreds of them, seemed to possess its face, coming and going rapidly, all fixing on him glances of malice and hatred: all hard-eyed and evil and sharp.

If he could only get away from the holes in the banks, he thought, there would be no more faces. He swung off the path and plunged into the untrodden places of the wood.

Then the whistling began.

Very faint and shrill it was, and far behind him, when first he heard it; but somehow it made him hurry forward. Then, still very faint and shrill, it sounded far ahead of him, and made him hesitate and want to go back. As he halted in indecision it broke out on either side, and seemed to be caught up and passed on throughout the whole length of the wood to its farthest limit. They were up and alert and ready, evidently, whoever they were! And he – he was alone, and unarmed, and far from any help; and the night was closing in.

Then the pattering began.

He thought it was only falling leaves at first, so slight and delicate was the sound of it. Then as it grew it took a regular rhythm, and he knew it for nothing else but the pat-pat-pat of little feet still a very long way off. Was it in front or behind? It seemed to be first one, and then the other, then both. It grew and it multiplied, till from every quarter as he listened anxiously, leaning this way and that, it seemed to be closing in on him. As he stood still to hearken, a rabbit came running hard towards him through the trees. He waited, expecting it to slacken pace, or to swerve from him into a different course. It stopped and looked at him, before dashing onwards. "Get out of this, you fool, get out!" the Mole heard him mutter as he swung round a stump and disappeared down a friendly burrow.

The pattering increased till it sounded like sudden hail on the dry leaf-carpet spread around him. The whole wood seemed running now, running hard, hunting, chasing, closing in round something or – somebody? In panic, he began to run too, aimlessly, he knew not whither. He ran up against things, he fell over things and into things, he darted under things and dodged round things. At last he took refuge in the deep dark hollow of an old beech tree, which offered shelter, concealment – perhaps even safety, but who could tell? Anyhow, he was too tired to run any further, and could only snuggle down into the dry leaves that had drifted into the hollow and hope he was safe for a time. And as he lay there panting and trembling, and listened to the whistlings and the patterings outside, he knew it at last, in all its fullness, that dread thing, which other little dwellers in field and hedgerow had encountered here, and known as their darkest moment – that thing which the Rat had vainly tried to shield him from – the Terror of the Wild Wood!

Meantime the Rat, warm and comfortable, dozed by his fireside. His paper of half-finished verses slipped from his knee, his head fell back, his mouth opened, and he wandered by the verdant banks of dream-rivers. Then a coal slipped, the fire crackled and sent up a spurt of flame, and he woke with a start. Remembering what he had been engaged upon, he reached down to the floor for his verses, pored over them for a minute, and then looked round for the Mole to ask him if he knew a good rhyme for something or other.

But the Mole was not there.

He listened for a time. The house seemed very quiet.

Then he called "Moly!" several times, and, receiving no answer, got up and went out into the hall.

The Mole's cap was missing from its accustomed peg. His goloshes, which always lay by the umbrella-stand, were also gone.

The Rat left the house, and carefully examined the muddy surface of the ground outside, hoping to find the Mole's tracks.

There they were, sure enough. The goloshes were new, just bought for the winter, and the pimples on their soles were fresh and sharp. He could see the imprints of them in the mud, running along straight and purposeful, leading direct to the Wild Wood.

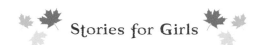

The Rat looked very grave, and stood in deep thought for a minute or two. Then he re-entered the house, strapped a belt round his waist, shoved a brace of pistols into it, took up a stout cudgel that stood in a corner of the hall, and set off for the Wild Wood at a smart pace.

It was already getting towards dusk when he reached the first fringe of trees and plunged without hesitation into the wood, looking anxiously on either side for any sign of his friend. Here and there wicked little faces popped out of holes, but vanished immediately at sight of the valorous animal, his pistols, and the great ugly cudgel in his grasp; and the whistling and pattering, which he had heard quite plainly on his first entry, died away and ceased, and all was very still. He made his way manfully through the length of the wood, to its furthest edge; then, forsaking all paths, he set himself to traverse it, laboriously working over the whole ground, and all the time calling out cheerfully,

"Moly, Moly, Moly! Where are you? It's me – it's old Rat!"

He had patiently hunted through the wood for an hour or more, when at last to his joy he heard a little answering cry. Guiding himself by the sound, he made his way through the gathering darkness to the foot of an old beech tree, with a hole in

it, and from out of the hole came a feeble voice, saying "Ratty! Is that really you?"

The Rat crept into the hollow, and there he found the Mole, exhausted and still trembling. "Oh Rat!" he cried, "I've been so frightened, you can't think!"

"Oh, I quite understand," said the Rat soothingly. "You shouldn't really have gone and done it, Mole. I did my best to keep you from it. We river-bankers, we hardly ever come here by ourselves. If we have to come, we come in couples, at least; then we're generally all right. Besides, there are a hundred things one has to know, which we understand all about and you don't, as yet. I mean passwords, and signs, and sayings that have power and effect, and plants you carry in your pocket, and verses you repeat, and dodges and tricks you practise; all simple enough when you know them, but they've got to be known if you're small, or you'll find yourself in trouble. Of course if you were Badger or Otter, it would be quite another matter."

"Surely the brave Mr Toad wouldn't mind coming here by himself, would he?" inquired the Mole.

"Old Toad?" said the Rat, laughing heartily. "He wouldn't show his face here alone, not for a whole hatful of golden guineas, Toad wouldn't."

The Mole was greatly cheered by the sound of the Rat's careless laughter, as well as by the sight of his stick and his gleaming pistols, and he stopped shivering and began to feel bolder and more himself again.

"Now then," said the Rat presently, "we really must pull ourselves together and make a start for home while there's still a little light left. It will never do to spend the night here, you understand. Too cold, for one thing."

"Dear Ratty," said the poor Mole, "I'm dreadfully sorry, but I'm simply dead beat and that's a solid fact. You *must* let me rest here a while longer, and get my strength back, if I'm to get home at all."

"Oh, all right," said the good-natured Rat, "rest away. It's pretty nearly pitch dark now, anyhow; and there ought to be a bit of a moon later."

So the Mole got well into the dry leaves and stretched himself out, and presently dropped off into sleep, though of a broken and troubled sort; while the Rat covered himself up, too, as best he might, for warmth, and lay patiently waiting, with a pistol in his paw.

When at last the Mole woke up, much refreshed and in his usual spirits, the Rat said, "Now then! I'll just take a look outside and see if everything's quiet, and then we really must be off."

He went to the entrance of their retreat and put his head out. Then the Mole heard him saying quietly to himself, "Hullo! hullo! here is a go!"

"What's up, Ratty?" asked the Mole.

"*Snow* is up," replied the Rat briefly; "or rather, *down*. It's snowing hard."

The Mole came and crouched beside him, and, looking out, saw the wood that had been so dreadful to him in quite a changed aspect. Holes, hollows, pools, pitfalls, and other black menaces to the wayfarer were vanishing fast, and a gleaming carpet of fairy was springing up everywhere, that looked too delicate to be trodden upon by rough feet. A fine powder filled the air and caressed the cheek with a tingle in its touch, and the black boles of the trees showed up in a light that seemed to come from below.

"Well, well, it can't be helped," said the Rat, after pondering. "We must make a start, and take our chance, I suppose. The worst of it is, I don't exactly know where we are. And now this snow makes everything look so very different."

It did indeed. The Mole would not have known that it was the same wood. However, they set out bravely, and took the line that seemed most promising, holding on to each other and pretending with cheerfulness that they recognized an old friend in every fresh tree that grimly and silently greeted them, or saw openings, gaps, or paths with a familiar turn in them, in the monotony of white space and black tree trunks that refused to vary.

An hour or two later they sat down on a fallen tree trunk to recover their breath and consider what was to be done. They were aching with fatigue and bruised with tumbles; they had fallen into several holes and got wet through; and the trees were thicker and more like each other than ever. There seemed to be no end to this wood, and no beginning, and no difference in it, and, worst of all, no way out.

"We can't sit here very long," said the Rat. "We shall have to make another push for it, and do something or other. The cold is too awful for anything, and the snow will soon be too deep for us to wade through." He peered about him and considered. "Look here," he went on, "this is what occurs to me. There's a sort of dell down here in front of us, where the ground seems all hilly and humpy and hummocky. We'll make our way down into that, and try and find some sort of shelter, a cave or hole with a dry floor to it, out of the snow and the wind, and there we'll have a good rest before we try again, for we're both of us pretty dead beat. Besides, the snow may leave off, or something may turn up."

So once more they got on their feet, and struggled down into the dell, where they hunted about for a cave or some corner that was dry and a protection from the keen wind and the whirling snow. They were investigating one of the hummocky bits the Rat had spoken of, when suddenly the Mole tripped up and fell forward on his face with a squeal.

"Oh my leg!" he cried. "Oh my poor shin!" and he sat up on the snow and nursed his leg in both his front paws.

"Poor old Mole!" said the Rat kindly. "You don't seem to be having much luck today, do you? Let's have a look at the leg. Yes," he went on, going down on his knees to look, "you've cut your shin, sure enough. Wait till I get at my handkerchief, and I'll tie it up for you."

"I must have tripped over a hidden branch or a stump," said the Mole miserably. "Oh, my! Oh, my!"

"It's a very clean cut," said the Rat, examining it again attentively. "That was never done by a branch or a stump. Looks as if it was made by a sharp edge of something in metal. Funny!" He pondered awhile, and examined the humps and slopes that surrounded them.

"Well, never mind what done it," said the Mole, forgetting his grammar in his pain. "It hurts just the same, whatever done it."

But the Rat, after carefully tying up the leg with his handkerchief, had left him and was busy scraping in the snow. He scratched and shovelled and explored, all four legs working busily, while the Mole waited impatiently, remarking at intervals, "Oh, *come* on, Rat!"

Suddenly the Rat cried "Hooray!" and then "Hooray-oo-ray-oo-ray-oo-ray!" and fell to executing a feeble jig in the snow.

"What *have* you found, Ratty?" asked the Mole, still nursing his leg.

"Come and see!" said the delighted Rat, as he jigged on.

The Mole hobbled up to the spot and had a good look.

"Well," he said at last, slowly, "I *see* it right enough. Seen the same sort of thing before, lots of times. Familiar object, I call it. A door-scraper! Well, what of it? Why dance jigs around a door-scraper?"

"But don't you see what it *means*, you – you dull-witted

animal?" cried the Rat impatiently.

"Of course I see what it means," replied the Mole. "It simply means that some *very* careless and forgetful person has left his door-scraper lying about in the middle of the Wild Wood, *just* where it's *sure* to trip *everybody* up. Very thoughtless of him, I call it. When I get home I shall go and complain about it to – to somebody or other, see if I don't!"

"Oh, dear! Oh, dear!" cried the Rat, in despair at his obtuseness. "Here, stop arguing and come and scrape!" And he set to work again and made the snow fly in all directions around him.

After some further toil his efforts were rewarded, and a very shabby door mat lay exposed to view.

"There, what did I tell you?" exclaimed the Rat in great triumph.

"Absolutely nothing whatever," replied the Mole, with perfect truthfulness. "Well now," he went on, "you seem to have found another piece of domestic litter, done for and thrown away, and I suppose you're perfectly happy. Better go ahead and dance your jig round that if you've got to, and get it over, and then perhaps we can go on and not waste any more time over rubbish-heaps. Can we *eat* a door mat? Or sleep under a door mat? Or sit on a door mat and sledge home over the snow on it, you exasperating rodent?"

"Do you mean to say," cried the excited Rat, "that this door mat doesn't *tell* you anything?"

"Really, Rat," said the Mole, quite pettishly, "I think we'd had enough of this folly. Who ever heard of a door mat *telling* anyone anything? They simply don't do it. They are not that sort at all. Door mats know their place."

"Now look here, you – you thick-headed beast," replied the Rat, really angry, "this must stop. Not another word, but scrape and scratch and dig and hunt round, especially on the sides of the hummocks, if you want to sleep dry and warm tonight, for it's our last chance!"

The Rat attacked a snow-bank beside them with ardour, probing with his cudgel everywhere and then digging with fury; and the Mole scraped busily too, more to oblige the Rat than for any other reason, for his opinion was that his friend was getting light-headed.

Some ten minutes' hard work, and the point of the Rat's cudgel struck something that sounded hollow. He worked till he could get a paw through and feel; then called the Mole to come and help him. Hard at it went the two animals, till at last the result of their labours stood full in view of the astonished and hitherto incredulous Mole.

In the side of what had seemed to be a snow-bank stood a solid-looking little door, painted a dark green. An iron bell-pull hung by the side, and below it, on a small brass plate, neatly engraved in square capital letters, they could read by the aid of moonlight: MR BADGER.

The Water Babies

An extract

by Charles Kingsley

Introduction

The Water Babies, *written by Charles Kingsley (1819–1875) in 1863, was as much for his youngest child as it was inspired by a government report on child employment that criticised the use of 'climbing boys' in the chimney-sweeping trade. One morning Tom is sent to Harthover, a huge great mansion with many chimneys. Tom loses his way in the dark and comes out in the bedroom of Ellie, the squire's daughter.*

How many Tom swept I cannot say; but he swept so many that he got quite tired, and puzzled too, for they were not like the town flues to which he was accustomed, but such as you would find – if you would only get up them and look, which perhaps you would not like to do – in old country-houses, large and crooked chimneys, which had been altered again and again, till they ran one into another. So Tom fairly lost his way in them; not that he cared much for that, though he was in pitchy darkness, for he was as much at home in a chimney as a mole is underground; but at last, coming down as he thought the right chimney, he came down the wrong one, and found himself standing on the hearthrug in a room the like of which he had never seen before.

Tom had never seen the like. He had never been in gentlefolks' rooms but when the carpets were all up, and the curtains down, and the furniture huddled together under a cloth, and the pictures covered with aprons and dusters; and he had often enough wondered what the rooms were like when they were all ready for the quality to sit in. And now he saw, and he thought the sight very pretty.

The room was all dressed in white – white window-curtains,

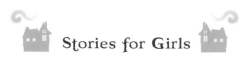

white bed-curtains, white furniture, and white walls, with just a few lines of pink here and there. The carpet was all over pretty little flowers; and the walls were hung with pictures in gilt frames, which amused Tom very much. There were pictures of ladies and gentlemen, and pictures of horses and dogs. The horses he liked; but the dogs he did not care for much, for there were no bull-dogs among them, not even a terrier. But the two pictures that took his fancy most were one of a man in long garments, with little children and their mothers round him, who was laying his hand upon the children's heads. That was a very pretty picture, Tom thought, to hang in a lady's room. For he could see that it was a lady's room by the dresses that lay about.

The other picture was that of a man nailed to a cross, which surprised Tom much. He fancied that he had seen something like

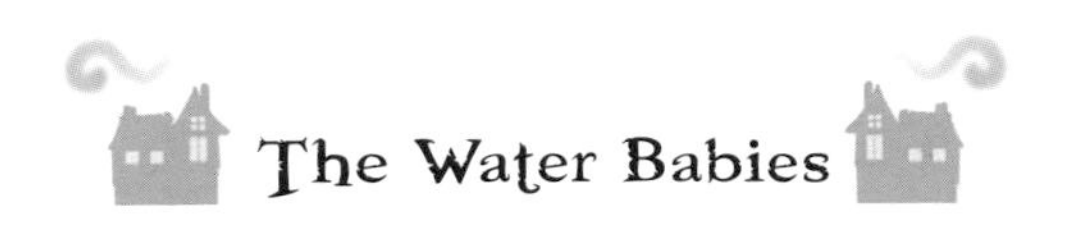

it in a shop window. But why was it there? 'Poor man,' thought Tom, 'and he looks so kind and quiet. But why should the lady have such a sad picture as that in her room? Perhaps it was some kinsman of hers, who had been murdered by the savages in foreign parts, and she kept it there for a remembrance.' And Tom felt sad, and awed, and turned to look at something else.

The next thing he saw, and that too puzzled him, was a washing-stand, with ewers and basins, and soap and brushes, and towels, and a large bath full of clean water – what a heap of things all for washing! 'She must be a very dirty lady,' thought Tom, 'by my master's rule, to want as much scrubbing as all that. But she must be very cunning to put the dirt out of the way so well afterwards, for I don't see a speck about the room, not even on the very towels.'

And then, looking toward the bed, he saw that dirty lady, and held his breath with astonishment.

Under the snow-white coverlet, upon the snow-white pillow, lay the most beautiful little girl that Tom had ever seen. Her cheeks were almost as white as the pillow, and her hair was like threads of gold spread all about over the bed. She might have been as old as Tom, or maybe a year or two older; but Tom did not

think of that. He thought only of her delicate skin and golden hair, and wondered whether she was a real live person, or one of the wax dolls he had seen in the shops. But when he saw her breathe, he made up his mind that she was alive, and stood staring at her, as if she had been an angel out of heaven.

No. She cannot be dirty. She never could have been dirty, thought Tom to himself. And then he thought, 'And are all people like that when they are washed?' And he looked at his own wrist, and tried to rub the soot off, and wondered whether it ever would come off. 'Certainly I should look much prettier then, if I grew at all like her.'

And looking round, he suddenly saw, standing close to him, a little ugly, black, ragged figure, with bleared eyes and grinning white teeth. He turned on it angrily. What did such a little black ape want in that sweet young lady's room? And behold, it was himself, reflected in a great mirror, the like of which Tom had never seen before.

And Tom, for the first time in his life, found out that he was dirty, and burst into tears with shame and anger; and turned to sneak up the chimney again and hide; and upset the fender and threw the fire-irons down, with a noise as of ten thousand tin

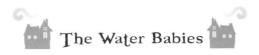

kettles tied to ten thousand mad dogs' tails.

Up jumped the little white lady in her bed, and, seeing Tom, screamed as shrill as any peacock. In rushed a stout old nurse from the next room, and seeing Tom likewise, made up her mind that he had come to rob, plunder, destroy, and burn; and dashed at him, as he lay over the fender, so fast that she caught him by the jacket.

But she did not hold him. Tom had been in a policeman's hands many a time, and out of them too, what is more; and he would have been ashamed to face his friends forever if he had been stupid enough to be caught by an old woman; so he doubled under the good lady's arm, across the room, and out of the window in a moment.

He did not need to drop out, though he would have done so bravely enough. Nor even to let himself down a spout, which would have been an old game to him; for once he got up by a spout to the church roof, he said to take jackdaws' eggs, but the policeman said to steal lead; and, when he was seen on high, sat there till the sun got too hot, and came down by another spout, leaving the policemen to go back to the stationhouse and eat their dinners.

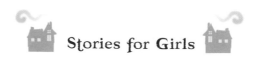

But all under the window spread a tree, with great leaves and sweet white flowers, almost as big as his head. It was magnolia, I suppose; but Tom knew nothing about that, and cared less; for down the tree he went, like a cat, and across the garden lawn, and over the iron railings and up the park towards the wood, leaving the old nurse to scream murder and fire at the window.

The under gardener, mowing, saw Tom, and threw down his scythe; caught his leg in it, and cut his shin open, whereby he kept his bed for a week; but in his hurry he never knew it, and gave chase to poor Tom. The dairymaid heard the noise, got the churn between her knees, and tumbled over it, spilling all the cream; and yet she jumped up, and gave chase to Tom. A groom cleaning Sir John's hack at the stables let him go loose, whereby he kicked himself lame in five minutes; but he ran out and gave chase to Tom. Grimes upset the soot sack in the new-gravelled yard, and

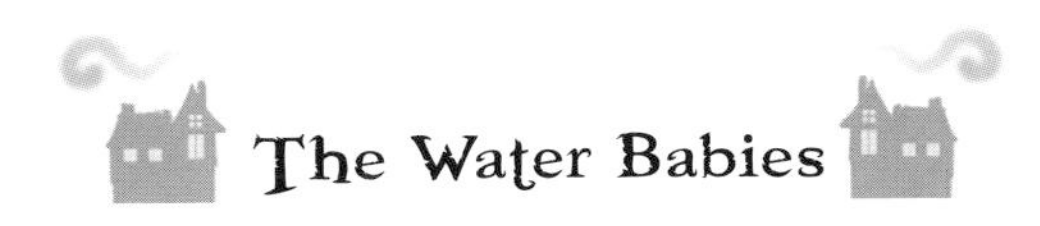

spoilt it all utterly; but he ran out and gave chase to Tom. The old steward opened the park gate in such a hurry, that he hung up his pony's chin upon the spikes, and, for aught I know, it hangs there still; but he jumped off, and gave chase to Tom. The ploughman left his horses at the headland, and one jumped over the fence, and pulled the other into the ditch, plough and all; but he ran on, and gave chase to Tom. The keeper, who was taking a stoat out of a trap, let the stoat go, and caught his own finger; but he jumped up, and ran after Tom; and considering what he said, and how he looked, I should have been sorry for Tom if he had caught him. Sir John looked out of his study window (for he was an early old gentleman) and up at the nurse, and a marten dropped mud in his eye, so that he had at last to send for the doctor; and yet he ran out, and gave chase to Tom. The cook too, who was baking in the kitchen, smoothed her apron, dropped her ladle and gave chase to

Tom. Only my Lady did not give chase; for when she had put her head out of the window, her night-wig fell into the garden, and she had to ring up her lady's-maid, and send her down for it privately, which quite put her out of the running, so that she came in nowhere, and is consequently not placed.

In a word, never was there heard at Hall Place – not even when the fox was killed in the conservatory, among acres of broken glass, and tons of smashed flower-pots – such a noise, row, hubbub, babel, shindy, hullabaloo, stramash, charivari, and total contempt of dignity, repose, and order, as that day, when Grimes, gardener, the groom, the dairymaid, Sir John, the steward, the ploughman, the keeper, and the Irishwoman, all ran up the park, shouting, "Stop thief," in the belief that Tom had at least a thousand pounds worth of jewels in his empty pockets; and the very magpies and jays followed Tom up, screaking and screaming, as if he were a hunted fox, beginning to droop his brush.

What Katy Did

An extract
by Susan Coolidge

Introduction

What Katy Did *was written by Susan Coolidge, the pseudonym of Sarah Chauncy Woolsey (1845–1905). Her younger sisters and brother William were the inspiration for the Carr family. Katy is always in trouble and is the despair of prim Aunt Izzie. The only person who has any influence on Katy is her Cousin Helen, and it is Helen who helps Katy through the dark days that follow the episode described in this extract.*

What Katy Did

Katy's name was Katy Carr. She lived in the town of Burnet, which wasn't a very big town, but was growing as fast as it knew how. The house she lived in stood on the edge of town. It was a large square house, white, with green blinds, and had a porch in front over which roses and clematis made a thick bower. Four tall locust trees shaded the gravel path that led to the front gate. On one side of the house was an orchard; on the other side were wood piles and barns, and an ice-house. Behind was a kitchen garden sloping to the south; and behind that a pasture with a brook in it, and butternut trees, and four cows – two red ones, a yellow one with sharp horns tipped with tin, and a dear little white one named Daisy.

There were six of the Carr children – four girls and two boys. Katy, the oldest, was twelve years old; little Phil, the youngest, was four, and the rest fitted in between.

Dr Carr, their Papa, was a dear, kind, busy man, who was away from home all day, taking care of sick people. The children hadn't any Mamma. She had died when Phil was a baby, four years before my story began. Katy could remember her pretty well; to the rest she was but a sad, sweet name, spoken on Sunday, and at prayer-times, or when Papa was specially gentle and solemn.

In place of this Mamma, whom they recollected so dimly, there was Aunt Izzie, Papa's sister, who came to take care of them when Mamma went away on that long journey, from which, for so many months, the little ones kept hoping she might return. Aunt Izzie was a small woman, sharp-faced and thin, rather old-looking, and very neat and particular about everything. She meant to be kind to the children, but they puzzled her much, because they were not a bit like herself when she was a child. Aunt Izzie had been a gentle, tidy little thing, who loved to sit as Curly Locks did, sewing long seams in the parlour, and to have her head patted by older people, and be told that she was a good girl; whereas Katy tore her dress every day, hated sewing, and didn't care a button about being called 'good,' while Clover and Elsie shied off like restless ponies when anyone tried to pat their heads. It was very perplexing to Aunt Izzie, and she found it quite hard to forgive the children for being so 'unaccountable,' and so little like the boys and girls in Sunday-school memoirs, who were the young people she liked best because they always seemed to behave so well, and who she understood most about.

Then Dr Carr was another person who worried her. He wished to have the children hardy and bold, and encouraged climbing and rough plays, in spite of the bumps and ragged clothes that resulted. In fact, there was just one half-hour of the day when Aunt Izzie was really satisfied about her charges, and that was the half-hour before breakfast, when she had made a law that they were all to sit in their little chairs and learn the Bible verse for the day. At this time she looked at them with pleased eyes, they were all so spick and span, with such nicely-brushed jackets and such neatly-combed hair. But the moment the bell rang her comfort was over. From that time on, they were what she called 'not fit to be seen.' The neighbours pitied her very much. They used to count the sixty stiff white pantalette legs hung out to dry every Monday morning, and say to each other what a sight of washing those children made, and what a chore it must be for poor Miss Carr to keep them so nice. But poor Miss Carr didn't think them at all nice; that was the worst of it.

"Clover, go upstairs and wash your hands! Dorry, pick your hat off the floor and hang it on the nail! Not that nail, the third nail from the corner!" These were the kind of things Aunt Izzie was saying all day long. The children minded her pretty well, but they didn't exactly love her, I fear. They called her 'Aunt Izzie' always, never 'Aunty.' Boys and girls will know what that meant.

I want to show you the little Carrs, and I don't know that I could ever have a better chance than one day when five out of the six were perched on top of the ice-house, like chickens on a roost. This ice-house was one of their favourite places. It was only a low roof set over a hole in the ground, and, as it stood in the middle of the side-yard, it always seemed to the children that the shortest road to every place was up one of its slopes and down the other.

They also liked to mount to the ridge-pole, and then, still keeping the sitting position, to let go, and scrape slowly down over the warm shingles to the ground. It was bad for their shoes and trousers, of course; but what of that? Shoes and trousers and clothes generally were Aunt Izzie's affair; theirs was to slide and enjoy themselves.

Clover, next in age to Katy, sat at one end. She was a fair, sweet dumpling of a girl, with thick pig-tails of light brown hair, and short-sighted blue eyes, which seemed to hold tears, just ready to fall from under the blue. Really, Clover was the jolliest little thing in the world; but these eyes, and her soft cooing voice, always made people feel like petting her and taking her part. Once, when she was very small, she ran away with Katy's doll, and when Katy pursued, and tried to take it from her, Clover held fast and would not let go. Dr Carr, who wasn't attending particularly, heard nothing but the pathetic tone of Clover's voice, as she said:

"Me won't! Me want Dolly!" and, without stopping to inquire, he called out sharply,

"For shame, Katy! Give your sister her doll at once!" which Katy, much surprised, did; while Clover purred in triumph, like a satisfied kitten. Clover was sunny and sweet-tempered, a little indolent, and very modest about herself, though, in fact, she was particularly clever in all sorts of games, and extremely droll and funny in a quiet way. Everybody loved her, and she loved everybody, especially Katy, whom she looked up to as one of the wisest people in the world.

Pretty little Phil sat at the other end. Elsie, a thin, brown child of eight, with beautiful dark eyes, and crisp, short curls covering the whole of her small head sat in the very middle. Poor little Elsie was the 'odd one' among the Carrs. She didn't seem to belong exactly to either the older or the younger children. The great desire and ambition of her heart was to be allowed to go about with Katy and Clover and Cecy Hall, and to know their secrets and be permitted to put notes into the little post-offices they were for ever establishing in all sorts of hidden places. But they didn't want Elsie, and used to tell her to 'run away and play with the children,' which hurt her feelings very much. When she wouldn't run away, I am sorry to say they ran away from her which, as their legs were longest, it was easy to do. Poor Elsie, left behind, would cry bitter tears and, as she was too proud to play much with Dorry and John, her principal comfort was tracking the older ones about and discovering their mysteries, which were her greatest grievance.

Katy, who had the finest plans in the world for being 'heroic' and of use, never saw, as she drifted on her heedless way, that here, in this lonely little sister, was the very chance she wanted for being a comfort to somebody who needed comfort very much. She never saw it, and Elsie's heavy heart went uncheered.

Dorry and Joanna sat on either side of Elsie. Dorry was six years old; a pale, pudgy boy, with rather a solemn face, and smears of molasses on the sleeve of his jacket. Joanna, whom the children called 'John,' and 'Johnnie,' was a square, splendid child, a year younger than Dorry; she had big brave eyes, and a wide rosy mouth, which always looked ready to laugh. These two were great friends, though Dorry seemed like a girl who had got into boy's clothes by mistake, and Johnnie like a boy who, in a fit of fun, had borrowed his sister's frock.

And now, as they all sat there chattering and giggling, the window above opened, a glad shriek was heard, and Katy's head appeared. In her hand she held a heap of stockings, which she waved triumphantly.

"Hurray!" she cried, "all done, and Aunt Izzie says we may go. Are you tired out waiting? I couldn't help it, the holes were so big, and took so long. Hurry up, Clover, and get the things! Cecy and

I will be down in a minute."

The children jumped up gladly, and slid down the roof. Clover fetched a couple of baskets from the wood shed. Elsie ran for her kitten. Dorry and John loaded themselves with two great bundles of green boughs. Just as they were ready the side-door banged, and Katy and Cecy Hall came into the yard.

I must tell you about Cecy. She was a great friend of the children's, and lived in the house next door. The yards of the houses were only separated by a green hedge with no gate, so that Cecy spent two-thirds of her time at Dr Carr's, and was exactly like one of the family. She was a neat, dapper, pink-and-white girl, modest and prim in manner, with light shiny hair, which always kept smooth, and slim hands, which never looked dirty. How different from my poor Katy! Katy's hair was forever in a snarl, her gowns were always catching on nails and 'tearing themselves' and – in spite of her age and size – she was as heedless and innocent as a child of six. Katy was the longest girl that was ever seen. What she did to make herself grow so, nobody could tell; but there she was – up above Papa's ear and half a head taller than poor Aunt Izzie. Whenever she stopped to think about her height she became very awkward, and felt as if she were all legs and elbows and angles and joints. Happily, her head was so full of other things – of plans and schemes and fancies of all sorts – that she didn't often take time to remember how tall she was. She was a dear, loving child, for all her careless habits, and made bushels of good resolutions every week of her life, only unluckily she never kept any of them. She had fits of responsibility about the other children, and longed to set them a good example, but when the chance came she generally forgot to do so. Katy's days flew like the wind; for when she wasn't studying lessons, or sewing and darning with Aunt Izzie (which she hated extremely) there were always so many delightful schemes rioting in her brains, that all she wished for was ten pairs of hands to carry them out. These same active brains got her into perpetual scrapes. She was fond of building castles in the air, and dreaming of the time when something she had done would make her famous so that everybody would hear of her and want to know her. I don't think she had made up her mind what this wonderful thing was to be; but while thinking about it she often forgot to learn a lesson, or to lace her boots, and then she had a bad mark, or a scolding from Aunt Izzie. At such times she consoled herself with planning how, by and by, she would be beautiful and beloved, and amiable as an angel. A great deal was to happen to Katy before that time came. Her eyes, which were black, were to turn blue; her nose was to lengthen and straighten, and her mouth – quite too large at present to suit the part of a heroine – was to be made over into a sort of rosy button. Meantime, and until these charming changes should take place, Katy forgot her features as much as she could, though still, I think, the person on earth whom she most envied was those ladies on the outsides of the shampoo bottles with the wonderful hair that sweeps the ground.

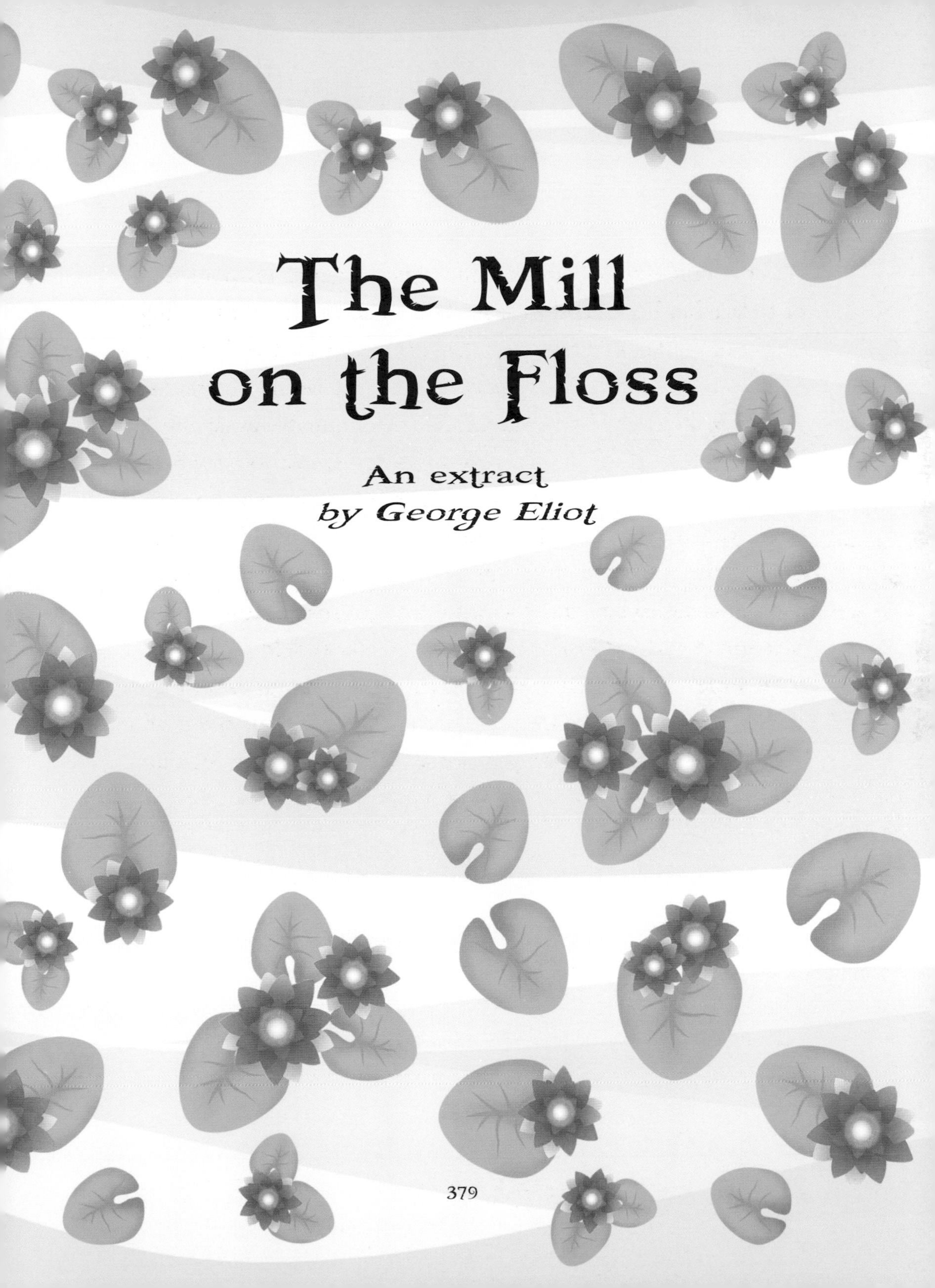

The Mill on the Floss

An extract
by George Eliot

George Eliot (1819–1880) was another female author who wrote under a man's name, her real name being Mary Ann Evans. In The Mill on the Floss, *Tom and Maggie are the children of an honest but uneducated miller. Tom is like his father but Maggie is intelligent and fiery, and becomes rebellious in the face of frustration. This extract highlights the conflict between Tom's sense of correctness, and Maggie's desire for freedom.*

Little Lucy, with her whole person – from her small feet to her bonnet-crown – wet and discoloured with mud, held out two tiny blackened hands, and made a very piteous face. To account for this unprecedented apparition in aunt Pullet's parlour, we must return to the moment when the three children went to play out of doors, and the small demons who had taken possession of Maggie's soul at an early period of the day had returned in all the greater force after a temporary absence. All the disagreeable recollections of the morning were thick upon her, when Tom, whose displeasure towards her had been considerably refreshed by her foolish trick of causing him to upset his cowslip wine, said, "Here, Lucy, you come along with me," and walked off to the area where the toads were, as if there were no Maggie in existence.

Seeing this, Maggie lingered at a distance looking like a small Medusa with her snakes cropped. Lucy was naturally pleased that cousin Tom was so good to her, and it was very amusing to see him tickling a fat toad with a piece of string when the toad was safe down the area, with an iron grating over him. Still Lucy wished Maggie to enjoy the

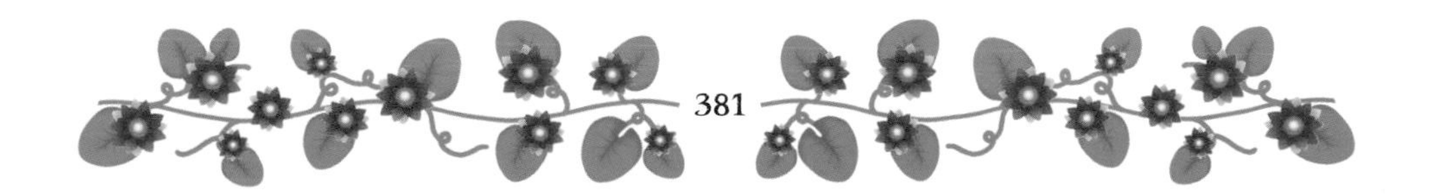

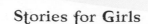

spectacle also, especially as she would doubtless find a name for the toad, and say what had been his past history; for Lucy had a delighted semi-belief in Maggie's stories about the live things they came upon by accident – how Mrs Earwig had a wash at home, and one of her children had fallen into the hot copper, for which reason she was running so fast to fetch the doctor. The desire to know the history of a very portly toad, added to her habitual affectionateness, made her run back to Maggie and say, "Oh, there is such a big, funny toad, Maggie! Do come and see!"

Maggie said nothing, but turned away from her with a deeper frown. As long as Tom seemed to prefer Lucy to her, Lucy made part of his unkindness. Maggie would have thought a little while ago that she could never be cross with pretty little Lucy, anymore than she could be cruel to a little white mouse; but then, Tom had always been quite indifferent to Lucy before, and it had been left to Maggie to pet and make much of her. As it was, she was actually beginning to think that she should like to make Lucy cry by slapping or pinching her, especially as it might vex Tom, whom it was of no use to slap, even if she dared, because he didn't mind it. And if Lucy hadn't been there, Maggie was sure he would have got friends with her sooner.

Tickling a fat toad who is not highly sensitive is an amusement that it is possible to exhaust, and Tom by and by began to look round for some other mode of passing the time. But in so prim a garden, where they were not to go off the paved walks, there was not a great choice of sport. The only great pleasure such a restriction suggested was the pleasure of breaking it, and Tom began to meditate an insurrectionary visit to the pond, about a field's length beyond the garden.

"I say, Lucy," he began, nodding his head up and down with great significance, as he coiled up his string again, "what do you think I mean to do?"

"What, Tom?" said Lucy, with curiosity.

"I mean to go to the pond and look at the pike. You may go with me if you like," said the young sultan.

"Oh, Tom, dare you?" said Lucy. "Aunt said we mustn't go out of the garden."

"Oh, I shall go out at the other end of the garden," said Tom. "Nobody'ull see us. Besides, I don't care if they do – I'll run off home."

"But I couldn't run," said Lucy, who had never before been exposed to such severe temptation.

"Oh, never mind. They won't be cross with you," said Tom. "You can say I took you."

Maggie saw them leaving the garden, and could not resist the impulse to follow. Anger and jealousy can no more bear to lose sight of their objects than love, and that Tom and Lucy should do or see anything of which she was ignorant would have been an intolerable idea to Maggie. So she kept a few yards behind them, unobserved by Tom, who was presently absorbed in watching for the pike – a highly interesting monster; he was said to be so very old, so very large, and to have such a remarkable appetite. The pike, like other celebrities, did not show when he was watched for, but Tom caught sight of something in rapid movement in the water, which attracted him to another spot on the brink of the pond.

"Here, Lucy!" he said in a loud whisper, "Come here! Take care! Keep on the grass – don't step where the cows have been!" he added, pointing to a peninsula of dry grass, with trodden mud on each side of it; for Tom's contemptuous conception of a girl included the attribute of being unfit to walk in dirty places.

Lucy came carefully as she was bidden, and bent down to look at what seemed a golden arrow-head darting through the water. It was a water-snake, Tom told her; and Lucy at last could see the serpentine wave of its body, very much wondering that a snake could swim. Maggie had drawn nearer and nearer – she must see it too, though it was bitter to her, like everything else, since Tom did not care about her seeing it. At last she was close by Lucy; and Tom, who had been aware of her approach, but would not notice it till he was obliged, turned round and said, "Now, get away, Maggie. There's no room for you on the grass here. Nobody asked you to come."

A rage possessed Maggie and with a fierce thrust of her small brown arm, she pushed poor little pink-and-white Lucy into the cow-trodden mud.

Then Tom could not restrain himself, and gave Maggie two smart slaps on the arm as he ran to pick up Lucy, who lay crying helplessly. Maggie retreated to the roots of a tree a few yards off, and looked on impenitently. Usually her repentance came quickly after one rash deed, but now Tom and Lucy had made her so miserable that she was glad to spoil their happiness. Why should she be sorry? Tom was very slow to forgive her, however sorry she might have been.

"I shall tell mother, you know, Miss Mag," said Tom, loudly and emphatically, as soon as Lucy was up and ready to walk away. Lucy was too entirely absorbed by the evil that had befallen her – the spoiling of her pretty best clothes, and the discomfort of being wet and dirty – to think much of the cause, which was entirely mysterious to her. She could never have guessed what she had done to make Maggie angry with her; but she felt that Maggie was very unkind and disagreeable, and made no entreaties to Tom that he would not 'tell,' only running along by his side and crying piteously, while Maggie sat on the roots of the tree and looked after them with her small cross face.

"Sally," said Tom, when they reached the kitchen door, and Sally looked at them in speechless amaze, with a piece of bread-and-butter in her mouth and a toasting-fork in her hand,"Sally, tell mother it was Maggie pushed Lucy into the mud."

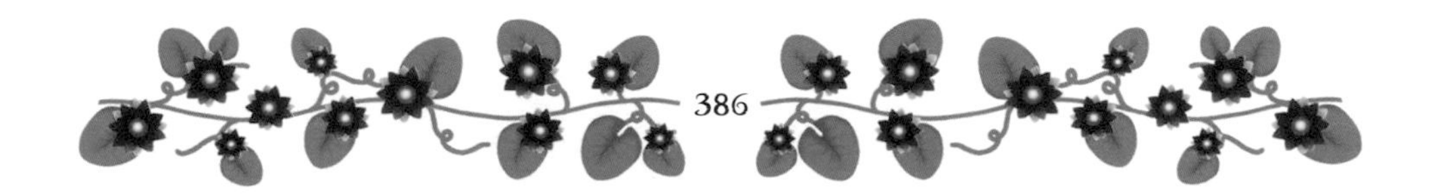

"But Lors ha' massy, how did you get near such mud as that?" said Sally, making a wry face, as she stooped down and examined the very dirty Lucy.

Tom's imagination had not been rapid and capacious enough to include this question among the foreseen consequences, but it was no sooner put than he foresaw whither it tended, and that Maggie would not be considered the only culprit in the case. He walked quietly away from the kitchen door, leaving Sally to that pleasure of guessing which active minds notoriously prefer to ready-made knowledge.

Sally, as you are aware, lost no time in presenting Lucy at the parlour door, for to have so dirty an object introduced into the house at Garum Firs was too great a weight to be sustained by a single mind.

"Goodness gracious!" Aunt Pullet exclaimed, after preluding by an inarticulate scream. "Keep her at the door, Sally!"

"Why, she's tumbled into some nasty mud," said Mrs Tulliver, going up to Lucy to examine into the amount of damage to clothes for which she felt herself responsible to her sister Deane.

"If you please, 'um, it was Miss Maggie as pushed her in," said Sally. "Master Tom's been and said so, and they must ha' been to the pond, for it's only there they could ha' got into such dirt."

"There it is, Bessy; it's what I've been telling you," said Mrs Pullet, in a tone of prophetic sadness. "It's your children – there's no knowing what they'll come to."

Mrs Tulliver was mute, feeling herself a truly wretched mother. Meantime tea was to be brought in by the cook, and the two naughty children were to have theirs in an ignominious manner in the kitchen. Mrs Tulliver went out to speak to these naughty children, supposing them to be close at hand; but it was not until after some search that she found Tom leaning with rather a hardened, careless air against the white paling of the poultry-yard, and lowering his piece of string on the other side as a means of exasperating the turkey-cock.

"Tom, you naughty boy, where's your sister?" said Mrs Tulliver.

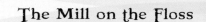

"I don't know," said Tom. His eagerness for justice on Maggie had diminished since he had seen clearly that it could hardly be brought about without the injustice of some blame on his own conduct.

"Why, where did you leave her?" said the mother, looking round.

"Sitting under the tree, against the pond," said Tom, apparently indifferent to everything but the turkey-cock.

"Then go and fetch her in this minute, you naughty boy. And how could you think of going to the pond, and taking your sister where there was dirt?"

The idea of Maggie sitting alone by the pond roused an habitual fear in Mrs Tulliver's mind, and she mounted the horse-block to satisfy herself by a sight of that fatal child, while Tom walked – not very quickly – on his way toward her.

"They're such children for the water, mine are," she said aloud, without reflecting that there was no one to hear her. "They'll be brought in drowned some day. I wish that river was far enough."

But when she not only failed to discern Maggie, but presently saw Tom returning from the pool alone, this hovering fear entered and took complete possession of her, and she hurried to meet him.

"Maggie's nowhere about the pond, mother," said Tom.

You may conceive the terrified search for Maggie. Mr Pullet, confused and overwhelmed by this revolutionary aspect of things – the tea deferred and the poultry alarmed by the unusual running to and fro – took up his spade as an instrument of search, and reached down a key to unlock the goose-pen, as a likely place for Maggie to lie concealed in.

Tom started the idea that Maggie was gone home, and the suggestion was seized as a comfort by his mother.

"Sister, for goodness' sake let 'em put the horse in the carriage. We shall perhaps find her on the road. Lucy can't walk in her dirty clothes," she said, looking at that innocent victim, wrapped up in a shawl, sitting with naked feet on the sofa.

It was not long before Mrs Tulliver was in the chaise, looking anxiously at the most distant point before her. What Maggie's father would say if Maggie was lost, was a question that predominated over every other.

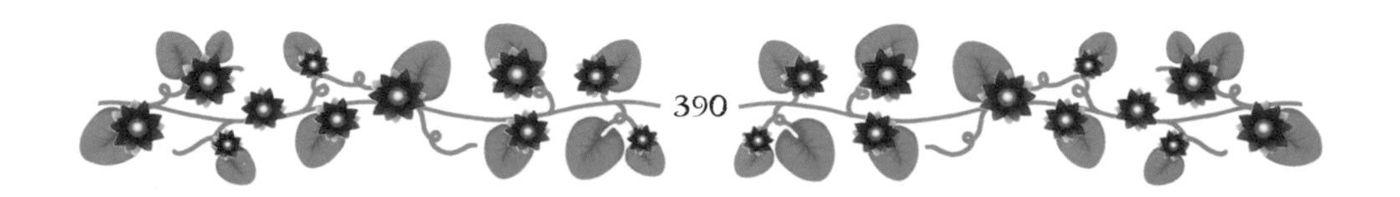

Rebecca of Sunnybrook Farm

An extract
by Kate Douglas Wiggin

Introduction

Kate Douglas Wiggin (1856–1923) trained as a teacher. She had no intention of taking up writing seriously, but her first book was so successful that she continued writing. Rebecca of Sunnybrook Farm *was written in 1903. Rebecca is sent to live with her two unmarried aunts. In this extract she and her friends have been selling soap in order to try and win the 'banquet lamp' that the soap company are giving away as a reward for sales.*

There had been company at the brick house to the bountiful Thanksgiving dinner that had been provided at one o'clock – the Burnham sisters, who lived between North Riverboro and Shaker Village, and who for more than a quarter of a century had come to pass the holiday with the Sawyers every year. Rebecca sat silent with a book after the dinner dishes were washed, and when it was nearly five asked if she might go to the Simpsons'.

"What do you want to run after those Simpson children for on a Thanksgiving Day?" queried Miss Miranda. "Can't you set still for once and listen to the improvin' conversation of your elders? You never can let well enough alone, but want to be forever on the move."

"The Simpsons have a new lamp, and Emma Jane and I promised to go up and see it lighted, and make it a kind of a party."

"What under the canopy did they want of a lamp, and where did they get the money to pay for it? If Abner was at home, I should think he'd been swappin' again," said Miss Miranda.

"The children got it as a prize for selling soap," replied Rebecca. "They've been working for a year, and you know I told you that Emma Jane and I helped them the Saturday afternoon you were in Portland."

"I didn't take notice, I s'pose, for it's the first time I ever heard the lamp mentioned. Well, you can go for an hour, and no more. Remember it's as dark at six as it is at midnight. Would you like to take along some Baldwin apples? What have you got in the pocket of that new dress that makes it sag down so?"

"It's my nuts and raisins from dinner," replied Rebecca, who never succeeded in keeping the most innocent action a secret from her aunt Miranda. "They're just what you gave me on my plate."

"Why didn't you eat them?"

"Because I'd had enough dinner, and I thought if I saved these, it would make the Simpsons' party better," stammered Rebecca, who hated to be scolded and examined before company.

"They were your own, Rebecca," interposed aunt Jane, "and if you chose to save them to give away, it is all right. We ought never to let this day pass without giving our neighbours something to be thankful for, instead of taking all the time to think of our own mercies."

The Burnham sisters nodded approvingly as Rebecca went out, and remarked that they had never seen a child grow and improve so fast in so short a time.

"There's plenty of room left for more improvement, as you'd know if she lived in the same house with you," answered Miranda. "She's into every namable thing in the neighbourhood, an' not only into it, but generally at the head an' front of it – especially when it's mischief. Of all the foolishness I ever heard of, that lamp beats everything; it's just like those Simpsons, but I didn't suppose the children had brains enough to sell anything."

"One of them must have," said Miss Ellen Burnham, "for the girl that was selling soap at the Ladds' in North Riverboro was described by Adam Ladd as the most remarkable and winning child he ever saw."

"It must have been Clara Belle, and I should never call her remarkable," answered Miss Miranda. "Has Adam been home again?"

"Yes, he's been staying a few days with his aunt. There's no limit to the money he's making, they say; and he always brings presents for all the neighbours. This time it was a full set of furs for Mrs Ladd – and to think we can remember the time he was a barefoot boy without two shirts to his back! It is strange he hasn't married, with all his money, and him so fond of children that he always has a pack of them at his heels."

"There's hope for him still, though," said Miss Jane smilingly. "I don't s'pose he's more than thirty."

"He could get a wife in Riverboro if he was a hundred and thirty," remarked Miss Miranda.

"Adam's aunt says he was so taken with the little girl that sold the soap – Clara Belle, did you say her name was? – that he declared he was going to bring her a Christmas present," continued Miss Ellen.

"Well, there's no accountin' for tastes," exclaimed Miss Miranda. "Clara Belle's got cross-eyes and red hair, but I'd be the last one to grudge her a Christmas present – the more Adam Ladd gives to her the less the town'll have to."

"Isn't there another Simpson girl?" asked Miss Lydia Burnham; "For this one couldn't have been cross-eyed – I remember Mrs Ladd saying Adam remarked about this child's handsome eyes. He said it was her eyes that made him buy the three hundred cakes. Mrs Ladd has it stacked up in the shed chamber."

"Three hundred cakes!" ejaculated Miranda. "Well, there's one crop that never fails in Riverboro!"

"What's that?" asked Miss Lydia politely.

"The fool crop," responded Miranda tersely, and changed the subject, much to Jane's gratitude, for she had been nervous and ill at ease for the last fifteen minutes. What child in Riverboro could be described as remarkable and winning, save Rebecca? What child had wonderful eyes, except the same Rebecca? And finally, was

there ever a child in the world who could make a man buy soap by the hundred cakes, save Rebecca?

Meantime the 'remarkable' child had flown up the road in the deepening dusk, but she had not gone far before she heard the sound of hurrying footsteps, and saw a well-known figure coming in her direction. In a moment she and Emma Jane met and exchanged a breathless embrace.

"Something awful has happened," panted Emma Jane.

"Don't tell me it's broken," exclaimed Rebecca.

"No! Oh, no! Not that! It was packed in straw, and every piece came out all right; and I was there, and I never said a single thing about your selling the three hundred cakes that got the lamp, so that we could be together when you told."

"*Our* selling the three hundred cakes," corrected Rebecca; "You did as much as I."

"No, I didn't, Rebecca Randall. I just sat at the gate and held the horse."

"Yes, but whose horse was it that took us to North Riverboro? And besides, it just happened to be my turn. If you had gone in and found Mr Aladdin you would have had the wonderful lamp given to you. But what's the trouble?"

"The Simpsons have no kerosene and no wicks. I guess they thought a banquet lamp was something that lighted itself, and burned without any help. Seesaw has gone to the doctor's to try if he can borrow a wick, and mother let me have a pint of oil, but she says she won't give me any more. We never thought of the expense of keeping up the lamp, Rebecca."

"No, we didn't, but let's not worry about that till after the party. I have a handful of nuts and raisins and some apples."

"I have peppermints and maple sugar," said Emma Jane. "They had a real Thanksgiving dinner; the doctor gave them sweet potatoes and cranberries and turnips; father sent a spare-rib, and Mrs Cobb a chicken and a jar of mince-meat."

At half past five one might have looked in at the Simpsons' windows, and seen the party at its height. Mrs Simpson had let the kitchen fire die out, and had brought the baby to grace the festive scene. The lamp seemed to be having the party, and receiving the guests. The children had taken the one small table in the house, and it was placed in the far corner of the room to serve as a pedestal. On it stood the sacred, the adored, the long-desired object; almost as beautiful, and nearly half as large as the advertisement. The brass glistened like gold, and the crimson paper shade glowed like a giant ruby. In the wide splash of light that it flung upon the floor sat the Simpsons, in reverent and solemn silence, Emma Jane standing behind them, hand in hand with Rebecca. There seemed to be no desire for conversation – the occasion was too thrilling and serious for that. The lamp, it was tacitly felt by everybody, was dignifying the party, and providing sufficient entertainment simply by its presence; being fully as satisfactory in its way as a pianola or a string band.

"I wish father could see it," said Clara Belle loyally.

"If he onth thaw it he'd want to thwap it," murmured Susan sagaciously.

At the appointed hour Rebecca dragged herself reluctantly away from the enchanting scene.

"I'll turn the lamp out the minute I think you and Emma Jane are home," said Clara Belle. "And, oh! I'm so glad you both live where you can see it shine from our windows. I wonder how long it will burn without bein' filled if I only keep it lit one hour every night?"

"You needn't put it out for want o' kerosene,' said Seesaw, coming in from the shed, 'for there's a great keg of it settin' out there. Mr Tubbs brought it over from North Riverboro and said somebody sent an order by mail for it."

Rebecca squeezed Emma Jane's arm, and Emma Jane gave a rapturous return squeeze.

"It was Mr Aladdin," whispered Rebecca, as they ran down the path to the gate. Seesaw followed them and handsomely offered to see them 'apiece' down the road, but Rebecca declined his escort with such decision that he did not press the matter, but went to bed to dream of her instead. In his dreams flashes of lightning proceeded from both her eyes, and she held a flaming sword in either hand.

Rebecca entered the home dining room joyously. The Burnham sisters had gone and the two aunts were knitting.

"It was a heavenly party," she cried, taking off her hat and cape.

"Go back and see if you have shut the door tight, and then lock it," said Miss Miranda, in her usual austere manner.

"It was a heavenly party," reiterated Rebecca, coming in again, much too excited to be easily crushed. "And oh! aunt Jane, aunt Miranda, if you'll only come into the kitchen and look out of the sink window, you can see the banquet lamp shining all red, just as if the Simpsons' house was on fire."

"And probably it will be before long," observed Miranda. "I've got no patience with such foolish goin's on."

Jane accompanied Rebecca into the kitchen. Although the feeble glimmer that she was able to see from that distance did not seem to her a dazzling exhibition, she tried to be as enthusiastic as possible.

"Rebecca, who was it that sold the three hundred cakes of soap to Mr Ladd in North Riverboro?"

"Mr Who?" exclaimed Rebecca

"Mr Ladd, in North Riverboro."

"Is that his real name?" queried Rebecca in astonishment. "I didn't make a bad guess," and she laughed softly to herself.

"I asked you who sold the soap to Adam Ladd?" resumed Miss Jane.

"Adam Ladd! then he's A. Ladd, too – what fun!"

"Answer me, Rebecca."

"Oh! excuse me, aunt Jane, I was so busy thinking. Emma Jane and I sold the soap to Mr Ladd."

"Did you tease him, or make him buy it?"

"Now, aunt Jane, how could I make a big grown-up man buy anything if he didn't want to? He needed the soap dreadfully as a present for his aunt."

Miss Jane still looked a little unconvinced, though she only said, "I hope your aunt Miranda won't mind, but you know how particular she is, Rebecca, and I really wish you wouldn't do anything out of the ordinary without asking her first, for your actions are very strange."

"There can't be anything wrong this time," Rebecca answered confidently. "Emma Jane sold her cakes to her own relations and to uncle Jerry Cobb, and I went first to those new tenements near the lumber mill, and then to the Ladds'. Mr Ladd bought all we had and made us promise to keep the secret until the premium came, and I've been going about ever since as if the banquet lamp was inside of me all lighted up and burning, for everybody to see."

Rebecca's hair was loosened and falling over her forehead in ruffled waves; her eyes were brilliant, her cheeks crimson; there was a hint of everything in the girl's face – of sensitiveness and delicacy as well as of ardour; there was the sweetness of the mayflower and the strength of the young oak, but one could easily divine that she was one of 'The souls by nature pitched too high, By suffering plunged too low.'

"That's just the way you look, for all the world as if you did have a lamp burning inside of you," sighed aunt Jane. "Rebecca! Rebecca! I wish you could take things easier, child; I am fearful for you sometimes."

Great Expectations

An extract

by Charles Dickens

Introduction

Charles Dickens (1812–1870) was the son of a clerk. His father was imprisoned for debt and young Charles found himself, aged 12, working in a blacking warehouse. This experience had a profound effect on him, and inspired much of his writing. Great Expectations *is narrated by Pip, and opens when Pip is summoned to the house of the wealthy Miss Havisham who has lived in seclusion since being jilted on her wedding day.*

The sound of my sister's iron shoes upon the hard road was quite musical, as she came along at a much brisker trot than usual. We got a chair out ready for her alighting, and stirred up the fire that they might see a bright window, and took a final survey of the kitchen that nothing might be out of its place.

The kitchen door opened, and my sister entered, saying, "Miss Havisham wants this boy to go and play at her house. And of course he's going. And he had better play there," she shook her head at me as an encouragement to be extremely light and sportive, "or I'll work him."

I had heard of Miss Havisham up town – everybody for miles round, had heard of Miss Havisham up town – as an immensely rich and grim lady who lived in a large and dismal house barricaded against robbers, and who led a life of seclusion.

"Well to be sure!" said Joe, astounded. "I wonder how she come to know Pip!"

My sister interrupted him: "Uncle Pumblechook, being sensible that for anything we can tell, this boy's fortune may be made by his going to Miss Havisham's, has offered to take him into town tonight in his own chaise-cart, and to keep him tonight, and to take him with his own hands to Miss Havisham's tomorrow morning. And Lor-a-mussy me!" – my sister, cast off her bonnet in sudden desperation – "Here I stand talking to mere Mooncalfs, with Uncle Pumblechook waiting, and the mare catching cold at the door, and the boy grimed with crock and dirt from the hair of his head to the sole of his foot!"

With that, she pounced upon me, like an eagle on a lamb, and my face was squeezed into wooden bowls in sinks, and my head was put under taps of water-butts, and I was soaped, and kneaded, and towelled, and thumped, and harrowed, and rasped, until I really was quite beside myself – I may here remark that I suppose myself to be better acquainted than any living authority, with the ridgy effect of a wedding-ring, passing unsympathetically over the human countenance.

When my ablutions were completed, I was put into clean linen of the stiffest character, like a young penitent into sackcloth, and was trussed up in my tightest and fearfullest suit. I was then delivered over to Mr Pumblechook, who formally received me as if he were the Sheriff, and who let off upon me the speech that I knew he had been dying to make all along: "Boy, be for ever grateful to all friends, but especially unto them which brought you up by hand!"

"Goodbye, Joe!"

"God bless you, Pip, old chap!"

Mr Pumblechook's premises in the high street of the market town, were of a peppercorny and farinaceous character, as the premises of a corn-chandler and seedsman should be. It appeared to me that he must be a very happy man indeed, to have so many little drawers in his shop; and I wondered when I peeped into one or two on the lower tiers, and saw the tied-up brown paper packets inside, whether the flower-seeds and bulbs ever wanted of a fine day to break out of those jails and bloom.

It was in the early morning after my arrival that I entertained this speculation. On the previous night, I had been sent straight to bed in an attic with a sloping roof, which was so low in the corner where the bedstead was, that I calculated the tiles as being within a foot of my eyebrows. In the same early morning, I discovered a singular affinity between seeds and corduroys. Mr Pumblechook wore corduroys, and so did his shopman; and somehow, there was a general air and flavour about the corduroys, so much in the nature of seeds, and a general air and flavour about the seeds, so much in the nature of corduroys, that I hardly knew which was which. The same opportunity served me for noticing that Mr Pumblechook appeared to conduct his business by looking across the street at the saddler, who appeared to transact his business by keeping his eye on the coach-maker, who appeared to get on in life by putting his hands in his pockets and contemplating the baker, who in his turn folded his arms and stared at the grocer, who stood at his door and yawned at the chemist. The watch-maker, always poring over a little desk with a magnifying glass at his eye, and always inspected by a group of smock-frocks poring over him through the glass of his shop-window, seemed to be about the only person in the high-street whose trade engaged his attention.

Mr Pumblechook and I breakfasted at eight o'clock in the parlour behind the shop, while the shopman took his mug of tea and hunch of bread-and-butter on a sack of peas in the front premises. I considered Mr Pumblechook wretched company. Besides being possessed by my sister's idea that a mortifying and penitential character ought to be imparted to my diet – besides giving me as much crumb as possible in combination with as little butter, and putting such a quantity of warm water into my milk that it would have been more candid to have left the milk out altogether – his conversation consisted of nothing but arithmetic.

On my politely bidding him 'Good morning', he said, pompously,

"Seven times nine, boy?" And how should I be able to answer, dodged in that way, in a strange place, on an empty stomach! I was hungry, but before I had swallowed a morsel, he began a running sum that lasted all through the breakfast. "Seven?" "And four?" "And eight?" "And six?" "And two?" "And ten?" And so on. And after each figure was disposed of, it was as much as I could do to get a bite or a sup, before the next came; while he sat at his ease guessing nothing, and eating bacon and hot roll, in (if I may be allowed the expression) a gorging and gormandising manner.

For such reasons I was very glad when ten o'clock came and we started for Miss Havisham's, though I was not at all at my ease regarding the manner in which I should acquit myself under that lady's roof. Within a quarter of an hour we came to Miss Havisham's house, which was of old brick, and dismal, and had a great many iron bars to it. Some of the windows had been walled up. Of those that remained, all the lower were rustily barred. There was a courtyard in front, and that was barred; so, we had to wait, after ringing the bell, until someone should come to open it. While we waited at the gate, I peeped in (even then

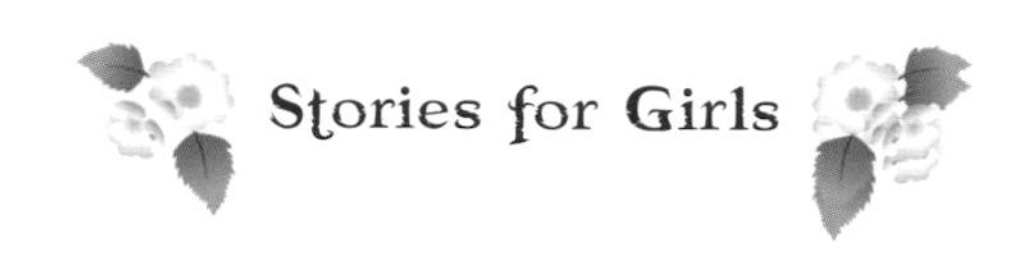

Mr Pumblechook said, "And fourteen?" but I pretended not to hear him), and saw that at the side of the house there was a large brewery. No brewing was going on in it, and none seemed to have gone on for a long long time.

A window was raised, and a clear voice demanded,"What name?"

To which my conductor replied, "Pumblechook."

The voice returned, "Quite right," and the window was shut again, and a young lady came across the courtyard, with keys in her hand.

"This," said Mr Pumblechook, "is Pip."

"This is Pip, is it?" returned the young lady, who was very pretty and seemed very proud; "Come in, Pip."

Mr Pumblechook was coming in also, when she stopped him with the gate.

"Oh!" she said. "Did you wish to see Miss Havisham?"

"If Miss Havisham wished to see me," returned Mr Pumblechook discomfited.

"Ah!" said the girl; "But you see she don't."

She said it so finally, and in such an undiscussible way, that Mr Pumblechook, though in a condition of ruffled dignity, could

not protest. But he eyed me severely – as if I had done anything to him! – and departed with the words reproachfully delivered: "Boy! Let your behaviour here be a credit unto them which brought you up by hand!" I was not free from apprehension that he would come back to propound through the gate, "And sixteen?" But he didn't.

My young conductress locked the gate, and we went across the courtyard. It was paved and clean, but grass was growing in every crevice. The brewery buildings had a little lane of communication with it; and the wooden gates of that lane stood open, and all the brewery beyond, stood open, away to the high enclosing wall; and all was empty and disused. The cold wind seemed to blow colder there, than outside the gate; and it made a shrill noise in howling

in and out at the open sides of the brewery, like the noise of wind in the rigging of a ship at sea.

We went into the house by a side door – the great front entrance had two chains across it outside – and the first thing I noticed was, that the passages were all dark, and that she had left a candle burning there. She took it up, and we went through more passages and up a staircase, and still it was all dark, and only the candle lighted us.

At last we came to the door of a room, and she said, "Go in."

I answered, more in shyness than politeness, "After you, miss."

To this, she returned: "Don't be ridiculous, boy; I am not going in." And scornfully walked away, and – what was worse – took the candle with her.

This was very uncomfortable, and I was half afraid. However, the only thing to be done being to knock at the door, I knocked, and was told from within to enter. I entered, therefore, and found myself in a pretty large room, well lighted with wax candles. No glimpse of daylight was to be seen in it. It was a dressing room, as I supposed from the furniture, though much of it was of forms and uses then quite unknown to me. But prominent in it was a draped table with a gilded looking glass, and that I made out at first sight to be a fine lady's dressing table.

Whether I should have made out this object so soon, if there had been no fine lady sitting at it, I cannot say. In an armchair, with an elbow resting on the table and her head leaning on that hand, sat the strangest lady I have ever seen, or shall ever see.

She was dressed in rich materials – satins, and lace, and silks – all of white. Her shoes were white. And she had a long white veil dependent from her hair, and she had bridal flowers in her hair, but her hair was white. Some bright jewels sparkled on her neck and on her hands, and some other jewels lay sparkling on the table. Dresses, less splendid than the dress she wore, and half-packed trunks, were scattered about. She had not quite finished dressing for she had but one shoe on – the other was on the table near her hand – her veil was but half arranged, her watch and chain were not put on, and some lace for her bosom lay with those trinkets, and with her handkerchief, and gloves, and some flowers, and a prayer book, all confusedly heaped about the looking-glass.

It was not in the first few moments that I saw all these things, though I saw more of them in the first moments than might be supposed. But, I saw that everything within my view which ought to be white, had been white long ago, and had lost its lustre, and was faded and yellow. I saw that the bride within the bridal dress had withered like the dress, and like the flowers, and had no brightness left but the brightness of her sunken eyes. I saw that the dress had been put upon the rounded figure of a young woman, and that the figure upon which it now hung loose, had shrunk to skin and bone. Once, I had been taken to see some ghastly

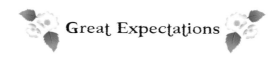

waxwork at the Fair, representing I know not what impossible personage lying in state. Once, I had been taken to one of our old marsh churches to see a skeleton in the ashes of a rich dress, that had been dug out of a vault under the church pavement. Now, waxwork and skeleton seemed to have dark eyes that moved and looked at me. I should have cried out, if I could.

"Who is it?" said the lady at the table.

"Pip, ma'am."

"Pip?"

"Mr Pumblechook's boy, ma'am. Come – to play."

"Come nearer; let me look at you. Come close."

It was when I stood before her, avoiding her eyes, that I took note of the surrounding objects in detail, and saw that her watch had stopped at twenty minutes to nine, and that a clock in the room had stopped at twenty minutes to nine.

"Look at me," said Miss Havisham. "You are not afraid of a woman who has never seen the sun since you were born?"

I regret to state that I was not afraid of telling the enormous lie comprehended in the answer 'No.'

"Do you know what I touch here?" she said, laying her hands, one upon the other, on her left side.

"Yes, ma'am."

"What do I touch?"

"Your heart."

"Broken!"

She uttered the word with an eager look, and with strong emphasis, and with a weird smile that had a kind of boast in it. Afterwards, she kept her hands there for a little while, and slowly took them away as if they were heavy.

"I am tired," said Miss Havisham. "I want diversion, and I have done with men and women. Play."

I think it will be conceded by my most disputatious reader, that she could hardly have directed an unfortunate boy to do anything in the wide world more difficult to be done under the circumstances.

"I sometimes have fancies," she went on, "and I have a fancy that I want to see some play. There, there!" with an impatient movement of the fingers of her right hand; "Play, play, play!"

For a moment, with the fear of my sister's working me before my eyes, I had a desperate idea of starting round the room in the assumed character of Mr Pumblechook's chaise-cart. But, I felt myself so unequal to the performance that I gave it up, and stood looking at Miss Havisham in what I suppose she took for a dogged manner, inasmuch as she said, when we had taken a good look at each other:

"Are you sullen and obstinate?"

"No, ma'am, I am very sorry for you, and very sorry I can't play just now. If you complain of me I shall get into trouble with my sister, so I would do it if I could; but it's so new here, and so strange, and so fine – and melancholy—" I stopped, fearing I might say too much, or had already said it, and we took another look at each other.

Before she spoke again, she turned her eyes from me, and looked at the dress she wore, and at the dressing table, and finally at herself in the looking glass.

"So new to him," she muttered, "so old to me; so strange to him, so familiar to me; so melancholy to both of us! Call Estella."

As she was still looking at the reflection of herself, I thought she was still talking to herself, and kept quiet.

"Call Estella," she repeated, flashing a look at me. "You can do that. Call Estella. At the door."

To stand in the dark in a mysterious passage of an unknown house, bawling Estella to a scornful young lady neither visible nor responsive, and feeling it a dreadful liberty so to roar out her name, was almost as bad as playing to order. But, she answered at last, and her light came along the dark passage like a star.

Miss Havisham beckoned her to come close, and took up a jewelled necklace from the table, and tried its effect upon her fair young neck. “Your own, one day, my dear, and you will use it well. Let me see you play cards with this boy.”

“With this boy! Why, he is a common labouring-boy!”

I thought I overheard Miss Havisham answer – only it seemed so unlikely: “Well? You can break his heart.”

“What do you play, boy?” asked Estella of myself, with the greatest disdain.

“Nothing but beggar my neighbour, miss.”

So we sat down to cards.

It was then I began to understand that everything in the room had stopped, like the watch and the clock, a long time ago. I noticed that Miss Havisham put down the necklace exactly on the spot from which she had taken it up. As Estella dealt the cards, I glanced at the dressing table again, and saw that the shoe upon it, once white, now yellow, had never been worn. I glanced down at the foot from which the shoe was absent, and saw that the silk

stocking on it, once white, now yellow, had been trodden ragged. Without this arrest of everything, this standing still of all the pale decayed objects, not even the withered bridal dress on the collapsed form could have looked so like grave-clothes, or the long veil so like a shroud.

So she sat, corpse-like, as we played at cards; the frillings and trimmings on her bridal dress, looking like earthy paper. I knew nothing then, of the discoveries that are occasionally made of bodies buried in ancient times, which fall to powder in the moment of being distinctly seen; but, I have often thought since, that she must have looked as if the admission of the natural light of day would have struck her to dust.

"He calls the knaves, Jacks, this boy!" said Estella with disdain, before our first game was out. "And what coarse hands he has! And what thick boots!"

I had never thought of being ashamed of my hands before, but I began to consider them a very indifferent pair. Her contempt for

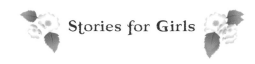

me was so strong, that it became infectious, and I caught it.

She won the game, and I dealt. I misdealt, as was only natural, when I knew she was lying in wait for me to do wrong; and she denounced me for a stupid, clumsy labouring-boy.

"You say nothing of her," remarked Miss Havisham to me, as she looked on. "She says many hard things of you, but you say nothing of her. What do you think of her?"

"I don't like to say," I stammered.

"Tell me in my ear," said Miss Havisham, bending down.

"I think she is very proud," I replied, in a whisper.

"Anything else?"

"I think she is very pretty."

"Anything else?"

"I think she is very insulting." (She was looking at me then with a look of supreme aversion).

"Anything else?"

"I think I should like to go home."

"And never see her again, though she is so pretty?"

"I am not sure that I shouldn't like to see her again, but I should like to go home now."

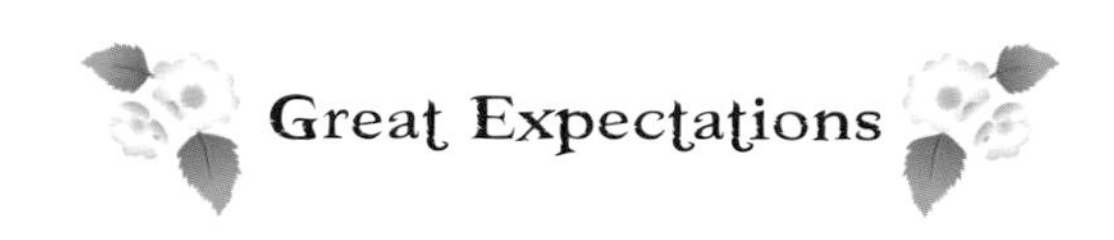

"You shall go soon," said Miss Havisham, aloud. "Play the game out."

Saving for the one weird smile at first, I should have felt almost sure that Miss Havisham's face could not smile. It had dropped into a watchful and brooding expression – most likely when all the things about her had become transfixed – and it looked as if nothing could ever lift it up again. Her chest had dropped, so that she stooped; and her voice had dropped, so that she spoke low, and with a dead lull upon her; altogether, she had the appearance of having dropped, body and soul, within and without, under the weight of a crushing blow.

I played the game to an end with Estella. She threw the cards down on the table when she had won them all, as if she despised them for having been won of me.

"When shall I have you here again?" said Miss Havisham. "Let me think."

I was beginning to remind her that today was Wednesday, when she checked me with her former impatient movement of the fingers of her right hand.

"There, there! I know nothing of days of the week; I know nothing of weeks of the year. Come again after six days. You hear?"

"Yes, ma'am."

"Estella, take him down. Let him have something to eat, and let him roam and look about him while he eats. Go, Pip."

I followed the candle down, as I had followed the candle up, and she stood it in the place where we had found it. Until she opened the side entrance, I had fancied, without thinking about it, that it must necessarily be night-time. The rush of the daylight quite confounded me, and made me feel as if I had been in the candlelight of the strange room for many hours.

"You are to wait here, you boy," said Estella; and disappeared and closed the door.

I took the opportunity of being alone in the courtyard, to look at my coarse hands and my common boots. My opinion of those accessories was not favourable. They had never troubled me before, but they troubled me now, as vulgar appendages. I determined to ask Joe why he had ever taught me to call those picture-cards, Jacks, which ought to be called knaves. I wished Joe had been rather more genteelly brought up, and then I should have been so too.

She came back, with some bread and meat and a little mug of beer. She put the mug down on the stones of the yard, and gave me the bread and meat without looking at me, as insolently as if I were a dog in disgrace. I was so humiliated, hurt, spurned, offended, angry, sorry – I cannot hit upon the right name for the smart – that tears started to my eyes. The moment they sprang there, the girl looked at me with a quick delight in having been the cause of them. This gave me power to keep them back and to look at her, so she gave a contemptuous toss – but with a sense, I thought, of having made too sure that I was so wounded – and left me.

But, when she was gone, I looked about me for a place to hide my face in, and got behind one of the gates in the brewery-lane, and leaned my sleeve against the wall there, and leaned my forehead on it and cried. As I cried, I kicked the wall, and took a hard twist at my hair – so bitter were my feelings, and so sharp was the smart without a name, that needed counteraction.

My sister's bringing up had made me sensitive. In the little world in which children have their existence, whoever brings them up, there is nothing so finely perceived and so finely felt as injustice. It may be only small injustice that the child can be exposed to; but the child is small, and its world is small, and its rocking-horse stands as many hands high, according to scale, as a big-boned Irish hunter. Within myself, I had sustained, from my babyhood, a perpetual conflict with injustice. I had known, from the time when I could speak, that my sister, in her capricious and violent coercion, was unjust to me. I had cherished a profound conviction that her bringing me up by hand, gave her no right to bring me up by jerks. Through all my punishments, disgraces, fasts and vigils, and other penitential performances, I had nursed this assurance; and to my communing so much with it, in a solitary and unprotected way – I in great part refer to the fact that I was morally timid and very sensitive.

I got rid of my injured feelings for the time, by kicking them into the brewery wall, and twisting them out of my hair, and then l smoothed my face with my sleeve, and came from behind the gate. The bread and meat were acceptable, and the beer was warming and tingling, and I was soon in spirits to look about me.

To be sure, it was a deserted place, down to the pigeon-house in the brewery-yard, which had been blown crooked on its pole by some high wind, and would have made the pigeons think themselves at sea, if there had been any pigeons there to be rocked by it. But there were no pigeons in the dove-cot, no horses in the stable, no pigs in the sty, no malt in the store-house, no smells of grains and beer in the copper or the vat. All the uses and scents of the brewery might have evaporated with its last reek of smoke. In a by-yard, there was a wilderness of empty casks, which had a certain sour remembrance of better days lingering about them; but it was too sour to be accepted as a sample of the beer that was gone – and in this respect I remember those recluses as being like most others.

Behind the furthest end of the brewery, was a rank garden with an old wall: not so high but that I could struggle up and hold on long enough to look over it, and see that the rank garden was the garden of the house, and that it was overgrown with tangled weeds, but that there was a track upon the green and yellow paths, as if someone sometimes walked there, and that Estella was walking away from me even then. But she seemed to be everywhere. For, when I yielded to the temptation presented by the casks, and began to walk on them, I saw her walking on them at the end of the yard of casks. She had her back towards me, and held her pretty brown hair spread out in her two hands, and never looked round, and passed out of my view directly. So, in the brewery itself – by which I mean the large paved lofty place in which they used to make the beer, and where the brewing utensils still were. When I first went into it and, rather oppressed by its gloom, stood near the door looking about me, I saw her pass among the extinguished fires, and ascend some light iron stairs, and go out by a gallery high overhead, as if she were going out into the sky.

It was in this place, and at this moment, that a strange thing happened to my fancy. I thought it a strange thing then, and I thought it a stranger thing long afterwards. I turned my eyes – a little dimmed by looking up at the frosty light – towards a great wooden beam in a low nook of the building near me on my right hand, and I saw a figure hanging there by the neck. A figure all in yellow white, with but one shoe to the feet; and it hung so, that I could see that the faded trimmings of the dress were like earthy paper, and that the face was Miss Havisham's, with a movement going over the whole countenance as if she were trying to call to me. In the terror of seeing the figure, and in the terror of being certain that it had not been there a moment before, I at first ran from it, and then ran towards it. And my terror was greatest of all, when I found no figure there.

Nothing less than the frosty light of the cheerful sky, the sight of people passing beyond the bars of the court yard gate, and the reviving influence of the rest of the bread and meat and beer, would have brought me round. Even with those aids, I might not have come to myself as soon as I did, but that I saw Estella approaching with the keys, to let me out. She would have some fair reason for looking down upon me, I thought, if she saw me frightened; and she should have no fair reason.

She gave me a triumphant glance in passing me, as if she rejoiced that my hands were so coarse and my boots were so thick, and she opened the gate, and stood holding it. I was passing out without looking at her, when she touched me with a taunting hand.

"Why don't you cry?"

"Because I don't want to."

"You do," said she. "You have been crying till you are half blind, and you are near crying again now."

She laughed contemptuously, pushed me out, and locked the gate upon me. I went straight to Mr Pumblechook's, and was immensely relieved to find him not at home. Leaving word with the shopman on what day I was wanted at Miss Havisham's again, I set off on the four-mile walk to our forge; pondering on all I had seen, and deeply revolving that I was a common labouring-boy;

that my hands were coarse; that my boots were thick; that I had fallen into a despicable habit of calling knaves Jacks; that I was much more ignorant than I had considered myself last night, and generally that I was in a low-lived bad way.

Pollyanna

An extract
by Eleanor H Porter

Introduction

Eleanor Hodgman Porter (1868–1920) wrote several popular novels but it was Pollyanna *that became an international best-seller. After the death of her father, Pollyanna comes to live with her sour Aunt Polly who is constantly thwarted in her efforts to discipline Pollyanna who has a perpetually happy outlook on life and is endlessly optimistic. In this extract the resourceful Pollyanna finds a way to keep cool in the heat of the night.*

At half-past eight Pollyanna went up to bed. The screens had not yet come, and the close little room was like an oven. With longing eyes Pollyanna looked at the two fast-closed windows, but she did not raise them. She undressed, folded her clothes neatly, said her prayers, blew out her candle and climbed into bed.

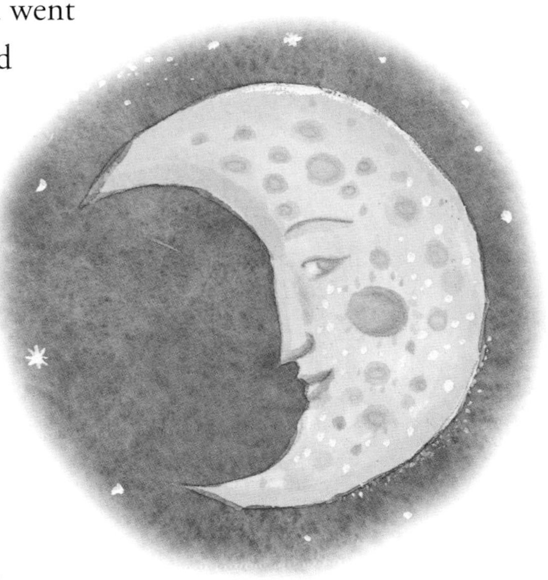

Just how long she lay in sleepless misery, tossing from side to side of the hot little cot, she did not know; but it seemed to her that it must have been hours before she finally slipped out of bed, felt her way across the room and opened her door.

Out in the main attic, all was velvet blackness save where the moon flung a path of silver half-way across the floor from the east dormer window. With a resolute ignoring of that fearsome darkness to the right and to the left, Pollyanna drew a quick breath and pattered straight into that silvery path, and onto the window.

She had hoped that this window might have a screen, but it did not. Outside, however, there was a wide world of fairy-like beauty, and there was, too, she knew, fresh, sweet air that would feel so good to hot cheeks and hands!

As she stepped nearer and peered longingly out, she saw something else: she saw, only a little way below the window, the wide, flat tin roof of Miss Polly's sun parlour. The sight filled her with longing. If only, now, she were out there!

Fearfully she looked behind her. Back there, somewhere, were her hot little room and her still hotter bed; but between her and them lay a horrid desert of blackness across which one must feel one's way with outstretched, shrinking arms; while before her, out on the sun parlour roof, were the moonlight and the cool, sweet night air.

If only her bed were out there! And folks did sleep out of doors. Joel Hartley at home, who was so sick with the consumption, *had* to sleep out of doors.

Suddenly Pollyanna remembered that she had seen near this attic window a row of long white bags hanging from nails. Nancy had said that they contained the winter clothing, put away for the summer. A little fearfully now, Pollyanna felt her way to these bags, selected a nice fat soft one (it contained Miss Polly's sealskin coat) for a bed; and a thinner one to be doubled up for a pillow, and still another (which was so thin it seemed almost empty) for a covering. Thus equipped, Pollyanna in high glee pattered to the moonlit window again, raised the sash, stuffed her burden through to the roof below, then let herself down after it, closing the window carefully behind her – Pollyanna had not forgotten those flies with the marvellous feet that carried things.

How deliciously cool it was! Pollyanna quite danced up and down with delight, drawing in long, full breaths of the refreshing air. The tin roof under her feet crackled with little resounding snaps that Pollyanna rather liked. She walked, indeed, two or three times back and forth from end to end – it gave her such a pleasant sensation of airy space after her hot little room; and the roof was so broad and flat that she had no fear of falling off. Finally, with a sigh of content, she curled herself up on the sealskin-coat mattress, arranged one bag for a pillow and the other for a covering, and settled herself to sleep.

"I'm so glad now that the screens didn't come," she murmured, blinking up at the stars; "else I couldn't have had this!"

Downstairs in Miss Polly's room next to the sun parlour,

Miss Polly herself was hurrying into dressing gown and slippers, her face white and frightened. A minute before she had been telephoning in a shaking voice to Timothy: "Come up quick! You and your father. Bring your lanterns. Somebody is up on the roof of the sun parlour. He must have climbed up the rose-trellis or somewhere, and of course he can get right into the house through the east window in the attic. I have locked the attic door down here – but hurry, quick!"

Some time later, Pollyanna, just dropping off to sleep, was startled by a lantern flash, and a trio of amazed exclamations. She opened her eyes to find Timothy at the top of a ladder near her, Old Tom just getting through the window, and her aunt peering out at her from behind him.

"Pollyanna, what does this mean?" cried Aunt Polly then.

Pollyanna blinked sleepy eyes and sat up.

"Why, Mr Tom – Aunt Polly!" she stammered. "Don't look so scared! It isn't that I've got the consumption, you know, like Joel Hartley. It's only that I was so hot in there. But I shut the window, Aunt Polly, so the flies couldn't carry those germ-things in."

Timothy disappeared suddenly down the ladder. Old Tom, with almost equal precipitation, handed his lantern to Miss Polly, and followed his son. Miss Polly bit her lip hard until the men were gone; then she said sternly:

"Pollyanna, hand those things to me at once and come in here. Of all the extraordinary children!" she exclaimed a little later, as, with Pollyanna by her side and the lantern in her hand, she turned back into the attic.

To Pollyanna the air was all the more stifling after that cool breath of the out of doors, but she did not complain. She only drew a long quivering sigh.

At the top of the stairs Miss Polly jerked out crisply:

"For the rest of the night, Pollyanna, you are to sleep in my bed with me. The screens will be here tomorrow, but until then I consider it my duty to keep you where I know where you are."

Pollyanna drew in her breath.

"With you? In your bed?" she cried rapturously. "Oh, Aunt Polly, Aunt Polly, how perfectly lovely of you! And when I've so wanted to sleep in the same room with someone, sometime – someone that belonged to me, you know; not a Ladies' Aider. I've *had* them. My! I reckon I am glad now those screens didn't come! Wouldn't you be?"

There was no reply. Miss Polly was stalking on ahead. Miss

Polly, to tell the truth, was feeling curiously helpless. For the third time since Pollyanna's arrival, Miss Polly was trying to punish Pollyanna, and for the third time she was being confronted with the amazing fact that her punishment was being taken as some kind of special reward of merit. No wonder Miss Polly was feeling curiously helpless.

The Wonderful Wizard of Oz

An extract

by Frank L Baum

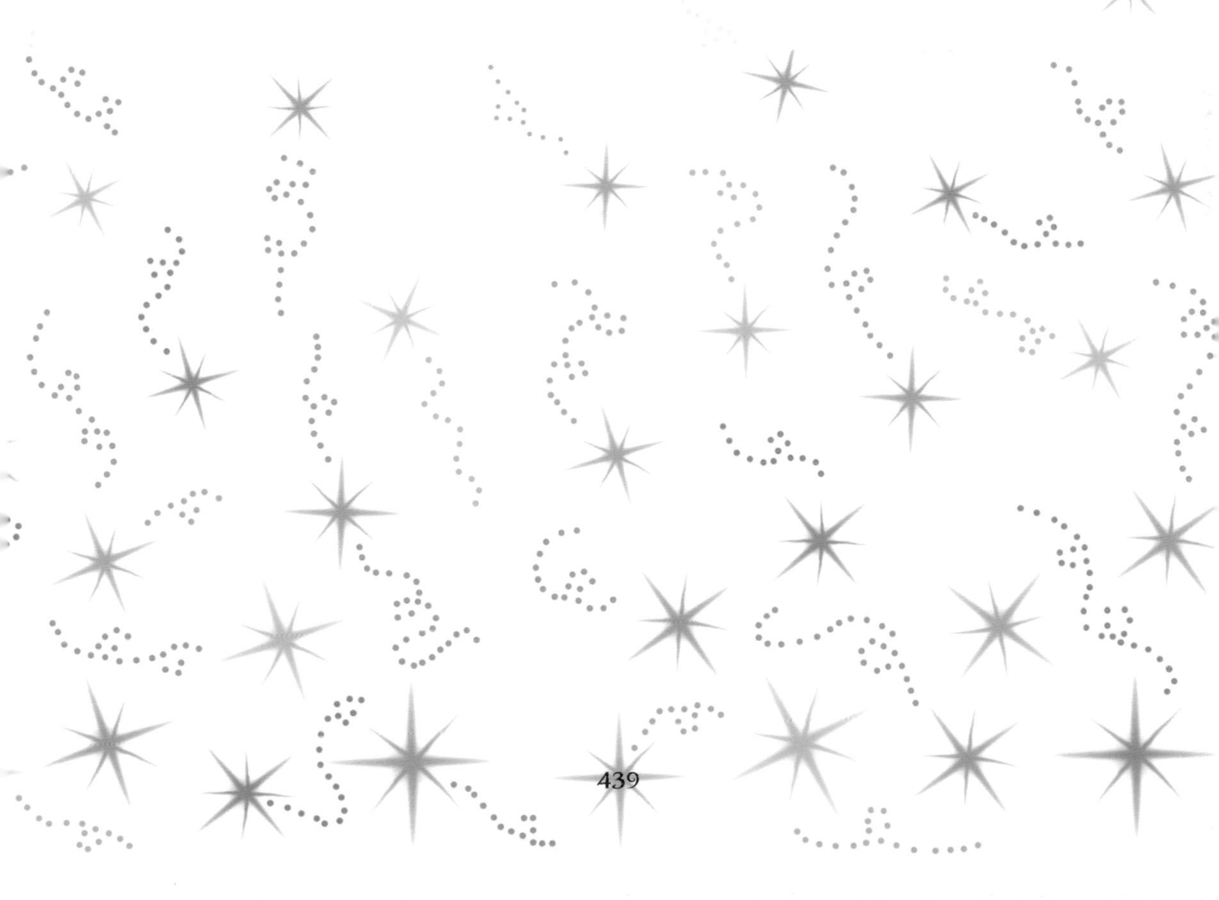

Introduction

Lyman Frank Baum (1856–1919) wrote The Wonderful Wizard of Oz *in 1900 as a bedtime story for his sons. Dorothy is carried in her house by a cyclone from Kansas to the land of Oz. When her house kills the Wicked Witch, Dorothy is hailed as a friend by the Munchkins. She is told that to find her way home she must ask for the help of the Wizard of Oz, who lives in the City of Emeralds at the end of the yellow brick road.*

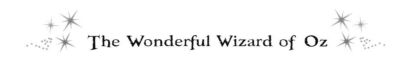

When Dorothy was left alone she began to feel hungry. So she went to the cupboard and cut herself some bread, which she spread with butter. She gave some to Toto, and taking a pail from the shelf she carried it down to the little brook and filled it with clear, sparkling water. Toto ran over to the trees and began to bark at the birds sitting there. Dorothy went to get him, and saw such delicious fruit hanging from the branches that she gathered some of it, finding it just what she wanted to help out her breakfast. Then she went back to the house, and having helped herself and Toto to a good drink of the cool, clear water, she set about making ready for the journey to the City of Emeralds.

Dorothy had only one other dress, but that happened to be clean and was hanging on a peg beside her bed. It was gingham, with checks of white and blue; and although the blue was somewhat faded with many washings, it was still a pretty frock.

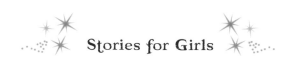

The girl washed herself carefully, dressed herself in the clean gingham, and tied her pink sunbonnet on her head. She took a little basket and filled it with bread from the cupboard, laying a white cloth over the top. Then she looked down at her feet and noticed how old and worn her shoes were.

"They surely will never do for a long journey, Toto," she said. And Toto looked up into her face with his little black eyes and wagged his tail to show he knew what she meant.

At that moment Dorothy saw lying on the table the silver shoes that had belonged to the Witch of the East.

"I wonder if they will fit me," she said to Toto. "They would be just the thing to take a long walk in, for they could not wear out."

She took off her old leather shoes and tried on the silver ones, which fitted her as well as if they had been made for her.

Finally she picked up her basket.

"Come along, Toto," she said. "We will go to the Emerald City and ask the Great Oz how to get back to Kansas again."

She closed the door, locked it, and put the key carefully in the pocket of her dress. And so, with Toto trotting along soberly behind her, she started on her journey.

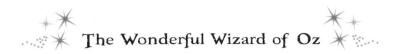

There were several roads nearby, but it did not take her long to find the one paved with yellow bricks. Within a short time she was walking briskly toward the Emerald City, her silver shoes tinkling merrily on the hard, yellow road. The sun shone bright and the birds sang sweetly, and Dorothy did not feel nearly so bad as you might think a little girl would who had been suddenly whisked away from her own country and set down in the midst of a strange land.

She was surprised, as she walked along, to see how pretty the country was about her. There were neat fences at the sides of the road, painted a dainty blue colour, and beyond them were fields of grain and vegetables in abundance. Evidently the Munchkins were good farmers and able to raise large crops. Once in a while she would pass a house, and the people came out to look at her and

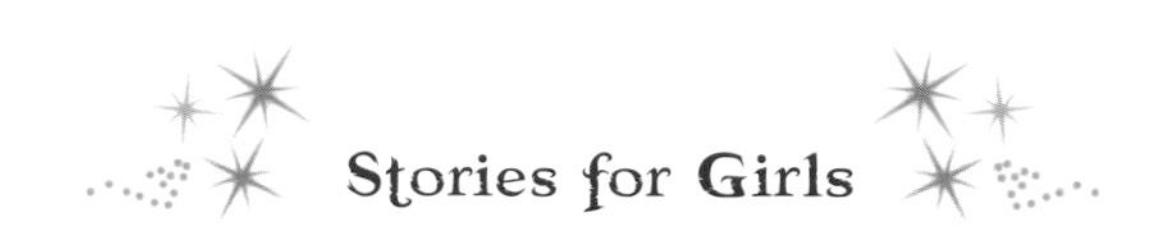

bow low as she went by; for everyone knew she had been the means of destroying the Wicked Witch and setting them free from bondage. The houses of the Munchkins were odd-looking dwellings, for each was round, with a big dome for a roof. All were painted blue, for in this country of the East, blue was the favourite colour.

Towards evening, when Dorothy was tired with her long walk and began to wonder where she should pass the night, she came to a house rather larger than the rest. On the green lawn before it many men and women were dancing. Five little fiddlers played as loudly as possible, and the people were laughing and singing, while a big table near by was loaded with delicious fruits and nuts, pies and cakes, and many other good things to eat.

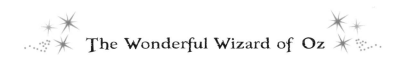

The people greeted Dorothy kindly, and invited her to supper and to pass the night with them; for this was the home of one of the richest Munchkins in the land, and his friends were gathered with him to celebrate their freedom from the bondage of the Wicked Witch.

Dorothy ate a hearty supper and was waited upon by the rich Munchkin himself, whose name was Boq. Then she sat upon a settee and watched the people dance.

When Boq saw her silver shoes he said, "You must be a great sorceress."

"Why?" asked the girl.

"Because you wear silver shoes and have killed the Wicked Witch. Besides, you have white in your frock, and only witches and sorceresses wear white."

"My dress is blue and white checked," said Dorothy, smoothing out the wrinkles in it.

"It is kind of you to wear that," said Boq. "Blue is the colour of the Munchkins, and white is the witch colour. So we know you are a friendly witch."

Dorothy did not know what to say to this, for all the people seemed to think her a witch, and she knew very well she was only

an ordinary little girl who had come by the chance of a cyclone into a strange land.

When she had tired watching the dancing, Boq led her into the house, where he gave her a room with a pretty bed in it. The sheets were made of blue cloth, and Dorothy slept soundly in them till morning, with Toto curled up on the blue rug beside her.

She ate a hearty breakfast, and watched a wee Munchkin baby, who played with Toto and pulled his tail and crowed and laughed in a way that greatly amused Dorothy. Toto was a fine curiosity to all the people, for they had never seen a dog before.

"How far is it to the Emerald City?" the girl asked.

"I do not know," answered Boq gravely, "for I have never been there. It is better for people to keep away from Oz, unless they have business with him. But it is a long way to the Emerald City, and it will take you many days. The country here is rich and pleasant, but you must pass through rough and dangerous places before you reach the end of your journey."

This worried Dorothy a little, but she knew that only the Great Oz could help her get to Kansas again, so she bravely resolved not to turn back.

She bade her friends goodbye, and again started along the road

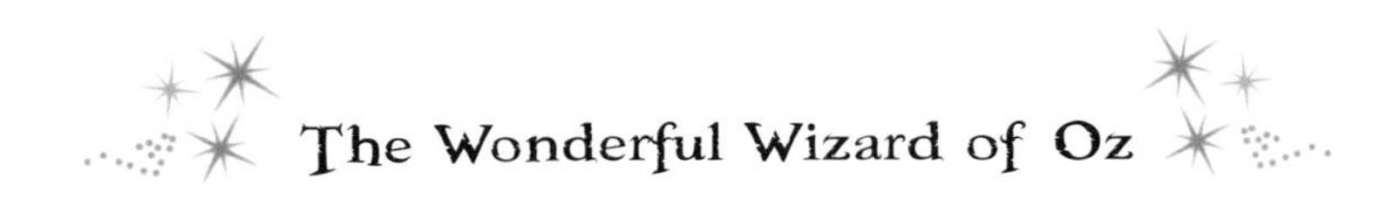

of yellow brick. When she had gone several miles she thought she would stop to rest, and so climbed to the top of the fence beside the road and sat down. There was a great cornfield beyond the fence, and not far away she saw a Scarecrow, placed high on a pole to keep the birds from the ripe corn.

Dorothy leaned her chin upon her hand and gazed thoughtfully at the Scarecrow. Its head was a small sack stuffed with straw, with eyes, nose, and mouth painted on it to represent a face. An old, pointed blue hat, that had belonged to some Munchkin, was perched on his head, and the rest of the figure was a blue suit of clothes, worn and faded, which had also been stuffed with straw. On the feet were some old boots with blue tops, such as every man wore in this country, and the figure was raised above the stalks of corn by means of the pole stuck up its back.

While Dorothy was looking earnestly into the queer, painted face of the Scarecrow, she was surprised to see one of the eyes slowly wink at her. She thought she must have been mistaken at first, for none of the scarecrows in Kansas ever wink; but presently the figure nodded its head to her in a friendly way. Then she climbed down from the fence and walked up to it, while Toto ran around the pole and barked.

"Good day," said the Scarecrow, in a rather husky voice.

"Did you speak?" asked the girl, in wonder.

"Certainly," answered the Scarecrow. "How do you do?"

"I'm pretty well, thank you," replied Dorothy politely. "How do you do?"

"I'm not feeling well," said the Scarecrow, with a smile, "for it is very tedious being perched up here night and day to scare away crows."

"Can't you get down?" asked Dorothy.

"No, for this pole is stuck up my back. If you will please take away the pole I shall be greatly obliged to you."

Dorothy reached up both arms and lifted the figure off the pole for, being stuffed with straw, it was quite light.

"Thank you very much," said the Scarecrow, when he had been set down on the ground. "I feel like a new man."

Dorothy was puzzled at this, for it sounded queer to hear a stuffed man speak, and to see him walk along beside her.

"Who are you?" asked the Scarecrow when he had stretched himself and yawned. "And where are you going?"

"My name is Dorothy," said the girl, "and I am going to the Emerald City, to ask the Great Oz to send me back to Kansas."

"Where is the Emerald City?" he inquired. "And who is Oz?"

"Why, don't you know?" she returned, in surprise.

"No, indeed. I don't know anything. You see, I am stuffed, so I have no brains at all," he answered sadly.

"Oh," said Dorothy, "I'm awfully sorry for you."

"Do you think," he asked, "if I go to the Emerald City with you, that Oz would give me some brains?"

"I cannot tell," she returned, "but you may come with me, if you like. If Oz will not give you any brains you will be no worse off than you are now."

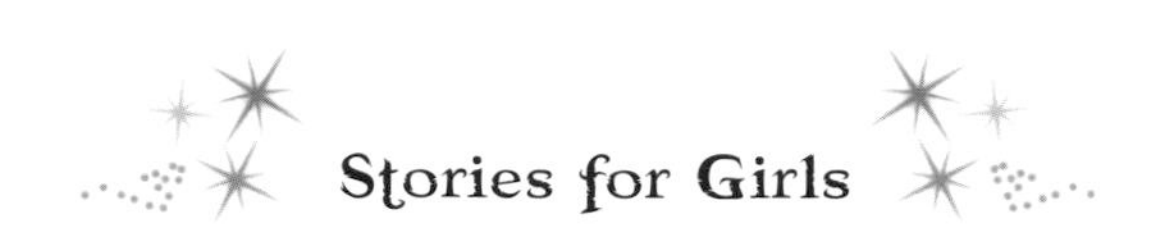

"That is true," said the Scarecrow. "You see," he continued confidentially, "I don't mind my legs and arms and body being stuffed, because I cannot get hurt. If anyone treads on my toes or sticks a pin into me, it doesn't matter, for I can't feel it. But I do not want people to call me a fool, and if my head stays stuffed with straw instead of with brains, how am I to know anything?"

"I understand how you feel," said the little girl, who was truly sorry for him. "If you will come with me I'll ask Oz to do all he can for you."

"Thank you," he answered gratefully.

They walked back to the road. Dorothy helped him over the fence, and they started along the path of yellow brick.

Toto did not like this addition to the party at first. He smelled around the stuffed man as if he suspected there might be a nest of rats in the straw, and he often growled in an unfriendly way at the Scarecrow.

"Don't mind Toto," said Dorothy to her new friend. "He never bites."

"Oh, I'm not afraid," replied the Scarecrow. "He can't hurt the straw. Do let me carry that basket for you. I shall not mind it, for I can't get tired. I'll tell you a secret," he continued, as he walked along. "There is only one thing in the world I am afraid of."

"What is that?" asked Dorothy; "the Munchkin farmer who made you?"

"No," answered the Scarecrow; "it's fire."

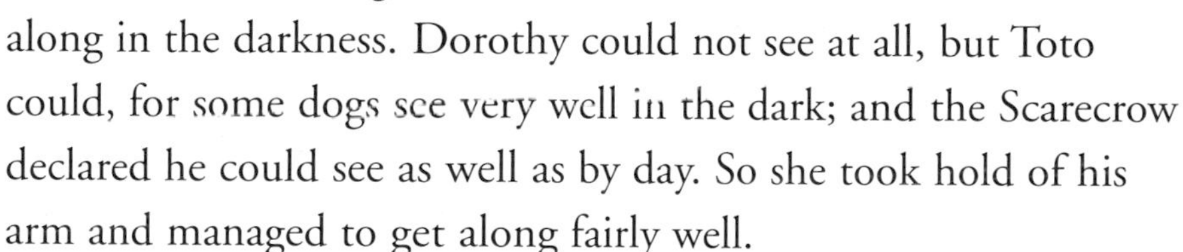

After many hours of walking the light faded away, and they found themselves stumbling along in the darkness. Dorothy could not see at all, but Toto could, for some dogs see very well in the dark; and the Scarecrow declared he could see as well as by day. So she took hold of his arm and managed to get along fairly well.

"If you see any house, or any place where we can pass the night," she said, "you must tell me; for it is very uncomfortable walking in the dark."

Soon after the Scarecrow stopped.

"I see a little cottage at the right of us," he said, "built of logs and branches. Shall we go there?"

"Yes, indeed," answered the child. "I am all tired out."

So the Scarecrow led her through the trees until they reached the cottage, and Dorothy entered and found a bed of dried leaves in one corner. She lay down at once, and with Toto beside her soon fell into a sound sleep. The Scarecrow, who was never tired, stood up in another corner and waited patiently until morning.

When Dorothy awoke the sun was shining through the trees and Toto had long been out chasing birds and squirrels. She sat up and looked around her. Scarecrow, still standing patiently in his corner, was waiting for her.

"We must go and search for water," she said to him.

"Why do you want water?" he asked.

"To wash my face clean after the dust of the road, and to drink, so the dry bread will not stick in my throat."

"It must be inconvenient to be made of flesh," said the Scarecrow thoughtfully, "for you must sleep, and eat and drink. However, you have brains, and it is worth a lot of bother to be able to think properly."

They left the cottage and walked through the trees until they found a little spring of clear water, where Dorothy drank and bathed and ate her breakfast. She saw there was not much bread left in the basket, and the girl was thankful the Scarecrow did not have to eat anything, for there was scarcely enough for herself and Toto for the day.

When she had finished her meal, and was about start walking again, she was startled to hear a deep groan nearby.

"What was that?" she asked timidly.

"I cannot imagine," replied the Scarecrow; "but we can go and see."

Just then another groan reached their ears, and the sound seemed to come from behind them. They turned and walked through the forest a few steps, when Dorothy discovered something shining in a ray of sunshine that fell between the trees. She ran to the place and then stopped short, with a cry of surprise.

One of the big trees had been partly chopped through, and standing beside it, with an uplifted axe in his hands, was a man made entirely of tin. His head and arms and legs were jointed upon his body, but he stood perfectly motionless, as if he could not stir at all.

Dorothy looked at him in amazement, and so did the Scarecrow, while Toto barked sharply and made a snap at the tin legs, which hurt his teeth.

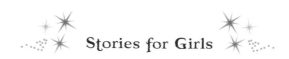

"Did you groan?" asked Dorothy.

"Yes," answered the tin man, "I did. I've been groaning for more than a year, and no one has ever heard me before."

"What can I do for you?" she inquired softly, for she was moved by the sad voice in which the man spoke.

"Get an oil-can and oil my joints," he answered. "They are rusted so badly that I cannot move them at all; if I am well oiled I shall soon be all right again. You will find an oil-can on a shelf in my cottage."

Dorothy at once ran back to the cottage and found the oil-can, and then she returned and asked anxiously, "Where are your joints?"

"Oil my neck, first," replied the Tin Woodman. So she oiled it, and as it was quite badly rusted the Scarecrow took hold of the tin head and moved it gently from side to side until it worked freely, and then the man could turn it himself.

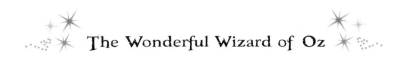

"Now oil the joints in my arms," he said. And Dorothy oiled them and the Scarecrow bent them carefully until they were quite free from rust and as good as new.

The Tin Woodman gave a sigh of satisfaction and lowered his axe, which he leaned against the tree.

"This is a great comfort," he said. "I have been holding that axe in the air ever since I rusted, and I'm glad to be able to put it down at last. Now, if you will oil the joints of my legs, I shall be all right once more."

So they oiled his legs until he could move them freely; and he thanked them again and again for his release, for he seemed a very polite creature, and very grateful.

"I might have stood there always if you had not come along," he said; "so you have certainly saved my life. How did you happen to be here?"

"We are on our way to the Emerald City to see the Great Oz," she answered, "and we stopped at your cottage to pass the night."

"Why do you wish to see Oz?" he asked.

"I want him to send me back to Kansas, and the Scarecrow

wants him to put a few brains into his head," she replied.

The Tin Woodman appeared to think deeply for a moment. Then he said, "Do you suppose Oz could give me a heart?"

"Why, I guess so," Dorothy answered. "It would be as easy as to give the Scarecrow brains."

"True," the Tin Woodman returned. "So, if you will allow me to join your party, I will also go to the Emerald City and ask Oz to help me."

"Come along," said the Scarecrow heartily, and Dorothy added that she would be pleased to have his company. So the Tin Woodman shouldered his axe and they all passed through the forest until they came to the road paved with yellow brick.

The Tin Woodman had asked Dorothy to put the oil-can in her basket. "For," he said, "if I should get caught in the rain, and rust again, I would need the oil-can badly."

It was a bit of good luck to have their new comrade join the party, for soon after they had begun their journey again they came to a place where the trees and branches grew so thick over the road that the travellers could not pass. But the Tin Woodman set to work with his axe and chopped so well that soon he cleared a passage for the entire party.

Dorothy was thinking so earnestly as they walked along that she did not notice when the Scarecrow stumbled into a hole and rolled over to the side of the road. Indeed he was obliged to call to her to help him up again.

"Why didn't you walk around the hole?" asked the Tin Woodman.

"I don't know enough," replied the Scarecrow cheerfully. "My head is stuffed with straw, you know, and that is why I am going to Oz to ask him for some brains."

"Oh, I see," said the Tin Woodman. "But, after all, brains are not the best things in the world."

"Have you any?" inquired the Scarecrow.

"No, my head is quite empty," answered the Woodman. "But once I had brains, and a heart also; so, having tried them both, I should much rather have a heart."

"And why is that?" asked the Scarecrow.

"I will tell you my story, and then you will know."

So, while they were walking through the forest, the Tin Woodman told the following story:

"I was born the son of a woodman who chopped down trees in the forest and sold the wood for a living. When I grew up, I too became a woodchopper, and after my father died I took care of my old mother as long as she lived. Then I made up my mind that instead of living alone I would marry, so that I might not be lonely.

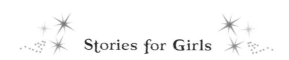

"There was one of the Munchkin girls who was so beautiful that I soon grew to love her with all my heart. She, on her part, promised to marry me as soon as I could earn enough money to build a better house for her; so I set to work harder than ever. But the girl lived with an old woman who did not want her to marry anyone, for she was so lazy she wished the girl to remain with her and do the cooking and the housework. So the old woman went to the Wicked Witch of the East, and promised her two sheep if she would prevent the marriage. Thereupon the Wicked Witch enchanted my axe, and when I was chopping away at my best one day, for I was anxious to get the new house and my wife as soon as possible, the axe slipped all at once and cut off my left leg.

"This at first seemed a great misfortune, for I knew a one-legged man could not do very well as a wood-chopper. So I went to a tinsmith and had him make me a new leg out of tin. The leg worked very well, once I was used to it. But my action angered the Wicked Witch of the East, for she had promised the old woman I should not marry the pretty Munchkin girl. When I began

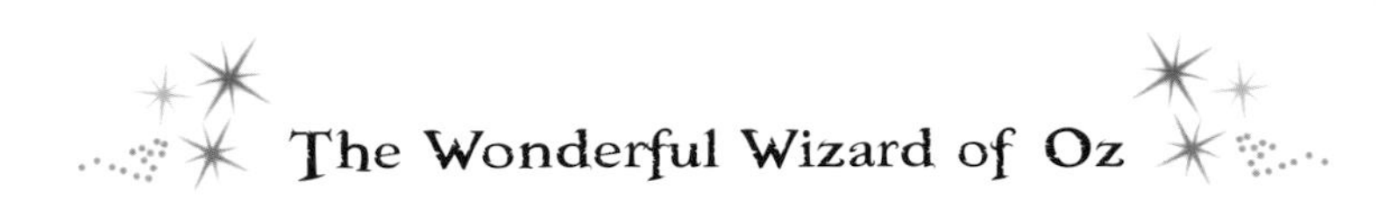

chopping again, my axe slipped and cut off my right leg. Again I went to the tinsmith, and again he made me a leg out of tin. After this the enchanted axe cut off my arms, one after the other; but, nothing daunted, I had them replaced with tin ones. The Wicked Witch then made the axe slip and cut off my head, and at first I thought that was the end of me. But the tinsmith happened to come along, and he made me a new head out of tin.

"I thought I had beaten the Wicked Witch then, and I worked harder than ever; but I little knew how cruel my enemy could be. She thought of a new way to kill my love for the beautiful Munchkin maiden, and made my axe slip again, so that it cut right through my body, splitting me into two halves. Once more the tinsmith came to my help and made me a body of tin, fastening my tin arms and legs and head to it, by means of joints, so that I could move around as well as ever. But, alas! I had now no heart, so that I lost all my love for the Munchkin girl, and did not care whether I married her or not. I suppose she is still living with the old woman, waiting for me to come after her.

"My body shone so brightly in the sun that I felt very proud of it and it did not matter now if my axe slipped, for it could not cut me. There was only one danger – that my joints would rust;

but I kept an oil-can in my cottage and took care to oil myself whenever I needed it. However, there came a day when I forgot to do this, and, being caught in a rainstorm, before I thought of the danger my joints had rusted, and I was left to stand in the woods until you came to help me. It was a terrible thing to undergo, but during the year I stood there I had time to think that the greatest loss I had known was the loss of my heart. While I was in love I was the happiest man on earth; but no one can love who has not a heart, and so I am resolved to ask Oz to give me one. If he does, I will go back to the Munchkin maiden and marry her."

Both Dorothy and the Scarecrow had been greatly interested in the story of the Tin Woodman, and now they knew why he was so anxious to get a new heart.

"All the same," said the Scarecrow, "I shall ask for brains instead of a heart; for a fool would not know what to do with a heart if he had one."

"I shall take the heart," returned the Tin Woodman; "for brains do not make one happy, and happiness is the best thing in the world."

Dorothy did not say anything, for she was puzzled to know which of her two friends was right, and she decided if she could only get back to Kansas and Aunt Em, it did not matter so much whether the Woodman had no brains and the Scarecrow no heart, or each got what he wanted.

What worried her most was that the bread was nearly gone, and another meal for herself and Toto would empty the basket. To be sure neither the Woodman nor the Scarecrow ever ate anything, but she was not made of tin nor straw.

All this time Dorothy and her companions had been walking through the thick woods. The road was still paved with yellow brick, but these were much covered by dried branches and dead leaves from the trees, and the walking was not at all good.

There were few birds in this part of the forest, for birds love the open country where there is plenty of sunshine. But now and then there came a deep growl from some wild animal hidden among the trees. These sounds made the little girl's heart beat fast, for she did not know what made them; but Toto knew, and he walked close to Dorothy's side, and did not even bark in return.

"How long will it be," the child asked of the Tin Woodman, "before we are out of the forest?"

"I cannot tell," was the answer, "for I have never been to the Emerald City. But my father went there once, when I was a boy, and he said it was a long journey through a dangerous country, although nearer to the city where Oz dwells the country is beautiful. But I am not afraid so long as I have my oil-can, and nothing can hurt the Scarecrow, while you bear upon your forehead the mark of the Good Witch's kiss, and that will protect you from harm."

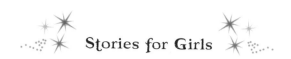

"But Toto!" said the girl anxiously. "What will protect him?"

"We must protect him ourselves if he is in danger," replied the Tin Woodman.

Just as he spoke there came from the forest a terrible roar, and the next moment a great Lion bounded into the road. With one blow of his paw he sent the Scarecrow spinning over and over to the edge of the road, and then he struck at the Tin Woodman with his sharp claws. But, to the Lion's surprise, he could make no impression on the tin, although the Woodman fell over in the road and lay still.

Little Toto, now that he had an enemy to face, ran barking toward the Lion, and the great beast had opened his mouth to bite the dog, when Dorothy, fearing Toto would be killed, and heedless of danger, rushed forward and slapped the Lion upon his nose as hard as she could, while she cried out:

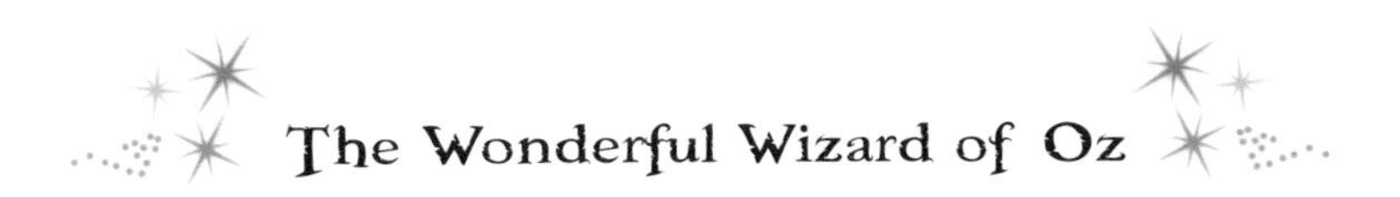

"Don't you dare to bite Toto! You ought to be ashamed of yourself, a big beast like you, to bite a poor little dog!"

"I didn't bite him," said the Lion, as he rubbed his nose with his paw where Dorothy had hit it.

"No, but you tried to," she retorted. "You are nothing but a big coward."

"I know it," said the Lion, hanging his head in shame. "I've always known it. But how can I help it?"

"I don't know, I'm sure. To think of your striking a stuffed man, like the poor Scarecrow!"

"Is he stuffed?" asked the Lion in surprise, as he watched her pick up the Scarecrow and set him upon his feet, while she patted him into shape.

"Of course he's stuffed," replied Dorothy, who was still angry.

"That's why he went over so easily," remarked the Lion. "It astonished me to see him

whirl around so. Is the other one stuffed also?"

"No," said Dorothy, "he's made of tin." And she helped the Woodman up again.

"That's why he nearly blunted my claws," said the Lion. "When they scratched against the tin it made a cold shiver run down my back. What is that little animal you are so tender of?"

"He is my dog, Toto," answered Dorothy.

"Is he made of tin, or stuffed?" asked the Lion.

"Neither. He's a – a meat dog," said the girl.

"Oh! He's a curious animal and seems remarkably small, now that I look at him. No one would think of biting such a little thing, except a coward like me," continued the Lion sadly.

"What makes you a coward?" asked Dorothy, looking at the great beast in wonder, for he was as big as a small horse.

"It's a mystery," replied the Lion. "I suppose I was born that way. All the other animals in the forest naturally expect me to be brave, for the lion is everywhere thought to be the 'king of beasts'. I learned that if I roared very loudly every living thing was frightened and got out of my way. Whenever I've met a man I've been awfully scared; but I just roared at him, and he has always run away as fast as he could go. If the elephants and the tigers and the bears had ever tried to fight me, I should have run myself – I'm such a coward; but just as soon as they hear me roar they all try to get away from me, and of course I let them go."

"But that isn't right. The 'king of beasts' shouldn't be a coward," said the Scarecrow.

"I know it," returned the Lion, wiping a tear from his eye with the tip of his tail. "It is my great sorrow, and makes my life very unhappy. But whenever there is danger, my heart begins to beat fast."

"Perhaps you have heart disease," said the Tin Woodman.

"It may be," said the Lion.

"If you have," continued the Tin Woodman, "you ought to be glad, for it proves you have a heart. For my part, I have no heart."

"Perhaps," said the Lion thoughtfully, "if I had no heart I should not be a coward."

"Have you brains?" asked the Scarecrow.

"I suppose so. I've never looked to see," replied the Lion.

"I am going to the Great Oz to ask him to give me some," remarked the Scarecrow, "for my head is stuffed with straw."

"And I am going to ask him to give me a heart," said the Woodman.

"And I am going to ask him to send Toto and me back to Kansas," added Dorothy.

"Do you think Oz could give me courage?" asked the Cowardly Lion.

"Just as easily as he could give me brains," said the Scarecrow.

"Or give me a heart," said the Tin Woodman.

"Or send me back to Kansas," said Dorothy.

"Then, if you don't mind, I'll go with you," said the Lion, "for my life is simply unbearable without a bit of courage."

"You will be very welcome," answered Dorothy, "for you will help to keep away the other wild beasts. It seems to me they must be more cowardly than you are if they allow you to scare them."

"They really are," said the Lion, "but that doesn't make me any braver, and as long as I know myself to be a coward I shall be unhappy."

So once more the little company set off upon the journey, the Lion walking with stately strides at Dorothy's side. Toto did not approve this new comrade at first, for he could not forget how nearly he had been crushed between the Lion's great jaws. But after a time he became more at ease, and presently Toto and the Cowardly Lion had grown to be good friends.

Five Children and It

An extract
by Edith Nesbit

Introduction

Five Children and It *by Edith Nesbit was published in 1902. Five children are left in the country while their parents are away. They discover a 'sand-fairy' (the Psammead), who is brown and hairy with bat's ears and snail's eyes, and seems to be permanently grumpy. He grants them daily wishes which are quite often disastrous but which are fortunately unmade at sunset.*

Five Children and It

Anthea woke in the morning from a very real sort of dream, in which she was walking in the Zoological Gardens on a pouring wet day without any umbrella. The animals seemed desperately unhappy because of the rain, and were all growling gloomily. When she awoke, both the growling and the rain went on just the same. The growling was the heavy regular breathing of her sister Jane, who had a slight cold and was still asleep. The rain fell in slow drops onto Anthea's face from the wet corner of a towel which her brother Robert was gently squeezing the water out of, to wake her up, as he now explained.

"Oh, drop it!" she said rather crossly; so he did, for he was not a brutal brother, though very ingenious in apple-pie beds, booby-traps, original methods of awakening sleeping relatives, and the other little accomplishments which made home happy.

"I had such a funny dream," Anthea began.

"So did I," said Jane, wakening suddenly and without warning. "I dreamed we found a Sand-fairy in the gravel-pits, and it said it was a Psammead, and we might have a new wish every day, and—"

"But that's what I dreamed," said Robert; "I was just going to tell you – and we had the first wish directly it said so. And I dreamed you girls were donkeys enough to ask for us all to be beautiful as the day, and we jolly well were, and it was perfectly beastly."

"But can different people all dream the same thing?" said Anthea, sitting up in bed, "because I dreamed all that as well as about the Zoo and the rain. And Baby didn't know us in my dream, and the servants shut us out of the house because the radiantness of our beauty was such a complete disguise, and—"

The voice of the eldest brother sounded from across the landing.

"Come on Robert," it said, "you'll be late for breakfast again – unless you mean to shirk your bath like you did on Tuesday."

"I say, come here a sec," Robert replied. "I didn't shirk it; I had it after brekker in father's dressing-room, because ours was emptied away."

Cyril appeared in the doorway, partially clothed.

"Look here," said Anthea, "we've all had such an odd dream. We've all dreamed we found a Sand-fairy."

Her voice died away before Cyril's contemptuous glance. "Dream?" he said; "You little sillies, it's true. I tell you it all happened. That's why I'm so keen on being down early. We'll go up there directly after brekker, and have another wish. Only we'll make up our minds, solid, before we go, what it is we want, and no one must ask for anything unless the others agree first. No more peerless beauties for this child, thank you. Not if I know it!"

The other three dressed, with their mouths open. If all that dream about the Sand-fairy was real, this real dressing seemed very like a dream, the girls thought. Jane felt that Cyril was right, but Anthea was not sure, till after they had seen Martha and heard her full and plain reminders about their naughty conduct the day before. Then Anthea was sure. "Because," said she, "servants never dream anything but the things in dream-books, like snakes and oysters and going to a wedding – that means a funeral, and snakes are a false female friend, and oysters are babies."

"Talking of babies," said Cyril, "where's the Lamb?"

"Martha's going to take him to Rochester to see her cousins. Mother said she might. She's dressing him now," said Jane, "in his very best coat and hat. Bread and butter, please."

"She seems to like taking him too," said Robert in a tone of wonder.

"Servants do like taking babies to see their relations," Cyril said; "I've noticed it before – especially in their best things."

"I expect they pretend they're their own babies, and that they're not servants at all, but married to noble dukes of high degree, and they say the babies are the little dukes and duchesses," Jane suggested dreamily, taking more marmalade. "I expect that's what Martha'll say to her cousin. She'll enjoy herself most frightfully."

"She won't enjoy herself most frightfully carrying our infant duke to Rochester," said Robert; "not if she's anything like me, she won't."

"Fancy walking to Rochester with the Lamb on your back! Oh, crikey!" said Cyril in full agreement.

"She's going by carrier," said Jane. "Let's see them off, then we shall have done a polite and kindly act, and we shall be quite sure we've got rid of them for the day."

So they did. Martha wore her Sunday dress of two shades of purple, so tight in the chest that it made her stoop, and her blue hat with the pink cornflowers and white ribbon. She had a yellow-lace collar with a green bow. And the Lamb had indeed his very best cream-coloured silk coat and hat. It was a smart party that the carrier's cart picked up at the Cross Roads. When its white tilt and red wheels had slowly vanished in a swirl of chalkdust, Cyril said:

"And now for the Psammead!"

And off they went.

As they went they decided on the wish they would ask for. Although they were all in a great hurry they did not try to climb down the sides of the gravel-pit, but went round by the safe lower road, as if they had been carts. They had made a ring of stones round the place where the Sand-fairy had disappeared, so they easily found the spot. The sun was burning and bright, and the sky was deep blue and without a cloud. The sand was very hot to touch.

"Suppose it was only a dream, after all," Robert said as the boys uncovered their spades from the sand-heap where they had buried them and began to dig.

"Suppose you were a sensible chap," said Cyril; "one's quite as likely as the other!"

"Suppose you kept a civil tongue in your head," Robert snapped.

"Suppose we girls take a turn," said Jane, laughing. "You boys seem to be getting very warm."

"Suppose you don't come shoving your silly oar in," said Robert, who was now warm indeed.

"We won't," said Anthea quickly. "Robert dear, don't be so grumpy – we won't say a word, you shall be the one to speak to the Fairy and tell him what we've decided to wish for. You'll say it much better than we shall."

"Suppose you drop being a little humbug," said Robert, but not crossly. "Look out – dig with your hands, now!"

So they did, and presently uncovered the spider-shaped brown hairy body, long arms and legs, bat's ears and snail's eyes of the Sand-fairy himself. Everyone drew a deep breath of satisfaction, for now of course it couldn't have been a dream.

The Psammead sat up and shook the sand out of its fur.

"How's your left whisker this morning?" said Anthea politely.

"Nothing to boast of," said it; "it had rather a restless night. But thank you for asking."

"I say," said Robert, "do you feel up to giving wishes today, because we very much want an extra besides the regular one? The extra's a very little one," he added reassuringly.

"Humph!" said the Sand-fairy. (If you read this story aloud, please pronounce 'humph' exactly as it is spelt, for that is how he said it.) "Humph! Do you know, until I heard you being disagreeable to each other just over my head, and so loud too,

I really quite thought I had dreamed you all. I do have very odd dreams sometimes."

"Do you?" Jane hurried to say, so as to get away from the subject of disagreeableness. "I wish," she added politely, "you'd tell us about your dreams – they must be awfully interesting."

"Is that the day's wish?" said the Sand-fairy, yawning.

Cyril muttered something about 'just like a girl,' and the rest stood silent. If they said 'Yes,' then goodbye to the other wishes they had decided to ask for. If they said 'No,' it would be very rude, and they had all been taught manners, and had learned a little too, which is not at all the same thing. A sigh of relief broke from all lips when the Sand-fairy said:

"If I do I shan't have strength to give you a second wish; not even good tempers, or common sense, or manners, or little things like that."

"We don't want you to put yourself out at all about these things, we can manage them quite well ourselves," said Cyril eagerly; while the others looked guiltily at each other, and wished the Fairy would not keep all on about good tempers, but give them one good rowing if it wanted to, and then have done with it.

"Well," said the Psammead, putting out his long snail's eyes so suddenly that one of them nearly went into the round boy's eye of Robert, "let's have the little wish first."

"We don't want the servants to notice the gifts you give us."

"Are kind enough to give us," said Anthea in a whisper.

"Are kind enough to give us, I mean," said Robert.

The Fairy swelled himself out a bit, let his breath go, and said "I've done that for you – it was quite easy. People don't notice things much, anyway. What's the next wish?"

"We want," said Robert slowly, "to be rich beyond the dreams of something or other."

"Avarice," said Jane.

"So it is," said the Fairy unexpectedly. "But it won't do you much good, that's one comfort," it muttered to itself. "Come – I can't go beyond dreams, you know! How much do you want, and will you have it in gold or notes?"

"Gold, please – and millions of it."

"This gravel-pit full be enough?" said the Fairy in an offhand manner.

"Oh yes!"

"Then get out before I begin, or you'll be buried alive in it."

It made its skinny arms so long, and waved them so

frighteningly, that the children ran as hard as they could towards the road by which carts used to come to the gravel-pits. Only Anthea had presence of mind enough to shout a timid "Good morning, I hope your whisker will be better tomorrow," as she ran.

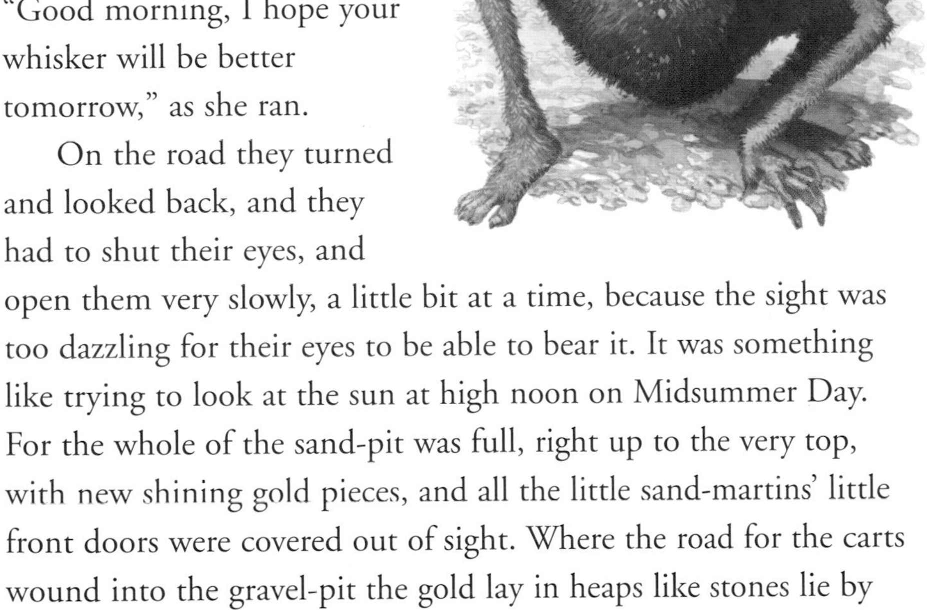

On the road they turned and looked back, and they had to shut their eyes, and open them very slowly, a little bit at a time, because the sight was too dazzling for their eyes to be able to bear it. It was something like trying to look at the sun at high noon on Midsummer Day. For the whole of the sand-pit was full, right up to the very top, with new shining gold pieces, and all the little sand-martins' little front doors were covered out of sight. Where the road for the carts wound into the gravel-pit the gold lay in heaps like stones lie by the roadside, and a great bank of shining gold shelved down from where it lay flat and smooth between the tall sides of the gravel-pit.

And all the gleaming heap was minted gold. And on the sides and edges of these countless coins the midday sun shone and sparkled, and glowed and gleamed till the quarry looked like the mouth of a smelting furnace, or one of the fairy halls that you see sometimes in the sky at sunset.

The children stood with their mouths open, and no one said a word.

At last Robert stooped and picked up one of the loose coins from the edge of the heap by the cart-road, and looked at it. He looked on both sides. Then he said in a low voice, quite different to his own, "It's not sovereigns."

"It's gold, anyway," said Cyril. And now they all began to talk at once. They all picked up the golden treasure by handfuls and let it run through their fingers like water, and the chink it made as it fell was wonderful music. At first they quite forgot to think of spending the money, it was so nice to play with. Jane sat down between two heaps of gold, and Robert began to bury her, as you bury your father in sand when you are at the seaside and he has gone to sleep on the beach with his newspaper over his face. But Jane was not half buried before she cried out, "Oh, stop, it's too heavy! It hurts!"

Robert said "Bosh!" and went on.

"Let me out, I tell you," cried Jane, and was taken out, very white, and trembling a little.

"You've no idea what it's like," she said; "it's like stones on you – or like chains."

"Look here," Cyril said, "if this is to do us any good, it's no good our staying gasping at it like this. Let's fill our pockets and go and buy things. Don't you forget, it won't last after sunset. I wish we'd asked the Psammead why things don't turn to stone. Perhaps this will. I'll tell you what, there's a pony and cart in the village."

"Do you want to buy that?" asked Jane.

"No, silly – we'll hire it. And then we'll go to Rochester and buy heaps and heaps of things. Look here, let's each take as much as we can carry. But it's not sovereigns. They've got a man's head on one side and a thing like the ace of spades on the other. Fill your pockets with it, I tell you, and come along. You can jaw as we go – if you must jaw."

Cyril sat down and began to fill his pockets.

"You made fun of me for getting father to have nine pockets in my Norfolks," said he, "but now you see!"

They did. For when Cyril had filled his nine pockets and his handkerchief and the space between himself and his shirt front with the gold coins, he had to stand up. But he staggered, and had to sit down again in a hurry.

"Throw out some of the cargo," said Robert. "You'll sink the ship, old chap. That comes of nine pockets."

And Cyril had to.

Then they set off to walk to the village. It was more than a mile, and the road was very dusty indeed, and the sun seemed to get hotter and hotter, and the gold in their pockets got heavier and heavier.

It was Jane who said, "I don't see how we're to spend it all. There must be thousands of pounds among the lot of us. I'm going to leave some of mine behind this stump in the hedge. And directly we get to the village we'll buy some biscuits – I know it's long past dinner-time."

She took out a handful or two of gold and hid it in the hollows of an old hornbeam. "How round and yellow they are," she said. "Don't you wish they were gingerbread nuts and we were going to eat them?"

"Well, they're not, and we're not," said Cyril. "Come on!"

But they came on heavily and wearily. Before they reached the village, more than one stump in the hedge concealed its little hoard of hidden treasure. Yet they reached the village with about twelve hundred guineas in their pockets. But in spite of this inside wealth they looked quite ordinary outside, and no one would have thought they could have more than a half-crown each at the outside. The haze of heat, the blue of the wood smoke, made a sort of dim misty cloud over the red roofs of the village. The four sat down heavily on the first bench they came to. It happened to be outside the Blue Boar Inn.

It was decided that Cyril should go into the Blue Boar and ask for ginger beer, because, as Anthea said, "It is not wrong for men to go into public houses, only for children. And Cyril is nearer to being a man than us, because he is the eldest." So he went. The others sat in the sun and waited.

"Oh, hats, how hot it is!" said Robert. "Dogs put their tongues out when they're hot; I wonder if it would cool us at all to put out ours?"

"We might try," Jane said; and they all put their tongues out as far as ever they could go, so that it quite stretched their throats, but it only seemed to make them thirstier than ever, besides annoying everyone who went by. So they took their tongues in again, just as Cyril came back with the ginger beer.

"I had to pay for it out of my own two-and-sevenpence, though, that I was going to buy rabbits with," he said. "They wouldn't change the gold. And when I pulled out a handful the man just laughed and said it was card-counters. And I got some sponge cakes too, out of a glass jar on the bar counter. And some biscuits with caraways in."

The sponge-cakes were both soft and dry and the biscuits were dry too, and yet soft, which biscuits ought not to be. But the ginger beer made up for everything.

"It's my turn now to try to buy something with the money," Anthea said; "I'm next eldest. Where is the pony-cart kept?"

It was at The Chequers, and Anthea went in the back way to the yard, because they all knew that little girls ought not to go into the bars of public houses.

"He'll be ready in a brace of shakes, he says," she remarked, when she came out. "And he's to have one sovereign – or whatever it is – to drive us in to Rochester and back, besides waiting there till we've got everything we want. I think I managed very well."

"You think yourself jolly clever, I daresay," said Cyril moodily. "How did you do it?"

"I wasn't jolly clever enough to go taking handfuls of money out of my pocket, to make it seem cheap, anyway," she retorted. "I just found a young man doing something to a horse's leg with a sponge and a pail. And I held out one sovereign, and I said, 'Do you know what this is?' He said, 'No,' and he'd call his father. And the old man came, and he said it was a spade guinea; and he said was it my own to do as I liked with, and I said 'Yes'; and I asked about the pony-cart, and I said he could have the guinea if he'd drive us in to Rochester. And his name is S Crispin. And he said, 'Right oh'."

It was a new sensation to be driven in a smart pony-trap along pretty country roads; it was very pleasant too (which is not always the case with new sensations), quite apart from the beautiful plans of spending the money that each child made as they went along, silently of course and quite to itself, for they felt it would never

have done to let the old innkeeper hear them talk in the affluent sort of way they were thinking in. The old man put them down by the bridge at their request.

"If you were going to buy a carriage and horses, where would you go?" asked Cyril, as if he were only asking for the sake of something to say.

"Billy Peasemarsh, at the Saracen's Head," said the old man promptly. "Though all forbid I should recommend any man where it's a question of horses, no more than I'd take anybody else's recommending if I was a-buying one. But if your pa's thinking of a turnout of any sort, there ain't a straighter man in Rochester, nor a civiller spoken, than Billy, though I says it."

"Thank you," said Cyril. "The Saracen's Head."

And now the children began to see one of the laws of nature turn upside down and stand on its head like an acrobat. Any grown-up person would tell you that money is hard to get and easy to spend. But the fairy money had been easy to get, and spending it was not only hard, it was almost impossible. The tradespeople of Rochester seemed to shrink, to a trades-person, from the glittering fairy gold ('furrin money' they called it, for the most part).

To begin with, Anthea, who had had the misfortune to sit on her hat earlier in the day, wished to buy another. She chose a very beautiful one, trimmed with pink roses and the blue breasts of peacocks. It was marked in the window, 'Paris Model, three guineas.'

"I'm glad," she said, "because, if it says guineas, it means guineas, and not sovereigns, which we haven't got."

But when she took three of the spade guineas in her hand, which was by this time rather dirty owing to her not having put on gloves before going to the gravel-pit, the black-silk young lady in the shop looked very hard at her, and went and whispered something to an older and uglier lady, also in black silk, and then they gave her back the money and said it was not current coin.

"It's good money," said Anthea, "and it's my own."

"I daresay," said the lady, "but it's not the kind of money that's fashionable now, and we don't care about taking it."

"I believe they think we've stolen it," said Anthea, rejoining the others in the street; "if we had gloves they wouldn't think we were so dishonest. It's my hands being so dirty fills their minds with doubts."

So they chose a humble shop, and the girls bought cotton gloves, the kind at sixpence three-farthings, but when they offered a guinea the woman looked at it through her spectacles and said she had no change; so the gloves had to be paid for out of Cyril's two-and-sevenpence that he meant to buy rabbits with, and so had the green imitation crocodile-skin purse at ninepence-halfpenny which had been bought at the same time. They tried several more shops, the kinds where you buy toys and scent, and silk handkerchiefs and books, and fancy boxes of stationery, and photographs of objects of interest in the vicinity.

But nobody cared to change a guinea that day in Rochester, and as they went from shop to shop they got dirtier and dirtier, and their hair got more and more untidy, and Jane slipped and fell down on a part of the road where a water-cart had just gone by. Also they got very hungry, but they found no one would give them anything to eat for their guineas. After trying two pastry-cooks in vain, they became so hungry, perhaps from the smell of the cake in the shops, as Cyril suggested, that they formed a plan of campaign in whispers and carried it out in desperation. They marched into a third pastry-cook's – Beale his name was, – and before the people behind the counter could interfere each child had seized three new penny buns, clapped the three together between its dirty hands, and taken a big bite out of the triple sandwich. Then they stood at bay, with the twelve buns in their hands and their mouths very full indeed. The shocked pastry-cook bounded round the corner.

"Here," said Cyril, speaking as distinctly as he could, and holding out the guinea he got ready before entering the shop, "pay yourself out of that."

Mr Beale snatched the coin, bit it, and put it into his pocket. "Off you go," he said, brief and stern like the man in the song.

"But the change?" said Anthea, who had a saving mind.

"Change!" said the man. "I'll change you! Hout you goes; and you may think yourselves lucky I don't send for the police to find out where you got it!"

In the Castle Gardens the millionaires finished the buns, and though the curranty softness of these were delicious, and acted like a charm in raising the spirits of the party, yet even the stoutest heart quailed at the thought of venturing to sound Mr Billy Peasemarsh at the Saracen's Head on the subject of a horse and carriage. The boys would have given up the idea, but Jane was always a hopeful child, and Anthea generally an obstinate one, and their earnestness prevailed.

The whole party, by this time indescribably dirty, therefore betook itself to the Saracen's Head. The yard-method of attack having been successful at The Chequers was tried again here. Mr Peasemarsh was in the yard, and Robert opened the business in these terms:

"They tell me you have a lot of horses and carriages to sell." It had been agreed that Robert should be spokesman, because in books it is always the gentlemen who buy horses, and not ladies, and Cyril had had his go at the Blue Boar.

"They tell you true, young man," said Mr Peasemarsh. He was a long, lean man, with very blue eyes and a tight mouth and narrow lips.

"We should like to buy some, please," said Robert politely.

"I daresay you would."

"Will you show us a few, please? To choose from."

"Who are you a-kidden of?" inquired Mr Billy Peasemarsh. "Was you sent here of a message?"

"I tell you," said Robert, "we want to buy some horses and carriages, and a man told us you were straight and civil spoken, but I shouldn't wonder if he was mistaken."

"Upon my sacred!" said Mr Peasemarsh. "Shall I trot the whole stable out for your Honour's worship to see? Or shall I send round to the Bishop's to see if he's a nag or two to dispose of?"

"Please do," said Robert, "if it's not too much trouble. It would be very kind of you."

Mr Peasemarsh put his hands in his pockets and laughed, and they did not like the way he did it. Then he shouted "Willum!"

A stooping ostler appeared in a stable door.

"Here, Willum, come and look at this 'ere young dook! Wants to buy the whole stud, lock, stock, and bar'l. And ain't got tuppence in his pocket to bless hisself with, I'll go bail!"

Willum's eyes followed his master's pointing thumb with contemptuous interest.

"Do'e, for sure?" he said.

But Robert spoke, though both the girls were now pulling at his jacket and begging him to 'come along'. He spoke, and he was very angry; he said:

"I'm not a young duke, and I never pretended to be. And as for tuppence – what do you call this?" And before the others could stop him he had pulled out two fat handfuls of shining guineas, and held them out for Mr Peasemarsh to look at. He did look. He snatched one up in his finger and thumb. He bit it, and Jane expected him to say, 'The best horse in my stables is at your service.' But the others knew better. Still it was a blow, even to the most desponding, when he said shortly:

"Willum, shut the yard doors," and Willum grinned and went to shut them.

"Good afternoon," said Robert hastily; "we shan't buy any of your horses now, whatever you say, and I hope it'll be a lesson to you." He had seen a little side gate open, and was moving towards it as he spoke. But Billy Peasemarsh put himself in the way.

"Not so fast, you young off-scouring!" he said. "Willum, fetch the pleece."

Willum went. The children stood huddled together like frightened sheep, and Mr Peasemarsh spoke to them till the 'pleece' arrived. He said many things. Among other things he said:

"Nice lot you are, aren't you, coming tempting honest men with your guineas!"

"They are guineas," said Cyril boldly.

"Oh, of course we don't know all about that, no more we don't – oh no – course not! And dragging little gells into it too. 'Ere – I'll let the gells go if you'll come along to the pleece quiet."

"We won't be let go," said Jane heroically; "not without the boys. It's our money just as much as theirs, you wicked old man."

"Where'd you get it, then?" said the man, softening slightly, which was not at all what the boys expected when Jane began to call names.

Jane cast a silent glance of agony at the others.

"Lost your tongue, eh? Got it fast enough when it's for calling names with. Come, speak up. Where'd you get it?"

"Out of the gravel-pit," said truthful Jane.

"Next article," said the man.

"I tell you we did," Jane said. "There's a fairy there – all over brown fur – with ears like a bat's and eyes like a snail's, and he gives you a wish a day, and they all come true."

"Touched in the head, eh?" said the man in a low voice, "All the more shame to you boys dragging the poor afflicted child into your sinful burglaries."

"She's not mad; it's true," said Anthea. "There is a fairy. If I ever see him again I'll wish for something for you; at least I would if vengeance wasn't wicked – so there!"

"Lor' lumme," said Billy Peasemarsh, "if there ain't another on 'em!"

And now Willum came back, with a spiteful grin on his face, and at his back a policeman, with whom Mr Peasemarsh spoke long in a hoarse earnest whisper.

"I daresay you're right," said the policeman at last. "Anyway, I'll take 'em up on a charge of unlawful possession, pending inquiries. And the magistrate will deal with the case. Send the

afflicted ones to a home, as likely as not, and the boys to a reformatory. Now then, come along, youngsters! No use making a fuss. You bring the gells along, Mr Peasemarsh, sir, and I'll shepherd the boys."

Speechless with rage and horror, the four children were driven along the streets of Rochester. Tears of anger and shame blinded them, so that when Robert ran right into a passer-by he did not recognise her till a well-known voice said, "Well, if ever I did. Oh, Master Robert, whatever have you been a-doing of now?"

And another voice, quite as well known, said, "Panty; want go own Panty!"

They had run into Martha and the baby!

Martha behaved admirably. She refused to believe a word of the policeman's story, or of Mr Peasemarsh's either, even when they made Robert turn out his pockets in an archway and show the guineas.

"I don't see nothing," she said. "You've gone out of your senses, you two! There ain't any gold there – only the poor child's hands, all over crock and dirt, and like the very chimbley. Oh, that I should ever see the day!"

And the children thought this very noble of Martha, even if rather wicked, till they remembered how the Fairy had promised that the servants should never notice any of the fairy gifts. So of course Martha couldn't see the gold, and so was only speaking the truth, and that was quite right, of course, but not extra noble.

It was getting dusk when they reached the police station. The policeman told his tale to an inspector, who sat in a large bare room with a thing like a clumsy nursery-fender at one end to put prisoners in. Robert wondered whether it was a cell or a dock.

"Produce the coins, officer," said the inspector.

"Turn out your pockets," said the constable.

Cyril desperately plunged his hands in his pockets, stood still a moment, and then began to laugh – an odd sort of laugh that hurt, and that felt much more like crying. His pockets were empty. So were the pockets of the others. For of course at sunset all the fairy gold had vanished away.

"Turn out your pockets, and stop that noise," said the inspector.

Cyril turned out his pockets, every one of the nine which enriched his Norfolk suit. And every pocket was empty.

"Well!" said the inspector.

"I don't know how they done it – artful little beggars! They walked in front of me the 'ole way, so as for me to keep my eye on them and not to attract a crowd and obstruct the traffic."

"It's very remarkable," said the inspector, frowning.

"If you've quite done a-browbeating of the innocent children," said Martha, "I'll hire a private carriage and we'll drive home to their papa's mansion. You'll hear about this again young man! I told you they hadn't got any gold, when you were pretending to see it in their poor helpless hands. It's early in the day for a constable on duty not to be able to trust his own eyes. As to the other one, the less said the better; he keeps the Saracen's Head, and he knows best what his liquor's like."

"Take them away, for goodness' sake," said the inspector crossly. But as they left the police station he said, "Now then!" to the policeman and Mr Peasemarsh, and he said it twenty times as crossly as he had spoken to Martha.

Martha was as good as her word. She took them home in a grand carriage, because the carrier's cart was gone, and, though she had stood by them so nobly with the police, she was very angry with them for 'trapseing into Rochester,' that none of them dared to mention the man with the pony-cart from the village who was still waiting for them. And so, after one day of boundless wealth, the children found themselves sent to bed in disgrace, and only enriched by two pairs of cotton gloves, an imitation crocodile-skin purse, and twelve penny buns, long since digested.

The thing that troubled them most was the fear that the old gentleman's guinea might have disappeared at sunset with all the rest, so they went down to the village next day to apologise for not meeting him in Rochester, and to see. They found him very friendly. The guinea had not disappeared, and he had bored a hole in it and hung it on his watch-chain. As for the guinea the baker took, the children felt they could not care whether it had vanished or not, which was not perhaps honest, but on the other hand was not unnatural. But afterwards this preyed on Anthea's mind, and at last she secretly sent twelve stamps by post to 'Mr Beale, Baker, Rochester.' Inside she wrote, 'To pay for the buns.' I hope the guinea did disappear, for that pastry-cook was really not a nice man and besides, penny buns are seven for sixpence in all respectable shops.

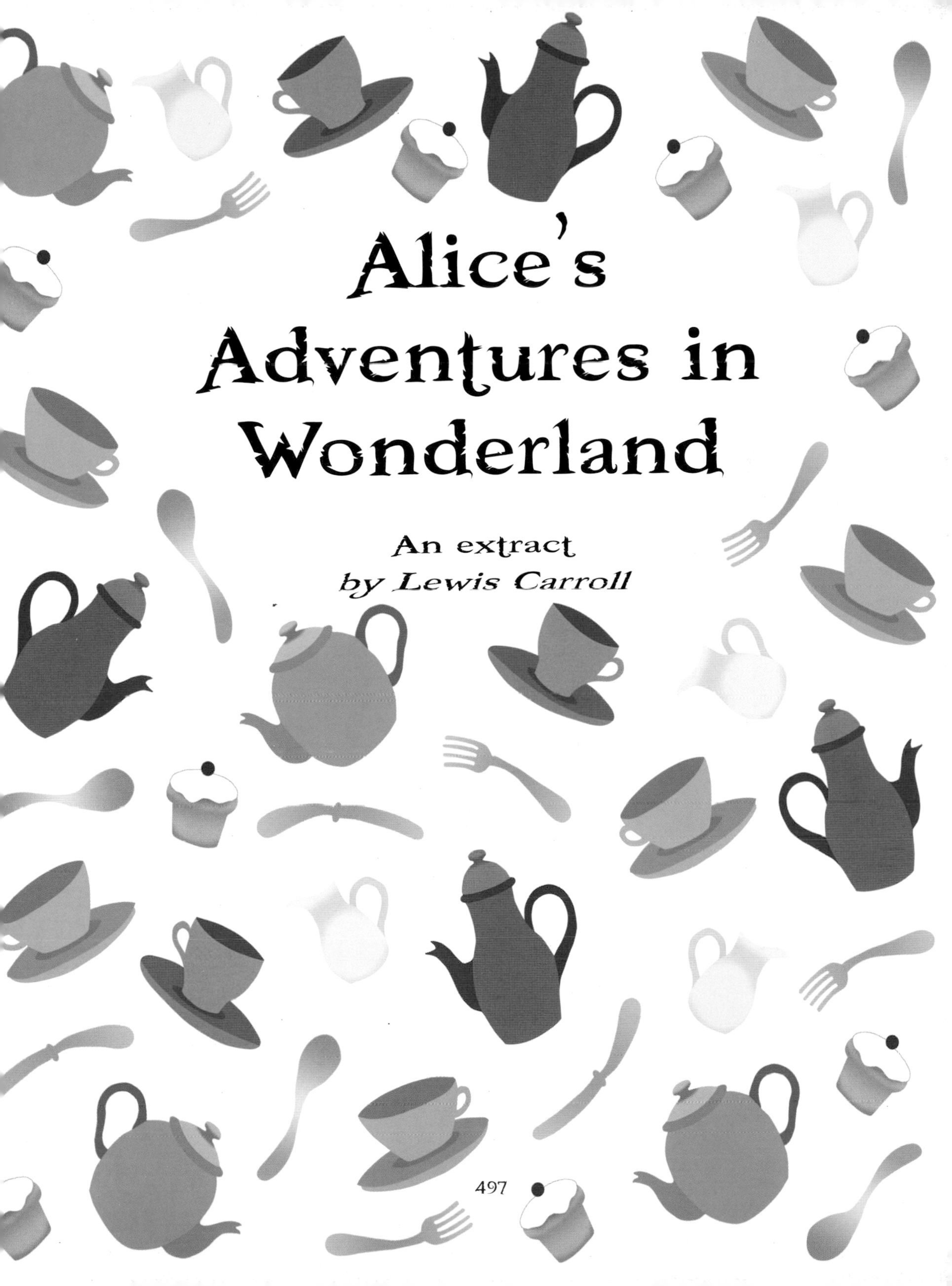

Alice's Adventures in Wonderland

An extract
by Lewis Carroll

Alice in Wonderland *was written by Lewis Carroll, and was the first book he wrote about Alice. It begins when Alice sees a white rabbit dash past, muttering to itself about being late, all the while peering at a large pocket watch. Alice followed the rabbit down a rabbit hole and found herself in a curious world. She began to feel very tired and thirsty when she came across a large table set for tea in front of the March Hare's house.*

There was a table set out under a tree in front of the house, and the March Hare and the Hatter were having tea at it. A Dormouse was sitting between them, fast asleep, and the other two were using it as a cushion, resting their elbows on it, and talking over its head. 'Very uncomfortable for the Dormouse,' thought Alice; 'only, as it's asleep, I suppose it doesn't mind.'

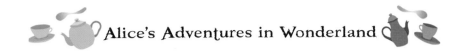

The table was a large one, but the three were all crowded together at one corner of it: "No room! No room!" they cried out when they saw Alice coming.

"There's *plenty* of room!" said Alice indignantly, and she sat down in a large armchair at one end of the table.

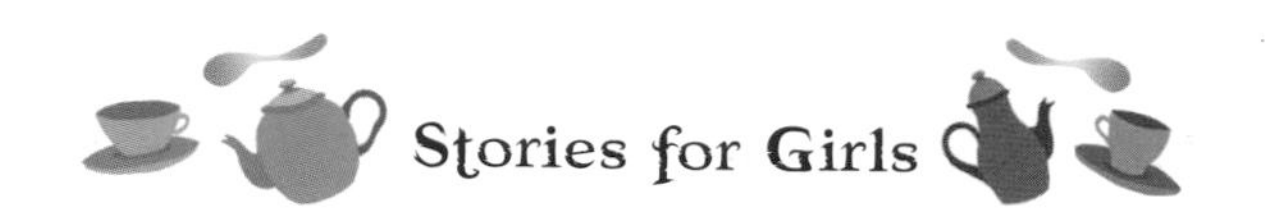

"Have some wine," the March Hare said in an encouraging tone.

Alice looked all round the table, but there was nothing on it but tea. "I don't see any wine," she remarked.

"There isn't any," said the March Hare.

"Then it wasn't very civil of you to offer it," said Alice angrily.

"It wasn't very civil of you to sit down without being invited," said the March Hare.

"I didn't know it was *your* table," said Alice; "it's laid for a great many more than three."

"Your hair wants cutting," said the Hatter. He had been looking at Alice for some time with great curiosity, and this was his first speech.

"You should learn not to make personal remarks," Alice said with some severity; "it's very rude."

The Hatter opened his eyes very wide on hearing this; but all he said was, "Why is a raven like a writing-desk?"

'Come, we shall have some fun now!' thought Alice. 'I'm glad they've begun asking riddles.'

"I believe I can guess that," she added aloud.

"Do you mean that you believe that you can find out the

answer to it?" said the March Hare.

"Exactly so," said Alice.

"Then you should say what you mean," the March Hare went on.

"I do," Alice hastily replied; "at least – at least I mean what I say – that's the same thing, you know."

"Not the same thing a bit!" said the Hatter. "You might just as well say that 'I see what I eat' is the same thing as 'I eat what I see'!"

"You might just as well say," added the March Hare, "that 'I like what I get' is the same thing as 'I get what I like'!"

"You might just as well say," added the Dormouse, who seemed to be talking in his sleep, "that 'I breathe when I sleep' is the same thing as 'I sleep when I breathe'!"

"It *is* the same thing with you," said the Hatter, and here the conversation dropped, and the party sat silent for a minute, while Alice thought over all she could remember about ravens and writing desks, which wasn't much.

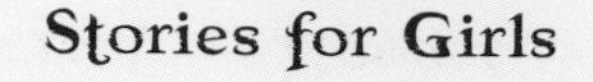

The Hatter was the first to break the silence.

"What day of the month is it?" he said, turning to Alice – he had taken his watch out of his pocket, and was looking at it uneasily, shaking it every now and then, and holding it to his ear.

Alice considered a little, and then said "The fourth."

"Two days wrong!" sighed the Hatter. "I told you butter wouldn't suit the works!" he added looking angrily at the March Hare.

"It was the *best* butter," the March Hare meekly replied.

"Yes, but some crumbs must have got in as well," the Hatter grumbled, "you shouldn't have put it in with the bread knife."

The March Hare took the watch and looked at it gloomily. Then he dipped it into his cup of tea, and looked at it again; but he could think of nothing better to say than his first remark, "It was the *best* butter, you know."

Alice had been looking over his shoulder with some curiosity. "What a funny watch!" she remarked. "It tells the day of the month, and doesn't tell what o'clock it is!"

"Why should it?" muttered the Hatter. "Does *your* watch tell you what year it is?"

"Of course not," Alice replied very readily: "but that's because it stays the same year for such a long time together."

"Which is just the case with *mine,*" said the Hatter.

Alice felt dreadfully puzzled. The Hatter's remark seemed to have no sort of meaning in it, and yet it was certainly English.

"I don't quite understand you," she said, as politely as she could.

"The Dormouse is asleep again," said the Hatter, and he poured a little hot tea upon its nose.

The Dormouse shook its head impatiently and said, without opening its eyes, "Of course, of course; just what I was going to remark myself."

"Have you guessed the riddle yet?" the Hatter said, turning to Alice again.

"No, I give it up," Alice replied. "What's the answer?"

"I haven't the slightest idea," said the Hatter.

"Nor I," said the March Hare.

Alice sighed wearily. "I think you might do something better with the time," she said, "than waste it in asking riddles that have no answers."

"If you knew Time as well as I do," said the Hatter, "you wouldn't talk about wasting *it.* It's *him.*"

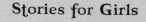

"I don't know what you mean," said Alice.

"Of course you don't!" the Hatter said, tossing his head contemptuously. "I dare say you never even spoke to Time!"

"Perhaps not," Alice cautiously replied: "but I know I have to beat time when I learn music."

"Ah! that accounts for it," said the Hatter. "He won't stand beating. Now, if you only kept on good terms with him, he'd do almost anything you liked with the clock. For instance, suppose it were nine o'clock in the morning, just time to begin lessons: you'd only have to whisper a hint to Time, and round goes the clock in a twinkling! Half past one, time for dinner!"

"I only wish it was," the March Hare said to itself in a whisper.

"That would be grand, certainly," said Alice thoughtfully; "but then I shouldn't be hungry for it, you know."

"Not at first, perhaps," said the Hatter: "but you could keep it to half past one as long as you liked."

"Is that the way *you* manage?" Alice asked.

The Hatter shook his head mournfully. "Not I!" he replied. "We quarrelled last March – just before *he* went mad, you know," (pointing with his tea spoon at the March Hare) " – it was at the great concert given by the Queen of Hearts, and I had to sing 'Twinkle, twinkle, little bat! How I wonder what you're at!' You know the song, perhaps?"

"I've heard something like it," said Alice.

"It goes on, you know," the Hatter continued, "in this way: 'Up above the world you fly, Like a tea tray in the sky. Twinkle, twinkle—'"

Here the Dormouse shook itself, and began singing in its sleep "Twinkle, twinkle, twinkle, twinkle..." and went on so long that they had to pinch it to make it stop.

"Well, I'd hardly finished the first verse," said the Hatter, "when the Queen jumped up and bawled out, 'He's murdering the time! Off with his head!'"

"How dreadfully savage!" exclaimed Alice.

"And ever since that," the Hatter went on in a mournful tone, "he won't do a thing I ask! It's always six o'clock now."

A bright idea came into Alice's head. "Is that the reason so many tea things are put out here?" she asked.

"Yes, that's it," said the Hatter with a sigh: "it's always teatime, and we've no time to wash the things between whiles."

"Then you keep moving round, I suppose?" said Alice.

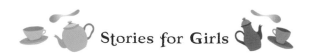

"Exactly so," said the Hatter; "as the things get used up."

"But what happens when you come to the beginning again?" Alice ventured to ask.

"Suppose we change the subject," the March Hare interrupted, yawning. "I'm getting tired of this. I vote the young lady tells us a story."

"I'm afraid I don't know one," said Alice, rather alarmed at the proposal.

"Then the Dormouse shall!" they both cried. "Wake up, Dormouse!" And they pinched it on both sides at once.

The Dormouse slowly opened his eyes.

"I wasn't asleep," he said in a hoarse, feeble voice. "I heard every word you fellows were saying."

"Tell us a story!" said the March Hare.

"Yes, please do!" pleaded Alice.

"And be quick about it," added the Hatter, "or you'll be asleep again before it's done."

"Once upon a time there were three little sisters," the Dormouse began in a great hurry; "and their names were Elsie, Lacie, and Tillie; and they lived at the bottom of a well—"

"What did they live on?" said Alice, who always took a great

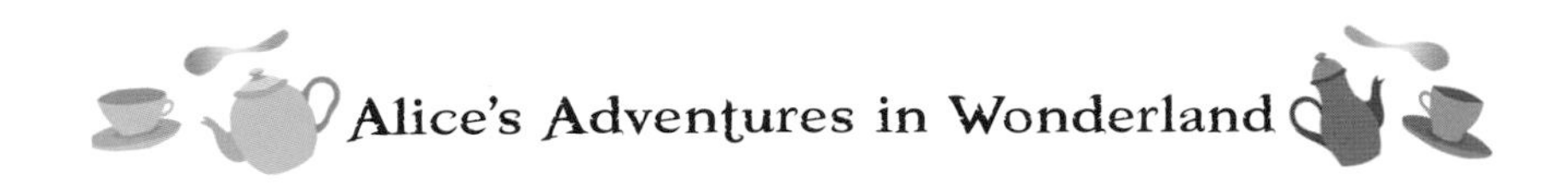

interest in questions of eating and drinking.

"They lived on treacle," said the Dormouse, after thinking a minute or two.

"They couldn't have done that, you know," Alice gently remarked; "they'd have been ill."

"So they were," said the Dormouse; "*very* ill."

Alice tried to fancy to herself what such an extraordinary ways of living would be like, but it puzzled her too much, so she went on: "But why did they live at the bottom of a well?"

"Take some more tea," the March Hare said to Alice, very earnestly.

"I've had nothing yet," Alice replied in an offended tone, "so I can't take more."

"You mean you can't take *less*," said the Hatter: "it's very easy to take *more* than nothing."

"Nobody asked *your* opinion," said Alice.

"Who's making personal remarks now?" the Hatter asked triumphantly.

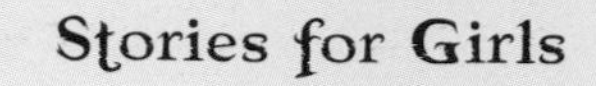

Alice did not quite know what to say to this, so she helped herself to some tea and bread and butter, and then turned to the Dormouse, and repeated her question. "Why did they live at the bottom of a well?"

The Dormouse again took a minute or two to think about it, and then said, "It was a treacle-well."

"There's no such thing!" Alice was beginning very angrily, but the Hatter and the March Hare went "Sh! sh!" and the Dormouse sulkily remarked, "If you can't be civil, you'd better finish the story for yourself."

"No, please go on!" Alice said very humbly; "I won't interrupt again. I dare say there may be *one.*"

"One, indeed!" said the Dormouse indignantly. However, he consented to go on. "And so these three little sisters – they were learning to draw, you know—"

"What did they draw?" said Alice, quite forgetting her promise.

"Treacle," said the Dormouse, without considering at all this time.

"I want a clean cup," interrupted the Hatter. "Let's all move one place on."

He moved on as he spoke, and the Dormouse followed him: the March Hare moved into the Dormouse's place, and Alice rather unwillingly took the place of the March Hare. The Hatter was the only one who got any advantage from the change; and Alice was a good deal worse off than before, as the March Hare had just upset the milk jug into his plate.

Alice did not wish to offend the Dormouse again, so she began very cautiously: "But I don't understand. Where did they draw the treacle from?"

"You can draw water out of a water well," said the Hatter; "so I should think you could draw treacle out of a treacle well – eh, stupid?"

"But they were *in* the well," Alice said to the Dormouse, not choosing to notice this last remark.

"Of course they were," said the Dormouse. "Well in."

This answer so confused poor Alice, that she let the Dormouse go on for some time without interrupting it.

"They were learning to draw," the Dormouse went on, yawning and rubbing its eyes, for it was getting very sleepy; "and they drew all manner of things – everything that begins with an 'M'—"

"Why with an 'M'?" said Alice.

"Why not?" said the March Hare.

Alice was silent.

The Dormouse had closed its eyes by this time, and was going off into a doze; but, on being pinched by the Hatter, it woke up again with a little shriek, and went on: "—that begins with an 'M', such as mousetraps, and the moon, and memory, and muchness – you know you say things are 'much of a muchness' – did you ever see such a thing as a drawing of a muchness?"

"Really, now you ask me," said Alice, very much confused, "I don't think—"

"Then you shouldn't talk," said the Hatter.

This piece of rudeness was more than Alice could bear: she got up in great disgust, and walked off. The Dormouse fell asleep instantly, and neither of the others took the least notice of her going, though she looked back once or twice, half hoping that they would call after her. The last time she saw them, they were trying to put the Dormouse into the teapot.

"At any rate I'll never go *there* again!" said Alice as she picked her way through the wood. "It's the stupidest tea party I ever was at in all my life!"

Just as she said this, she noticed that one of the trees had a door leading right into it. "That's very curious!" she thought. "But everything's curious today. I think I may as well go in at once." And in she went.

Once more she found herself in the long hall, and close to the little glass table. "Now, I'll manage better this time," she said to herself, and began by taking the little golden key, and unlocking the door that led into the garden. Then she went to work nibbling at the mushroom (she had kept a piece of it in her pocket) till she was about a foot high: then she walked down the little passage; and *then* she found herself at last in the beautiful garden, among the bright flower-beds and the cool fountains.

Acknowledgements

The publisher would like to thank the following artists whose work appears in this book:

Shirley Bellwood/B L Kearley, Julie Cornwall,
Peter Dennis/Linda Rogers Associates,
John Dillow/Beehive Illustration,
Pamela Goodchild/B L Kearley,
Richard Hook/Linden Artists,
Iole Rose/Beehive Illustration,
Eric Rowe/Linden Artists, Mike Saunders,
Elena Selivanova/Beehive Illustration,
Colin Sullivan/Beehive Illustration,
Roger Wade Walker/Beehive Illustration,
Mike White/Temple Rogers

All other artworks from the Miles Kelly Artwork Bank